LIFE
SENTENCE

A.K. Turner's latest crime fiction series features forensic sleuth Cassie Raven, who was first introduced in two short stories broadcast on BBC Radio 4. She also works as a TV producer and writer making documentaries on a range of subjects from history to true crime. A.K. has lived in East London since its pre-hipster days and recently qualified as a City of London walks guide so that she can share her passion for the city's 2,000-year history; her specialist subject – crime and punishment!

Also by A.K. Turner
Body Language

LIFE
SENTENCE

A. K. Turner

ZAFFRE

First published in the UK in 2022 by
ZAFFRE
An imprint of Bonnier Books UK
4th Floor, Victoria House, Bloomsbury Square, London WC1B 4DA
Owned by Bonnier Books
Sveavägen 56, Stockholm, Sweden

A CIP catalogue record for this book is
available from the British Library.

ISBN: 978-1-83877-478-3

Also available as an ebook and an audiobook

1 3 5 7 9 10 8 6 4 2

Typeset by IDSUK (Data Connection) Ltd
Printed and bound in Great Britain by Clays Ltd, Elcograf S.p.A.

MIX
Paper from
responsible sources
FSC® C018072

Zaffre is an imprint of Bonnier Books UK
www.bonnierbooks.co.uk

For Philip

Chapter One

'He was always such a *happy* little boy.'

Bradley's mum was looking straight at Cassie, but her pupils were wide and unfocused – her thoughts miles away.

'His Year One teacher used to call him Sunshine,' she added, a sudden smile bringing her tear-blurred features into focus.

A fervent hope gripped Cassie: that Mrs Appleton was remembering her son aged five or six, on a trike, laughing – anything rather than the image she would forever have of the fifteen-year-old Bradley: lying on his bed with the cord of his laptop tight around his neck, half-suspended from the light fitting on the wall above his head.

The two women were sitting in the mortuary's family viewing suite, close enough for their knees to touch. 'I just don't understand it.' Kim Appleton blinked, bumping back down to reality. 'He didn't seem unhappy. He never mentioned bullying or anything. I mean, he would have told me . . . wouldn't he? We always got on.' Her gaze flickered to her husband Steve – ceaselessly prowling the pastel-painted room like a man looking for someone to punch. 'As well as you'd expect, anyway, with a teenage boy.'

Cassie's only response was an understanding murmur: five years as a mortuary technician had taught her that what grieving relatives needed was a sounding board, not conversation. Anyway, what could she possibly say that would offer any consolation? For whatever reason, Bradley Appleton had ended his life before it had really begun. *The selfish little twat* . . . But her spurt of anger dissolved swiftly into pity. It was only ten years since Cassie had been Bradley's age herself, struggling to stay afloat in an emotional maelstrom – the not-knowing who you were yet, intractably at odds with the world. A fifteen-year-old was barely able to grasp the consequences of his actions, let alone foresee the brutal and unassuageable grief he had bequeathed to his parents – a life sentence with no chance of parole.

That morning Cassie had retrieved Bradley from the refrigerated body store and made him look nice, ready for his mum and dad's visit. Now he lay out of sight behind the curtained glass doors that bisected the viewing room. When his parents were ready she would draw back the drapes to reveal his body, the dark red coverlet pulled up high enough to cover the ligature mark that creased his neck. She would encourage them to go in, to be close to him, to touch him if they wanted to – the shrinks said that it helped with the grieving process. It was important not to rush things, to give his mum and dad time to prepare for the finality of that moment. This bit was like waiting for curtain-up at the theatre, but with a terrible twist.

Kim Appleton must have been talking about her son for at least ten minutes straight, trying to stave off the reality behind the curtains – to keep him alive for just a little longer. But now she fell silent.

'Are you ready?' Cassie asked, careful to include both parents in the question.

A nod from Kim; a bitter shrug from her husband.

Minutes later they were on the other side of the glass doors, standing around Bradley's body, his mum bent over him stroking his hair as if trying to lull him to sleep.

Bradley's longish hair was an unnatural black, which stood out against the pallor of his face, and one of his eyebrows and both ears had been multiply pierced. In goth-speak, Bradley had been a 'baby bat' – just like Cassie had been at his age. When she'd asked his mum on the phone whether she should remove his body jewellery for the viewing Kim had swiftly said yes, adding, 'I'm afraid his dad hated all that.'

Cassie understood – she always took out her own facial piercings before a family viewing and rearranged her black-dyed hair to cover her shaved undercut. Although she'd toned down the full-on goth look after leaving school, she knew that some people still found her appearance challenging. The last thing she wanted was to weird anyone out on top of what they were already going through.

Cassie had cleaned up the smudged black kohl liner that had panda-ed Bradley's eyes when he'd been brought in, so that now he looked more or less like any other fifteen-year-old boy: touchingly young, his skin peach-fuzzed and clear, bar a sprinkle of zits on his chin. The red pinpricks scattered across both eyelids and cheeks weren't spots, though; they were superficial haemorrhages called petechiae – tiny blood vessels burst by increased venous pressure.

Kim Appleton glanced up at Cassie. 'Just before . . . it happened, I was showing him how to make cupcakes – he'd bought black colouring to put in the sponge mix.' She smiled, back in the moment. 'Funnily enough, he's really into baking' – unable to consign her child to the past tense just yet. 'You wouldn't think that was a goth thing.'

'That's why he did this!' The first words Bradley's dad had spoken burst out of him in a fierce hiss, his finger jabbing towards his son. 'All that skulls-and-death . . . *bullshit* that him and his so-called friends are into!'

Kim's face fell – literally – the groups of muscles around the mouth and jaw suddenly slackening, as if the wires supporting them had been cut. Her husband eyed her face, breathing heavily, before looking away. 'Sorry, love. I can't do this. I'll see you at home.'

'Steve!' Kim threw out a hand, but the door was already closing behind him.

Cassie left a moment before putting a tentative hand on Kim's forearm, ready to withdraw if it seemed unwelcome. 'Bradley and his dad, did they have a difficult relationship?'

'Sometimes.' Her voice was hoarse. 'Until a few months ago they loved going to the football together – you know, dad-and-son stuff. Steve has a season ticket for Arsenal. But then Bradley got into this whole goth business and wouldn't go anymore. Steve . . . well, he found it all very difficult to handle.'

'And they had a bit of a falling-out last night?'

'Steve had a go at him about him wearing eyeliner . . . Implied he was gay.' They shared a look. 'There was a row. The last thing Bradley said was that he wished . . . he wished he could go to sleep and never wake up.'

Her eyes strayed back to Bradley's face. 'But this . . . this is all *my* fault. Like I told the woman police officer, we've been worried recently, thinking that he might have been smoking cannabis. He'd been acting a bit . . . fuzzy sometimes? So now if he's up in his room for any length of time I go and check on him. But we were watching a film and . . . *drinking wine.*' She turned haunted eyes on Cassie. 'If only I'd gone up ten minutes earlier I might have saved him . . .'

If only. The self-scourging litany of those who had lost someone they loved to sudden unexpected death. *If only I hadn't let them get in the car that night. If only we'd called an ambulance out to Mum sooner. If only we'd pushed the GP harder for a test.* A never-ending catechism that Cassie wouldn't wish on her worst enemy. But trying to challenge that kind of thinking at this stage was pointless; the best advice she'd ever got, from a bereavement counselling course early in her training: *Don't tell a grieving person how they should feel.*

'Listen, Kim, we don't know anything for sure yet,' she said carefully. 'We'll probably get some more information after the lab tests, and the pathologist's examination.' *Examination:* her go-to euphemism for the deconstruction that their son's body was about to undergo in the search for answers.

Cassie allowed herself to hope that Bradley really had been off his face on something when he'd strangled himself – if he hadn't been in his right mind it would make his death a little easier for his parents to bear.

Kim nodded vaguely, her eyes glued to her son's face.

Cassie had always thought that she had a good grasp of how important it was for people to know why their loved ones had died, but six weeks ago that understanding had acquired a new and scalpel-like edge.

That was when she'd made the discovery that demolished at a stroke everything she thought she knew about her life to date.

Cassie's mother hadn't died in a car crash – the story she'd been told since the age of four. She had been murdered by Cassie's father.

Chapter Two

In the loo, Cassie replaced her eyebrow piercings and lip ring and scraped her hair back up into its topknot before wheeling Bradley out of the 'clean side' and back into the autopsy suite. First thing in the morning the foreground smell was the harsh chemical reek of bleach and formalin, but in a couple of hours' time the odours of blood, sweat and urine would get the upper hand.

Bradley's mum had left an old soft toy tucked into the curve of his neck, a battered and faded penguin he'd apparently loved when he was little. As Cassie retrieved it, to stow somewhere safe until after the post-mortem, she found the plush fur still damp with his mother's tears.

People got it all wrong about her job – the hard part wasn't cutting up dead bodies; it was looking after the poor bastards they left behind. Two or three traumatic viewings in a row could leave her totally wrung-out by going-home time. But it was also a privilege. When she sat with a grieving relative like Kim she was often reminded of the Latin origin of the formal-sounding word 'condolences'. *Condolore* meant 'to suffer with another'.

The new technician, Jason Begby, was standing at his autopsy table, singing along to some cheesy pop track playing too loud on the radio. Background music did help make a shift spent up to your elbows in blood and viscera go faster but Jason must be fifty, twice her age, and his taste for Nineties house had made it clear that they would never be musical soulmates. Or soulmates of any kind, come to that.

Cassie was still missing her old colleague and drinking buddy Carl, who'd done an unscheduled midnight flit six weeks ago, after getting himself into trouble with some local gangsters. In fact, it felt like everything in her life had gone to shit around then, those few traumatic weeks that had culminated in Cassie's grandmother, Weronika, dropping her bombshell about how her mum had really died.

Cassie's gran had raised her from the age of four to believe that both her parents had died in a car accident – a head-on collision with a drunk-driver. It was only after Weronika suffered a mini-stroke that she had finally revealed the truth: Cassie's dad, Callum, had beaten her mother, Katherine, to death in a jealous rage, a crime for which he'd spent seventeen years behind bars.

Why had he not contacted her – his only daughter – even after he'd got out of prison four years ago? The question that had nagged at Cassie incessantly since she'd learned the truth, always swiftly followed by another: *Why would you even want him to?* She gave her head a shake to dislodge this pointless mental loop – knowing the power it had to knock her off-beam.

She went over to Jason's table. 'How's it going?' she asked, lifting her chin towards the body that he was working on. The desiccated Marmite-brown carcase was the incinerated remains of an old gentleman who'd fallen asleep with a lit cigarette in his hand and turned his bed into a funeral pyre.

Jason wafted the air above the body towards him, inhaling ostentatiously. 'Aaah. The great smell of KFC.'

Cassie managed a tight smile: it was true that badly burned bodies smelled disturbingly like fried chicken and Jason's tasteless gaggery was the norm in many mortuaries, especially among older technicians. But talking about a body in that disrespectful way still made her hackles rise.

'Sorry I had to give you Mr Siddiqui. I knew my viewing would take a while.'

The fierce heat had literally cooked Mr Siddiqui's long muscles, shortening them and contorting his body into the 'pugilist stance' – arms flexed at the elbow and raised in front of him, fists clenched, his legs drawn up. The body looked half human, half praying mantis. His body would be difficult to repair after the post-mortem: the cooked flesh tearing easily when you tried to close the incision.

'Oh, I don't mind the occasional crispy critter,' said Jason with a grin. 'But I'll be in the mood for a bargain bucket by lunchtime.'

Cassie turned away to hide her expression. Carl had unquestioningly followed her lead in treating the dead who they looked after with dignity – which meant always calling them guests or bodies and never stiffs, floaters, jumpers or crispy critters. She always referred to them by name – the older ones by their title – treating them, in other words, as if they were a living person. The difference was that Carl had just turned nineteen and Cassie had overseen his on-the-job training. As senior technician she theoretically stood above Jason in the pecking order but she couldn't bring herself to lecture a guy who'd been eviscerating bodies when she was still in primary school.

Returning to her own autopsy station she locked the stainless-steel trolley carrying Bradley into position and started to undress him. His black T-shirt emblazoned with the face of Nosferatu was raggedly scissored up the front where paramedics had exposed his chest to attempt defibrillation. But she already knew from the notes that he'd been asystolic by that time – his heart showing no shockable rhythm. Game over. She folded the T-shirt away into a clear plastic bag. No doubt Bradley's dad would be glad to see the back of his goth gear, but his mum would treasure it: the things someone was wearing when they died were the closest you'd ever get to them again.

'Well, you can tell *them* I'm not *remotely* happy with their accommodation plan.'

Dr Curzon. The sound of the familiar, self-important voice behind her made Cassie's blood pressure spike. Philip Curzon was their new regular pathologist, replacing her friend and mentor Professor Arculus, who'd taken a sabbatical to write a book about the Somme. As substitutions went, it was like swapping a premium Polish vodka for Asda's value brand.

'I am growing weary of repeating myself . . .' Curzon went on. 'I will accept a Hyatt or a Hilton, at the minimum. Are we perfectly clear? Good. Fix it.'

Putting his phone away he turned his perpetually irritated gaze on Cassie – apparently finding nothing there to improve his mood. 'These people. They spend weeks pleading with me to present my paper at their blessed conference, and now they try to fob me off with a *Radisson.*'

His gaze swivelled down to Bradley. Taking in the curtain of coal-black hair and the skull amateurishly inked on the milk-pale skin of his forearm, he made a scoffing sound. 'Another druggie, I assume?'

'Probable suicide, Doctor.' She turned Bradley's jaw to reveal the ligature mark on the right-hand side of his neck, a brownish-red streak that finished beneath his ear. She caught the masseter muscle in Curzon's jaw clenching, his face twisting briefly in what looked like anger before he turned away to take off his camel coat.

While he started his external examination of Bradley, she ran her own eye over Curzon. His shirt was expensive, densely woven cotton, the cufflinks personalised with his initials, but one cuff bore a tiny smear of what could be ketchup. No, he wasn't a ketchup sort of guy. More likely the tomato sauce off an M&S pizza. He'd shaved hastily, leaving an patch the size of a fifty-pence piece unshaven in front of one ear, and the aggressive smell of mouthwash coming off him didn't entirely erase the sour tang of last night's red wine.

What was the score with Curzon? His platinum wedding band looked uncomfortably tight, the flesh raised around it in a ruff. A man of his vintage, hungover, in the grip of some private fury, and wearing yesterday's shirt? It all said 'recently separated'. Perhaps he hadn't got round to having the ring cut off – or maybe he was still in denial.

'There's evidence of self-harm, Doctor,' said Cassie, turning Bradley's arm to reveal the soft inner skin of his upper arm with its ladder of pink horizontal scars, incised where they wouldn't easily be spotted. 'Razor cuts, I'd say, but not recent – probably three or four months old.'

Curzon paused to send her a look. 'Well, I'm indebted to you for your *expert opinion'* – his voice loaded with elaborately polite scorn. Any sympathy she'd allowed herself to feel for him evaporated.

Professor Arculus was at the very top of his profession, and posher than the Queen, but in the five years Cassie had worked with him he had never once failed to ask her opinion – and it wasn't simply out of good manners.

In a forensic post-mortem – conducted when there was evidence of foul play – the pathologist could spend the best part of a day dissecting and investigating the body, but for the day-to-day 'routine' version, like the one Bradley was getting, they typically spent no more than forty minutes with the body. In these cases it was the anatomical pathology technician (APT) who performed the evisceration, weighed the organs, and took many of the samples. Unlike the pathologist they also dealt with the deceased's loved ones. All of which could give an experienced technician like Cassie clues to the likely cause of death.

If it had been the Prof standing next to her she'd have raised Bradley's waxy pallor and his lack of facial congestion and asked whether he thought the mechanism leading to death might involve the vagus nerve.

But Philip Curzon wasn't the Prof. He had made it crystal clear to Cassie from the off that he had zero interest in the views of the lower orders – or maybe he just disliked her personally. He clearly didn't approve of her alternative look, and she suspected that his height – he was barely five foot six, an inch or two shorter than her – probably didn't help. Not long after he started she'd overheard him describe her to Doug the mortuary manager as 'a chippy female'.

Dinosaur.

When Curzon was ready to examine Bradley from the back, he flipped him over casually – like he was a side of beef, rather than somebody's much-loved child. Cassie was still seething when he left her to go over to Jason's table, on the other side of the room.

'And what do we have here, my good man?' Curzon's tone turned nauseatingly matey.

'Can I interest you in the barbecue special, Dr Curzon?' said Jason – his lame joke rewarded with a chuckle from Curzon. Jason never got above himself by offering an opinion, just the basic facts, seasoned with a series of toadying remarks.

Tuning out of their conversation, Cassie leaned closer to Bradley's ear.

'We need to find out exactly how you died, Bradley, for the sake of your mum and dad,' she said, her voice a low murmur.

Talking to the dead bodies in her care had always felt natural. To Cassie, the mortuary was a shadow land where her charges hung in a kind of limbo between life and death. Objectively, she had no truck with the supernatural and yet there was an irrational corner of her that believed the dead could hear her words. And that now and again, they would even reply.

'I was miserable, too, when I was your age. It sucks, doesn't it, being fifteen?' She scanned the soft contours of Bradley's face, his adult jawline yet to emerge from beneath its layer of puppy fat.

Would Bradley be one of those who 'spoke'? Might he tell her something of what he'd been feeling in his last minutes, why he had done what he did? But no message rose from Bradley's youthful lips, and she experienced none of the dislocated dreaminess that usually preceded her moments of communion with the dead.

She'd not had one of those experiences for weeks now – in fact, now she came to think of it, they had ended on the day she'd learned the truth about how her mum had really died. A horrible thought struck her: what if that discovery had killed off forever what she saw as her sacred gift – the thing that gave her job meaning?

Get a move on! Cassie told herself, reaching for her trusty PM40, into which she'd screwed a brand-new scalpel blade, from the serried ranks of instruments lined up on the counter. Her task, which she must have carried out a couple of thousand times in the last five years, was to open Bradley's body and remove his organs intact.

Because of the way Bradley had died she was using a high Y-shaped incision, the arms of the Y starting right up by the ears either side of the neck. This would avoid any damage to the structures at the front of his neck – especially a bony structure called the hyoid which often got fractured in a hanging.

As Cassie's blade met Bradley's perfect satiny skin she was aware of the shift in outlook she always experienced at this moment – the pulling of a mental lever so tangible she could almost hear the swish-clunk. Now she was no longer seeing Bradley Appleton the loved son and troubled fifteen-year-old, but the body of a juvenile male that had to be deconstructed in order to deliver the answers needed by the living.

Once the uppermost arms of her Y incision met at the base of Bradley's throat, she began the midline incision, sweeping down over the chest and abdomen, the blade eagerly parting the tender skin. What lay beneath was a layer of golden fat above tissue the precise colour and texture of sirloin steak – the uncanny similarity the reason she'd given up meat five years ago, right after witnessing her first evisceration. Once past the sternum she automatically let up the pressure so as not to risk lacerating any of the organs in the abdominal cavity, before making a practised detour around the umbilicus, and coming to a halt just above the pubic bone.

Cassie was using the Letulle Method, in which the viscera were removed in a single block, from tongue to rectum, ready for dissection by the pathologist. It was fast – Cassie had the process down to around ten minutes.

Bradley's youth made her task easier: the bone shears chomped through the costal cartilage, the softest bit of the ribs where they met the sternum, with none of the effort it took when they were ossified by age. His heart and the lungs were a moist and healthy pink without any adhesions sticking them to the body cavity; with two swift incisions she was able to scoop them free.

Returning to the neck area she peeled the Y-shaped flap of skin from Bradley's throat up over his face to reveal the neck structures. Severing the strap muscles which supported the hyoid bone, she murmured the ditty Prof Arculus had taught her for remembering their individual names: 'TOSS my gravy spoon, darling'. It was actually just the TOSS bit you needed to remember: thyrohyoid, omohyoid, sternothyroid and sternohyoid.

Looking more closely at the omohyoid stretching down the left-hand side of Bradley's neck, she made out bruising across the muscle in line with the external marks caused by the ligature. Some of the bruising looked darker than she'd have expected from a fresh injury, but it was hard to tell against the deep-red muscle tissue.

By the time Curzon had returned in full scrubs, Bradley's viscera and brain were waiting on his dissecting bench. He separated each of them out for dissection, before Cassie carried them away to be weighed.

Watching him dissect the bony structures of the neck she asked, 'Should we take a section from the contusions in the strap muscles, Dr Curzon?' – knowing from experience that if she gave them their proper anatomical name he'd probably slap her down. She wanted Bradley's report to be as comprehensive as possible, so his parents would know no stone had been left unturned.

'Waste of time,' snapped Curzon without even turning around.

He recorded his verdict on his phone, propped at a safe distance from the blood and guts. 'Minimal damage to hyoid or cartilaginous structures. No sign of venous congestion. Marked facial pallor. A textbook case of vagal inhibition.'

It was the verdict Cassie had suspected the minute she'd laid eyes on Bradley. People tended to think of hanging as pretty straightforward – close off the airway and you starve the lungs of oxygen. In fact, death was more usually caused by the compression of the neck veins and carotid arteries which cut off the blood supply to the brain, and left the face dark with congested blood.

But Bradley's pallor was a tell-tale sign of vagal inhibition – an even less well-known route to death.

As a kid, with her nose buried in *Gray's Anatomy*, Cassie had marvelled at the weird and wonderful journey of the vagus nerve – starting out in the brain it travelled all the way down to the gut, branching off into several organs en route. Later, while studying for her classics A Level, it gave her a buzz to discover that *vagus* was Latin for 'wandering' – a linguistic root shared by the terms 'vagrant' and 'vagabond'. One of the key roles of the vagus was regulating blood pressure – a vagal reflex was what made some people faint at the sight of blood.

When Bradley had tightened the cable around his neck he had compressed the carotid sinus, a crucial bundle of nerves sited where the carotid artery branches in the neck. That sent a signal to his brain which would have responded by instructing the vagus to lower blood pressure. Maintaining that compression would have caused Bradley's blood pressure to plunge catastrophically and stopped his heart in as little as two minutes.

Cassie remembered Kim torturing herself with the image of Bradley slowly strangling to death while she and Steve drank wine downstairs.

Addressing Curzon's back she said, 'Well, at least we can tell his mum and dad it was fast – that there wasn't time for them to save him.'

He whipped round to face her – his eyes hot and angry-looking. 'This selfish idiot didn't deserve a quick death.'

Bemused by Curzon's flash of hostility, Cassie gathered Bradley's organs into a blue plastic bag and went back to where he lay. After heaving it into his body cavity she started to massage the contents back inside their owner, which was a bit like trying to get a sleeping bag back inside its cover. Dissection always seemed to double the size of the viscera.

Once that was done, she set a bloodied gloved hand on Bradley's shoulder. 'I just need to close you up, sweetheart, and give you a wash, and you'll be as good as new.'

She was just reaching for one of the big curved needles she'd lined up, already threaded with strong white twine, when something made her stop. Bradley's head was turning slowly to face her, his eyes half open.

She knew it was only the weight of his head settling on the neck block, but it still spooked her.

Reaching out to close his eyelids she got a zip of static to her fingertips that made her whole body tingle, followed by a familiar feeling. She was slip-sliding into an altered state, the overhead fluorescent lights flaring on her retina, the iron filings smell of blood catching at the back of her throat.

Her vision dimmed, darkening from the edges, combined with a light-headedness that was almost enjoyable. A bit like the rush off a hit of skunk. The air crackled with static and out of the fuzziness, she heard a young male voice.

'Trippy!'

Chapter Three

'You're putting too much brine in!'

Cassie made a superhuman effort to keep her voice calm. 'Look, Babcia. Why don't you go sit down and watch the telly and leave the dinner to me?' She was making a Polish salad to go with the pierogi simmering on the stovetop, but during these last few weeks cooking for her convalescent grandmother she'd had to call on all her reserves of self-control.

'I'm just saying, you can always put more in but you cannot take it back out.'

Always so indomitable, Weronika seemed diminished after her mini-stroke, not just physically but also in herself. Before the – thankfully tiny – fragment of arterial plaque had travelled to her brain she'd been unfailingly sharp and decisive, even at seventy-nine, but now she was often irritable or fretful, and found it hard to settle.

'I tell you what, could you lay the table?' Cassie nodded at a tray which held cutlery and condiments.

Weronika fixed a piercing look on her granddaughter that was a bit more like her old self. 'Do you think I am too old and foolish to see what you're up to, *tygrysek*? "Keep the old woman feeling useful."' Nodding to herself, she picked up the tray. 'I know when I'm not wanted in my own kitchen.' But

Cassie had seen one corner of her mouth crook upwards. She felt a little surge of relief every time she saw these little signs that her grandmother – the unshakeable rock in her life – was recovering.

After Cassie's father was jailed for the murder of her mother more than twenty years earlier, Weronika had stepped in – together with her husband – to bring up the four-year-old daughter of her beloved only child. The 'car accident' that had killed both parents had simply been a fiction to protect Cassie from the truth, but Weronika's stroke had made her realise she couldn't take the truth to her grave. Even though Callum Raven had never attempted to contact his daughter, Cassie needed to be prepared in case he ever did turn up out of the blue.

Until her grandmother's revelations, Cassie hadn't dwelt much on her parents' deaths. She'd always told herself that losing them so young – too early to lay down many memories or to properly understand her loss – had the advantage of sparing her any long-lasting emotional fall-out. But discovering the truth had left her reeling, especially coming on top of the murder of her much-loved teacher Geraldine Edwards – the surrogate parent who had persuaded Cassie to return to education, and steered her through science A levels at evening classes.

Twenty-one years after losing her parents Cassie had realised something: she was only just starting to deal with what was an unhealed lifelong wound. A legacy that might help to explain the trouble she had forming long-lasting relationships.

Unresolved grief. That's what the shrinks called it.

Since her grandmother had left hospital Cassie had been staying at her flat to cook and clean for her and make sure she took her daily dose of warfarin. But living in the overheated old-lady home that she'd viewed as a prison cell during her teenage years had reawakened feelings of being trapped and desperate for adult freedoms. Whenever she went out after dinner and came back late – sometimes drunk, stoned or both – Weronika was on her case. Just like the old days.

'Too much brine in the salatka,' the old lady said, as they ate. 'But the pierogi are nice and light.'

Cassie's eye fell on what she'd always thought of as the mantelpiece icon – the now-faded photo of her mother at eighteen – her prettiness given a touch of grit by a hint of challenge in her eyes, her long centre-parted hair cascading over a ruffle-necked blouse. Apparently, Katherine had wanted to study psychology at uni, before marriage and a baby came along to permanently derail that idea.

It was a bitter irony that while Cassie could barely remember her mum beyond a few fleeting impressions – a dress she wore bedecked with giant orange poppies, a perfume that smelled a bit like watermelon – her memories of her dad were far richer. She remembered him as an engaged and loving father: playing aeroplane with a spoonful of food to persuade her to eat; hoisting her up onto his shoulders in the park; or pretending to be a monster chasing her. Memories horribly contaminated now by the knowledge of what he had gone on to do.

'How are you getting on with the new people at work?' Her grandmother fixed her with a beady look.

'OK, I guess.' Putting her fork down Cassie pushed away her plate, half the pierogi uneaten. 'I miss Carl – and the Prof. But I'll get over it.'

Cassie could hear the sourness curdling her voice. These days she often found herself getting angry for no apparent reason. It didn't help, knowing that she was simply following the well-known stages of grief – even a slumbering grief re-awoken after two decades. After denial there was the whole 'if only' stage to look forward to – the concocting of fantasies about how she could have averted her mother's death – all topped off by a dose of depression. The supposed final state of 'acceptance' seemed like a distant fairy tale right now. Anyway, knowing all this shit in theory was one thing, living it was another.

'What about that young body doctor, the one you made friends with, after thinking he was a snobby fellow to start with?'

Picturing Archie Cuff, the newbie pathologist who helped cover the routine PMs, Cassie suppressed a smile. It was true that she'd put him down as an insufferably arrogant posh boy at the start – a Dr Curzon in the making – but after she'd helped him out during his first post-mortem, he'd been so touchingly grateful that she'd been forced – grudgingly – to change her mind about him. They'd even been out for a drink a couple of times, just as friends, but the banter had been good and she'd detected a spark of attraction both ways.

Recognising her grandmother's speculative look she decided to head off any further interrogation. 'You were saying you were feeling better enough to think about a little outing? With Barbara?'

'*Tak*. If I feel up to it tomorrow morning we're going out for a walk. We might even go for a coffee.'

Seeing her grandmother's face light up gave Cassie a little lift: she was definitely on the mend. But how long before she could safely start to broach the questions she had about her mum and dad?

When Cassie returned from the fridge with a second bottle of beer her grandmother said nothing at first. But after a loaded silence she put her knife down and took Cassie's hand in her warm leathery grip. 'When I'm a little stronger we will have a proper talk about everything, I promise. I know what a dreadful thing it was for you, *tygrysek*, finding out what happened to your mama. God rest her soul.' She crossed herself, her voice sounding hoarse. 'But . . . you know, don't you, that the answer isn't in there.' She tipped her birdlike head towards the bottle.

Cassie squeezed her hand back. It was uncanny, the way Weronika always seemed to know what was on her mind.

Before the stroke her grandmother had never once voluntarily mentioned her son-in-law nor given any real explanation for her antipathy towards him, beyond describing him as uncouth and work-shy. Growing up, Cassie had wondered why she'd never seen a single photograph of her dad, but now she understood: after the murder Weronika would have destroyed all mementoes of him.

Cassie knew only the basic facts. Callum had been a heavy drinker who used his fists on Katherine and had gone on to murder her after getting it into his head that she'd been having an affair. Despite his protestations of innocence the jury had found him guilty and he'd gone on to serve seventeen years of a life sentence, before his release on licence, at which point he'd returned to his home town, somewhere in Northern Ireland.

The question that wouldn't stop looping the loop in Cassie's head: *why in all these years had he never so much as sent her a birthday card?*

She couldn't shake the bitter irony that after twenty-one years as an orphan, her father had been returned to her – and yet his crime meant that he remained completely out of reach.

As she loaded the dishwasher, she wondered what Kim and Steve Appleton were doing right now, as they started a lifetime of grieving for their only child, knowing that Bradley had taken his own life – far worse than losing him to an accident or fatal illness. What was it she had heard him 'say' earlier that day?

'*Trippy!*'

These moments of connection with the dead meant a lot to her but she always resisted analysing them in case it all might simply evaporate when exposed to sunlight. After all, she didn't buy the idea of ghosts, or an afterlife. If sometimes these 'messages' turned out to carry clues to the cause of death it was probably just the ability she had to pick up things that others missed.

Bradley's mum had mentioned him using weed, so it wasn't much of a leap to imagine him trying out something more risky. Had he killed himself while having a bad trip? Camden was awash with nasty psycho-actives knocked up using recipes from the dark web and a single dodgy pill could tip a developing brain into a psychotic state. For Kim and Steve's sake, she hoped the lab would find something in his blood or urine that might have affected his grasp on reality.

Drugged or not, maybe Bradley had simply been playing around with the *idea* of suicide – death being a bit of a goth preoccupation – rather than having any genuine desire to kill himself.

Or maybe she was grasping at straws. The fact remained that Bradley had looped a flex around his neck and hanged

24

himself from a light fitting. The idea that someone you loved would deliberately absent themselves from you forever must be unbearable.

Just like her father had done after leaving prison.

Archie Cuff's text message couldn't have arrived at a better time. He was 'in the area', he said, and wondered if she was free.

Pulling on her leather jacket she avoided her grandmother's gaze. 'Don't forget your drugs, Babcia, I'm popping out for a drink.'

Weronika appeared engrossed in a cowboy movie, her favourite genre, and didn't issue Cassie with her usual lecture about not drinking too much, or even ask who she was meeting. But as Cassie made to go she said, 'Thank Dr Cuff for me would you, *tygrysek*?'

The old fox.

'Umm. Why?'

'He reminds you how to smile.'

Chapter Four

It was Friday night and despite the chill January air the weekend was in full swing, a conga line of people spilling out of Camden Town Tube to hit the bars, clubs and gigs, the air already thick with the smell of *ganja* and doner kebab. Stood outside, Archie was easy to spot amid the punk haircuts, chains and leather, piercings and tattoos of Camden's motley after-dark crowd – six foot two of spotless blue Barbour jacket, with what appeared to be an actual rugger scarf looped round his neck, and gleaming brogues poking out from jeans that looked suspiciously like they'd been ironed.

As she passed the two lads stationed against the wall, one of them sent her an upward nod of enquiry. Cassie gave an imperceptible headshake – she was smoking a lot more recently but she wasn't about to buy weed in front of Archie. She noticed the dealers weren't in their usual spot and guessed they were keeping as far away from Archie as possible. Daft really. A plain-clothes cop would attract less attention if he wore a full clown suit.

'Hello, you,' said Archie. The way his eyes lit up as he scanned her face gave her a buzz. Despite the little jaw-skimming ginger beard he'd grown, which made him look even more like Prince Harry than before. *Jesus.* Wasn't it bad enough, fancying a public schoolboy – let alone a ringer for a royal?

'There's a pretty good wine bar nearby?' she said, stamping her feet against the cold.

'Not likely!' he retorted. 'I get plenty of wine bars in Guildford. No, I'm expecting the full Camden experience.'

A couple of minutes later Archie was chivalrously craning a long arm over her to open the door to The Black Heart, a backstreet boozer in a soot-bricked Victorian warehouse. Inside, the vibe was cosy, lit by festoons of fairy lights, but undercut by a dark glamour: an orange neon cross loomed over the bar, and in a glass case on one wall stood a kitsch plaster Jesus and various goth knick-knacks including the compulsory skull. Cassie had been coming here ever since she could lay her hands on fake ID: and she still liked a place where her job was considered cool instead of weird.

Despite some lingering looks from a couple of regulars sitting at the bar, Archie appeared unfazed.

'All right, Cass?' said Zed, a shaven-headed guy she knew, raising a pierced eyebrow at her date like a skinhead Lady Bracknell.

After ordering the beers – two bottles of Rogue Dead Guy seemed appropriate – they managed to find a table.

As Archie surveyed the place, she noticed, not for the first time how the boyishness of his face was offset by a broken nose, probably a legacy of rugby. 'So, this is the real Camden,' he said, with anthropological relish.

'I don't know what the *real* Camden is anymore. It's not like it used to be, back when there were still more squats than Starbucks. Now every empty building is being turned into flats for people with half a mill to spare.' She grinned. 'Listen to me – twenty-five and already going on about the good old days.'

'You'll be saying a pint of milk costs ten bob next . . .' He took a slug of beer from the bottle, his eyes resting comfortably on hers. 'You used to live in a squat, didn't you?'

'Just for a year or so, when I was seventeen.'

'*Seventeen!* Wowser! That must have been . . . tough?'

Picturing her favourite squat, the one in the disused pub, she remembered the winter mornings she'd woken to find frost icing her sleeping bag, cooking on a primus stove, the siren of an ambo turning up when someone overdosed, the inevitable eviction . . . but also the magical times when they'd sat round a backyard bonfire looking at the stars.

'In some ways, yeah. But it was also the happiest I've ever been. The feeling of freedom – and the camaraderie. Like we were all in it together. It's hard to explain.'

Archie nodded in frowning agreement. 'It was like that on my rugby team at Harrow.'

She was tempted to take the piss, before remembering her new resolution not to be so judgy of people like Archie. After all, he had never so much as mentioned her piercings or tattoos – and nor had Prof Arculus, come to that. Maybe the self-confidence of the properly posh – as opposed to the simply loaded – meant they didn't feel the need to pass judgement on others.

'So, what kind of people frequent this place?' He leaned towards her, his sandy-coloured eyebrows conspiratorial.

'Oh, a few different tribes. Goths, emos, skins, punks, the odd greaser . . .'

Her eye fell on a nearby table of young wannabe goths, most of them still with the soft features of early adolescence. The girls and boys alike had black bird's nest hair and wore full white foundation with lips painted blue and purple – a look that reminded her of poor dead Bradley Appleton lying in his steel bed a half-mile away. One of the younger girls had put flashes of turquoise in her hair just like Cassie used to. They were holding hands around a black candle burning on the table and they all looked gloomy as hell. The default goth mood, supposedly – except she knew different. Being into the dark side didn't make you a misery-guts twenty-four/seven, quite the reverse; when she'd been an angry, depressed teen her little bat-tribe had been a lifesaver.

'How did you end up as an APT?' Archie asked. 'I mean, when did you first get interested in the idea?'

'When I was about four I used to bring dead animals home – my gran was always finding dead pigeons under my bed. Then I saw an autopsy in an American crime drama, when I was about thirteen. The idea that a dead person was like a puzzle that you could solve by taking it to pieces, that stuck with me, I guess.'

'So why did you never consider medicine? I remember you showing me the C-spine fracture I missed on my first PM.' He angled his bottle at her, smiling. 'You notice things.'

She smiled back, not liking to say that his failure to spot it was a standard rookie error. How to find the words to explain to someone like Archie that for a girl like her, brought up in a tower block, who'd spent her high school years winding up the teachers, medical school hadn't remotely figured on her radar. Even after she'd gone on to get good A level grades at evening classes, she just knew she would never fit in with all those hyper-confident posh boys and girls who went into medicine.

In any case, she loved her job – to her, dealing with the dead was a sacred vocation. 'The thing is, you guys dash in, dissect, and disappear,' she told him. 'I get to spend quality time with the guests – and to look after their families.' She took a slug of her beer. 'What about you? Why medicine?'

He ran a hand through his copper curls. 'My father was a heart surgeon so I suppose I was always marked out for it, and pathology seemed a good bet for making consultant by thirty-five. But unlike you, cutting up bodies in a freezing cold mortuary at 7 a.m. is *not* my idea of fun.' He pantomimed a shiver. 'Once I've done the compulsory two years of post-mortems I'll concentrate on diagnostic pathology. I can see myself sitting in a nice warm lab looking at slides of rare cancers with the odd trip to an international conference at a swanky hotel.'

Archie's boyish grin took the edge off any cynicism in his plan. He raised an eyebrow. 'Fancy coming with me to a five-star hotel somewhere when that happens? Or are you *far* too alternative for something so lamestream?'

She laughed. She liked the way Archie took the piss out of her, the way he didn't take her – or life – too seriously. It made him relaxing to be around. *Unlike Phyllida Flyte.* Out of nowhere Cassie got a vivid image of her pale beauty, those sharp cheekbones, the serious ice-blue gaze. She had formed an unexpected . . . what to call it – alliance? – with the uptight cop during the investigation of her old teacher's death; a relationship which had occasionally felt like it teetered on the edge of more dangerous territory. Dangerous because there was no way she could see herself dating a cop, however hot.

Later, when Cassie went to the loo, she encountered the girl with the turquoise streaks coming out of one of the stalls, blowing her nose on some bog roll. She didn't like to stare but the girl had clearly been crying – hard: her eyes were bloodshot and twin trails of kohl had left sooty tracks through her pale makeup. *Poor thing.*

By the time Cassie returned, the Goth kids had gone. Amid the dirty glasses on the table the stump of their candle sat in a pool of black wax, its wick still smoking. She stared at it a moment before going over to Zed, still at his bar stool. 'What was the story with those baby bats, do you know?' – giving a backward nod to where they'd been sitting.

He shook his shaved head slowly and Cassie was taken aback to see him blinking rapidly. 'One of their mates topped himself.'

Some part of her had known all along that they must be Bradley's mates, she realised. Was the girl who'd been crying in the loo his girlfriend? 'That's terrible.'

'Yeah, he was only fifteen.'

Later, she refused Archie's repeated offers to walk her back to her grandmother's place: the thought of the two of them meeting gave her the heebie-jeebies. On the way to the Tube he took her by the hand and tugged her round the corner to a quiet alleyway. Taking her by the shoulders he bent to kiss her, his lips barely touching hers.

Then he murmured in her ear, 'Stand on my feet, shorty'. She was about to protest, to say she was nearly five foot eight, *actually*, but instead found herself complying. He walked her backwards on his feet, his eyes locked on hers, until she was up against the wall. Then he kissed her, properly this time, his body long and hard against hers. Cassie felt her eyebrows shoot up.

For a ginger hooray, Archie was a helluva kisser.

It had turned properly cold so she took the fastest way back to the flat, along the canal, still replaying that kiss – which was probably why she wasn't running the full radar scan on her surroundings as she usually would at night.

On the last stretch of towpath before the stairway up to the safety of the street above, something made her throw a cautionary glance over her shoulder. Here, far from the high street, the towpath was empty – except for the outline of a figure thirty or forty metres behind, silhouetted against the glowering lamplight. A tall, thin man, shabbily dressed – probably homeless, which in her experience usually meant harmless. But there was something about the way this guy was walking that niggled her. It was too purposeful for a drunken down-and-out – almost as if he was trying to catch up with her.

He was probably just after a handout, the usual spiel about needing cash for a hostel place, but she was taking no chances. Doubling her pace towards the stairway, she checked behind her again. And saw that he had speeded up, too, a sight that made her go cold to the tips of her fingers.

She broke into a run. He called out then, his voice a ragged wheeze – but she didn't plan on hanging around to find out what he'd said. Properly scared now, she told herself she could outrun an ageing drunk.

Reaching the stairs she tried to take the first two steps in one stride but missed her footing, and felt her ankle buckle. As she went down she put out a hand to save herself, in the same instant twisting her body round to face whatever was coming.

The man had stopped a few feet away, bent over, struggling for breath.

He raised his head. 'Catkin' – his voice a rasp – 'I didn't do it.'

Only one person had ever called her that.

Chapter Five

If Cassie had walked past him in the street she wouldn't have given him a second glance; but once she'd seen those dark blue eyes, so like her own, she was in no doubt who he was.

Her father hadn't stopped looking at her since getting his breath back.

She leaned back against the balustrade of the stairway and folded her arms across her chest. 'Will you stop staring at me?' Although her heart was still going nineteen to the dozen she also felt strangely numb. Like someone had just punched her full in the face but the endorphin rush was warding off the inevitable pain.

'Sorry.' Dropping his eyes, he dug in his pocket, and pulled out a packet of tissues. 'Here, you're bleeding.'

The blood from her grazed palm was smeared all over the front of her T-shirt but she just crossed her arms tighter, shaking her head.

'I'm sorry I frightened you, sweetheart.'

'Don't call me that.' Cassie was still trying to process how he looked. His denim jacket hung off his emaciated frame, his chain-store jeans baggy on broomstick-thin thighs, and the sharp jawline of the wedding photo had gone, the skin there hanging down like a pair of swagged curtains. Together with the breathing that sounded like a busted accordion he looked easily a decade older than his actual age of forty-eight – and a million miles from the strong, handsome dad who used to hoist her up on his shoulders.

Apparently guessing her thoughts he said, 'I know I look like crap, Catkin.'

'Don't call me that either!'

A bout of coughing bent him double. It was a minute or more before he spoke again. 'Sharing a cell with a sixty-a-day smoker for nine years left me with chronic bronchitis.' A bitter smile. 'Which is kind of ironic considering I never smoked.'

She shivered in the cold, not wanting to speak but silently urging him to explain what he'd said.

I didn't do it.

A treacherous little voice in her head said, *Convince me.*

'Will you take my jacket at least?' His voice was deeper, rougher – his Northern Irish accent stronger than she remembered, but then according to her grandmother, he'd been living back there since his release.

She shook her head.

'Listen, Cat—Cassie. I had to see you. To tell you the truth.' He put his right hand flat on his chest. 'I swear on all that's holy that I didn't kill your mum.'

So why wait all these years to come find me? The urge to ask the question rose from somewhere deep inside her but she clamped down on it: unwilling to reveal her feelings to this . . . stranger.

'She's the only woman I ever loved,' he went on. 'That night, the first time I saw her out in the crowd at a gig?' He opened his hand like a firework bursting. 'Kapow. I was in. I was done.'

34

A lopsided smile crept over his long face, giving her a glimpse of the confident, good-looking dad she remembered, and she felt like someone had sheared open her ribs and was squeezing her heart.

'I swear to you, Cassie, when your mum was being attacked, I was at my mate Barney's watching the footie and getting battered.'

'The jury's verdict was unanimous,' she snapped, remembering what her grandmother had told her.

'Only because the barrister made Barney look like a liar! You've got to believe me. I didn't kill Kath!' He beat out the last words on his chest with the flat of his hand, making a hollow sound.

'I suppose you're going to deny hitting her as well?

He shuffled from one foot to the other. 'Look, I don't deny I had a temper on me back then. But I would never have laid a finger on Kath. She was the only woman I ever loved.'

He sounded sincere, but dropped his eyes as he spoke.

Cassie got a sudden image of her mum, her beautiful long auburn hair, her open smile with its hint of challenge. What the fuck was she doing standing here listening to the man who'd murdered her?

Something else struck her.

'How did you find me? Have you been you following me?' He might not know her address but he would still know where her grandmother lived. He must have been lurking at the foot of the block, waiting for her to go out.

He opened both hands, looking shamefaced. 'I could hardly knock at your gran's door, could I?'

Cassie started to tremble with fury. Not, in truth, for the sake of her mum, but for his weak, pathetic failure to come and find her, his only child, all these years. Followed by a backwash of guilt.

She turned abruptly and grasped the rail of the stairway.

'Cassie. Do you believe me?' He scrabbled in the pocket of his anorak. 'Can I see you again? I'm staying at a B&B in Kentish Town, The Bay Leaf.' She ignored the card he held out, his hangdog but hopeful expression only intensifying her anger.

'No. And no. Stay away from me. Or I'll call the cops.'

Chapter Six

'Don't cry!'

Cassie heard herself mumbling the words as she surfaced from sleep the following morning.

She scrabbled to hold onto her dream, to stop herself waking, but felt it slipping away, and the harder she tried the faster it evaporated. All she was left with was the vivid sense of her mother weeping inconsolably.

It was impossible to know whether the dream sprang from a real childhood memory, or whether her sleeping brain had simply coloured in the outline of an unhappy and abusive marriage. Even after the dream had ebbed completely away she still felt distressed – and confused. Why had she dreamed about her mum when she'd only just laid eyes on her father after a twenty-one-year absence?

Then it dawned on her: she felt guilty. Because seeing her dad had set up a tiny treacherous voice in her head that wouldn't shut up – *what if he was telling the truth*?

Then something else floated up from her dream: she had smelled something acrid. *Burning.* But try as she might she couldn't identify the source or make sense of it.

Was the memory real? It wouldn't be surprising if her sub-conscious had made a night-time trip into her early childhood.

The box room had been her bedroom from the age of four until the day after her seventeenth birthday, when she'd left home to seek freedom and adventure in a Camden squat. There was her tattered Nine Inch Nails poster still tacked to the wall, and the kingfisher print of the old wallpaper coming ghost-like through the midnight-blue paint job she'd given the room as a teenager. She'd even painted the ceiling the same intense blue, splodged with a few crude yellow stars of the Vincent variety here and there.

Callum turning up like that had ratcheted up her yearning to understand why her parents' marriage had gone bad, what had caused it to spiral into murderous violence. At least it was a Saturday and since she wasn't on call she didn't have to rush into work.

From the smell of baking bread, Babcia must have been up early – as usual. Then there came the soft click of the front door being closed. When she went to investigate she found a note on the kitchen worktop, propped against a still-hot loaf of half-rye sourdough. '*I've gone out to meet Barbara. Back in an hour or so,*' it read, followed by '*Let the bread cool a little or you'll get stomach-ache!*' Cassie smiled at the figure sketched underneath – on stick legs stood two circles, a tiny head above a distended belly.

She pulled a bread knife from the drawer, about to risk indigestion, when a thought sidled into her head. It was too soon to press her grandmother into talking about her daughter's marriage – that would have to wait until she was fully recovered. But she had to do something to quell the clamour of questions in her head.

Moments later she was opening the elaborately carved door of her gran's second wardrobe, the one where she kept her out-of-season clothes but also – as Cassie knew – her mementoes of

Katherine Liliana Raven, her only child. The smell that wafted out was a mix of old clothes and her grandmother's favourite perfume – *l'Air du Temps*. As a young student in 1950s Poland, Weronika had scraped together enough illegal foreign currency to buy a bottle of the stuff from the caretaker at her college who ran a sideline in contraband Western goods. But after the police had caught her pasting up flyers for a demo against the Communist regime they'd searched her room and confiscated it. It amused Cassie, the way this seemed to aggrieve Weronika more than the six months she'd been sentenced to spend in an unheated prison cell through a Warsaw winter.

Spotting the faded blue velvet of her gran's photo album sitting on top of a cardboard box she pulled it out and leafed through until she found the photo of her mother she remembered.

It had been taken at the canal end of Camden Market: in the background you could make out the decks of narrowboats in the lock. These days this spot was overrun with tourists, out-of-towners and overseas students come to rubberneck at Camden's subculture, but back then it looked low-key, with just a handful of people browsing the vintage clothes stalls in the background. From the hot-looking light and Katherine's cut-down jeans, which revealed enviably long and slender legs, it had been high summer. Her wavy auburn hair reached down her back and she looked perhaps twenty, before Cassie was born. Although Cassie's dark hair and blue eyes had clearly come from her father, it always gave her a jolt seeing her mum's wide forehead and delicate nose, so like her own.

But it was the look on her mum's face that had stuck in Cassie's mind – shyly half laughing towards the camera, with a hint of complicity you would only send a lover. Cassie's dad, in other words.

Retrieving the cardboard box the album had been sitting on, she found a smaller, fancier box within. Inside that was a treasure trove from her mother's childhood years including a bundle of school report cards. Cassie suppressed her guilty feelings by reasoning that Babcia had tried to show her these mementoes many times over the years – overtures that, as her memory of her mother faded, she'd resisted more and more strongly.

Skimming Katherine's secondary school reports she was intrigued to find the teachers' early glowing write-ups turning less complimentary as the years progressed, with the words 'sulky' and 'distracted' starting to figure and her year-end grades plummeting to Cs and Ds. *Well, well.* They sounded a lot like Cassie's own teenage school reports, and yet her grandmother had always painted her mum as a paragon – sweet-natured, a diligent student, always kept her room tidy . . . and so on *ad infinitum*. It had clearly been a propaganda ploy – although one doomed to fail – designed to improve Cassie's behaviour.

The box also held relics of Katherine's childhood: a painting of a rainbow, a bracelet of bright plastic beads, and a home-made birthday card with *To Mama from Katerina* in halting pink crayon. Although formally baptising her daughter Katherine, Weronika had always called her Katerina in the Polish way. There was a later picture postcard of wooded hills, unmistakably English, undated and addressed to the flat with a short message: *Dearest Ma & Pa. It's beautiful here and I am fine, so please don't worry about me! Love, Katherine.*

At the bottom of the box, she found a yellowed newspaper cutting about some music festival and a card-backed manila envelope. Inside it, a photograph that stopped the breath in her throat. Her mum standing in front of an official-looking arched stone entrance, arm in arm with Cassie's father. Her parents' wedding.

This was the father of her childhood, not the broken old man she'd seen last night. Drop-dead gorgeous, with a long and lean face, a crooked but sexy smile, and deep-blue eyes almost the same shade as her own. The near-black hair falling in his eyes was hers, too – a phenotype that was apparently the legacy of Mediterranean sailors plying the trade routes to Ireland for millennia. It was weird to see a face so familiar and at the same time so *un*familiar – like looking at some celebrity from the 90s.

Katherine wore her hair shorter by now, the auburn curls just brushing the shoulders of a 20s-style cream lace dress, and she held a bunch of the sort of lame flowers you might buy from the petrol station in an emergency. They made an attractive couple, but Cassie picked up something new in her – a sort of bruised prettiness, an anxiety around her eyes. The camera had caught them looking in opposite directions – probably just an accident of timing, but knowing how the story would end, it made Cassie shiver.

Turning the photo over she stared for a moment at the date written there in her grandmother's crabbed hand. *October 1992.* Six months before Cassie was born. So Katherine was pregnant when they'd got married – a fact that her Catholic grandmother had kept to herself – probably horrified at the thought of her daughter giving birth to a child 'out of wedlock'.

Had Weronika put the screws on Callum to make 'an honest woman' of her daughter? Did the terrible trajectory that would end in murder start with a shotgun wedding?

41

Putting things back in the box in what she hoped was more or less the same order Cassie came across the newspaper cutting again. From the *Camden Gazette*, June 1992, the piece said that local band *Poitín*, was to headline a benefit gig in High Wycombe for the 'Save Oakwood Common Campaign'. She was still trying to figure out what it was doing there when she heard her grandmother's key in the front door.

Chapter Seven

Cassie had managed to return the box and its contents to the wardrobe and get out of the bedroom without being caught. Now she was striding down the canal towpath – the fastest route into central Camden whether from her gran's or her own place, twenty minutes' walk in the other direction.

Out here, a mile west of the market, tranquility reigned – the traffic rumble tamed to a distant backdrop, the canal's stillness broken only by the paddling of ducks and the occasional chirrup of a moorhen. This was usually her haven, a calming headspace where she could prepare for the day ahead, but since the encounter with her father her thoughts wouldn't stop churning, like dirty clothes on a never-ending wash cycle.

She kept looking around, half-expecting to see Callum's gaunt outline on the towpath or one of the bridges crossing the canal.

Half hoping to see it, too. She pushed the thought away.

After seeing the wedding photo, a new and unwelcome idea had shouldered its way into Cassie's consciousness. *Her mother hadn't wanted her.* The younger Katherine the camera shutter had captured in the market had looked so happy – keen to go to university, with an exciting future ahead of her – before discovering she was pregnant. That had narrowed her horizons to a single narrow path: a shotgun wedding and a marriage that went sour. Together with Cassie's recurring dream of her mother weeping, it was impossible not to draw the obvious conclusion: that her unwanted arrival had ruined her parents' relationship.-

The sun had come out, burning off the morning mist and softening the winter chill. Cassie slowed for a moment to check the best route to Holborn Library.

The cutting from the local paper she'd found in her grand-mother's mementoes box had given her an idea. She had already searched online for details of her mother's murder and her father's trial – in vain: the national papers had digitised their back editions, but apparently, yet another wife-murder wasn't big enough news to make their pages in the first place. But she'd discovered that hard copies of the local rag, the *Camden Gazette*, going back to the 90s were archived at Holborn Library, and it was open on Saturdays.

The sound of traffic and human hubbub mounted as she reached the footbridge just before the lock. Pausing in the middle to look towards the market she tried to locate the spot where her mum had been standing in the photo, but it was now home to a sprawl of hot food stalls sending up a spicy cloud of Indian, Korean and Moroccan aromas. In a couple of hours the aisles of the market would be heaving with sightseers. Self-respecting locals avoided the place – the original traders who had sold an eclectic mix of antiques, decent leather goods, home-made jewellery, and vintage clothes were now outnumbered by stalls flogging mass-produced tat from China which you might as well buy off Amazon. Worse, only a handful of the original clubs and music venues survived in the Victorian warehouse buildings that ringed the market.

Jesus, listen to yourself, woman. Moaning on about a lost golden era again.

Passing a busker murdering 'Another Day in Paradise' reminded Cassie of the band mentioned in the newspaper cutting. Something her grandmother had said years ago, in one of her rare comments about Callum, came back to her: 'Singing wasn't a proper job for a husband and father.'

Of course! Poitín must have been her father's band. He was a Northern Irish Catholic and the name looked like one of those unpronounceable Gaelic words. The cutting was the souvenir of a proud girlfriend in love with the front man in a rock band.

A sign in the lobby of the shabby 60s-era library directed her to the archive up on the first floor but there she found the door locked. After knocking at the wired glass she saw a girl get up from the reception desk to come to the door.

'I'm sorry, but we're closed for stocktaking,' she said. 'It should say so on the website.'

Cassie must have looked gutted because she didn't close the door.

'What is it you need to see?'

A few minutes later she was in, and the kind-hearted librarian was setting down a pile of eight oversized bound books holding the *Camden Gazette* for 1997 and 1998 – Cassie having figured that while the murder would have been reported straight away, the case would have taken a while to reach court.

'You're in luck,' said the librarian. 'Anything earlier is on microfiche and I can't spare the time today to show you how to use the machine.'

Cassie nodded knowledgeably. *What the fuck was a microfish?*

The smell of the old newspaper was the first thing that hit her. Musty but not unpleasant, it made her feel . . . nostalgic. At first she couldn't figure out why, but then she remembered, it smelled a bit like the second-hand copy of *Gray's Anatomy* her grandmother had given her on her eleventh birthday. Picturing herself lying on her bed, poring over its intricate illustrations of organs and musculature, memorising the names, she smiled. How many other grandmas would have handled a childhood fascination with the dead so matter-of-factly?

Although Cassie had visited her mum's grave she couldn't remember the exact date of her death, recalling only that she had died in the autumn of 1997, so she started with the September '97 editions. Entering the Camden of two decades ago felt like descending in a diving bell into a lost world.

The Parkway Cinema, now an Odeon, had been showing *Trainspotting* and *Dead Man Walking*, two of her favourite films. Then *Toy Story*. Yes! She remembered her father taking her to see it. When the little boy had mothballed his old favourite, the cowboy Woody, she'd been inconsolable. Hadn't her dad given her some sweets to comfort her?

Fizzy cola bottles. She could still recall the transgressive thrill when they landed on your tongue. Why hadn't had her mum been with them?

In the music listings, legendary venues like the Roundhouse and Electric Ballroom were still going strong but she was disappointed to see them hosting mostly metal, indie, funk, and jazz acts – or raves. She'd stupidly been expecting to see her personal heroes like The Clash, The Cure, Siouxsie and the Banshees, The Ramones … when of course the punk/post-punk scene had waned at least a decade earlier.

Even the good old days had a good old days.

Leafing past ads for flats on sale at 90k – which would now go for five times that – she was amused to find an actual Lonely Hearts page – *Attractive lady, 39, seeks professional gentleman for theatre visits and possible marriage.* No swiping right back then: you had to write to a box number, which sounded a bit filthy.

The crime coverage was dominated by drug-dealing busts, but there were none of the drug-related knifings that all too often ended up on her mortuary table; the only report of a stabbing – non-fatal – arose out of two guys having a fight outside a pub over a girl.

The biggest story was about a local police corruption case – a Camden detective, who had pocketed twenty-five grand for turning a blind eye to organised crime activity, caught in a sting by an anti-corruption unit.

Cassie paused to stretch. She'd reached the end of September without finding any mention of her mother's murder.

Halfway through the seventh volume she reached the front page for October 6, 1997 – and met her mother's trusting gaze.

BRUTAL MURDER OF CAMDEN MOTHER, 26

She suddenly knew what they meant when they said a headline screamed. The block capitals jumped off the page in a shriek that raised the hairs on her forearms. Then her eye fell on the black-and-white photo down the page – a cobbled street under a railway bridge, and one of those white tents the police used to

47

cover bodies. She pushed her chair back from the table with a grating screech.

Next thing she knew, someone was telling her to take deep breaths. She opened her eyes to see the criss-crossed laces of her own DMs. Lifting her head cautiously she met the librarian's wide-eyed gaze.

'I'm OK. Sorry about that.' She managed a weak smile. 'No breakfast.'

'Are you sure?' After casting a glance at the headline, the girl retreated.

Christ. Fancy throwing a whitey! Scooping up people who fainted was usually her job.

Once the initial shock had passed, Cassie found herself able to read the article more coolly, as if the two-decade-old crime had happened to someone else.

Local mother of one, Katherine Raven, twenty-six, was found dead in Prowse Place early on Sunday morning. Police are treating it as murder. 'This was a brutal crime and Camden Police offer our sincere condolences to Katherine's family,' DCI Stanley Neville told the Camden Gazette. *'We will not rest until the perpetrator has been brought to justice.' He appealed to anyone who saw Katherine in the area around Camden Road station on Saturday night or has any other information, to contact him or DS Gerald Hobbs directly.*

The cops didn't reveal how Katherine had died – which Cassie knew was standard procedure at the early stage of an investigation.

Barely three weeks later the paper ran the headline **TRAGIC KATHERINE – HUSBAND CHARGED WITH MURDER** above a close-up of a smiling Callum, which looked like it had been cropped from a publicity shot of his band. The piece, which was only three paragraphs long, repeated the basic facts; reporting restrictions presumably preventing the paper saying more before the trial.

The first day of Callum Raven's trial was 13 April 1998. It had been held at Snaresbrook Crown Court from where the paper's crime correspondent filed detailed reports.

First up in the witness box was DS Hobbs. He described how he'd arrived at Prowse Place after a 999 call from the early morning dog walker. He had found Katherine bludgeoned to death, evidently many hours previously – and had recovered the presumed murder weapon, a bloodied half-brick that lay nearby. Later that day, when he and his DCI Stanley Neville had interviewed Callum Raven, Hobbs said they found his account of what had happened as 'confused and defensive'.

The case put by the prosecution over the following ten days was this: Callum and Katherine had gone for a rare evening out, and – in a detail that brought Cassie up short – had left their four-year-old daughter on a sleepover at her grandparents'. Callum said that the couple were drinking in The Hawley Arms until just before 9 p.m. when he'd left his wife there, to go to a mate's house to watch football – stopping for a 'quick pint' at a second pub on the way. But when the prosecution called the barman at the Hawley, he reported that he'd had to eject Callum after he started shouting at Katherine. Distressed and tearful, she had stayed for another drink before also leaving around 10 p.m.

From the time she was last seen alive leaving the pub and the pathologist's calculations, Katherine's murder was estimated to have happened between 10 p.m. and midnight. A key witness for the prosecution was a middle-aged male eyewitness who reported looking out of his window and seeing a man running down Prowse Place just before midnight – a man he later ID-ed as Callum in a line-up.

Damningly, when his wife failed to return home that night Callum hadn't even called the police, claiming that he'd assumed she'd gone to her mother's.

The name of the final witness for the prosecution was unexpected. Weronika Janek. Cassie's grandmother was called to give a picture of the marriage and was quick to paint her son-in-law as a work-shy drunk, prone to angry outbursts, before going on to report the time she'd called unexpectedly at the couple's flat to find her daughter nursing a black eye. Kath claimed she'd fallen over and hit her face on the edge of the bath. 'And what did you make of her account?' asked the barrister. 'It was an untruth,' she said. 'My daughter was always a hopeless liar, from when she was a tiny girl.' The defence barrister couldn't leave the jury to draw the obvious conclusion, so on cross-questioning he asked whether Katherine had given Weronika any reason at all to believe that Callum had hit her. Her response had been succinct but effective: 'She didn't need to.'

Hearing an echo of her dream – the distant sound of her mother weeping – Cassie felt her whole body tense with rage. As a child she had no doubt heard the sound of her mother crying after just such a beating.

'Sorry to interrupt—'

Cassie jumped in her seat. It was the librarian.

'Oh, sorry! But I need to go into the archive now and I can't leave anyone here unattended.' Her kind eyes looked anxious.

She let Cassie make photocopies of the relevant articles, including the ones she hadn't had a chance to read yet, and gave her a couple of rubber bands to make them into an easy-to-carry scroll. She declined Cassie's attempt to pay with a little 'don't worry' wave before unlocking the door for her. 'Good luck with your research' – her tentative smile recognising that Cassie's quest was personal and important.

Chapter Eight

Back in Camden, Cassie took her precious scroll to her favourite coffee shop in a quiet backstreet off the high street.

Reading the reports of her father's trial was an unsettling experience. Despite knowing the outcome she felt strangely torn: wanting to see him punished, while also nursing the irrational hope that he might be exonerated Hollywood-style, by some last-minute courtroom revelation. It was a bit like one of the alternative narratives – all those what-ifs – that tormented the newly-bereaved.

Pressed by the prosecution barrister to explain his wife's bruised face, Callum repeated what his wife had told her mother – that she'd simply fallen over. When confronted by the pathologist's report, which also mentioned bruising to Katherine's arms, he claimed neither to have seen the bruises nor to have any explanation for them. The barrister also produced a record of the police attending a domestic – a noisy argument at their flat reported by neighbours just days before the murder.

Callum admitted that they'd been having arguments because he believed Katherine was seeing another man. She had denied it, and when Callum was invited to share any evidence of an affair with the court, all he could say was that she'd been 'acting suspiciously'. His testimony ended with him losing his rag, shouting that the police should be trying to find his wife's mystery lover – the man he claimed must have killed her. It wasn't hard to imagine how Callum would have come across to the jury: as a volatile young man with a hair-trigger temper.

Cassie remembered his protestation the previous night that he would never hurt her mother. He had *sounded* sincere, but had avoided her gaze. As if he was hiding something.

Ironically, it was a witness for the defence who helped to hammer the final nail into her father's coffin. Barney Cotter was Callum's best friend but had apparently also been both *Poitín*'s manager and drummer. It was his house Callum had gone to after being thrown out of the pub and Barney said that they'd watched the end of the Arsenal match before sitting drinking beer and chatting. Crucially, he said that Callum was there 'past midnight' – which wouldn't have given him enough time to reach Prowse Place and attack his wife. But when cross-questioned by the prosecution, Barney contradicted himself over the time Callum had actually left. The prosecuting barrister carried on needling him about his vagueness over the timing, finally triggering a damning admission: 'I'd had a lot to drink!'

Barney was forced to admit that he couldn't be one hundred per cent sure that Callum had still been there at midnight – which left enough time for his mate to encounter Kath and commit the murder.

In his summing-up, the prosecution counsel demolished Callum's alibi faster than a cut-price shed, and painted him as a heavy drinker with a violent temper. The accused's belief in his wife's infidelity, albeit 'wholly erroneous', had become an obsession, he claimed. After the row in the pub, Callum had intercepted his 'beautiful and innocent young wife' on her way home before beating her to death in a jealous rage and being seen running away after the crime. Rather than confessing, Callum had compounded his crime by besmirching Katherine's name in a last-ditch bid to divert the blame from himself to a fictitious lover.

At the sound of rapping, Cassie looked up and grinned to see her old squatting buddy Kieran, the closest thing she had to a best friend, waving through the window of the coffee shop. She'd called him right after leaving the library. Cassie had always found confiding in people difficult: the living were so much more complicated than the dead. But for once, her need to talk things over had outweighed her reticence.

He made his way over, his dipping limp the legacy of a bad fall he'd had years ago while off his head, which had trashed his knee. 'Thanks for coming, Kieran,' she told him. 'It's great to see you.' She eyed him with a smiling frown 'Wow, you look . . .'

'Like a proper straight, right?' Striking a model-ish pose, Kieran waved both hands over his outfit.

When they'd last met a few weeks back, he'd still been sleeping rough and pursuing his twin hobbies of special brew and ketamine. Now in place of his usual stained and raggedy-arsed tracksuit, he wore new jeans and trainers and a brand-new black puffa jacket. The sores on his face were healed, and his strawberry-blond frizz had been clipped almost to a buzzcut – although his wide smile revealed gaps in his teeth from years of living on the street.

After she'd ordered him a hot chocolate, Kieran brought her up to date. He'd been sober a month and had a long-term place in a dry hostel run by a homeless charity, which had not only given him money for new clothes but set him up with basic training in accounts and marketing.

'That's brilliant news,' she said. 'What made you take the leap?'

'To be honest, the booze and ket was doing my head in. And I'm not getting any younger. One more winter sleeping out would probably have killed me.' His ever-present grin broadened as he contemplated his own demise. He was probably right: last time they met Kieran had looked like a forty-year-old with too many miles on the clock, but now he looked a bit closer to his actual age of twenty-nine. 'If I can stay straight and get through the training I'm going to get a share in a market stall.'

'What are you going to sell?'

'I've been talking to a supplier of those novelty rubber duckies.' He laughed at Cassie's bemused expression. 'Haven't you seen them? They're designed to look like Batman, or the Queen. I reckon the tourists would love 'em.'

Cassie would never have described the old Kieran as entrepreneur material, but she could imagine novelty ducks selling well on the market. And if he could just stay sober, she could see his eternal optimism taking him a long way.

'The last of the squatting generation goes straight, eh, Kieran?'

They shared a rueful smile. Camden had once offered a decent supply of closed-down pubs, semi-derelict offices, and light industrial units just begging to be squatted by those who couldn't afford, or didn't want the ties of, a rental agreement. But now that Camden property prices had gone stratospheric, developers were in a tearing hurry to get their investment back and wouldn't tolerate squatters even on a temporary basis.

Her own place – a hard-to-let council flat in a dilapidated tower block – was earmarked for demolition and replacement by a shiny public-private housing development. The council would have to rehouse her but it was unlikely to be in central Camden. If she was lucky she might get something in the grimmest bit of Gospel Oak; if not, she faced exile from her beloved Camden to some God-awful suburb.

He nodded to the sheaf of paperwork under her elbow. 'What's all this then, Cassie Raven?'

When he hadn't been off his face, Kieran had always been smart, and a good listener. After she gave him the rundown on what had happened to her mum he screwed his face up in sympathy and said, 'Bummer.'

She passed him the articles covering the key moments of her father's murder trial.

After reading through it all in silence he leaned back and met her eye. 'So, do you think he did it?'

That brought it home to her. Her interest in the coverage of the trial wasn't just a need to understand events leading up to her mother's death. From the moment her father had turned up to protest his innocence she'd nursed a subconscious desire to uncover some flaw in the case. It was obvious why – if Callum Raven really had been falsely accused she got her father back. But for the sake of her mother, she had to stay objective.

'Well, the jury certainly thought so,' she said. 'They took less than an hour to find him guilty.'

'Your mum never actually said it was him who hit her though, did she?' said Kieran, frowning at one of the articles. 'It's all insinuation.'

In his summing-up the judge had reminded the jury that there was no evidence that Callum was responsible for his wife's bruises, but her grandmother's heavy hint had clearly hit home.

'And there weren't any forensics against him, was there?' he went on.

She shook her head. Although the police lab had reported a match between her mother's blood and the blood from the half-brick murder weapon, the tests hadn't yielded any other usable DNA which might have identified her attacker.

'No, but he was seen running away from the murder scene at the right time.'

'Witnesses are shit at identifying people.' Kieran frowned. 'A couple of years back, somebody swore to the feds he'd seen me half-inch some lady's handbag from under her table at The White Lion. It was just dumb luck I could prove I was in a DSS interview at the time.'

'Maybe. Then there was the row they had that was so bad the neighbours called the police, and the one in the pub – and her mysterious bruises. If I was one of the jurors I think I'd buy that he was a violent man.'

Kieran frowned down at the photocopied articles. 'You said you were what, four, when your mum died? Do you remember him being aggressive? Were you scared of him?'

She shook her head. 'Never. In fact, out of the two of them he's the one I remember best, and he was lovely – smiley, kind, patient . . .' She shrugged. 'But then he could have been nice to me but violent to her, right?'

Kieran's smile grew crooked. 'In my experience, if the dad is a wifebeater the kids get their share too.' Eyeing his face, Cassie realised that Kieran had never talked about why he had dropped out of straight life and ended up with serious booze and gear issues: it was the kind of thing you didn't ask people in the squat. Anyway, she couldn't explain what had made her drop out at seventeen, swapping a loving home for Camden's alternative subculture, even if her own interlude squatting with a bunch of druggie vagabonds hadn't lasted long.

'I'm sorry, Kieran,' she murmured.

He shrugged before picking up one of the photocopies. 'It sounds to me like the feds made up their minds from the off that your dad was their man. You know what I think really tipped things against him?'

'Go on?'

'The alibi from his buddy Barney that fell over in court. I reckon that's worse than not having one in the first place. If I was on that jury I'd assume your dad got his mate to cover for him but then it all went Pete Tong on the day.'

Cassie frowned. 'Maybe that's exactly what happened.'

Kieran tipped his head, conceding the point.

'You were always a bit of a muso,' she said. 'I remember you also knew chapter and verse on what gigs happened where round here. You ever hear of this band he was in? Poi-tin?'

'Poi . . . ? Oh, *Puuh-cheen*. It's Gaelic for moonshine.' Kieran's hundred-watt grin was back. 'No, I can't say as I have. But there were probably fifty Irish rock bands playing the pubs and clubs round here in the Nineties. I can ask around if you like?'

After they left the coffee shop Kieran nodded towards the roll of photocopies she carried. 'This is heavy shit you're getting into, Cassie Raven. Maybe it's not for me to say but . . . are you sure you wouldn't be better off letting the past alone?'

She thought about it for a moment.

'The way it feels to me, Kieran, it's the past that won't let me alone.'

Chapter Nine

Around 7.45 a.m. on Monday and the sky was only just starting to lighten as Cassie made her way to the mortuary, squinting through the winter fog that cocooned the canal. She liked the uncanny sensation of hearing the slap of water against the banks while only glimpsing its black surface intermittently through the mist.

Others might find it an unwelcoming spot, the post-weekend towpath strewn with fast-food debris, the graffiti that screamed from the walls of the foot tunnels, but for as long as she could remember the canal had been a source of fascination and mystery – so that it had become almost a part of her. Recently, whenever she thought about having to move to the suburbs, and imagined losing the daily sight and earthy scent of its dark waters, she felt a little leap of panic.

She had spent the rest of the weekend trying to follow Kieran's advice, but had found the only surefire way to stop herself constantly going over her mum's murder and her dad's trial was to drown her thoughts in vodka. Like unwanted puppies. It had worked, up to a point, and had at least granted her two nights of dream-free sleep, but now she was paying the price in an epic cumulative hangover.

As she neared the mortuary entrance she was digging in her bag for her swipe card when she heard somebody call her name.

'Long time no see.' Phyllida Flyte raised a perfect eyebrow. As ever, her tone was dry, borderline sarky. Was it something they taught wannabe cops during training?

'DS Flyte,' said Cassie, stupidly, noting the flutter in the pit of her stomach. Probably just the after-effects of too much vodka.

'Oh, I thought we were on first-name terms these days,' she said, tipping her head to one side and pulling a tight smile. She had a new haircut – gone was the tightly wound chignon from which not a single hair had dared to escape; now her wheat-blonde hair hung in a slanted chin-length bob, perfectly cut, of course. The style emphasised the geometrical planes of her face – the wide cheekbones and clean jawline. She put Cassie in mind of a cubist painting of a beautiful woman.

'Phyllida then.' Swiping her card Cassie pushed open the door. 'What brings you here?'

'I wanted to check some details on a young suicide who came in last week. I'm the family liaison officer.'

So Flyte must be the female cop who Kim Appleton mentioned attending after Bradley's death. *Just my luck*, thought Cassie.

They headed down the corridor towards the body store.

At the threshold Flyte paused, frowning down at her smart black jacket, before picking an invisible piece of fluff off the lapel and discarding it.

Cassie took in what she was wearing: a wool crepe trouser suit, undeniably well cut, but too conservative, too *middle-aged* for someone in her mid-thirties – especially teamed with those mother-of-the-bride court shoes. 'Jaeger sale?' she asked, nodding to her outfit.

Flyte's eyes narrowed. 'How did you know?'

Cassie shrugged. 'I don't know, it's January. Just a good guess.'

When the two of them had first met a couple of months back they couldn't have got off to a worse start. Cassie's visceral mistrust of the cops had only been affirmed when Flyte treated her as a suspect for the theft of a body from the mortuary. Then, after Cassie had been cleared of any involvement, she had gone on to persuade Flyte – OK, *blackmailed* might be a more accurate word – to investigate the supposedly natural death of her former teacher Geraldine Edwards. By the time the killer had been charged with Mrs E's murder, the mutual suspicion between the two of them had been replaced by a wary respect.

Be honest. It was more than that.

OK, so Cassie had sensed a certain edgy frisson between them from the off, but when it reached a tipping point she had backed off. Not because Flyte was female – Cassie had dated girls as well as boys since her teens – but because she was a cop. The animosity dated from the time a male police officer had manhandled her during an ugly eviction from one of the squats. Only a few months later, the cops had busted her for a tiny wrap of speed – a conviction which could have derailed her application to become a mortuary technician.

Cassie handed Flyte the coroner's report and the summary of Bradley's medical notes to read before pulling his drawer out on its castors and unzipping the body bag as far as his waist. Over the weekend his skin had acquired a distinct bluish tinge.

'Why do they go that colour?' asked Flyte.

'It's the oxygen in blood that gives tissue its pink colour. Deoxygenated blood is dark which makes the skin appear blue.'

Flyte pointed to a purple patch, like a vivid bruise, just visible on the underside of Bradley's body. 'That's just the blood settling to the back of the body, right?'

'Yep. It's called hypostasis.' The manual for the human body had been written in Latin and Greek, and Cassie's final night school A level in classics had helped to fix thousands of anatomical terms in her memory. Hypostasis, for instance, was easy to remember once you knew it came from the Greek for sediment – *matter which settles.*

She eyed Bradley's repaired Y-incision with a critical eye, knowing that his mum would be wanting to view him again once he went to the undertakers. Having to cut both sides of his throat had made the repair impossible to hide, but she was as happy as she could be with the results: the stitching was neat and even, with no bobbling or distortion of the skin.

'Why did you want to see him again?' Cassie asked.

She read in Flyte's expression a rare admission of having no good answer.

'I just feel so sorry for his parents,' she said, pink tingeing her pale cheeks – reminding Cassie of the compassionate side that occasionally peeked out from beneath Flyte's chilly composure. 'I don't suppose you found anything at the PM to suggest that he didn't really intend to kill himself?'

Cassie shook her head. 'Intent isn't our strong point, I'm afraid. I wondered at first whether it might have been an auto-erotic experiment, but I hear there was nothing at the scene to suggest that?' She'd seen a handful of such cases over the years – all of them men. Self-strangulation could increase the intensity of a climax, apparently – at the risk of getting a bigger finale than you bargained for.

Flyte shook her head. 'No. He was fully clothed and there was no history of porn searches on his laptop.'

Cassie shrugged. 'I'm hoping toxicology will find he took something that sent him a bit crazy, so he didn't really understand what he was doing.'

'Unlikely,' said Flyte. 'We didn't find any evidence of drugs, or drug paraphernalia in his room, and when I interviewed his friends – they all swore that the most he ever did was smoke a bit of cannabis.'

Seeing the lip curl that followed the word cannabis, Cassie pictured Flyte interviewing Bradley's goth pals in her Jaeger suit. As if they would 'fess up to a cop – let alone a five-star straight like Flyte – any more than she would have at their age. An image of the tear-stained girl with the turquoise-streaked hair came into her head.

'What about his girlfriend?'

Flyte pinned her gaze on Cassie. 'What girlfriend?'

A shrug to gain time. 'I suppose I was just assuming he'd have one.'

Flyte's unusually pale blue eyes – the corneas like fallen discs of winter sky – remained fixed on Cassie, who held the look without blinking.

'Anything else?' asked Flyte after a moment.

Cassie turned Bradley's arm to show her the ladder of razor scars he'd incised in his soft skin.

'Right,' Flyte sighed. 'I'm probably wasting my time.' She closed her notebook with a resigned gesture. 'According to the research, a third of goth youngsters self-harm and they're six times as likely to suicide as a normal kid.'

Normal kid ... Cassie felt a thrill of irritation run up her neck. 'Actually, those scars are a few months old, so they're from before Bradley got into the goth scene. Has it occurred to you he might have *stopped* cutting himself because he'd found people who understood him?' She could hear her voice getting heated. 'As for the research, I've read it too, and it seems to me the study authors are confusing cause and effect. Goths are probably drawn to dark stuff because they're already sad and the straight world gives them zero outlet for those feelings.'

There was a long silence as Flyte eyed her face. 'Anyway. Thanks for letting me see him.'

As Cassie saw Flyte out, she said to the back of that gleaming blonde head. 'By the way, if I wanted to find out more about a murder case from the Nineties, how would I go about it?'

Flyte sent a smile back over her shoulder. 'Why? I hope you're not planning on mounting another freelance murder investigation.'

When she smiled it illuminated and softened her usually severe expression. Cop or no cop, she was certainly a looker.

'No, nothing like that, it's just an old local case I'm interested in.' As she closed the door on Flyte's curious expression, Cassie pulled what she hoped would pass as an innocent smile.

It was only then that it struck her. Investigating her mother's murder was exactly what she was planning to do.

FLYTE

Flyte took a sip of her Earl Grey tea – watery and, at £3.50, criminally overpriced. Sadly, her policing powers didn't extend to the impertinent pricing policies of Shoreditch hipster cafes.

Matt, her ex-husband, had named the rendezvous because it was close to his office in the City. Not quite yet ex in fact, not until the divorce had wended its way through the tortuous judicial labyrinth. All of which it had – naturally – fallen to her to navigate. Because Matt's job as a middle manager in a City fintech firm – the tribulations of which he'd been holding forth on since he arrived – was obviously far more important and demanding than that of an inner-city police detective.

Their divorce was as straightforward as these things could be – they'd agreed a straight split of the profits on their little house in Winchester – but it had nonetheless generated a snowstorm of legal forms and documents.

And on almost every form, the question that she dreaded lay in wait.

Children?

None.

She was only starting to face the fact of that absence – if not yet quite full on. For more than two years she'd managed to keep it at arm's length, simply in order to be able to function day-to-day. That necessity had become even more pressing after she'd taken up her new post in Camden CID four months ago – intended as a fresh start, far from any reminders of her old life.

After three and a half years of marriage and only twenty-eight weeks of pregnancy Flyte had given birth to a baby girl.

Stillborn. *But still born.*

'Phyllida?'

She must have muttered the last bit out loud.

When he picked up his monologue where he'd left off – something about some promotion he deserved – she felt the old rage rising inside her. But almost as swiftly, it ebbed. She knew that Matt talked to fill the chasm that their daughter's death had opened between them. Deep and wide as the Marianas Trench.

And yet.

She found these occasional meetings unsettling, and not just because Matt studiously avoided any allusion to Poppy. It was because their former life – their former love – kept flitting into her peripheral vision. One moment Matt was just some over-weight City stranger in a chalk-stripe suit – the extra stone and double chin he'd gained since the separation making him look older than his thirty-seven years – but then he would smile and she'd see the drily funny and fundamentally sweet man she'd fallen for. Images of him from their old life kept surfacing: the silly straw hat he used to wear to mow the lawn, or the way he'd always say 'Yammas!' when popping the cork on a bottle, a habit acquired on a holiday to Santorini. And the memory that she most wished she could dislodge – him balancing on a step ladder reaching up to fix a mobile to the nursery ceiling, white bunny rabbits circling wildly below . . .

Unless she shut him up he would talk forever, and now that he'd signed the latest batch of divorce paperwork she was impatient to broach the subject she really needed to talk about.

66

'Matt.' Hearing the note in her voice, he stopped and sent her a wary look. 'I need to ask you something, to do with Poppy.'

'I never agreed to a name.' His lips pushed out in that familiar stubborn gesture.

'You didn't want a ceremony – or anything to mark her life. The least I could do was give her a name.' Struggling to keep her voice low, non-accusing. Stopping herself from asking him what the hell he'd been thinking when he persuaded her, just days after their daughter's death, to allow her little body to be cremated with no ceremony, alongside two other stillborn babies, their intermingled ashes scattered in the crematorium memorial garden. And asking herself for the thousandth time why she had agreed to it.

'Matt, you remember that medical report, the one saying why we lost her? I was half-crazy at the time and I just couldn't face reading it – but now I really want to and I can't find it anywhere. I could try the hospital but that would probably take forever. You must still have it?'

APH, they had called it. Antepartum haemorrhage. In human-speak, their baby girl had bled to death during the birth. After they had cleaned her up, she'd looked perfect, but pale as a marble cherub. Flyte could dimly recall a doctor telling them something about the umbilical cord having grown in the wrong place. The only other thing seared into her memory was him saying that if it had been picked up earlier in the pregnancy, a Caesarian might have saved her. *If.*

He looked away, frowning. 'It's a long time ago, Phyll.'

'I just wanted to ask. I didn't have any weird symptoms, did I? Before they rushed me in that night, I mean. Do you recall me ever mentioning any bleeding early in the pregnancy?' These last couple of months, since she'd started allowing herself to think about the pregnancy, about losing Poppy, a fear had been gnawing away at her. Had she missed something, some twinge or sign that she should have reported to the GP which might have saved her daughter? Their daughter.

After a pause, she pushed something across the table. 'I took a photograph of her that day, before the nurse took her away. I had a print made for you. I haven't been able to look at it until recently but ... well, when you feel ready, you might find it's kind of a comfort.'

Matt looked down at the tabletop – probably trying not to cry. But when he lifted his head his eyes weren't tearful but hot and angry, his lips thinned to a bitter line. 'What possible good can it do, digging it all up again?' he asked in a fierce undertone. 'A bad thing happened; it was an incredibly rare syndrome. It was just terrible luck, the doctor said.'

He shucked his sleeve to look at his watch. 'I've got to go.' His chair grated on the floor – a brutal sound. 'It's been two years, Phyllida. You really should be getting over it by now, like I have. That might sound harsh but it needs to be said. I'll pay the bill on my way out.' And he walked away, leaving the photo untouched on the table.

Two years, two months and nine days, actually, she wanted to say. She had spent most of that time in the same state as Matt – refusing to accept what had happened and furious with the world, and herself. He wasn't 'over it', that was for sure. As if one could ever 'get over' such a thing.

She picked up the photo and pressed her cheek against Poppy's. All you could really hope for was to make peace with the absence, to have it walk alongside you the rest of your life, to endure.

Chapter Ten

Cassie kept her head down at work all day, determined to avoid any clashes with Jason or the ghastly Dr Curzon.

First on the PM list was Mrs Perlman, eighty-six, a widowed Jewish lady who'd died after falling in her kitchen while recovering from a knee replacement op. A PM was needed to see whether her death was the result of a stroke or heart attack, for instance, or from injuries sustained in the fall.

When Cassie unzipped the body bag to reveal her face she had to put out a hand to steady herself. Beneath Mrs P's blue-rinse fringe her left eye was puffed up like a golf ball and a fresh purple bruise enveloped much of the left-hand side of her face, stretching from the eye socket almost down to the jawline.

Without warning she was pitched back to her grandmother's witness box account of her father: an angry man with a drink problem who shouted at his wife in public and knocked her about in private. Picturing her mother's sweet, trusting face battered and bruised like Mrs P's she clenched her fists so hard that the nails bit into her palms. Why had she allowed her father to sow seeds of doubt about his guilt when her poor mother wasn't around to speak up for herself?

Pull yourself together. 'Hello there, Mrs Perlman.' Her voice a murmur, she set a hand on her shoulder, the bones there as fragile as a bird's. She chatted on, telling Mrs P where she was and why she needed to be examined, but still she felt like there was a boulder sitting in her stomach. Had her usual professional detachment deserted her? Would every body bag she opened risk pouring salt in an open wound?

Ten minutes later, as Cassie lifted off the top of her skull, Mrs P's cause of death became blindingly obvious: a fatal sub-arachnoid haemorrhage. Arachnoid: from the Greek *arachne* for spider. The obvious clotting distorting the spider-like formation of veins on the surface of Mrs P's brain was typical of this type of cerebrovascular accident. This time, though, she knew better than to mention her observation to Dr Curzon.

Later, after she'd reconstituted and repaired Mrs P's body, Cassie left the other three bodies to Jason so she could clear a backlog of forms from the coroner's office.

Heading out at lunchtime to grab a sandwich, she glimpsed a figure in black disappearing round the side of the mortuary towards the main road. Somebody had been standing there and had hastily made themselves scarce on seeing Cassie open the door.

Remembering the gang who'd stolen a body from the mortuary a couple of months back, she broke into a jog – the narrow lane to the main road was long enough for her to catch up with whoever it was. But when she got there: *nada*. Whoever it was must have had to sprint to reach the road that fast. Picturing the figure again in her mind's eye, Cassie upped her speed.

Reaching the main road she found the pavement empty in both directions. She headed north to the nearest turning, which she knew to be a cul-de-sac. And there, leaning against the tall brick wall of an old warehouse, she found her.

The goth girl from Bradley's wake. The giveaway had been the long black coat and the flash of blue in her hair. Panting and clutching her side, she raised her head and Cassie was taken aback by the look of fear in her eyes.

Joining her against the wall and getting her own breath back, Cassie gave her a moment to recover.

'You OK?'

The girl gave a wary nod at the pavement. Under the black coat she was wearing a long floaty black lace dress and a monochrome scarf with a spooky winged insects design around her neck. Her makeup was full goth white face – her mouth a slash of purple, a bolt through the upper lip. She was pretty but a lot of people would read her look as in-your-face, designed to shock or challenge. Cassie knew better. It was camouflage. A look that you put on to retreat from a hostile world, to cover up your angst and confusion. And a badge of solidarity with a different tribe – people who understood.

'What's your name?' Cassie asked her.

'Naenia, spelt with an "ae".'

Cassie had to stop herself smiling.

'Dark name,' she said approvingly. 'Goddess of funerals, right?'

'And funeral laments.' Naenia was cautiously eyeing Cassie now, her gaze lingering on her piercings.

'Look, Naenia, you haven't done anything wrong. If a friend of mine died I'd be haunting the place where he lay too.'

Naenia looked confused for a moment, then she lifted her chin. 'I want to see him.'

Tricky.

'How old are you?'

'Seventeen.'

71

Cassie let it hang there.

'Fifteen.'

'That's going to make it difficult. Would your parents be cool with you seeing Bradley?'

A scornful little puff through her lips. 'There's only my mother, and she wouldn't give a fuck either way.'

As a former black belt in teen bravado Cassie sensed the hurt beneath the tough chat. 'I'm sorry to hear that, Naenia. You'd also need permission from his mum and dad. Do you know them?'

A little headshake. 'Bradley's dad was really harsh on him and his friends.' Naenia's fingers went to her hairline where she plucked out a hair and discarded it, before tugging sideways on the scarf at her neck. The gestures reflexive and seemingly unconscious.

In the past, Cassie had relayed viewing requests to the next of kin, but visualising Kim and Steve Appleton she hesitated: would it be right to intrude on that raw grief?

'You were his girlfriend, I'm guessing?'

'No. Yes. Sort of.' The girl looked confused. 'We'd . . . kissed, but we weren't official yet.' She blushed so fiercely that pink patches appeared through her foundation.

'Had you known him long?'

'Since the middle of autumn term. Nearly three months.'

She had to ask. 'Naenia. Do you have any idea why—'

'No,' Naenia broke in.

'Was he unhappy about something in particular?' Cassie persisted.

'No! He was in a great mood. We were going to the Whitby Goth weekend in April!'

Bram Stoker's *Dracula* had been set in Whitby and the festival was the goth equivalent of the Hajj. Whatever ructions Bradley had been having with his dad, and with a hot girlfriend and a cool event to look forward to, why would he want to kill himself? It didn't make sense.

'Because you know it would really help his mum and dad if they had some idea of why he did it.' Cassie got a flash of Kim Appleton tucking a faded stuffed penguin into her son's neck. And reached a decision. She couldn't pass on Naenia's request to see Bradley. The brutal truth was that Kim and Steve's loss of their only child would stalk them until their dying day, whereas there was a good chance Naenia would have a new boyfriend within six months.

The young moved on. And rightly so. She could always go to his funeral.

She heard Naenia take a gulping breath and saw tears spilling down her face.

'I'm so sorry,' Cassie told her. 'It's terrible what happened to Bradley. It's not your fault.' She remembered a shrink on one of the courses she'd attended saying that the bereaved often turned the blame on themselves – however irrationally.

But her words only seemed to add to Naenia's distress.

'You don't understand!' Her hand flew up to pluck another hair, then to the scarf again. *Tug*. An automatic gesture that seemed to mirror the way Bradley had died. Cassie noticed that her repeated plucking had left a line of red dots along her hairline.

Had Naenia unwittingly given Bradley a bad pill? Was that it?

Before she could work out how to ask without pushing her into an outright denial, Naenia had pushed herself away from the wall. 'I've got to go.'

'Look, Naenia, call me at the mortuary any time if you want to talk. Ask for Cassie Raven.'

But all she got back was a half-nod over Naenia's shoulder as she hurried away, black coat fluttering out behind her like the cape of a pantomime villain.

Chapter Eleven

When Cassie let herself in at her gran's at around five she was met with a sight that brought her up short: her rucksack, packed, beside the front door. She took it into the kitchen, where her grandmother stood at the worktop mixing something with a return of her old vigour.

'What's all this then?' Cassie grinned. 'I know my salatka isn't up to your standards but does it really justify eviction?' The gunpowder smell of dried ginger in the air told her there was piernik – Polish gingerbread – for afters.

'I washed and packed your clothes. It's time you went home,' said the old lady firmly, turning to her. 'You have your own life and I don't want you wasting it here. I am fine now – fit as a fish.'

'But Babcia ...' Cassie felt unexpectedly crestfallen. Sure, these weeks spent back in her childhood home had felt stifling sometimes, but there had been a comfort in it, too.

Weronika took her hands. 'Life's too short to waste it on the old, *tygrysek*. You need to be back in your own place' – she raised one eyebrow – 'where you can entertain your friends.'

Archie Cuff, in other words.

'But before you go, I know you wanted to talk about your mama and ... and your father. Let's have supper first.'

Throughout the meal Cassie felt her gaze drawn towards her mother's face in the mantelpiece photo. For the thousandth time she tried to remember her but all that surfaced was the same old memories like pebbles worn smooth by the tide: the watermelon-scented perfume, the orange poppies on a dress. To which she could now add the sound of inconsolable weeping from her dream.

After they'd cleared away the dinner things, Weronika said, 'Would you like to see the mementoes I have of your mama?'

As she led the way into her bedroom and opened the wardrobe Cassie hoped that her guilty secret wasn't written all over her face.

Luckily, Weronika was lost in her own thoughts. 'Where is it . . . ?' Shuffling aside some hangers she unhooked a plastic clothes protector from the rail and unzipped it. 'This was her favourite blouse' – a long cotton shirt, so fine as to be almost muslin, in a pale dove-grey sprigged with tiny pink roses. Not Cassie's style, but kind of cute – it must have been vintage even in the Nineties.

Weronika pressed the blouse to her face, inhaling, before bending down with the caution of the elderly, to retrieve the mementoes box. She put it in her granddaughter's hands.

Cassie picked out the child's drawing of the rainbow and the home-made birthday card first, awkwardly aware that she'd seen them before. 'These are so sweet. She must have loved you very much, Babcia.'

'Oh, when she was little we were inseparable. She was a shy little thing then, scared of her own shadow – not like you. You came out of the womb with your fists up.'

The bracelet of beads had been a gift for Katherine's fifth birthday that she had apparently worn every day and wouldn't take off 'even at bedtime'.

After listening to her gran's recollections of Katherine's childhood, Cassie pulled out her mother's final school report card. She read a section out loud, '*I am sorry to say that Katherine's attention span and general attitude have gone dramatically downhill this year . . .*' before sending her gran a questioning look.

'Let me see that . . .' Pulling reading glasses from a pocket she scanned the whole report, a frown growing on her face. It was clear that a settled memory, buffed to a sheen over many decades, was struggling to survive in the face of an objective fact. After a moment she lowered the card and met Cassie's eyes. 'It's true. She had always been a good girl at school, but in her middle teens she became . . . rebellious. Like most teenagers.'

Cassie knew that her mother had left school with seven GCSEs and gone to sixth form college to study for A levels, with the aim of doing a psychology degree – a plan that never came off. But how long she'd lasted at college and precisely when she'd met Callum was hazy. 'So did she drop out of college when she met Dad?'

Weronika's eyelids lowered at the mention of her son-in-law. 'No, he came later. I pleaded with her to stick with her studies but by then she was going out every night and wanted to earn some money.' She raised one hand, let it fall. 'I . . . couldn't reach her anymore. She dropped out of college after a year or so and went to work in . . . in a second-hand record shop.' From her grandmother's tone she might have said 'brothel'. She shot a sharp look at Cassie. 'You might make fun of me, but she was a clever girl. Not as clever as you, maybe, but far too good to work in a shop.'

So the paragon had worked in a shop selling second-hand vinyl! Cassie didn't say so, but she found this impossibly cool.

Her eye fell on the postcard with its picture of typically English countryside and she picked it up. 'Where did she send this from? And why does she say that you and Grandpa shouldn't worry?' Cassie's grandfather – a reserved but kindly presence in her childhood – had died within a year of his daughter's murder.

Weronika took the postcard and read the back. She let the hand holding it fall in her lap.

'Babcia, if you don't want to—'

'It's all right. You deserve to know it all. How my Katerina came to meet a man like your father.'

She told Cassie that, after working at the record shop for a year or more, Katherine had announced she was leaving home to join an anti-roads protest in the Chilterns. 'We couldn't stop her – she was twenty years old. She took a rucksack and a sleeping bag – and told us she would be sleeping in a tent in the forest! Ever since she was a little girl she had a *fantazja* about moving to the countryside to live on a farm.'

Wow. So the demure-looking Katherine Janek had dropped out of college to work in a record shop, and then turned eco-warrior! Cassie recalled an older guy called Enzo from her squatting days speaking wistfully about the road protests of the 90s – apparently it had been a massive movement to try to stop the government concreting over the countryside. Their poster boy was some guy called Swampy.

'We saw it every night on the news,' her grandmother went on, staring into space. 'Terrible hippy people with long matted hair or shaved heads, sleeping outdoors, with nowhere to go to the toilet or wash!'

Save Oakwood Common. The benefit gig by her father's band in the newspaper article she'd found in her gran's mementoes box.

'It must have been really tough for you.' Cassie experienced a surge of guilt as she realised something: when she'd upped and left home the day after her seventeenth birthday it must have felt like history repeating itself.

Her grandmother stared inwardly. 'There were no portable phones back then so all we got was a call from a public phone box now and again. Nearly a year she was gone from us. For a while we thought we had lost her for good.'

'So, was it at the camp she met Dad?'

A grim nod. 'When she finally came back to Camden she brought this *Callum*' – freighting the word with contempt – 'this long-haired *gbur*.'

Knowing the word meant 'yob', Cassie had to suppress a sudden impulse to speak up for the smiling dad she remembered, the one who'd taken her swimming in the lido up at Gospel Oak, who'd carried her on his shoulders in the park – the parent who was more vivid in her handful of memories of life up to the age of four than her mother.

Right, she told herself. *Now who's choosing rose-tinted memories over objective facts?*

'She wasn't the same after meeting him, my Katerina,' her grandmother went on. 'Before, she had troubles sometimes, but her moods were like summer storms – here and gone in a blink. She was a happy outgoing child. But after she started with him . . .' Weronika's hand patted the bedspread absent-mindedly.

'Sometimes she would just sit on the sofa looking up at him, while he did all the talking. *Brag brag.* Full of schemes he was, but they all came to nothing. He was going to be a pop star!' she hooted derisively. 'The only money he ever earned was from labouring on building sites, and selling vegetables at the market.

And if you gave him a drink he would' – she upended an imaginary glass into her mouth.

'I'm guessing you didn't approve of them getting married?' – wondering whether her gran would admit to Katherine being pregnant.

Instead, she ducked the question. 'It was inevitable. She was besotted with him. And then you came along.' Her face lit up. 'They got a little council flat and for a while your mama seemed happy enough. But it didn't last very long. Your father kept being sacked from jobs, so I would give Katerina money to pay the rent. Sometimes after my shift at Safeway I would go to the flat to help clean up and look after you so your mama could get some rest.'

Recalling the smell of burning from her dream, Cassie asked, 'Did their flat have an open fire?'

'A hearth, you mean? Bless you, no. Just electric radiators. Anyway, one day I found two empty vodka bottles when I was taking the bins out.' Her hand gripped a handful of bedspread. 'She tried to protect him but when I confronted him on his own he lost his temper and confessed that he'd been drinking too much.'

Cassie got a flash image of Mrs Perlman's poor bruised face. 'And he was . . . violent?'

She saw her grandmother crimp her lower lip, to stop it trembling. 'One lunchtime I turned up as a surprise, with some felt pens I'd got for you at the market. Katerina hadn't put her makeup on and there was a bruise here' – she touched her cheekbone as tenderly as if it were her daughter's – 'and she'd hurt her wrist. She said that she tripped and hit her face on the bath. But that child could never tell a lie. It was written on her face that it was him who did it.'

'Did you, or Grandpa, say anything to Callum?'

Weronika's expression twisted in a self-torturing grimace that tore at Cassie. 'She made me swear not to say anything to him. Your *dziadek* and I were frantic, *naturalnie*. We didn't know what to do.' She stared at Cassie but it was Katherine she was seeing. 'A few days later she was dead. May God forgive me for not putting a stop to it, for not getting you both away from that man.'

If only.

Cassie felt her training kick in. She took her grandmother's hand. 'You were only trying to respect your daughter's wishes. That was a loving impulse. What happened – what he did – that was one hundred per cent his responsibility. It wasn't your fault.'

They sat there like that for a long moment.

'The police were marvellous, you know,' said Weronika. 'The young one – Dżerek something? – he came to see us half a dozen times!' Dżerek sounded like a Polish approximation of the name Gerry, so Cassie guessed she meant DS Gerald Hobbs, the investigating officer. Then she clasped Cassie's knee, remembering something. 'Do you remember the time he brought you a Barbie doll?'

'That was from a detective?' Cassie couldn't picture Hobbs, but she remembered the doll. In fact, Barbie had been the subject of her very first evisceration, although the doll's insides had been a major disappointment – as plastic and hollow as her external persona.

'Your grandfather and I met his boss at the police station as well. Mr Neville? A lovely man. Do you know what he said to me? "Mrs Janek, I can't bring back your lovely daughter, but I promise you this, we won't rest until we put that scumbag behind bars for what he did to her."' She'd clearly memorised the little speech word for word – like a catechism.

'And they told me something in confidence.' She leaned towards Cassie. 'You know your father was Irish? Well, Dżerek told me he was mixed up with the IRA.'

'Really?' To Cassie the IRA was a hazy bit of ancient history; all she knew was that they had been happy to plant bombs that killed civilians.

'He said there was no point bringing it up in court. But it confirmed everything I always thought about him.'

Cassie was itching to ask more about her dad – most of all whether he'd ever tried to get in touch to ask about her, either from prison or after his release – but a quick scan of Babcia's drawn face dissuaded her. This trip down memory lane had clearly drained her emotionally.

'Let's have a cup of tea,' she said, getting up to put her mother's rose-sprigged shirt back inside its cover. She had started to zip it up – like closing a body bag – when Weronika said, 'Why don't you take the blouse? You are about the same size. Maybe you will wear it sometimes, in remembrance?'

'I'll wear it now,' she said on impulse.

In the bathroom she checked out her reflection in the long mirror.

It kind of worked: her vintage 501s and DMs lending the girlie blouse a bit of necessary edge. Turning around she looked over her shoulder to check how it looked from the back – and blinked a couple of times.

Where had her piercings gone?

What she saw looking back at her wasn't her own face – but the softer curves and sad hazel eyes of her mother.

Chapter Twelve

When Cassie stepped out of her gran's flat onto the eighth-floor walkway she still had the uncanny feeling that she was inhabiting her mother's skin. It was unusually mild for a January night and on reaching street level she peered at the parked cars under the streetlights, half-expecting to find them morphed into the unfamiliar colours and shapes she'd seen on reruns of old cop shows.

She replayed the moment when she'd seen her mother's sad, soft eyes looking back at her from the bathroom mirror – the banal backdrop of the ancient green bath suite and flowered shower curtain making it seem even more real. In half a second her mum's face had dissolved swiftly back into her own, but it left her feeling spacy – like she'd been untethered from reality.

She was still getting her head round this new image of her mother as an eco-warrior who'd slept in the woods with crusties and lay down in the path of bulldozers. Although she could never say so to her grandmother, it gave her a buzz – finding that she and her mum had something in common, having both dropped out of the straight world at a young age to take a walk on the wild side.

Cassie often took the towpath all the way home – the fastest route to her flat at the other end of Camden – but this time she found herself mounting the footbridge that crossed the canal heading towards the high street. Her feet seemed to know where she was going before her brain caught up.

Minutes later she had reached the entrance to Prowse Place, the spot where the local paper had reported her mum's body being found. Hovering at one end, she looked down the empty cobbled street – so narrow it resembled a mews – lined with modest little Victorian cottages. At the far end the houses ended, the road narrowing into a darkened tunnel under the railway.

That's where it happened.

Hefting the rucksack higher on her back, she started walking towards the darkness. Her rubber-soled DMs made barely any sound on the cobbles and although the light from TVs glimmered mutely through the windows of some of the houses, no sound escaped through the double glazing.

At the entrance to the tunnel she paused to let her eyes acclimatise to the gloom and felt her heart was working overtime, thump-thumping away in her chest. *Don't be such a fuckwit*, she told herself, forcing herself to concentrate on picturing the cone-shaped receptor cells on her retina – the ones that worked best in bright conditions – shutting down, while the rod-like cells adapted to darkness started to wake up.

Adapted to darkness, she thought. *A bit like my life.*

Once the outlines of the tunnel had emerged from the gloom she went on. Her ears too seemed to have developed a heightened sensitivity. She could hear the sound of an individual car changing gear in the distance, a wisp of someone playing piano scales as a window was opened and then closed, bottles clinking against each other in a carrier bag a street away.

Coming to a stop by a section of tunnel wall she noticed something on the dark grey brick – the long-faded graffiti of a smiley face, an image she'd always found vaguely sinister, possibly a relic from the 90s. Her gaze dropped to the cobbles beneath. Was that darker area a bloodstain? The kind that might be left after someone had their head caved in?

Yeah, right. After more than two decades . . .

All at once, her nostrils crimped at the sudden acrid whiff of burning, like there was a bin fire close by. Then the distant sound of a woman weeping – just like in her dream. She whipped around. No one in sight. A moment of city silence. Then the volume of the crying cranked right up, to just inches from her ear. Followed by a voice she knew to be her mother's, ragged and keening.

'It's all my fault . . . All my fault!'

Not daring to move she stood there, rigid, her breathing closed down. Then, *bang*, it was over. The sense of someone at her shoulder had gone. She looked down, tried to find the bloodstain – but could no longer make it out.

Fuck! Not caring if anyone saw her, Cassie legged it to the end of the tunnel.

Even ten minutes later, under a brightly lit streetlamp with people going to and fro, she could feel her heart still doing its impression of a jackhammer.

Seeing the welcoming lights of The Hawley Arms up ahead she ducked inside, grateful for the crush of warm bodies, the booze-fuelled racket, the comforting smell of stale beer.

It was so noisy at the bar she had to mouth 'Grey Goose' at the barman while pointing to the bottle. When he lifted two enquiring fingers, she raised him to three. Taking her vodka she found a corner where she could drop the rucksack and lean against a spare section of wall.

I don't believe in ghosts, she reminded herself. Her training and experience had taught her that the recently bereaved often felt the presence of their lost loved ones, and she herself had 'seen' or sensed her old teacher Mrs E several times after her death. She had put these apparitions down to emotional over-load, and this latest experience had to be the same: no more than her traumatised subconscious working overtime, trying to make sense of all the stuff she was unearthing about her mum's death.

'All my fault' . . . As if her mother blamed herself for her own murder. In what dark corner of Cassie's psyche had such an idea had been born?

As she drained the last of her vodka a thought popped into her head.

She might not believe in ghosts – but what if ghosts believed in her?

Chapter Thirteen

The next morning, as Cassie woke in her own bed after a sweaty and restless night, all that remained of her recurring dream was the smell of something burning. It was only then that she remembered it: the acrid gust of what she'd initially thought was a bin fire in Prowse Place the previous evening, just before hearing her mother say it was all her fault.

The brightness of the room hurt her eyes, but then she had kept on drinking vodka after getting home. Then her gaze fell on the curtained bedroom window and she sat bolt upright.

Nasty smell. Flames licking up the curtains. Black snowflakes.

The window into the past had cracked open before slamming shut again. But it left Cassie with a settled conviction: she had witnessed some sort of house fire when she was little.

Visiting the spot where her mum died had unlocked something in Cassie's brain. Childhood memories that had lain submerged for years were now rising to the surface like a badly weighted corpse.

Once she was up and dressed, Cassie knocked next door, a sense of anticipation taking the edge off her hangover. Her neighbour Desmond had been looking after her cat Macavity while she'd been at her gran's and she was looking forward to getting him back.

'Oh, there's no need for that, darlin', said Desmond, as she pressed a bottle of Laphroaig – his favourite – into hands the size of soup bowls. 'It's been a pleasure having His Highness about the place.'

Catching the very tip of a black tail disappearing into the kitchen she called out, 'Macavity!'

Desmond followed her. Despite his shuffling gait and near-totally grey hair, he was only in his fifties. His dad had hailed from Montserrat, his mum was local white Irish, and up until ten years ago he'd had a decent job as a security guard. Then a gang of robbers had turned up at the tobacco warehouse he was guarding and tried to beat the entry code out of him with an iron bar. The siren of a passing squad car probably saved his life, but after the compensation money ran out Desmond had been left relying on benefits.

Whenever the story came up he always just grinned, flashing a gold tooth, and said, 'They didn't get one cigarette – *not one!*'

She found Macavity, lurking under the kitchen table. Black from nose to tail-tip except for his golden-green eyes, he surveyed her – unblinking and imperious. When she reached down to stroke him he bowed his spine away from her, his belly nearly touching the floor, before trotting over to Desmond and threading himself through his legs – a rejection that left her feeling stupidly crushed.

Desmond laughed, but after catching her look said, 'Just you wait till it's you giving him his dinner again. I'll be long forgotten.'

That only made her more melancholy, struck by a stark truth. With the sole exception of her grandmother, couldn't all her relationships be described as contingent, transient, temporary?

Her longest romantic relationship to date had been with Rachel, a trainee psychotherapist who she'd lived with the previous year for just five months. Rachel had ended things by saying what all Cassie's boyfriends and girlfriends had said in the end: that she was 'hard to reach', not affectionate enough – or not often enough – distracted, distant . . . *Yada yada*. Rachel liked to share her theory about these failings: that far from being unaffected by losing her parents at such an early age, the four-year-old Cassie had lacked the emotional equipment to process it, to properly grieve. It was Rachel who had diagnosed her as suffering from 'unresolved grief'.

Well, she thought grimly, *I'm processing things properly now.*

She managed to carry a struggling Macavity to her own flat and inside without him escaping. But as she lowered him to the ground in the hallway, he made a hissing swipe at her, claws out, leaving a red furrow down her forearm.

She dropped to a crouch, her back against the wall, fighting the hot sting of tears. Most of the time she was pretty content with her own company, but sometimes, like right now, she missed having somebody around. Being in love. The intoxicating temptation of submerging yourself in another person. She remembered the snog with Archie, and the banter they'd had on WhatsApp since – his last message that morning asking when she was free that week.

After dabbing some TCP on the scratch and putting down food for her ungrateful flatmate – who was sulking under the sofa – she got the bottle of vodka from the freezer and stretched out on the sofa. Reaching for her phone she smiled at the open, uncomplicated face on Archie's profile pic. After a long moment of hesitation – she tapped out a message.

Bit busy this week. Can I get back to you? Cx

Opening her contacts she messaged Phyllida Flyte to ask for a meeting.

Archie would have to wait. Duty before pleasure.

FLYTE

'Sorry?' Making a huge effort Flyte surfaced from her thoughts. What had Josh been saying?

'I said, what a pair of gorillas, Sarge.'

'Quite.' She was still fuming from what they'd just witnessed.

She and Josh, the brightest of Camden's DCs, were driving back from a cannabis farm up in Gospel Oak. The 'gorillas' were a pair of uniforms who had attended after passers-by reported a man getting beaten up in the street. The 'man' had turned out to be a seventeen-year-old kid called Minh, trafficked from Vietnam by a drug gang and forced into tending a farm in a derelict council estate. When one of his gang minders had dropped in, Minh had grabbed the chance to escape, but only made it as far as the street. After passers-by intervened, his attacker had disappeared.

Minh had led the officers through the estate to a block of disused lock-up garages – inside, crude doorways had been knocked through the walls to create a space filled with a forest of cannabis plants. In cannabis farm terminology Minh was a 'gardener', tending the lighting and feeding system, sleeping on an airbed, locked in round the clock with no natural light. Minh's backstory was depressingly familiar: his parents had borrowed ten thousand pounds to pay a gang of people smugglers who promised a guaranteed job on a building site in the UK.

91

Instead he was handed over to the drug gang who told him he had to work off the 'extra costs' of his journey.

Josh grinned. 'That older cop won't forget what you told him in a hurry.'

She gripped the steering wheel. 'Well, seriously, how could he be unaware of the protocol for dealing with a likely victim of trafficking? One: involve social services. Two: refer to the NRM.'

The National Referral Mechanism was there precisely to identify those who weren't criminals but victims of trafficking and slavery, but getting that distinction across to some of the beat cops wasn't easy. Flyte usually prided herself on keeping her cool, but arriving on scene to see two uniforms bundling a terrified skinny kid, all five foot four of him, in cuffs, into a squad car had tested her powers of self-control.

'I just can't abide the kind of officer who doesn't know – or chooses to ignore – the correct protocols. The rules are there for a reason.'

If the police didn't respect that, what hope was there for anyone?

'What was it you told him again?' Josh chuckled. '"If you don't get the cuffs off him in the next ten seconds I'll have you up on a misconduct charge by teatime."'

'OK, that's enough, Josh.'

'Sorry, Sarge.'

Flyte was aware that during her first couple of months in Camden CID her colleagues had viewed her as a bit of a joke – the by-the-book ice maiden with a serious case of OCD – but recently, after her persistence on the case of Cassie's dead teacher had led to a suspect being charged with murder, she sensed a shift in attitude. They might still view her as a bit of weirdo, but she sensed a new edge of respect.

Josh had managed to find a social services caseworker to look after Minh. Flyte had decided that since he was still distressed and hadn't eaten for twenty-four hours his statement could wait.

'You know what I'd really like to do?' she fumed. 'Bring all those so-called alternative types who buy their cannabis around the market down to that garage to see how Minh has been living for the last four months – just so they can get stoned. They get all sanctimonious about a T-shirt made by kids in Pakistan, but drug slavery? So long as they can get their weekend spliff, that's just collateral damage.'

Flyte was no killjoy – she enjoyed a couple of glasses of sauvignon from time to time – but the idea of ceding control of your brain to drugs? She just couldn't understand it.

Josh just nodded, ducking what had become a well-worn argument between them. He took the view that decriminalising the so-called soft drugs would reduce crime – and their workload. *Win-win.*

A view that Cassie Raven would unquestionably share. She was clearly a habitual user of cannabis – or worse. Recreational drug use was practically compulsory for Camden types, along with the regulation piercings, tattoos, bizarre clothes and hair, and screw-you attitude.

Despite it all, she had found herself agreeing to meet up that evening, intrigued to learn what the morgue girl had to say. Did she know something about Bradley Appleton's death that she hadn't shared? Or was it something else? Either way she couldn't deny that seeing last night's message had made her heart skip a beat.

Chapter Fourteen

Jason was handling the single PM booked for that day which meant Cassie was able to get on with some admin, starting with the regular inventory of guests in the body store. Winter was always peak season in the mortuary – bad weather and dark evenings brought a spike in road traffic accidents, viruses morphed into pneumonia in elderly lungs – all of which meant a constant battle to prevent a backlog of bodies building up.

As she opened each drawer to check the identity tag on the occupant's body bag against the inventory she murmured a few words of greeting. 'Good morning, Mr Khan, you'll be leaving us tomorrow . . .' 'Hello, Mrs Perlman, you've got your daughter Becca coming to see you later . . .' Simple words of human comfort. The way that she hoped a mortuary technician might have treated her mum when her broken body had come in that night twenty-one years ago.

She was impatient to meet Phyllida Flyte that evening. Going by his picture in the local paper, Gerry Hobbs, the investigating officer on her mother's case had only been in his late twenties in 1997, so he could still be a cop – might even still work at Camden nick. If Flyte could be persuaded to put a word in, maybe he would answer her questions about her mother's murder – and settle any lingering doubts about her father's guilt.

Reaching the drawer marked Bradley Daniel Appleton, DOB 06/07/2003, she rolled it out on its castors. 'I'm going to chase up the toxicology department today, Bradley,' she told him. 'Hopefully we can get your mum and dad some closure.' She pictured Bradley's girlfriend, Naenia, again – her nerviness, the hair plucking and scarf tugging: the very image of a girl with a guilty secret. Again, she experienced that niggle at the back of her mind: the feeling that Bradley's death wasn't a straightforward suicide.

Her check revealed just four unoccupied berths out of twenty-four – which could fill up in a heartbeat with the next surge of check-ins. She'd have to inform the coroner's office so they could chase up collection of the bodies that had already been autopsied; it was they who paid the mortuary guests' 'board and lodging' – the daily storage fees.

Having made her calls, she changed back into civvies before heading out to buy lunch. On her way down to central Camden she got a call from Kieran, her old squatting buddy.

'Cass! Can you meet me?' He sounded so hyped that she wondered for a bad moment if he was using again.

'What, right now?'

'Yeah. It's a surprise!'

He named a backstreet a good way off the main drag, but would say only that their meeting point was 'a shop' next to a solicitor's. On reaching the parade, she realised with a little jolt of excitement why he'd brought her here. Under a storefront sign that read HONEST BOB'S VINYL she could see a half-dozen hipsters inside, their heads bent, expressions as devout at monks at prayer, leafing through racks of old albums. According to her gran, Cassie's mum had done a stint in a second-hand record shop; Kieran knew she was keen to find out more about her mum. *Ipso facto* this must be the place where the young Katherine had worked.

Cassie had passed Honest Bob's many times; it was one of a handful of indie shops and bars that had survived Camden's colonisation by chain stores and upmarket apartment blocks. Until the vinyl revival came along, the place must have limped along on the custom of a few nerds but now she noticed its recent paint job and the addition of a cafe area with gleaming espresso machine at the back of the shop.

This was where she found Kieran, chatting over coffee with an older guy – tall and lean, wearing a waistcoat, his long steel-grey hair tied back in a ponytail. He had the seamed look of an old rocker but his age was hard to pin down – one of those guys who could be anything between a dissolute late fifties and a well-preserved early seventies. A set of chunky amber-coloured Greek worry beads hung loosely from his right hand.

It wouldn't have occurred to Kieran to perform introductions, bless him, so she said, 'Hi, I'm Cassie Raven.' He introduced himself as Bob, his eyes flicking over her chest before acquainting themselves with her face.

'"Honest Bob", I assume?' she asked.

His half-smile, half-grimace revealed a platinum incisor. 'It's what people have called the place since the Stone Age.' His voice sounded like gravel marinated in Jim Beam.

Kieran stood up. 'I'm off to have a browse. I'll leave you two to talk.'

Bob turned to the girl behind the counter. 'Make us some coffees, would you, darling?' which gave Cassie the chance to run an eye over him. A repaired hole in one ear from wearing a tunnel piercing and, climbing one side of his neck, the ghost of a lasered-off tattoo. Probably the wrong look when it came to trying to swing a business overdraft at the bank.

'So you're Kath and Callum's daughter? Who'd have thought it?' He let his gaze rest on her, flipping the worry beads over his knuckles. *Clack . . . clack*. 'It was terrible, her dying so young – and a tragic loss for you, of course.'

He sounded insincere, but then people reached for these phrases – overused to the point of being meaningless – because they had no idea what to say to the bereaved.

'How long did Kath work here?' asked Cassie, trying out the shortened version of her mother's name.

'Now you're asking . . . Probably about a year, off and on? She was a lovely girl, your mum' – he flashed his platinum tooth – 'almost as pretty as you.'

Yecch, she thought, managing what she hoped would pass for a grateful smile.

'Kath was passionate about music – about everything, really. That girl didn't do anything by halves.' The worry beads clacked over his hand. 'I remember when Van Morrison played Glastonbury, she was desperate to see him but it was sold out. Off she went anyway. When she came back she said she'd got someone to smuggle her through the gate in the boot of their car. It was the same with the whole anti-roads thing.'

'Oakwood Common, you mean?'

'Yeah, Oakwood Common. Most people would just go down for the day when there was an action on, you know? Not Kath. Said she was off to go and live there.'

His expression was neutral, but a stillness around his eyes made Cassie wonder if he'd been pissed off at the time.

'Were you sorry to lose her? I mean, was she good at her job?'

'She wasn't the greatest for turning up on time but she knew her stuff – especially new folk, folk rock – that was her bag, really. And her being so pretty didn't hurt with the customers. But Kath was a free spirit.' He broke into a rusty chuckle. 'I just realised something. If it wasn't for me, you might not ever have been born.'

Cassie just stared at him.

'A few months after Kath left she came back into the shop with some bloke on her arm. Not Callum' – he shook his head at her questioning look – 'and she told me, pleased as Punch, that she'd been made one of the organisers at Oakwood. The guy was her boyfriend, and the pair of them were in charge of putting on a benefit gig down there.'

Another nugget of her mum's past – she had an eco-warrior boyfriend before she met Callum.

'She wanted a favour – could I put them in touch with any local bands who might be up for doing a free gig. I gave the guy some numbers, including the manager of your dad's band.'

'Barney Cotter.'

'Yeah, that's right. Anyway, that's how *Poitín* ended up head-lining the Oakwood gig a few months later – which is how your mum and dad met. So you see, if I hadn't made the introduction you might not be here!'

Bob looked chuffed, seeming to have forgotten that his accidental matchmaking had ended in murder.

'What about after Oakwood Common? Did you see much of her after she came back with Callum?'

'Not really. After she had you, I only saw her now and again in the street pushing a buggy.' It was clear from his expression that he'd lost interest once Kath the 'free spirit' had morphed into the harassed young mother.

'She was too young to have a baby, don't you think?'

'Well, she didn't strike me as particularly happy. She'd got very thin, and I dunno, it was like she'd lost her . . . sparkle.'

Cassie allowed the misery to settle within her – her suspicion solidified into a bitter conviction: having a baby had been the biggest mistake of Katherine Raven's life. She had been happy – sweet and lovable, if a little wild – until Cassie had come along. If she hadn't got pregnant she might still be alive today.

'How well did you know Callum?' she asked.

'Only by reputation. People whose opinion I respected said Callum Raven could sing and played a tidy lead guitar. I suppose it was inevitable your mum would end up with a good-looking rock musician.'

Picking up a trace of jealousy in Bob's voice, Cassie was eyeing his face when something landed on the table between them. 'Look what I found!' Kieran crowed.

It was an old-school album, the cover showing a moody black-and-white image of two men and a woman, shot beside the canal, which gleamed like mercury in the light. Her father stood at the back, the other two sat on a low wall in front of him, the man – who must be Barney Cotter – in profile, smoking a cigarette, the girl facing camera. Under the picture, in an Irish-style typeface, the single word *POITÍN*.

Bob leaned forward. 'That's a rare one. They pressed it themselves. They had quite a following and I remember there being some chatter about a record deal until . . .' He didn't need to finish the thought. 'Irish folk rock was never really my cup of tea, but it was huge in the 90s, y'know?'

'I don't suppose you still have Barney Cotter's number?'

'Nah. Afraid not.' Then he tapped a gnarled nail on the image of the woman, her dark curls cascading around a heart-shaped face. 'I met her once or twice, good-looking girl. I think she still sings round here, pub gigs. Maria something.'

Cassie turned the cover over. 'Maria Maguire, vocals.'

'That's her. Decent blues voice she had.'

'I'd like to buy this.'

'Have it.' Bob waved a munificent hand. 'It's the least I can do for Kath's girl.'

Leaving Kieran paying for an old Metallica album she went outside and took the *Poitín* album out of its bag. Staring at her dad's curly hair and long lean face she felt her insides churn like they did after a big love affair went sour.

When Kieran emerged she offered to buy him lunch in return for his sleuthing.

'Ah, sorry, Cass, I've got a webinar on social media for small businesses in half an hour.'

Seeing the way he stood a little taller as he said this, Cassie reached out to squeeze his arm. 'That's brilliant, Kieran. I'm so proud of what you're doing . . . So, how did you find out about my mum working here?'

'It was a lucky break,' he said modestly. 'A mate at the hostel put me on to Bob – said he knew every band who played Camden, going back to the Seventies. But when I mentioned *Poitín*, he said your mum had worked there and that he'd love to meet you.'

She looked down at the album. 'I wish I had a way to play this.'

He frowned. 'I think there might be a record player in the social room at my hostel.'

'Great! Could you record it for me? I'd love to hear my dad sing and none of their stuff is online.'

'Sure, Cass, not a problem' – jerking his head back towards Honest Bob's. 'I was chatting to the guy on the till, and guess what?' A little grin on his face.

She shook her head.

'Maria Maguire sings at The Dublin Castle every other Wednesday – and she's on tomorrow. Fancy going?'

'Yeah, love to.' But the chance to meet someone who had known her dad – and probably her mum, too – set up conflicting emotions. Excitement, but with an edge of panic – like she was walking in slow motion into a quagmire from which she might never escape.

Kieran must have seen something in her face because his perpetual smile faded to a look of concern and he gave her shoulder a rub. 'Are you doing OK, Cassie Raven? All this stuff about your poor mum, that's some pretty heavy shit you're churning up.'

'I'll survive.' She dredged up a grin. 'Remember what you used to call me, back when we were squatting?'

'Yeah!' he chuckled. '"Teflon". You were the youngest one there but you were the toughest one of us all.'

'There you go.' She smiled reassuringly.

Then a thought struck her: Teflon was unarguably tough – but it was just a layer.

Chapter Fifteen

'I thought you'd want to know asap, the tox report on Bradley Appleton is going to come back negative,' Cassie told Flyte. 'No chemical signature for psychoactives, or narcotics, not even a smidge of cannabis.'

It was 5 p.m. and they were in the same coffee shop where she had once asked Flyte to investigate the death of Geraldine Edwards. Now she was building up to ask her another favour.

'Really?' Flyte looked at her over the rim of her cup of Earl Grey. From the sceptical expression in those ice-blue eyes she was ahead of Cassie and trying to work out what she was up to.

In fact, her entire body language – bolt upright, elbows on the table – took Cassie back to the wariness of their early interactions. She had to admit it was understandable. After manipulating Flyte into launching the investigation, she'd put her in the awkward position of having to hush up a break-in that Cassie had committed. Cops could be funny about stuff like that.

Any whisper of romantic interest looked to be firmly back in the box. Not for the first time, Cassie wondered whether the vibe she sometimes sensed between them was all in her imagination. If so, it was just as well. Flyte was intriguing, and unquestionably hot, but Cassie already had enough on her plate with the emotional maelstrom stirred up by delving into her parents' past.

'It usually takes longer to get a tox report back, doesn't it?' Flyte raised a perfectly plucked eyebrow.

'I know someone over in the lab at Hammersmith who owed me one.' Cassie lowered her eyes to take a demure sip of espresso. No need to mention that the favour had been giving Marco the number of a weed dealer in Ealing.

A shadow fell across Flyte's face like a sudden eclipse. 'So that's that then. We have to tell his mum and dad that he was stone-cold sober when he killed himself.'

'I'm afraid so.' Flyte's emotional investment in the Bradley Appleton case seemed more visceral than you'd expect from a cop, even in a child suicide, but Cassie had worked out some time ago that Flyte had lost someone very close to her and had barely begun to deal with it. She left a respectful pause before making her move.

'By the way, I was wondering whether you'd come across a Gerry Hobbs at the station – he used to be a detective sergeant there back in 1997? I should think he'd be in his early- to mid-fifties by now.'

Flyte shot her a drily amused look that said, *So that's why you wanted to meet.*

'Doesn't ring any bells, I'm afraid,' she said. 'He's not in CID, that's for sure. But if he was a sergeant by the 90s he might already have retired – after thirty years' service you can draw the full pension.' As she picked up the slice of lemon from her tea and tore the flesh off with her teeth, Cassie remembered being surprised the first time she'd seen this animalistic gesture from someone so apparently self-controlled. 'Why do you want to know?'

Cassie hesitated. All her instincts rebelled against confiding in a cop, even one she'd grown to trust, up to a point. But her father's reappearance, together with the resurfacing memories and waking apparitions of her mother, had left her feeling off-kilter and struggling to focus at work. The only hope of getting back to some kind of normal was to reassure herself that her mother's murder had been properly investigated and that her father hadn't been wrongly convicted.

She told Flyte the story in a rapid monotone, eyes fixed on the table – finding the task getting harder rather than easier with each retelling. The only detail she left out was her father turning up, in case it broke some post-release restriction.

'I'm so sorry,' said Flyte after she'd finished. 'What an absolutely ghastly time you must be having.'

Cassie had seen Flyte's hand clench reflexively on the table and sensed that she'd reined in an impulse to reach out and touch her arm.

Instead Flyte reached into her bag and pulling out her phone, made a call.

'Gary? It's Phyllida Flyte. Can I pick your brains?' A brief exchange followed. After hanging up she said, 'OK, so DS Gerald Hobbs retired last year, just a couple of months before I arrived. Apparently, he took a post as head of security for a children's charity. Nice job to have on top of his pension.'

'Still a DS? Does it mean anything, him staying at sergeant level all those years?'

Flyte pursed her lips – still painted the pale candy-pink that Cassie loathed – considering the question. 'It's probably less usual nowadays, with so many detectives joining the force from uni. But back then there were plenty who'd be happy to stay a career sergeant. The higher up the ladder you go, the more you're dealing with politics instead of police work.'

'What about you? Do you want to carry on climbing the ladder?'

'I . . . I don't know.' Flyte blinked, like she hadn't thought about it for a while. 'I used to have it all mapped out. DS by thirty-five, DI by forty, and so on up to Commissioner.' A sardonic smile. 'But the longer I've been in the job the more I think that career progression is less important than enjoying the day-to-day policing.'

'And do you enjoy it? The day-to-day policing?'

'I'm starting to. I lost sight of it for a while . . .' she tailed off, and Cassie was aware of her loss as an almost-physical presence between them. She seemed about to say more, but the moment passed. Instead, she went on, 'I'm thinking of applying for a job in Major Crimes, actually. I miss working murder cases.' A sudden stricken look. 'Oh! I'm sorry! That was a thoughtless thing to say.'

Cassie raised a hand. 'It's fine. Anyway, I totally get it. With a murder there's a bit more at stake than a stolen smartphone, right?' She paused, before taking the leap. 'I don't suppose you could get me the records of my mother's murder investigation?'

'Not a chance.' She looked sympathetic but her words were final-sounding. 'Look, Cassie, I'm really sorry, but even accessing a file without authority could get me in trouble. Serious trouble.'

Fuck it.

They drained their cups in silence before Flyte asked, 'When will Bradley Appleton's body be released? I think a funeral . . .' She dropped her gaze to the table for a moment before going on, 'Being able to have a funeral for him would help his parents.'

The realisation sprang on Cassie like a camera flash.

A child. Flyte had lost a child.

'We should get the release documentation from the coroner's office in a few days.' Cassie's thoughts turned to Bradley's parents and she wondered if his goth girlfriend Naenia would turn up to the funeral. Since the tox results had ruled out Bradley having any drugs in his system – she'd been wondering about that word 'Trippy' which she'd got from his body. Was it just her over-active imagination? Probably. But remembering how flustered Naenia had become when questioned, she felt her doubts solidify.

There was more to Bradley's death than Naenia was letting on. Had she dumped Bradley just before he took his life? Was that why she felt so guilty?

'You obviously checked his phone for messages he sent, or received, that might explain what he did?' she asked Flyte.

'There was nothing. Just chit-chat.'

She and Flyte knew that the absence of a final message wasn't unusual – and male suicides were even less likely than females to leave any explanation to their loved ones.

Cassie made a decision. She had to see Naenia again, to try to get her to 'fess up whatever it was that was torturing her – for the girl's own sake as well as for Bradley's parents. But how to find her? Simply hoping to bump into her drinking in The Black Heart wasn't much of a plan.

As they got up to go, Cassie said casually, 'Bradley went to my old school, Camden High, didn't he?'

A frown line appeared between Flyte's brows. 'No, he was at St Crispin's. The Catholic school.'

Cassie felt a mixture of emotions: triumphant but also guilty at having suckered Flyte so easily.

FLYTE

Flyte made her way home through the chill evening, feeling ruffled by her encounter with Cassie – and, as ever, not entirely sure why.

One the one hand she found her infuriating. Why couldn't she tone down that 'teenage rebel' look she insisted on sporting? What message exactly was the workman's boots, gruesome piercings and half-shaved haircut intended to send? That people should not judge her by her looks? As for the tattoo on her chest – the top edge of which Flyte had glimpsed when she'd bent to pick up her bag – however skilfully depicted the image, it wouldn't look so attractive when her skin was no longer smooth and wrinkle-free.

Still.

Having witnessed more than once the respectful – no, *tender* – way that she handled the dead, she had also come to realise that Cassie's challenging look was a front of sorts. A few weeks earlier she'd discovered that Cassie had been breaking a host of rules and putting her job at risk by staying in the mortuary overnight whenever a child was admitted. Apparently, it had started when she had bedded down alongside the drawer holding the body of a drowned nine-year-old called Oliver – because his mum had told her he was afraid of the dark.

Ever since, Flyte had sometimes found herself fantasising about Cassie sleeping beside the fridge that had held her baby daughter, holding vigil.

Darling Poppy. For more than two years she hadn't so much as glanced at the single photo she'd taken of her baby before the nurses took her away; now she looked at it a dozen times a day. There was something about Poppy's serene and preternaturally wise expression which always made her feel as though her daughter was watching over her, telling her everything would be all right.

It was a comfort, but it couldn't quell the questions that clamoured in her head.

Starting to face the reality of her loss had only made her more anxious to know what had happened between the apparently healthy foetus with a strong heartbeat on the twenty-week scan and the stillborn baby who had been put into her arms eight weeks later. She remembered the attending obstetrician saying that Poppy had lost most of her blood during the delivery, but after that she must have tuned out when he was explaining the complication that had caused it. Matt too said he had no recall of the details – but claimed he had no wish to 'keep going over it'.

Poppy's cause of death had been signed off by the same doctor, which meant that no post-mortem had been required. Not that she had wanted one – who would willingly put their baby put through that? But now she wondered if it mightn't have given her the thing she craved – certainty that the death had been unavoidable.

Since her disastrous drink with Matt, he had neither been in touch nor emailed over the medical report she'd asked for. Should she call him? Medical report aside, she was also aware of an urge to help him. But equally, she knew there would be no point. Just as she had been until recently, Matt was still in the bunker, intent on burying his grief.

She made a decision. Although she was nearly at her doorstep, she didn't even wait to get into the warm. She tapped out an email to him – it felt more appropriate than a text. Deleted it. Redrafted it. In the end she just put 'medical report' in the subject bar, and a one-word message.

Please?

Feeling relieved but also exposed, she recalled the rare flash of vulnerability that had crossed Cassie's face when she had asked about her mother's case file.

It struck Flyte with cold force that the two of them were in the same boat – both desperate to find answers to questions about the death of somebody they loved.

Chapter Sixteen

It was 10 a.m. and in the body store Cassie was pulling out a drawer in the giant fridge to check in her latest guest who the hospital porters had brought over in the early hours.

After checking the name tag and dob on the side of the body bag – which revealed that Harjinder Singh had only been twenty-eight – she unzipped the bag as far as his chest. The pads from the paramedics' defibrillator were still stuck to him: all IV lines, cannulas and so on had to stay in place until the post-mortem; they were important artefacts of any unexplained death.

'Hello there, Harjinder,' she murmured, feeling a pang at how young and handsome he looked. 'You are in the mortuary. Your sister, Ruha, just called. She wasn't there when you passed so she's on her way in to see you.' She touched his cheek: it had started to stiffen but full rigor mortis had yet to set in. *Good.* Most people felt the need to touch their dead loved ones and once his body reached peak rigor it would display all the pliancy and warmth of a telegraph pole.

The notes from the coroner said that Harjinder's parents – he'd still been living at home – had heard a crashing sound in the night and found him unconscious on the bathroom floor, not breathing. His father had performed CPR for fifteen minutes until the ambulance came but the paramedics were unable to save him.

Twenty minutes later she was showing his sister into the viewing room. Ruha Singh was in her twenties and a head-turner: she had expressive dark eyes and thick black hair plaited and coiled around her head, and wore a figure-hugging business suit. Seeing the closed drapes that covered the glass doors to where her brother was lying she turned her intelligent gaze on Cassie. 'I'm ready to see him,' pre-empting Cassie's usual preparation speech.

Inside the viewing room she immediately reached out to touch her brother's hair, dark and glossy like hers, before resting her hand on his chest which was covered by the deep-red coverlet.

'I left home three months ago, which was a bit of a sore point as he's two years older than me,' she told Cassie with a quick smile. 'Now I wish I'd still been there. I might have noticed he wasn't right that evening and insisted on taking him to A&E.'

Cassie just nodded, knowing there was little point in trying to divert that train of thought. In fact, Harj's mum had said that after coming home late from a post-work gym session he'd seemed fine and had eaten a plateful of his mum's paneer makhana with a couple of roti before going to bed.

'What kind of work did he do?'

A flash of pride crossed Ruha's face. 'He got a job as an analyst at an investment bank in the City a couple of months ago. He was loving it, but it was tough. When he had a report to deliver he'd start at 7 a.m., have lunch at his desk, then work through the night. In the morning he'd have to go to M&S to buy a fresh shirt.' She widened her eyes – half disapproving, half admiring. 'We had our ups and downs, you know, but I'll say this for my big brother – he was never afraid of hard work.'

Hard work alone never killed a twenty-eight-year-old and Cassie had seen no red flags in his medical notes – his blood pressure was normal, he didn't smoke or drink, and hadn't suffered from diabetes or any other chronic condition. Three of the top candidates for sudden death were cardiovascular blockages of one kind or another leading to heart attack, stroke, or pulmonary embolism – a blood clot that travelled to the lung. Failures of the wall of the aorta, the largest artery in the body, could cause catastrophic internal bleeding. But in younger adults, the likeliest culprit was Sudden Arrhythmic Death Syndrome.

In SADS, death was down to an undiagnosed and usually inherited heart condition, but the abnormal cardiac rhythm that caused death left no post-mortem calling card. In the absence of any other clear cause, the coroner would return a finding of SADS on a balance of probabilities and advise the family to undergo genetic testing to detect any underlying heart problems.

'You must have seen other cases like this.' Ruha dragged her gaze from her brother to meet Cassie's eyes. 'What do you think happened?'

Another possible trigger for Harj's death had occurred to Cassie. An ambitious young City boy who sometimes worked through the night might have been tempted to use something stronger than caffeine to stay alert – and stimulant drugs like Ritalin and Modafinil could prove fatal on top of any underlying heart issue. But she wasn't about to mention the possibility before the tox lab ran their tests.

'It wouldn't be helpful for me to speculate, Ruha, but I can tell you that the pathologist will explore every possible option.'

She hoped she'd injected the right level of confidence into her words, but picturing Curzon's grumpy face and casual approach she mentally crossed her fingers.

Ruha fell silent, her hand patting her brother's chest. She was clearly a tough cookie but now Cassie saw her shoulders slump: no doubt starting to absorb the reality of never seeing her brother alive again.

'Let me go get a chair so you can sit with him,' Cassie told her. 'Then I'll make you a cup of tea.'

After Ruha had left, Cassie returned Harj to his drawer to await his PM, scheduled for two days' time. Before closing his body bag she looked into his face for a long moment, wondering if he might give her some clue to what had happened. But there was nothing.

In the autopsy suite Jason was mopping the floor.

She found herself running what was known about Harj's out-of-the-blue death past him. 'What do you think?' she asked. 'You've seen a ton more sudden deaths in young people than me. SADS? An aortic rupture caused by some congenital weakness? Could overdoing it at the gym have triggered something he'd had since birth?'

Leaning on his mop he sent her a patronising half-smile, shaking his head. 'Why waste your time on guessing games? My advice is – leave the rocket science to the pathologists.'

'Yes, but—'

'You know what our job is, don't you?' He leaned his big face towards hers to deliver his words of wisdom: 'Cut and shut, sweetheart. Cut and shut.'

Chapter Seventeen

When Cassie arrived at The Dublin Castle for Maria Maguire's gig at 6.30 p.m., the bar stood half-empty, but by seven, every table had been taken and the queue at the bar was three-deep. A long-limbed guy, his hair worn up in a topknot had started setting up an amp and mic stand on the little stage opposite the main bar and an anticipatory buzz was building.

A glance around told her she was among the youngest there: most of the clientele were old enough to have seen Maria sing in her *Poitín* days – and Cassie's father, too. Her eye fell on a woman with short-cut hair in her fifties speaking intently to her male partner and, seeing her eyes widen for dramatic emphasis, Cassie had a sudden intuition: she was reminding him of the murder that had brought an end to *Poitín*. Perhaps Maria's dubious celebrity still acted as a macabre draw.

After Kieran arrived she was relieved when he asked for a half of shandy, suggesting his rehab was still on track. Like she could talk, seeing as she was already on her second large vodka – unusual for her on a school night, until recently, at least.

At their table he leaned close, a look of delighted intrigue on his face. 'I found out that there was a bunch of 'zines that covered the Camden music scene back in the day—'

'Zeens?'

'Fanzines,' he grinned. 'You must have heard of 'em? They were written by fans and musos and had all the listings and gossip on local bands. They used to sell them in record shops. Nothing fancy, just black-and-white photocopies.'

'Like a blog but on paper?'

'Yeah! So, Bob put me in touch with this guy Pete who used to write one and who's got quite a collection from the 80s and 90s. I've asked him to have a look through for any mention of *Poitín*.'

He stopped to nod over her shoulder towards the door. A woman with dark curly hair had just come in from the street and as she surveyed the bar area, her eyes swept over Cassie. From her heart-shaped face she was instantly recognisable as Maria Maguire, the young woman from the *Poitín* album cover. Assuming she was around the same age as Cassie's mum would have been, she had to be in her mid-forties by now, but with her tall, willowy figure and still-sharp jawline, could pass for a decade younger.

After a chat with the guitarist, Maria shucked off her leather jacket and stepped up to the mic, curly head bent. 'One two, one two,' she murmured, her voice low and self-effacing, before raising the mic to the right height. The guitarist twiddled a few knobs on the amp and without preamble struck up a series of unhurried lines. Maria angled the mic towards her and with a backward smile at the guy, went straight into a haunting bluesy number, about a man who'd left her all alone. Something about cold eyes and a cold, cold bed.

By the time she'd reached the chorus, Cassie was exchanging a surprised look with Kieran, eyebrows raised – *This is good shit!* It wasn't the kind of thing she'd usually go for, but the languorous twang of the bass and a yearning quality to Maria's surprisingly deep voice stirred something inside her. And not just her – the whole pub had quieted, everyone's attention focused on the figure of Maria, standing almost motionless, eyes half-closed as she sang, cupping the mic like the face of a lover. During the bits where the guitar took over she stepped to one side, putting him centre stage, one hand tapping out a rhythm on her thigh.

But Cassie's eyes kept drifting back to Maria's face – a bit shop-worn around the eyes but still beautiful. Her floaty indigo-blue asymmetric dress was offset by boots with criss-cross lacing up the front, channelling early Stevie Nicks, and she wore a black, faintly goth ribbon around her neck. A thought struck Cassie like a punch in the gut: she would never know what her mother might have looked like if she'd lived to Maria's age.

Maria wasn't the type to chit-chat between numbers, only murmuring a brief 'thank you' once the applause had died down. After half a dozen songs she unleashed a more rocky number, belting it out, one boot heel rapping out percussion on the stage. Once the clapping and appreciative hoots had died down, the guitarist stepped to the mic to say they were taking a break and Kieran gave Cassie a big nudge.

Maria was taking a drink from a water bottle, but when she saw Cassie approach, her gaze became guarded – she'd probably had a lifetime of fangirls and -boys wanting selfies – but when Cassie mentioned the name Katherine Raven, her eyes widened and her hand shot out to touch her shoulder.

'Seriously? You're Callum's little girl?' The hand stayed there as she scanned Cassie's face, her eyes growing sad. 'Ah, now I see it, you've got Kath's nose and mouth.'

'Look, I hate to bug you, but I had a few questions . . . ?'

'Of course, sweetheart. Shall I come and find you after the set?'

Despite the butterflies in her stomach which cried out for another large vodka, Cassie decided to move onto tonic water: this was too big an opportunity to screw up by being half-cut.

Once Maria's set was finished, she came over to where they were sitting. Gazing at Maria with a starstruck expression, Kieran leapt up to give her his seat. 'I'll go hang out at the bar, give you ladies some space.'

The feeling in Cassie's stomach reminded her of the time in her last year at primary school when she'd had to stand up at assembly and recite a Ted Hughes poem about a fox.

'I suppose I just wanted to find out a bit more about my mum and dad – and what went wrong between them. You must have seen quite a bit of Kath back then?'

Maria nodded. 'I knew Callum better, but sure, Kath used to come hear the band pretty much every week. She was a beautiful woman, your mum, inside and out.'

But from the way she dropped her eyes right after saying it, Cassie sensed a 'but' hanging in the air. It was a vibe that she sometimes got at the mortuary from people who had just seen their dead father, mother, spouse.

De mortuis nil nisi bonum. Of the dead, say nothing but good.

Sometimes people would literally purse their lips.

'Look, Maria, I know she wasn't a saint, but I'd honestly rather hear the truth about her. From what Bob, her boss at the record shop, told me, she could be a bit . . . unpredictable?'

Maria met her gaze, an uncertain look in her peat-brown eyes. 'She could wind Bob round her little finger. He let her get away with murder.'

Ignoring the unfortunate turn of phrase, Cassie tried another tack. 'I'm guessing that living with a heavy drinker like Callum – the marriage must have been volatile?'

Maria shook her head slowly. 'Bless you, sweetheart. I suppose there's no way you'd know.'

'Know what?'

'Your dad wasn't the one with the drink problem, that was Kath.'

'Really? How do you know?' Cassie blinked rapidly, trying to take it in.

'I'm sorry. I wouldn't have said anything, but I can see you're not the kind of girl who wants palming off with platitudes. Callum never said a word against your mum to me, but he did confide in Barney a couple of times.'

She said that Callum had told Barney Cotter, his best friend as well as manager and bandmate, about the time Cassie's grandmother found empty vodka bottles in the bin.

'When your gran put Callum on the spot, he told her the bottles were his – but he was just covering for your mum. Don't get me wrong, sure Callum was no teetotaller himself, we saw him roaring plenty of times' – her original Irish accent ruffling the flat surface of the Londonese – 'but he was more of a binge drinker than an alcoholic.'

'Why would he do that? Cover for her, I mean.'

Maria gave a sad shrug. 'He was a very sweet man, your dad . . .' she trailed off, no doubt reluctant to sing his praises given what he had gone on to do. 'Your mum was a troubled soul, Cassie. These days they'd have her on Prozac. But back then nobody talked about post-natal depression, mental health issues. All poor Kath had to tame her demons was vodka and a script for Valium off some dodgy doctor.'

All my fault.

Cassie recalled hearing her mother's plaintive words in Prowse Place where she'd been murdered. Accompanied by the acrid reek of burning.

'What about the fire?' she asked.

Maria's gaze shot up to meet Cassie's. 'You know about that? Yeah, Callum told Barney that one time Kath got drunk and set fire to the flat.' She raised her hand palm outwards. 'Don't get me wrong, it was an accident – obviously. But it was lucky your dad came home in time to put it out.'

'I was there.' More of a statement than a question.

Maria nodded.

So it was starting the fire that Kath had blamed herself for – not her own murder. Tempting as it was to think that her mum had somehow reached out to communicate with her, Cassie knew it was more likely that a fragmented childhood memory of her mother's self-recrimination and distress had floated to the surface. She was startled to discover how empty the realisation made her feel.

Cassie struggled to absorb this latest shift in her worldview. The portrait of her mother as the innocent teenager that she'd seen on the mantelpiece every day while she was growing up, accompanied by her grandmother's litany about Katherine the diligent student and devoted mother, lay in tatters.

Maybe it had held some truth when she'd been younger but one thing was becoming clear: after marrying and having a baby Kath had clearly undergone some sort of psychological crisis.

'Can I ask you something?' Maria's expression was apprehensive.

'Sure.'

'Do you know how Callum is doing, since he got out?'

'I have no idea.' Cassie shrugged, deciding not to reveal that he had followed her.

'I wrote to him in prison a couple of times,' Maria said, 'to tell him that Barney and I were still his friends, but he never replied. I suppose he just wanted to be left alone to do his time, try to forget the past.'

Do you think he did it? Cassie was trying to find a way to formulate the question, but at that moment a vaguely familiar-looking guy appeared at their table. Late fifties, his wiry frame clad in a cool black suit with mod overtones, his face was thinner and older than the version on the album cover, but Cassie recognised him as Callum's former best mate, Barney Cotter.

Before Cassie could process what he was even doing there, he'd put a proprietorial hand on Maria's shoulder.

'This is Barney,' said Maria. 'He manages me. But I refuse to pay him commission.'

Cassie looked confused.

'Which is fair enough,' Maria smiled. 'We've been married for over twenty years.'

She caught them sharing the kind of look you only saw between people who'd been together for a very long time. It held affection mixed with forbearance, underpinned by a rock-solid dependence on one another.

'Barney, this is Cassie – she's Kath and Callum's daughter.'

Barney literally took a step back – an understandable enough reaction to meeting the daughter of a woman who your best mate had murdered. 'Wow, Cassie. Great to meet you. You grew up good-looking.' From his accent, hard and flat as a granite worktop he was clearly London born and bred.

But after a few polite enquiries about what she was doing these days, he turned to Maria. 'Sorry, doll, but we're gonna have to make tracks – I said we'd be there at nine thirty.'

'Dinner party,' Maria told Cassie, with an apologetic eye-roll at how it sounded. Barney looked impatient to get going but his wife seemed reluctant to leave. She touched the back of Cassie's hand. 'Will you come back so we can chat some more?'

As they left Barney put an arm round Maria before throwing a look back at Cassie. At first, she couldn't decipher his expression. Picking up her drink she decided it held curiosity, but also defensiveness. Was it because he had screwed up her dad's alibi at his trial? Or because the alibi was a lie in the first place, dreamed up to get his mate off the hook for murdering her mum?

Kieran came to sit down again, bringing her another vodka. 'How'd it go?'

'Fine. Awful. I don't know. Jesus, Kieran, the more I find out the more fucked-up it all gets.'

Kieran sent her a sympathetic grin. 'Sounds a lot like life.'

Chapter Eighteen

The morning after meeting Maria – and Barney – Cassie did something she'd never done in her entire five years at the mortuary and pulled a sickie. As she hung up after calling in to report a bout of food poisoning she sent a silent apology to her guests lying in their chilly dormitory. At least there were no PMs that day, she told herself.

To be fair, she had barely slept the previous night, going over and over Maria's revelations about her mum being a problem drinker. *An alcoholic.* You had to call it that when someone got pissed enough to let a fire start around her kid, right? It had set a whole new wash-load of questions churning in her mind.

Had her grandmother not clocked that her daughter had a drink problem? Or chosen not to see it? But why hadn't Callum told the truth at his trial, to explain his wife's black eye? As Cassie absent-mindedly opened a pouch of cat food for Macavity he surveyed her balefully from his now-usual spot under the kitchen table. This morning she couldn't even be bothered to try to coax him out – knowing that he would only emerge to eat after she left the room.

Slumped on the sofa in the oversized T-shirt she'd slept in – the legacy of an ex-boyfriend – she drank her nuclear-strength black coffee, and examined again how Maria's revelations made her feel about her father's guilt.

The fact that she was the drinker didn't get him off the hook –
he and her mum had been having flaming rows, serious enough
to have the neighbours call the cops, after all. And then there
were the claims he'd made in court that she was having an affair –
which if not just a tactic to shift the blame elsewhere arguably just
gave him a solid motive for murder.

The jury had been able to hear his account first-hand before
deciding he was guilty. Was it wrong of her to want to do the
same?

Closing her eyes she pictured her mum's face, and sent her a
question. Would contacting her father be a betrayal?

Nothing for a moment, and then the words:

You're a big girl now.

Was it simply her imagination? A projection of what she
wanted to hear? Either way it brought a sad smile to her lips.

Cassie made a decision. If her father was still in town she
needed to look him in the eye and hear what he had to say –
while maintaining a strict sceptical distance.

Pulling out her phone, she googled the name of the place
where he'd said he was staying. There was no 'Bay Leaf' B&B
in Kentish Town but there was a Bay *Tree* – clearly more hostel than B&B from the images and the £22 per night rate for a
shared room. The receptionist answered with an uninterested
'Hello' and when she asked him to check if they had a guest
called Callum Raven he sucked his teeth expressively. He confirmed Callum was still staying there but she had to sweet-talk
him into taking her name and number in the vague hope he
might pass it on.

As she hung up, Macavity slunk into the room and headed
for his daytime hidey-hole under the coffee table without a
glance at her.

'Seriously?' she told him. 'I was only gone a couple of weeks and you dump me for Desmond?'

The cat settled down, lining up his paws neatly together in front of him before fixing his accusatory stare on her. 'Oh, fuck this,' said Cassie. 'I'm going out.'

She just wandered, hoping vaguely that no one from the mortuary would spot her on her sickie. After walking east for twenty minutes, the Victorian red-brick chimneys of St Crispin's – Bradley Appleton's school – came into view and Cassie felt a needle-prick of guilt: she'd been so preoccupied with her mum and dad that she'd given barely a thought to Bradley and his poor parents, Kim and Steve.

Naenia's school, too. She felt a sudden desire to do something that might help them, to find out if Naenia really was hiding something that might explain Bradley's suicide. An ironwork school gate came into view and through it a steady stream of kids in dark green uniforms making their way to a day of mind-numbing incarceration. She parked herself next to a hedge which hid her from view but let her see out and pretended to be checking her phone. She didn't want anyone to think she was some kind of school-gate paedo.

It was a good fifteen minutes before the lone figure of Naenia came into view – one of the last stragglers, shoulders slumped, dragging her feet and clearly not worried about arriving late. Cassie had to check her over a couple of times to be sure it was her – minus the full Goth makeup she looked like any other slightly pudgy teen girl, except for the flash of blue in her hair and the ever-present insect-patterned scarf around her neck.

Cassie walked towards her, and when their eyes finally met, Naenia physically flinched.

She knew something.

Breaking into a trot, the girl went through the gate but Cassie followed, catching up with her at the chain-link perimeter of a netball court. Seeing her come alongside, Naenia looked horrified. 'You can't come in here!' She nodded towards a middle-aged woman fifty yards ahead at the school entrance who was busy interrogating some boy. 'Mrs Spindler will throw you out!'

Cassie's smile was unconcerned. 'I'm happy to tell Mrs Spindler why I'm here, if you like, Naenia.'

The girl opened her mouth and closed it again.

Cassie nodded towards a timber-built hut. 'Let's go in here for a quick chat.'

'But . . .'

The girl's distress made Cassie feel bad but she summoned up an image of Kim Appleton to harden her heart. 'It'll only take a few minutes.'

The hut housed a changing room, smelling of pine resin, girl sweat, and old plimsolls. Sitting down on one of the benches, Cassie waited for Naenia to take the seat opposite her.

'Look, Naenia, I'm going to be completely straight with you. We aren't very happy about Bradley's cause of death. Something doesn't add up. So we might have to run more tests.'

Silence. But from the rise and fall of the girl's chest her breathing was rapid and shallow.

'Whether those tests find anything or not, I can promise you the coroner will get to the bottom of it all at Bradley's inquest. You do realise he has the legal right call you for questioning?'

Naenia's fingers flew to her hairline to pluck out a hair before dropping to neck level to fiddle with her scarf. Cassie met her eyes. 'Listen to me. I don't want you to get into trouble. And if you tell the truth I promise you won't. Bradley's mum and dad, they really need to know what happened.'

Naenia dropped her gaze. 'I . . .'

It was then that Cassie noticed. Naenia had slapped on some foundation but it didn't entirely conceal a sprinkle of red dots across her eyelids. *Just like the ones on Bradley's lids.*

Petechiae? On a living person?

Of course. Meeting Naenia's eyes, Cassie indicated the scarf. 'May I?'

Naenia gave a helpless nod.

Underneath a brownish line bordered by a yellow haze of old bruising ran across her throat, disappearing up behind her ear.

'How long had you and Bradley been playing the choking game?'

Chapter Nineteen

'I told him never *ever* to play it on his own! I swear!'

Naenia rubbed punishingly hard at her reddened eyes with the tissue Cassie had given her. The truth had emerged between sobs and accompanied by a stream of self-recrimination. Naenia had first heard about the 'game' – which she called Flatliner – a couple of months earlier, when a girl at school shared a video on some alternative social media app Cassie had never even heard of.

Naenia had deleted it after Bradley died but she told Cassie it showed a goth boy choking himself with a bungee cord in a multi-storey car park, a mate filming him as he went limp, his face becoming congested. He didn't quite lose consciousness and a couple of minutes later, after loosening the cord, he had raved about the 'trip'. Cassie had to work hard to maintain a neutral expression but the whole thing turned her stomach.

'So, you and Bradley tried it together?'

Naenia nodded, unable to meet Cassie's eye. 'I know how crazy it sounds now. But I didn't want to . . . you know . . .' She blushed.

'You didn't feel ready to have sex and this felt like an experience you could try together.'

'A few kids at school had done it and it seemed safer than pills, y'know?'

Cassie kept her voice level. 'That euphoria you felt? It's a by-product of your brain being starved of the oxygen carried in the blood. It's called hypoxia and it annihilates your brain cells. It can cause long-term mental health issues – if you survive.'

Tears welled in the girl's eyes again. 'It's all my fault!' If I hadn't shown him that video, if I hadn't played the game with him . . .'

Cassie thought back to what she was like at fifteen. Would she have strangled herself to get high? She couldn't imagine it. Weed seemed incredibly benign by comparison. She reached out and took Naenia's hand, the girl's fingers curling gratefully around hers. 'Look, you said that people at school were playing it? So chances are he'd have heard about it from someone else anyway. And boys tend to take more risks than girls.' Her eye fell on the spray of red dots across Naenia's eyelids and she pictured the capillaries just under the skin bursting under venous pressure. It occurred to her that if they were old they probably would have disappeared by now. 'You've done it in the last couple of days, am I right? In spite of what happened to Bradley?' The girl dropped her eyes. 'You were hoping the same thing might happen to you.'

'I wanted to properly pass out, but every time I got close I chickened out' – her voice heavy with self-disgust. 'I'm such a coward.'

'Listen to me.' Cassie squeezed her hand. 'Bradley's dead and there's no bringing him back. What would another pointless death achieve? Just a load more pain and misery – for your family, all your friends. You know now what it's like to lose someone.' The girl gave a little shrug of reluctant agreement. 'Look, Naenia, it's great you're still alive – because you can make some good come out of this.'

'Some *good*?'

'Absolutely. Letting Bradley's mum and dad know that it was just a stupid accident, that he didn't kill himself because he was unhappy. That'll make a huge difference to them, honestly it will. And you can tell the kids at school what a dangerous dumbass game Flatliner is.'

'My mum'll kill me and I'll get expelled!' Her voice had risen to a wail.

'No, you won't.' Cassie was gambling this was true. 'Your only crime is being fifteen years old and not believing you can die.'

'I can't face his mum and dad, I just can't.' She started shaking her head vehemently.

Cassie gave her a moment before going on. 'You don't need to. I know the cop who's looking after Bradley's family. You can talk to her. She'll be sympathetic, I promise. She'll deal with his mum and dad – and I'm sure she'd be happy to be there when you tell your mum.'

Naenia bit her lip – still not convinced.

'You know how crap you've been feeling? Telling the truth will make you feel one thousand per cent better, I promise.'

A few minutes later, Cassie watched Naenia continue on up the path to school. Unless it was just wishful thinking on Cassie's part, her posture seemed less hunched, the burden of her terrible secret already lightened by telling someone the truth about the accidental death of Bradley Appleton.

Chapter Twenty

That afternoon Cassie took the bus to Hampstead Heath, contradictory feelings bubbling up in her chest. Doubt and guilt, but also an undeniable undertow of anticipation. When Callum had phoned back she'd been curt with him, determined that he shouldn't misread her willingness to meet as an acceptance of his claims of innocence.

The meeting place she'd named was carefully chosen: a park bench in a quiet corner at the Gospel Oak end of the Heath. Meeting outdoors felt less . . . intimate somehow, and on a winter weekday, even though weak sunshine was filtering through the clouds, there were unlikely to be many people about and less risk of being seen by anyone she knew.

She turned the corner to the bench having passed no more than a handful of dog walkers. Seeing Callum sat there, she felt a horrible mixture of pity and disappointment as the big strong dad who still lived in her mind's eye dissolved into this hunched and skinny old guy.

Taking a seat at the other end of the bench from him, she perched on the edge to signal this was no social call, and cut to the chase.

'I've been remembering stuff from when I was little,' she said, her tone businesslike. 'And I know that Mum started a fire in the flat.' Telling him she'd got the intel from Maria would only complicate things.

He looked shocked. 'You remember the fire?' He looked down at his hands, his jaw muscle working for a long moment before looking up at her again. 'Listen, Cat—Cassie, it was an accident. Your mum suffered with her nerves and she said a little drink helped her to cope, but sometimes she would get . . . a bit tipsy. That was how she got the black eye that got brought up at the trial – taking a fall in the bathroom.' He looked pained at the memory. Cassie remembered him seeming shifty when he'd denied hitting Kath – now she realised it might have been an understandable reluctance to tell her that her mum had been an alcoholic.

Stay sceptical, she told herself.

'Tell me about the fire.'

'OK. Kath had been drinking that afternoon and gone for a nap, leaving you parked in front of the TV and a candle burning on the windowsill. The flame caught the curtains.' He stared into the distance as if reliving the sight. 'If I'd come home even ten minutes later . . .'

'You just happened to come home?'

'Not exactly. By then I'd started to worry about leaving you alone with her. So I would call her from work and if she didn't answer I'd rush home. It got me fired from a couple of jobs.'

Cassie studied Callum's long, thin face. He appeared to be telling the truth, but she reminded herself that since Maria had only been relaying what he'd told Barney, he was still the only source for this version of events.

'So why didn't you say all this in court? About her drinking, and how she really got the black eye?'

'My brief told me not to. He said that bad-mouthing my dead wife wouldn't go down well with the jury. Especially after your nana tore me a new arsehole in the witness box.' Glancing at her face he added, 'Sorry, sweetheart, seventeen years inside didn't do a lot for my manners. Look, this must be horrible for you to hear, but alcoholics are devious and your mum, well, she let your nana think that it was me who blackened her eye.'

'But you *did* bad-mouth her,' said Cassie. 'You claimed in court that she was screwing some other guy – without a shred of evidence!'

His shoulders dropped. 'That day was the first time I'd mentioned it to anybody – I hadn't even told my brief. But when I saw the way the trial was going I *had* to tell the truth. Not to save my skin like they made out – but to get the cops to go looking for the guy.' He thumped a fist on his skinny thigh. 'He *had* to be her real killer. You must see that.' The look he turned on her was so intense it scared her.

'So where did you get this idea that she was being unfaithful?'

He plucked at the thin denim of his jeans, lost in a memory. 'Everything was great to start with. You, me and Kath, we were a happy little family. The Ravenettes? Do you remember us calling ourselves that?' One side of his mouth lifted in a hopeful smile.

She didn't – but his wistful expression made something twist in her chest. She had to suppress the urge to reach out and touch him, to brush his over-long fringe out of his eyes.

'Then, just after you turned four, we hit a rough patch. The band was getting a load of gigs and it was tough on Kath, me being out so many evenings. That was when her drinking got bad. A few weeks before ... before it happened, I just *knew*

132

something was going on. Two or three times I walked in and she put the phone down with some pathetic excuse.'

'That's it?'

'We'd been married long enough for me to know that something was up, that she was hiding something. That's why we were having rows – why we had the row in the pub that night. I begged her; said that if she would just tell me the truth, I would forgive her.' He craned towards her. 'Cassie, sweetheart. I'll never forgive myself for leaving her there that night. If I'd known she was going to stay out late and walk home on her own . . .' He let the thought trail off, his jaw clenching and re-clenching.

'So how come somebody saw you, coming out of Prowse Place where—'

He shook his head 'Look that guy must have mixed me up with someone else. I didn't even go home that way, I swear! I wish to God I had – she might still be alive.'

'What about the cops? Why were they so convinced you were guilty?'

'Because they bought what your nana said about me hitting Kath, added in the rows we'd been having – and made five. Being Irish didn't help. In London back then, there were still bombs still going off and a guy like me couldn't get a fair shake. When I was eighteen the cops threw me in a cell just because my roommate's family in Derry had some IRA connection.' His face hardened, the eyelids hooding, and she could imagine him in a temper. 'Those bastards made up their minds I did it on day one – after that they just couldn't see past it being me.'

Cassie tucked her freezing hands under her armpits to warm them. She couldn't suppress the feeling that had been bubbling up

133

while her father talked – the growing sensation that he appeared to be telling the truth.

'I want you to know that I never blamed her,' he went on, 'not for the drinking, not even for the affair. She was always a fragile creature, my Kath.' He thumped his own chest with unnecessary force. 'But I loved her more than I loved my own life.'

Suddenly angry, she thought, *And what about me?*

'Why did you wait so long to come looking for me?' Her words icy-cold. 'If you really didn't kill her, why wait twenty-one years to say so? Why turn up now?'

He rubbed his thighs to warm them. 'You probably don't remember but I used to work on a fruit and veg stall at the market and I'm still in touch with the fella who runs the stall. Your gran shops there now and again, without knowing our connection – obviously – so when she disappeared a few weeks back he asked another customer who said she'd had a stroke.

'That was it. I realised that if your gran had died you'd have to face it alone, without any family. I knew then I had to come and find you, tell you face to face that I didn't kill your mum – whether you believed me or not. I borrowed enough cash for the trip' – he shrugged his bony shoulders – 'and here I am.'

The light was beginning to fail and with it the last glimmer of warmth from the winter sun. She chafed her upper arms through her leather jacket. His hands went to his jacket, clearly about to offer it to her. She shook her head but softened the refusal with a smile.

'That still doesn't explain why you didn't come earlier,' she said, but more gently.

'Ah, Cassie, I've wanted to get in touch a thousand times. But I couldn't bear the thought of seeing you while you still believed

134

it was me who killed your mum. I just kept praying that *something* would happen to clear my name. When I was inside I read all those cases from the 80s and 90s getting solved years later through DNA. I even wrote to my MP about it, to see if he could help to clear my name.' He made a scornful sound. 'He said I would need "significant new evidence" to bring an appeal. Like that's ever going to happen. So I just gave up.'

He paused, sending her a look she couldn't decipher. 'I know I have no right to ask this. But once you turned eighteen, did you ever think . . . I mean, did you ever consider . . . contacting me?'

She stared at him, momentarily confused. *Of course. How would he know?* 'From the start, Babcia told me that you both died in a car accident. She said I'd been "too young" at four to go to the funeral. She only told me a few weeks ago what really happened to Mum.'

He stared at her for a moment. 'Jesus, Cassie! I had no idea. All these years you thought I was dead?'

'She did what she thought was best for me.' Even she could hear the defensive note in her own voice.

He put up a hand. 'Whatever went on between your nana and me, I don't deny she did a great job bringing you up.' He smiled his crooked smile at her, piercing her heart. 'I looked you up online, and I'm so proud of what you've achieved. You must have passed a string of exams to get that job at the mortuary. But I wasn't surprised – you always were such a smart little thing. Always into everything.'

Unsettled by the wave of warmth she felt at her dad's approving gaze, Cassie stood to go. But looking down at his crestfallen face she found herself reaching out to touch his shoulder. The

135

contact only lasted a couple of seconds – but in that moment it was as if all their years apart fell away.

Before she turned the corner to disappear out of view she glanced back and saw him looking after her, his hand resting on the shoulder she had touched. He was sitting taller, more upright than before, like a condemned man who'd just been given a reason to hope.

Chapter Twenty-One

Cassie struggled to sleep that night, manacled to a never-ending switchback ride of guilt and hope. Guilt that she'd given airtime to the man who a jury had found guilty of killing her mother. Guilt, too, that her birth had left her mum with undiagnosed post-natal depression and struggling with a child who Babcia had described as 'a handful', or who, in her father's euphemism, was 'into everything'.

Was it any surprise that Kath took to the bottle? It must have been torture for such a free spirit, ending up stuck in a flat with a hyperactive kid while her husband worked all day and gigged by night. A pressure-cooker scenario that could easily have led to rows, violence and ultimately to murder.

If he really did do it.

Seeing him again – even so physically diminished – had revived her memory of the loving and patient father he'd been when she was tiny. The hope that he was telling the truth kept elbowing its way to the front of her mind.

The next morning, waking from fractured sleep Cassie admitted something to herself for the first time: she was desperate to find proof that her father had been wrongly convicted. If she succeeded it would mean her only surviving parent being returned to her.

Picking up her phone to check the time she remembered something else she needed to do. After her day 'off sick' she was on a late shift at the mortuary, which gave her time to get hold of Phyllida Flyte and tell her what Naenia had revealed about Bradley Appleton's death.

'You look terrible.' Flyte's glacier-blue eyes raked Cassie's face through the open front door. 'Are you sick?'

Heartsick, thought Cassie. Again she pictured the figure of her dad, the question *Did he do it?* running through her mind for the thousandth time.

'I'm fine. You need to get to Naenia before anyone else ends up as another casualty of this stupid fucking game.'

Flyte's eyelids came down a notch in disapproval of her swearing. 'Yes, well, I already called the school and arranged to interview her, with her teacher as chaperone.'

'Not the mother?'

'No.' A purse of the lips. 'She said she couldn't get any time off work.'

Cassie had given Flyte the basics over the phone but she had wanted to hear the full story face to face, so Cassie had told her to come to the flat.

As Flyte's gaze took a tour of the living room, Cassie had second thoughts about that plan: looking at the place afresh under that pitiless scrutiny she could see that she'd been letting things go. OK, so at least there was no eviscerated squirrel on the kitchen worktop like the first time Flyte had come here, but Cassie's hasty clear-up had missed a grease-stained pizza box sticking out from under the sofa, and when Flyte's searchlight gaze found the empty vodka bottle on the windowsill along-side the cairn of animal skulls her eyebrows went up a half-centimetre.

'Right. So the coroner is bound to ask how we acquired the information about this choking game, and how I came to interview Sophie Kerrow. Remember she calls herself Naenia.'

'Why?' Flyte frowned in confusion. 'Sophie is such a pretty name.'

Already anxious about the way Flyte would handle the girl, Cassie wasn't about to explain that Naenia was her goth name, taken in honour of the goddess of funerals. 'You do know she's a goth, like Bradley?'

'Yes, you already said.' A sharp look. 'Why do you mention it?'

'It's just . . . she already blames herself for Bradley's death. Don't take this the wrong way, but you will go easy on her, won't you?'

Cassie watched as Flyte performed a mime of the verb 'to bristle' – her broom-handle spine stiffening, a quiver running through her shoulders.

'Of course I will,' she snapped. 'She's just a child – and as much a victim of this so-called game as Bradley was.'

'OK. I'm just saying she's vulnerable.' Cassie paused, wondering how much to reveal. 'Look, she as good as said she tried to kill herself over Bradley's death.'

Concern momentarily softened the severe beauty of Flyte's face. 'Good to know,' she said crisply before her eyes narrowed. 'At the mortuary you seemed convinced that Bradley was a straightforward suicide. What was it that led you to go looking for Soph . . . for Naenia?'

He told me that his dying thought was 'Trippy' ... ? Cassie imagined how that would play.

'I don't know. Sometimes I just get . . . a feeling?'

'A feeling . . .' It was impressive, the way Flyte could distil a ton of meaning into a raised eyebrow. 'Oh yes, your famous intuition. Sorry, but you'll have to do better than that.'

Cassie thought back to the moment when she'd heard Bradley 'speak'. As real as these episodes always felt at the time, *rationally* she knew that the dead couldn't communicate with the living. So, assuming she had projected the word 'Trippy' onto Bradley, where had it come from?

Had some of the petechiae on Bradley's eyelids looked darker and therefore older, indicating that his self-strangulation wasn't a one-off? Then she remembered asking Dr Curzon if he wanted samples of the strap muscles in Bradley's neck taken for microscopic analysis – an idea he'd dismissed as unnecessary.

'I think I probably noticed that some of the subcutaneous bruising to his neck muscles wasn't fresh – in other words, it wasn't the first time he'd choked himself.' She shrugged. 'I've read about kids impeding their airway to get high, so maybe my subconscious was working overtime to join the dots.'

Flyte made a note in her neat schoolgirl hand. 'Is there any way objectively to confirm that Bradley had played this game before?' Cassie had to press a smile from her lips at Flyte's refusal to split the infinitive. 'It would be useful to give the coroner something concrete, in case Naenia changes her story.'

Cassie nodded 'Bruises produce a substance called haemosiderin as they break down, and we can stain the samples with a chemical to show up any pre-mortem bruising as a brown pigment under the microscope.'

Flyte had her spell out 'haemosiderin' for her notes.

'By the way,' Cassie went on. 'When you ask the coroner's office to request the extra testing, could you leave my name out of it? I'm not exactly flavour of the month with the new pathologist.'

Flyte looked at her. 'Let me guess. He doesn't like the underlings getting ideas above their station?'

'Yeah. Especially ones with piercings and tatts.' She sent Flyte a wry look, reminding her of her own knee-jerk reaction to Cassie's look.

The way Flyte pursed her pretty lips, she'd taken the point. 'All right, I'll keep you out of it. Once I have the full story from Naenia, I'll be advising the headteacher that her pupils need an urgent talking-to about this so-called game.' Flyte returned the notebook to her bag. 'I might even do it myself.'

Cassie left a beat before saying, 'Why not suggest to Naenia that she do it? It'd make her feel useful, and the message might come better from someone their own age . . .' *Rather than an uptight cop . . .*

Flyte surveyed her through lidded eyes before giving a micro-nod. 'Fair point.' After stowing her notebook in her bag she said, 'You really don't look well, you know, Cassie. How are you doing, dealing with your mum's death?'

It was the concern in her voice that floored Cassie. Unable to trust herself to speak, she got up and went into the kitchen. She was running a glass of water at the sink when she heard Flyte behind her at the doorway. 'Listen. About your mum's case

141

file' – her voice sounding more awkward, more *human* than its usual robocop setting. 'I really can't promise anything, but I'll see what I can do. Strictly on the QT. OK?'

Cassie didn't turn but managed to nod her head.

Chapter Twenty-Two

Flyte was efficient, Cassie had to give her that. By the time Cassie reached the mortuary the coroner's instruction to conduct extra tests on Bradley had already come through. At least she was forewarned when Dr Curzon swept in like a stormfront that afternoon. After a glance at his face, even Jason didn't risk his usual jokey greeting.

He came straight over to her table where she was laying out her instruments ready for the PM list. 'I hear that I am required to undertake further examination of the strap muscles of the hanged boy?'

She did a little mime of surprise. 'Oh yes?'

'Something I recall you suggesting at the PM' – his stare a flat challenge.

'Did I?' she said mildly, pretending to be busy lining up the instruments in her preferred order: her PM40 knife, and selection of scalpels, followed by the rib shears, bowel scissors and the toothed forceps.

'Yes, I am quite certain of it.' His words simmered with repressed fury. 'And now some female detective has been on to the coroner asking for the same thing. A remarkable coincidence, wouldn't you agree?'

She shrugged. 'I wouldn't know, I've been off sick, with food poisoning' – remembering in the nick of time the story she'd given Doug – 'I guess the police must have a new line of enquiry.' Frowning down at her instruments she swapped the dura stripper with the skull key for no good reason.

She could feel waves of frustrated anger coming off Curzon but they both knew he couldn't prove anything. After a moment he said, 'Either way, we shall be prioritising the *real* work before I waste my valuable time on some overexcited policewoman's pet theory.'

Curzon barely spoke as he conducted his external exam of her first customer – Harjinder Singh, the twenty-eight-year-old City analyst who'd collapsed and died at home two nights ago. The only sign of anything amiss was a deep purple haematoma over Harj's sternum, a poignant reminder of the chest compressions his dad had performed until the paramedics arrived. It hadn't been there when Harj first came in but Cassie could hear her much-missed mentor Prof Arculus addressing her over the top of his specs: 'Remember. Bruises continue to develop after death.'

Cassie was relieved to feel her brain letting up on its endless loop – whether her father had been wrongly convicted – to focus on the task in hand: what could have caused the sudden death of a young and apparently healthy man?

Half an hour later she was noting down the weight of Harj's liver – just under 1,600 grams, within the normal range for his age. His heart had looked normal and healthy too, with Curzon finding no obvious signs of defect or disease.

Heading back to Curzon's dissecting bench she watched as he pulled Harj's lungs towards him and started slicing into one of them with all the enthusiasm of a man doing his tax return.

'No evidence of PE,' he intoned into his phone a couple of minutes later, simultaneously pushing the lungs to one side.

Scooping them into a pail Cassie took them over to the scales to be weighed. As she manhandled Harj's lungs into the weighing pan something caught her eye. Craning closer she saw a deep-red blood clot edging its way out of one of the tiny peripheral arterial vessels. Clots were a commonplace sight as the blood congealed after death but when she squished this one between her fingers it felt wrong. After death the cellular and plasma components of the blood separated, which gave post-mortem clots the consistency of chicken fat. This one had a distinctly spongy consistency, a sign that it might have formed pre-mortem, while Harj was still alive.

Pulmonary embolism – a clot in the main artery of the lung – was a fairly common cause of sudden death, but she had just heard Curzon specifically rule it out.

Remembering the bruising to Harj's chest Cassie got the fizzy feeling in her own chest that came when she was on to something. Going back to his body, face down on the autopsy table, she stood at his feet and studied his calves through half-closed eyes, before reaching for a tape measure. Her eyes hadn't deceived her: the diameter of his left calf was one and a half centimetres bigger than the right.

Taking her scalpel she swiftly cut a rectangular flap in the back of the left calf before carefully separating the gastrocnemius muscles. After a minute of delving, she hit paydirt. The posterior tibial vein, normally smooth and slender inside its semi-opaque creamy covering, was dark and bulging. She made a transverse cut across the vein and saw a fat crimson worm crawl out. *A classic deep vein thrombosis.* For a moment she surfed the dopamine rush that came with finding the probable cause of death, before it was cut short by a realisation: technically, she should have asked Curzon's permission before doing any further investigation of the body.

She approached him with a deference she didn't really feel. 'Ah, Dr Curzon?'

'Hmm?'

'There's something you should have a look at.'

Curzon stood silently surveying the offending vein, which she had hooked clear of Harj's calf muscles over her scalpel handle. 'Did I ask you to further dissect the body?' His polite formality was more chilling than his default grumpiness.

'I know you didn't find a PE in the main pulmonary artery but I saw a clot in one of the peripheral vessels. Then I remembered that Harj's father did chest compressions for fifteen minutes and I realised that might have dispersed the main clot – although obviously not in time to save him.' She knew that she was gabbling.

Curzon held up a hand to silence her. 'So you thought that you would go *fishing around* in this poor young man's body for the origin of a pulmonary embolism – without my express instruction?'

'I'm really sorry, Dr Curzon. It's what I would usually do if I was working with Professor Arculus . . . I suppose I just forgot about the formalities.'

'Formalities?' He widened his eyes. 'You'll be hearing more about this, young lady.'

And with that he returned to his bench with a new spring in his step.

Twat.

As soon as Curzon had left, Jason sidled over to her PM table where she was using the flexible hose to wash the blood and

146

debris from Harj Singh's now-reconstructed body into the drain hole between his feet.

Jason's expression aimed for commiseration but his eyes sparkled with schadenfreude. 'Bad luck with Curzon.'

'I was an idiot,' she admitted. 'He's already got it in for me and I just handed him a PM40 to stick between my ribs.'

'Well, what do I always say? Let them do our job, and us do ours.'

Told you so, in other words. His delight at seeing the jumped-up girlie get her comeuppance was so obvious that she wanted to slap his meaty face.

'Well, at least Curzon will have to give PE and DVT as cause of death,' she retorted. 'If I hadn't opened Harj's leg, the family might have been left never knowing why he died.'

'Better an unascertained death than a disciplinary.' Jason shrugged.

He disappeared, whistling, and Cassie turned back to her task, playing the hose over the bloodied but neat line of stitches she'd used to close the back of Harj's leg. 'Apologies for thinking you might have taken drugs, Harj,' she murmured. 'Anyway, now we can tell Ruha and your mum and dad that you wouldn't have suffered.' She paused to pat his shoulder. 'And the whole family will be screened, to see if any of them are vulnerable to abnormal clotting – it might even save another unnecessary death in the family.'

Once Cassie had found the deep vein thrombosis in Harj's leg, reconstructing the cascade of events that had led to his unexpected death was straightforward. Sitting immobile at his desk for long hours at a stretch to meet a deadline – probably combined with a pre-existing tendency to thromboembolic disease – had caused the blood to pool in his vein, where it formed a clot or thrombus. It could have sat there for weeks, before something – maybe Harj's final gym workout – dislodged a large chunk of it. Once it was on the move it turned from a thrombus to a life-threatening embolism – the word came from the Greek for plug. True to its name, on reaching the lung it had blocked an artery, triggering a catastrophic cardiac arrest.

Harj was one of the unlucky few who'd had no symptoms to prompt him to go to the GP. Or maybe he'd put down any pain in his leg to a pulled muscle. To the young, death was a vague and distant concept, she reflected – unless of course you happened to work in a mortuary.

After the debacle over Harj, Cassie had been careful to await Curzon's icy instruction before retrieving Bradley from the body store to take samples from his neck muscles. Now she knew that he'd been playing the choking game for weeks, the darker areas seemed to scream pre-mortem bruising.

She returned him to his berth in the body store. Before zipping the body bag closed over his waxy face she murmured, 'We all do dumb things at fifteen, Bradley. God knows I did. But your mum and dad will know now that this was just a stupid accident. And I'd take bets that there won't be too many more kids at your school playing this dumbass game.'

It was probably just her imagination but as she zipped the bag up she thought she heard Bradley say, '*Cool.*'

Later, Cassie had just showered and changed ready to head home when Doug intercepted her in the corridor wearing a harassed expression. After beckoning her into his office, he revealed that Curzon had dropped her in it over Harj Singh.

'Honestly, Doug, I can hear every note he records and he ruled out a pulmonary embolism – until I found the DVT.'

Doug opened his hand – a gesture that accepted her version of events while simultaneously signalling how little difference it made. 'You know what the rules say, Cassie. Any further investigation of the body has to be explicitly requested by the attending pathologist.'

'I didn't need to ask Prof Arculus for permission – he trusted me to get on with it.'

'You and the Prof had an unusual relationship. Whereas you and Dr Curzon – well, you didn't exactly hit it off from the start – and now he's seen a way to punish you.'

'Is he going to report it to the HTA?' A sudden chill ran through her as she realised she might lose her job. The Human Tissue Authority regulated mortuary practice and issued the iron-clad protocols surrounding dissection of bodies and the handling of tissue and organ samples. Would an undirected dissection break their rules? Very probably, if the pathologist made a complaint.

'Look, I think I've managed to talk him out of that – largely by pointing out the shedload of work it would involve if he wanted to bring an official complaint.'

'Thank God.'

Doug raised a hand. 'But he wants me to give you a written warning.'

'What? And have a black mark on my record forever? Because *he* wasn't thorough enough? It's just not fair, Doug.'

Doug looked like someone had shot his dog. He clearly hated being torn between loyalty to his senior technician and the demands of the pathologist.

'Between you and me, I plan to play for time. Maybe when he's cooled down he'll see sense. Nobody wants a poisonous atmosphere in an autopsy suite.'

'Not with all those offensive weapons to hand,' muttered Cassie darkly.

'That's enough now!'

They stared at each other.

Doug blew out a breath. 'Look, Cassie, you've got a stack of holiday owed that you can't carry over. Why not take a few days off, keep out of his way? I can get a locum in to help Jason.'

Cassie crimped her lips shut, to stop herself saying anything she would regret.

'I think you could do with a break anyway – you've not been yourself lately.' The genuine kindness in his voice making it ten times worse.

She shut the office door with a bang behind her, furious tears springing into her eyes. Until now, Doug had always backed her when there had been any tension with the pathologists – Curzon wasn't the first whose feathers had been ruffled by a twenty-five-year-old technician who had the cheek to actually know something. Now, without her old ally Prof Arculus there to defend her she had never felt so alone.

FLYTE

Flyte had spent most of her morning working out how to access the case file on Katherine Raven's murder. Locating it wouldn't be difficult, but explaining why she was accessing a case from the 90s, if anyone caught her, was another matter. Putting aside the to-do list on her current job – a minor-league embezzlement at a dry-cleaners in Kentish Town – she logged on to the Police National Computer Names File where all UK arrests and convictions were recorded.

Her fingers hovered over the keyboard. What she was about to do was a sackable offence. Only last week she had read about an officer who'd been thrown out of the force for repeatedly accessing the PNC illicitly to search for criminal records on his lovers, friends and family members.

It was some comfort that the cops who got into trouble with Professional Standards tended to be repeat offenders, the scale of their trawling presumably triggering some kind of alert. But she had taken the precaution of consulting the open investigations file, and found a fraudster by the name of Craven. If anyone were to challenge her, she would claim that she'd simply miskeyed the name.

The basic info page recorded the dates and details of Callum Raven's trial and conviction for the murder of his wife, and his life sentence. Scrolling down to find the location of the case file she saw the initials MIRSAP – Major Incident Room Standard Administrative Procedures. *Hurrah!* Just as she'd hoped, the case was old enough for the files to be in hard copy form which meant that they would be filed in the local document store rather than electronically. Claiming to have 'accidentally' stumbled on Raven's record on the PNC was one thing, trying to explain away why she'd accessed and downloaded e-files would be quite another.

'Cuppa?'

Flyte literally jumped in her seat.

'You all right, Sarge?' asked Josh, one of the DCs, eyeing her with a quizzical half-smile.

She resisted the guilty urge to close the window on her screen. 'I'd love one.'

'Earl Grey, no milk, one sweetener, leave the bag in, and a slice of lemon out of your little placcy box?' He grinned – apparently the amusement value of her tea order never wore thin.

Unable to come up with a witty comeback Flyte just smiled. It was the one aspect of the job she doubted she would ever master. *Bants.* Or worse, *Bantz.* Even the word irritated her.

As Josh walked away she could feel her heart still bumping along in double time. It wasn't just an entirely logical anxiety about the risk of being caught, she realised: it was excitement. Excitement at breaking the rules – rules that she'd always been so scrupulous in observing.

Except once. The time she had deliberately ignored evidence that Cassie Raven had illegally gained access to the house of her dead teacher. And now here she was again, risking a disciplinary on the girl's behalf.

Whenever she tried to work out why she was prepared to stick her neck out for this infuriating creature, Flyte was unable to come up with a convincing answer. Admittedly, in spite of the whole tiresome Camden look, there were times she'd almost felt . . . attracted to her – but since Phyllida Flyte was most definitely not lesbian, nor bisexual, nor any of the multiplicity of sexual orientations people seemed to go in for these days, that didn't really explain anything.

What about Eleanor? The name flew into her mind.

Eleanor had been a fellow pupil at her boarding school, on whom Flyte had nursed a bit of a crush when she was fourteen – but then that was a well-known phase that plenty of teenage girls went through. The memory of her blurted declaration of love one night over the midnight feast she'd organised, just for the two of them – and the way Eleanor responded – had haunted her for years. If Eleanor had scoffed or even said something mean it might have been better; instead, she had literally behaved as though Flyte hadn't spoken. The only evidence that she'd actually heard her was the graffiti that appeared a few days later, scrawled on the wall of the girls' lavatories.

Phyllida is a LEZZA.

Flyte's first ambition had been to follow her father into the army but after enduring the constant house and school moves that came with his job – ending with the Cyprus posting that had sentenced her to four years of boarding school – she'd switched her focus to the police. By the age of eighteen she had added three personal goals to her life agenda: a white church wedding by the age of thirty, a husband at least two inches taller than her and – once her career allowed it – two children, ideally one of each sex, their arrivals sensibly spaced.

Five weeks before her thirty-first birthday, dearest Pops, wearing his dress uniform, had walked her down the aisle of a Norman church in a Hampshire village to marry Matt (five foot eleven). As she recited her vows, she had recalled Eleanor's rebuff, and found herself able for the first time to smile at her own teenage confusion. And she really had loved Matt, no question about it, even if the sex had, for her at least, been more of the cosy intimacy kind than the unrealistic passion promoted in pop songs and movies.

As for her warm feelings towards Cassie, there was a perfectly simple explanation. She identified with her desperate need for information about her mother's murder, just as Flyte needed to know why she had lost Poppy.

At lunchtime she took herself off to the document store a couple of blocks away. The PC manning the desk was in his forties and not bad-looking, although he'd already started laying in some middle-aged padding around the neck and torso. He was eating a Greggs pasty and watching what sounded like an American cartoon on a smartphone propped up in front of him.

Flyte had put on some lipstick – a deeper, redder shade than her usual pink – and practised her smile outside before coming in.

'Marcus, isn't it?' – remembering to crinkle her eyes.

He looked up at her and did that little eye-widening thing she sometimes prompted in men. *Idiots.*

'DS Flyte from CID. I'm doing a bit of deep background on a fraud case from '97/'98. Pain in the proverbial. How does this work again?'

Simultaneously brushing crumbs from his lips and sucking in his stomach, Marcus waved a proprietorial arm at the rows of metal shelves stretching behind him into the gloom. 'Cases are filed by month and year, earliest to the left. '97 and '98 will be in aisle seventeen at the back.' He smiled up at her. 'I'd love to help you to find it but I can't leave the desk – we lost a post in the cuts.'

They exchanged a look bemoaning a system that could decimate police numbers while entire classes of 'minor' crimes went uninvestigated and the guilty unpunished.

'Do I need to sign in?'

He handed her an old-fashioned ring binder file holding forms with a column for visitor names plus sign-in and sign-out times. *Good grief!* Still, the ancient technology should help her get away with her misdemeanour.

'You don't need the URN?' she asked without looking up. The Unique Reference Number would identify the Raven case to anyone inclined to check up on her.

'Nah. Only if you physically check out any files.'

Phew.

In the dark labyrinth of tall metal shelves the overhead strip lights flickered automatically into life as she entered each new aisle. The familiar smell of old paper whisked her back to the library at her boarding school, where she'd spent so much of her teen years closeted away, avoiding the other girls and their catty, shallow chit-chat. Whilst they'd been obsessing over Rachel off *Friends*' haircut, or whether they'd rather be Posh or Baby Spice, she'd been losing herself in the Agatha Christie and Ngaio Marsh novels her dad sent from Cyprus. Still, sometimes she wondered: had she been a bit more of an airhead in her teens – or at least played along with the daft chatter – would she find her adult dealings with people a bit easier?

Aisle seventeen was rammed to the rafters with cardboard boxes each bearing a URN number and case name. She prayed that the Raven case wasn't on too high a shelf: she couldn't ask Marcus for help. Every contact with him raised the possibility of further chat and therefore lies – not her natural forte.

After a few minutes squinting into the packed shelves she saw *R v RAVEN* inscribed in black marker on a large box at shoulder height. Her heart sank as she counted nine boxes marked with the same URN number.

Fishcakes.

She should have anticipated the volume of paperwork a major crime would generate. Hauling one towards her she opened it and found a stack of ring binders containing what looked like admin bumf. The next one contained more of the same. The third held what must be Katherine Raven's personal effects: clear plastic evidence bags containing the clothes she'd been wearing and at the bottom a bagged half-brick, dark with old blood, obviously the murder weapon.

Finally, she found the box she was looking for: the one containing the case summary and witness statements. In one of the binders she came across Callum Raven's arrest mugshot. He was good-looking in a rough-hewn sort of way, although he had trouble written all over him. Cassie must have inherited her delicate features from her mother. In the same box were the Home Office pathologist's post-mortem report on Katherine Raven and photographs of the body.

With a quick look up and down the aisle she whipped out her iPhone and snapped the first page of the PM report. A bright light illuminated the aisle. *Buggeration!* Turning off the flash function she flicked swiftly through the rest of it before moving on to the other documents, all fingers and thumbs. She muttered as she worked, cursing whatever it was that made her do these crazy things for a tattooed goth girl with the darkest blue eyes she'd ever seen.

When she reached the images from the post-mortem, she hesitated, aware that she'd need to use the flash in order to give Cassie the detail she'd expect. Then the overhead lights came on in the next aisle, accompanied by the even tread of Marcus's size nines. She made a snap decision. Stuffed the sheaf of PM photos inside the waistband of her skirt, relying on her knicker elastic to keep them in place. Hoisted the box back onto the shelf just as a shadow rounded the corner. Spun around to scour the shelf opposite.

'Did you see a flash? A couple of minutes ago?' asked Marcus.

'Yes, I did. I think it was from the next aisle.' This was not the right moment to pick him up for omitting to use her rank.

He squinted up at the fluorescent strip light overhead. 'Probably one of the lights playing up.' He nodded to the shelf she was scanning. 'Any joy?'

'Nope. I reckon I've been given the wrong number.'

'Do you want a hand? Two pairs of eyes . . . ?' His pair of eyes wandered, seemingly of their own accord, to her chest before drifting hopefully back to her face.

'That's so sweet of you! But you know, I think it'll be quicker if I go back and get the right number.'

He nodded, clearing his throat. *Oh Lord, he wasn't about to ask her out, was he?* She headed him off with, 'Golly, look at the time! I've got a briefing with my DI in ten minutes.' The mention of a senior officer with its subtle reminder of her own rank did the job.

'Well, pop back any time,' he said. 'Sarge.'

He walked ahead of her down the aisle – just as well since she felt the photos edging up out of her knickers and had to reach a hand back to shove them in more securely.

Once back outside in the darkening twilight, she had to lean against the wall for a moment to recover, before striding off in the direction of the nick.

She didn't hear the door to the document store opening behind her.

Marcus stepped outside, a pack of cigarettes in his hand. Putting one between his lips he lit it, his gaze trained on her departing back, an assessing look on his face.

Chapter Twenty-Three

'Carpe vinum!'

Archie set the drinks down on the table with a flourish. A pint of some gruesomely cloudy-looking real ale for him, a beer and a large vodka chaser for Cassie. He had passed no comment on her order, which she was grateful for – but then she should know by now that in spite of the rugger scarf and Harrow School accent Archie was a pretty cool guy. When she'd called him after the Curzon/Harj clusterfuck he had immediately agreed to schlep over from Walthamstow where he'd been giving evidence at an inquest.

Cassie ran a discreet but appreciative eye over him: it must be a couple of years since she'd come close to dating a guy. The trouble with men was they didn't think like girls. But that was also their appeal.

She took a slug of her Sol. 'If Curzon makes a report to the HTA, the trust could give me the heave-ho.'

'Crikey,' said Archie, pulling a face. 'I've never had anything to do with the dreaded HTA but I hear they can be termagants.'

Terma-what?

It had been the Alder Hey scandal of the late 90s that prompted the HTA's formation. A maverick pathologist was found to have retained hundreds of babies' organs – and even whole foetuses – for his research without asking the parents' permission. The result had been strict rules governing the treatment of all human remains in mortuaries – down to the tiniest scrap of tissue.

'From what I've heard, things did need tightening up,' said Cassie, remembering some of the horror stories Jason had told her about the bad old days. 'Some pathologists kept organ samples they wanted to study in their home freezer.'

'I heard that, too,' Archie chuckled. 'Imagine reaching in for the Ben and Jerry's and bringing out a gall bladder.'

'I've never been *anything* but respectful towards our guests. Curzon knows that. But he just . . . hates me.'

Archie nodded sympathetically. 'I suppose what happened with his wife probably didn't help.'

She stared at him. 'What do you mean?' Remembering Curzon's habit of turning up in yesterday's shirt, smelling of stale booze. 'Did she leave him?'

Archie's expression became serious. 'In a manner of speaking, yes. She committed suicide.'

'You're kidding!' Cassie's hand shot to her mouth.

'I'm afraid not. She had severe depression, apparently – had battled it on and off her entire life. Coming home from work one night he opened the garage door to park his car' – he pressed thumb to finger, mimicking a remote control – 'and there she was, hanging from a ceiling joist.'

Cassie pictured again the too-tight wedding ring Curzon still wore. The anger that lurked at the back of his eyes like a caged animal.

'Christ. How long ago?'

'Less than a year, I think. A bad business.'

Curzon had struck her as dismissive and cruel at Bradley Appleton's PM but now she felt a wave of pity and comprehension: *of course* he'd be furious with anyone who committed suicide, even a child. Unfortunately, the discovery only made it more likely that he would make good on his threat to drop her in it. She'd seen at first hand the way the bereaved could lash out, to deflect some of their hurt and pain onto others.

Still, an evening of Archie's uncomplicated bonhomie had a relaxing effect on her – assisted by the alcohol. By closing time she realised she was half-cut, unsteady on her feet when they got up to go.

This time she accepted Archie's offer to walk her home, but when she put her face up to his after reaching her front door, all she got was a chaste kiss and a brotherly hug. She frowned into the warmth of his neck, before murmuring, 'Do you want to come in?' – her meaning impossible to misunderstand.

Pulling back to look at her, he smiled, regretful. 'I have a very early start.'

'Oh, don't be such a buzzkill.' She tugged him closer, trying to close the distance between them, but he set both hands on her shoulders.

'Listen, Cassie, you're a bit squiffy and I wouldn't want you to do anything you might regret. Another time?'

The kindly look in his deep brown eyes only made it worse. Furious with him – *no,* with herself – she turned on her heel. 'Fine. Bye then.'

Opening her front door, she was already picturing the misted bottle of Polish vodka in the freezer compartment, when she saw a brown envelope lying on the doormat. It had no address, just her name and the words in marker pen: *Check your email before opening!! PF.*

The message had been sent from Flyte's personal address and said: *The envelope I left contains hard copies of some upsetting images from your mum's PM. I knew you would want them but PLEASE, think carefully whether you really ought to look at them.*

After feeding Macavity, whose frostiness had thawed a little, she settled herself at the kitchen table. For a long moment she stared at the envelope, feeling suddenly a lot less drunk.

She told herself that she'd seen dozens of murder victims on the mortuary slab over the years. She could handle it, right?

Pulling the envelope towards her she pulled out the photo-copied colour images.

Seconds later she was arched over the sink puking up beer, vodka and the bag of peanuts that had passed for dinner. Trying to blot out the image she'd just glimpsed.

A face that was the wrong shape, caved-in, obliterated with blood. The only recognisable feature, her mother's beautiful auburn hair.

It was a while before she was able to shove the photo back into the envelope and pour herself a steadying shot. *She couldn't do it.* When it came to her own mother her ability to distance herself, honed by thousands of eviscerations, had deserted her.

Chapter Twenty-Four

'You look like shit,' said Kieran cheerfully. 'Bender last night?'

Cassie gave a rueful affirmative shrug.

The vodka had helped to blur the image of her mother burned on her retina but it was no longer helping her to sleep. After another wakeful night, the face scowling back at her from the bathroom mirror this morning had been paper-pale and hollow-eyed, set off by a volcanic zit on her chin.

They were in one of Camden's last surviving greasy spoons – still the real deal down to the brutal strip lighting and blue formica tables topped with squeezy bottles of ketchup and brown sauce – but now run, like so many of North London's old-school caffs, by Turkish Cypriots. The head-scarfed waitress had just delivered Kieran's fry-up and Cassie's fried egg sandwich.

'Since I got clean I've never slept so well.' Kieran raised his mug of tea. 'You should try it, Cass.'

He did look irritatingly healthy – his face had filled out and his skin had lost the perpetually dirt-grained look of the homeless user.

'All right, St Kieran. Spare me the motivational pep talk.'

But she had to admit she'd been overdoing it on the booze front lately. The memory of last night – and the total arse she'd made of herself with Archie – still made her cringe. *Of course* he wouldn't screw a woman who was halfway to hammered – that was part of his appeal. They'd exchanged friendly messages that morning, but she still reckoned she'd blown it, practically begging him for a shag. Not that she had the time or headspace for a romantic entanglement right now . . .

Pulling a sheaf of photocopied articles from a carrier bag Kieran selected one to push across to her.

'Check that out,' he said, wearing a big grin.

'RECORD DEAL FOR *POITÍN*?' she read out the headline before squinting at the grainy photos that illustrated the full-page article – images of the band playing live with Maria at the mic, Callum beside her on guitar, Barney in the background on drums. A second head-and-shoulders shot showed Barney on his own wearing a suit and a mod haircut that was pure 90s Liam Gallagher.

'It's from the *NME*!' said Kieran through a mouthful of bacon and beans.

'I've heard of them,' she murmured.

'Heard of them?!' He widened his eyes. 'They were THE music paper before the world went digital.'

'So what does it say?' Picking up the egg sandwich she forced herself to take a bite.

'It's an interview with Barney Cotter. Remember he took over as manager while carrying on playing drums in the band? So, up until then your dad's band had a bit of a psychedelic vibe. Have you heard of My Bloody Valentine?'

She pulled a blank face.

'Anyway, *Poitín*'s sound was similar. They had a proper cult following but it was all a bit fringe.' He pulled the article back across the table. 'So Barney tells this reporter that the band are "taking a new creative direction"' – he made ironic quote marks in the air – 'but when the reporter pushes him he admits they're going more mainstream, looking for a wider fanbase.'

Cassie's stomach instructed her to put the sandwich down. 'So . . . they were going after the big bucks?'

'Exactly. You have heard of The Cranberries, right?'

She screwed her face up. 'Irish folk-rock, right?'

'Yeah. They were *huge* in the 90s. The journalist compares Maria's voice to their lead singer Dolores O'Riordan. Anyway, Barney tells him that they've written some new material, and hints that they've got interest from a big label.'

'Does it say what Callum and Maria thought about that?'

'Uh-uh.' Kieran piled a heap of beans onto a square of fried bread and picked it up. 'But they had to've been onside for any recording contract – the band would be nothing without those two.'

Her head had started to pound. Pressing fingers to her temples she massaged the temporal muscles. 'If *Poitín* was a cult band, their fans would consider a move to the mainstream a sell-out, am I right?'

'Yeah, I need to chase the guy with the 'zine collection – see what the fans made of it.'

Giving up on the sandwich she pushed her plate away, and took another look at the article. I just can't see how a record deal could explain what happened to my mum.'

Nodding towards the remains of her breakfast, Kieran said, 'Okay if I—?' before taking a big bite.

Then he reached out his free hand to tap a finger on the small print in the bottom margin and said through a mouthful 'See the date?'

'Third of October, 1997.' Cassie's gaze snapped up to meet his. 'That's . . . three days before Mum died. Could just be coincidence, though.'

'Could be. Or maybe the record deal caused trouble between your mum and dad. Signing with a big label would have meant Callum doing a lot more touring – leaving her at home on her own with a little kid for weeks on end.'

Her father hadn't mentioned any recording contract, and their rows had seemed to centre solely on Kath's supposed affair, which both cops and jury had dismissed as a fiction – a last-ditch attempt by Callum to pin the blame for her murder on a fictional boyfriend.

'Where did he storm off to, after getting thrown out of the pub?' Kieran asked meaningfully.

She shrugged. 'To see Barney. What are you suggesting?'

'I don't know, exactly. But I just think this record deal timing and your mum getting killed? Maybe it's more than just coincidence.'

Pulling a pack of Nurofen Max out of her bag Cassie knocked a couple back with the last of her coffee and tried to view it objectively. If Kath had demanded that Callum choose between her and the band could it have tipped a man with a violent temper into a murderous rage?

She squeezed her fingers against her temples. 'Are you saying he killed her in a row over the record deal, and not some imagined lover? Either way, it would just be another motive for murder, wouldn't it?'

'I don't know. But I'll keep digging. What about you, pardner? Found anything interesting?'

'I tracked down the investigating officer Gerry Hobbs. He's agreed to see me.'

'Cool!'

It had been straightforward to track Hobbs to the charity where he worked and he'd known right away who she was – almost like he'd been waiting for her call all these years. The trouble was, the one thing she wanted to ask him about was more or less impossible to raise without dropping Flyte in it.

Cassie still hadn't been able to bring herself to look again at the photographic images from the PM but she had read the pathologist's report – and picked up something weird. Of the many samples recorded as having been taken from her mum's body for testing, one was a vaginal swab, aimed at detecting semen from any recent sexual contact. Had it come back positive, and if DNA testing had revealed a recent sexual encounter with someone other than her husband, then it could back Callum's allegation of an adulterous affair. And the police would presumably have wanted to trace and eliminate the man as a potential suspect.

The lab results were listed in an addendum at the back of the report and noted blood alcohol of three times the drink-drive limit, and the presence of prescription tranquillisers.

But there was no mention of the vaginal swab, or whether it had tested negative or positive for semen. It was like it had never existed.

Chapter Twenty-Five

A misty moon hung over the mortuary, which was a single-storey building crouched behind a screen of leylandii as if apologising to the living for its existence. The midnight air felt like an iced vodka bottle pressed against Cassie's cheeks, and the only sound was the distant whinge of traffic on the North Circular.

Swiping her card at the entrance, Cassie heard the *tock* of the lock opening. Technicians had round-the-clock access to the mortuary so they could check in any out-of-hours deaths in the community.

She changed into fresh scrubs, wellies and a plastic apron, just as she would for an evisceration, feeling every layer that she donned enveloping her in a cocoon of professionalism. Never before had the description Personal Protective Equipment seemed so apt.

In the autopsy suite, she flicked on the lights and went over to her stainless-steel table. After pulling on a pair of nitrile gloves, she took the post-mortem images of her mother out of the envelope, murmuring, 'Just another body' to herself like a mantra. Only after laying them all out on the stainless-steel surface of the autopsy table did she let her eyes rest on one.

Just another body.

So far so good. Just as she'd hoped, viewing the images in a workplace context gave her the emotional distance which had eluded her at home. She was no longer looking at her mother, but an anonymous body to be analysed, an anatomical puzzle to be solved.

The photographic record began with a shot of the victim's fully clothed body lying on a white plastic sheet to capture any fibres or other evidence, taken from above using a stepladder, a practice still used in forensic post-mortems.

The next images recorded the body lying on the autopsy table, supine and prostrate – aka face up and face down – and in various stages of undress. The jacket had been removed before the next photo was taken, then the floaty Laura Ashley-style dress, underwear and so on – the grim striptease of a forensic PM designed to record any clues to the events leading up to death.

Once the bra and knickers had been removed, the contrast between the smashed and bloodied face and the pale young body was startling.

Just another body.

Cassie turned to the big close-ups of the face aimed at identifying the individual injuries inflicted by the murder weapon. The blood had been washed off for this exercise and the images were so close-up they felt impersonal, like the details of some geographical feature. In any case with injuries this extensive it was a struggle to identify the victim's sex, let alone recognise her.

A series of images of the back of the skull, the hair shaved off, showed further contusions, and a sizeable skull depression just above the occipital bump. Cassie already knew from the PM report that it was this blow, delivered from the rear, which caused the acute subdural haematoma recorded as the cause of death. According to the pathologist, the multiple blows to the face came after this injury and were delivered when the victim was already unconscious and lying on her back. The roughly broken half-brick used as a murder weapon had also been captured from every angle – the business end evident from the amount of blood soaked into its rough surface.

Close-ups of the upper arms showed the bluish-purple bruises that she remembered being mentioned at Callum's trial – bruises which he had denied any knowledge of. They were grip marks in the distinct shape of fingers, just turning yellow at the edges, which fitted the pathologist's finding of them being between three and four days old. Was it credible that a husband wouldn't notice such bruises on a wife in bed, or while she was undressing?

It was only at the very end that something threatened to pierce Cassie's bubble of professional detachment – and it came from an unexpected source. A set of photos recorded the jewellery her mother had been wearing that night: silver earrings shaped like scallop shells, her plaited gold wedding ring, and a torn black leather choker designed to look like barbed wire – the kind of thing you could still pick up on the market.

She got a vivid image of her mum getting dolled up for her date night with her husband, humming as she applied her makeup, looking forward to a rare evening at the pub, praying that there would be no more jealous outbursts.

Suddenly Cassie's field of vision darkened, narrowing to a tunnel and the air crackled so loudly she gripped the edge of the table. From the photos spread on the autopsy table she heard her mother's voice rise in a distinct whisper.

Not my style.

Chapter Twenty-Six

The following day Cassie went to her grandmother's for Sunday lunch. At first it looked like Weronika had gone along with her request for something light – serving up Polish rolmopsy, salad and miseria, proudly pointing out the substitution of crème fraîche for full-fat sour cream in the latter. But then she went and blew it with dessert.

Cassie had just finished her second slice of home-made kremowka.

'Another little piece maybe?' Weronika wheedled. 'You are looking so thin in the face!'

'Are you kidding?' Cassie pushed the plate away. 'And remind me, when did multiple layers of pastry, buttercream, *and* real cream, count as "light"?'

'A little treat is good for the soul.'

Cassie suppressed a smile at this exchange – worn to a soft shine by a thousand repetitions. It was good to see her grandmother apparently fully restored to her old self.

The buzz she'd got last night at the mortuary after hearing – or imagining she'd heard – her mum's voice had faded, leaving her feeling depressed and deflated.

Not my style. To what? To get gruesomely murdered? Or to have an affair?

It wasn't much help. She realised what had been lurking half-consciously at the back of her mind during the photographic post-mortem she'd conducted on her mum. The dumbass idea that she would find some big fat clue to clear her dad of the murder.

After lunch, she and her grandmother shared a comfortable silence, listening to the hiss and pop of the gas fire. Cassie was close to dozing off on the sofa when Weronika asked, 'How are you, *tygrysek*? I know how hard it must have been for you, learning what happened to your mama.'

Surprised into a candid reply she said, 'The hardest thing is finding out my father was alive all those years.' She blinked. 'Sorry, Babcia—'

Weronika raised a hand. 'No, it is I who should be making the apology. I have been thinking it over and I realise now what a very wrong thing it was for me to do. I had no right to rob you of the knowledge that you still had a father.'

'You had good reason after what he did.' *If he did it.*

'No.' A firm headshake. 'Whatever kind of man he is, whatever he did, you had the right to know you still had a parent living once you were old enough. What you chose to do with the knowledge should have been up to you.'

That partly assuaged Cassie's guilt about having seen her father – not that she had asked him to pop up out of nowhere after a twenty-one-year absence.

'It was probably for the best, given that he showed zero interest in me while he was in prison.'

Her grandmother set her hands on the arms of her chair to lever herself up, before going to retrieve something from the old mahogany bureau where she kept her correspondence. She put a sheaf of envelopes into Cassie's hands, which were all addressed to Weronika Janek, here at the flat.

'Go on, take a look.'

Opening one, Cassie found a single sheet of notepaper and written in a looping hand, '*For Cassandra*'. Just those two words.

'I don't get it.'

'After your mama died, they came in the post every year on your birthday, together with a postal order made out to me.' Seeing Cassie's blank look she went on, 'Postal orders are anonymous, not like a cheque. It was fifty pounds at first, but later on it grew to two, three hundred pounds a time.'

Cassie started to pull out more of the notes, always finding those two words in the same hand.

'There was never any more than that,' said Babcia. 'Always just "*For Cassandra*".'

'When did they stop?'

The old lady dropped her eyes. 'They never stopped. The last one came just before your birthday last year. Four postal orders totalling a thousand pounds.'

'The five hundred quid you gave me, that you said came from some endowment policy payout?'

Babcia's smile made her look like a naughty five-year-old. 'I always gave you half and invested the rest.'

'In what?'

'Tech stocks, mostly,' she said crisply. 'It's quite a little pile now. There for you whenever you need it.'

'You invested on the stock market?' Of course, she'd seen the *Investors Chronicle* magazines that had been delivered over the years – but had thought they were just another of her gran's eccentric interests, like her love of cowboy movies.

'I might just be a silly old lady to you but before Stalin ended my education with a stay in prison, I was studying for an economics degree. I wanted to work in an investment bank.'

'Could you not still have done? After you escaped and came to London?'

Weronika shrugged. 'I had no money for college and in the 60s it wasn't easy for a woman, let alone one straight off the North Sea ferry, to get a job in the City.'

Cassie did a quick count of the envelopes. *Twenty-one.* 'So they came every year after Callum went to jail?' She checked the postmarks. Kentish Town, Camden, King's Cross. 'They were all posted from round here or a few Tube stops away.'

'At the beginning I thought they must have been sent by a well-wisher.'

'A *well-wisher*? Like who?'

'After your mama died we got such a lot of cards – and even flowers – from kind people who read about her in the paper. Some even sent sweets or a toy for you – like that nice policeman.'

Cassie felt a little leap of hope: had her father found a way to send cash anonymously? Perhaps through that guy who ran the fruit and veg stall where he used to work?

'Could it have been my father?'

The old lady shrugged. 'I don't know, darling. I never liked to think so – we didn't need any money from that . . .' She closed her lips over the insult. 'But I suppose it's possible.'

If the birthday cash came from Callum, where would he have got the money? Savings? Royalties from *Poitín*'s only album?

Cassie picked up the sheaf of notes. 'Can I keep these?'

'Of course. It felt wrong to throw them away,' said Weronika.

'I wanted to ask you something, Babcia. Did you know that Callum might have been about to sign a record deal just before Mama died?' Frowning, Weronika turned down her mouth doubtfully. 'You don't recall her being upset about it? It would have meant him being away a lot, although it would have brought in a lot of money.'

Weronika scoffed. 'My Katerina wasn't interested in money.' She smiled at a memory. 'You know the only dream she ever talked about? To have a little farm with a vegetable garden and some chickens.'

Cassie couldn't suppress an unwelcome thought: here was another dream her mother never lived to achieve – one that might have come to pass if having a baby hadn't plunged her into depression and drink.

Chapter Twenty-Seven

Cassie tugged at the collar of her jacket. It was Monday morning and she was wearing the suit she'd bought from Next for her job interview at the mortuary. It still fitted just fine round her waist and bust but had become uncomfortably tight across the shoulders: six years of manoeuvring bodies beat the gym hands down as an upper-body workout.

The charity where former DS Gerry Hobbs now worked as head of security occupied two floors of a smart-looking office block in Farringdon. Cassie gave her name at the reception desk and a few minutes later she saw a man in his fifties – about the right age – emerge from the lift. His upright bearing, single-breasted black wool coat and highly polished brogues gave off the unmistakable vibe of lifelong cop. When he clocked her, he performed 'the look' she sometimes got from people over forty – eyes widening as they flickered from her black-dyed hair and eyebrow bolt to her lip piercings. Just as well she'd worn her hair down to cover her shaved undercut.

'Cassie?' He recovered with an uncertain smile.

Did he expect to find her still rocking the tartan pinafore and plaits her gran had her wearing at the age of four?

'I thought we'd go out for coffee?' he went on. 'Saves on all the bureaucracy you need to do to get a pass these days.'

As he went to speak to the reception lady Cassie ran a discreet inventory on him. A big man, but not fat, with one of those open, freckled faces and the sandy colouring she recognised from Camden residents with Irish roots – like a Sligo farmer who'd just climbed off his tractor. He'd clearly been good-looking in his youth, and was still pretty presentable now, in what, his mid- to late-forties?

They played small-talk ping-pong until reaching the cafe – a smart little independent place near Smithfield market, but as soon as they sat down he cleared his throat and donned the frowning expression she was getting used to from people about to offer their condolences.

'It's the kind of case you never forget,' he went on, shaking his head. 'Kath was such a lovely looking girl – and so young. And you, just a tiny little thing.' His eyes skittered over her pierced lip again.

'You brought me a Barbie doll – in a pink princess frock,' she said, picturing Barbie's empty eyes and moronic smile, and the wasp-waist which even then had struck her as unrealistic compared to a real grown-up lady.

'You remember that, do you?' He looked delighted.

'Oh, I loved that doll!' she lied. After the disappointing results of Barbie's post-mortem, she had pushed her dismembered remains out of sight under her bed, to hide the evidence of her crime.

'It must have been just terrible for you, losing your mother like that, but at least you had Weronika to raise you. What a remarkable woman. You say she's still active?'

Kath, Weronika . . . Either the case had left a deep impression on him or he had read up on it ahead of meeting her.

'She had a small stroke but she's on the mend now.' Cassie took a sip of her espresso. 'Obviously, I don't want to upset her by stirring up traumatic memories – and the case is too old to come up in online searches.'

'I completely understand. Well, look, feel free to ask me whatever you like. I've got a pretty sharp memory.'

'I think you were first on the scene? Could you tell me about . . . finding her? You got a call from someone walking their dog, right?'

A nod. 'Yes, a call from a phone box, around 6 a.m. We raced out there. It was a foggy morning, I recall, you know how it gets sometimes around the canal.'

'"We?"'

'Yes, me and a PC. When we got there she was lying on the cobbles in a tunnel under the railway.'

Cassie remembered seeing – or imagining – the bloodstained cobbles.

'And the dog walker?'

'He was standing guard over the body.'

It was nice to know that a stranger had done that – not wanting to leave her mother's body alone.

'We taped off the street and put a tent up right away to protect her dignity. The pathologist got there pretty quickly and declared life extinct – sorry, it's just the jargon.'

'Sure, no problem. Then you took her to the mortuary, I assume?' She hadn't mentioned her job – deciding he'd be less guarded if he thought she was just a civilian.

'Back then it was the old local authority mortuary down at King's Cross.'

Not her mortuary. *Thank Christ for that.* She could do without picturing her mum's battered body every hour of the working day.

She hesitated, chewing on her thumbnail, a gesture for his benefit.

'What is it? Please ask me anything.'

'Umm. It might sound weird but . . . was there any evidence of, y'know, anything sexual?'

'I . . .' He blinked twice. *Interesting.* Then dropped his gaze, a thoughtful expression on his face. 'I don't recall anything like that. The poor thing was fully clothed. From the moment I saw her I knew she'd been killed by someone close to her.'

'How come?'

'There were . . . serious facial injuries which usually suggest a personal motive – that her attacker knew her intimately. This was no stranger murder.'

'Intimately, right.' Dropping her eyes as though embarrassed, she continued, 'I just wondered if any samples were taken, to, you know, rule out any . . . recent sexual contact?'

Again, that double-blink. 'I honestly don't recall,' he said, shaking his head slowly.

Sharp memory deserting you? she wanted to ask. Saying instead, 'It is a very long time ago.'

'In any event, it was blindingly obvious who our main suspect was. The police had already been called out to a domestic at the flat, your grandmother told us that Callum had given your mum a black eye, she had bruised arms – and they'd had an almighty row that night. Then we found the eyewitness who'd spotted him running away from Prowse Place that night.'

'Right. And Callum's best mate – the one who said they were watching football at the time Kath was killed – what made you suspicious about his story?'

'Barney Cotter?' Hobbs leaned forward, his eyes animated by conviction. 'The moment I clapped eyes on him I knew he had something to hide. It was as clear as' – he tapped the jam-jar filled with winter pansies on the table – 'as clear as water, that he was covering up for his mate. When he got in that witness box the prosecution only had to poke his story and it crumbled.'

On the bus back to Camden she closed her eyes to replay her encounter with Hobbs, analysing his body language, the moments he'd paused or broken eye contact – the way she would examine a body on her autopsy table. Why was she even remotely suspicious of him? Probably because there was a part of her which had taken on board what her dad had said: about the cops having it in for him from day one.

When she'd asked about the possibility of sexual assault, he had appeared to react shiftily – was it just embarrassment? Or something more? And could it be connected to the vaginal swab taken by the pathologist which had apparently vanished without trace?

Something else occurred to her. Gerry Hobbs had called her mother 'a lovely looking girl' – when the only time he'd seen Kath Raven in the flesh was after her pretty face had been obliterated by a half-brick.

FLYTE

'Is that Phyllida Flyte?'

The voice alone, a laidback yet commanding baritone that belonged unmistakably to someone of higher rank, rang alarm bells in Flyte's head.

'This is she.'

'DCI Capaldi here. You logged on to the PNC recently to look up' – there was a pause – 'a Callum Raven?'

'Sir?' Her own voice sounding surprisingly composed in spite of her blood crashing like surf in her ears.

'It was a murder case – the vic was his wife,' Capaldi went on. 'Sorry, I should have said, I'm calling from the DPS.'

Buggeration.

It felt as though somebody had thrown open the door of a blast chiller in front of her. The Directorate of Professional Standards was the body that investigated not just police corruption, but also misconduct – such as accessing the criminal records database for personal reasons.

'I'm just wondering, what is your interest in the case?' his voice silky.

'Callum Raven? I don't . . .' she said musingly. 'Oh, hang on. I remember now!' Injecting a smile into her voice as she had taught herself to do. 'It was when I was looking up a fraudster we're investigating, name of *Craven*.'

A moment of worrying silence, before that deep voice came back on the line. 'So you're saying, what, that you typed in Raven by mistake?' This was said without any trace of suspicion, which only made it worse. She'd used the same technique herself while interviewing suspects.

'Exactly. It was a miskey!'

'Right.' He sounded disappointed. 'You've only been at Camden CID a few months, am I right? Up from Hampshire?'

She gave a wary affirmation. *How did he know all this*?

'I need to ask you something in complete confidence, Sergeant Flyte. Understood?'

'Of course, sir.'

'Have you heard any gossip during your time there about a DCI Stanley Neville, nicknamed Spud, died a few years back? Or a DS Gerald, aka Gerry, Hobbs – recently retired?'

What the focaccia?!

She instantly recalled both names from the Kath Raven murder file. Thank God she had managed to return the PM photos to the document store that morning on her way to work, having checked ahead that Marcus was off-duty – no point pushing her luck with a second encounter.

'I don't recall anyone mentioning those names at work. Can I ask in what context?'

He hesitated, clearly deciding whether to trust her. 'Strictly off the record, I'm investigating certain ... irregularities in another Camden case – a major crime they worked on in 1995. It's likely to end up going to the CCRC.'

The Criminal Cases Review Commission. The body which re-examined possible miscarriage of justice cases.

'Have you picked up any . . . chatter about Neville or Hobbs at all?' he went on. 'Not that I'm suggesting they are in any way under suspicion. It's just standard practice to ensure everything is squeaky-clean our end when these cases go to review.'

She allowed herself to relax just a smidgen. It sounded as though Capaldi's motive for contacting her wasn't her accessing of Callum Raven's record, but Neville's and Hobbs' involvement with this other case. Evidently, he had decided that it was safe to quiz a recently arrived out-of-towner about any gossip at the nick.

'No, nothing,' she said. 'Hobbs retired before I got here.'

Whoops.

'Because now I think about it I have heard his name,' she added as smoothly as possible – relieved that Capaldi wasn't able to see her expression.

He didn't seem to pick up on it.

'OK. Well, keep your ears open, would you? You can call me anytime in total confidence.'

Chapter Twenty-Eight

Despite not having to go in to work, and a nightly vodka intake that would shame a Soviet salt miner, Cassie was still waking up at her usual time of 6 a.m. Lying in bed the morning after her encounter with Gerry Hobbs, she turned this way and that, trying to get back to sleep, but her thoughts wouldn't stop whirring.

She couldn't shake the feeling that Hobbs had something to hide – something to do with that missing swab. Evidence of sexual contact between Kath Raven and someone other than her husband would have backed up her father's claim that she was having an affair. And although it would arguably have strengthened his motive for killing his wife, the police should clearly have traced any other contact as a possible suspect.

But there had been no mention of the missing result in the press reports, which suggested that her father's defence had either failed to notice the omission or to understand its possible significance.

Dragging herself out of bed she found Macavity sitting silently but meaningfully by the fridge. Over the last week he'd gradually got over his epic sulk, and as she squeezed the rest of the pouch of cat food onto a plate, he actually deigned to press his furry body against her bare legs.

'Hmm. I know cupboard love when I see it.' She reached down to stroke his silken head, hearing his lawnmower purr. 'But I'll take it all the same, you heartbreaker, you.'

Knocking back a couple of Nurofen Max with a mug of water she went into the living room and wrinkled her nose: on the coffee table lay two tinfoil curry boxes, half-empty, two beer bottles, and a half-drunk bottle of vodka.

Gripped by a sudden compulsion, she gathered it all up and took it into the kitchen. Going over to the sink, she unscrewed the cap of the vodka bottle and without giving herself time to reconsider, upended it, pouring the contents straight down the plughole.

Inhaling the last of the delicious vapour as it evaporated she smelled something else. Something she couldn't place at first.

Watermelon. The perfume her mum had worn. And had once dabbed behind the four-year-old Cassie's ears.

The scent disappeared within seconds but it left her feeling strangely warmed. It struck her that there was something she hadn't asked herself. What would Kath think about her daughter digging around in the harrowing events of the past?

Remembering hearing her voice in the mortuary – even if she wasn't sure what the words had meant – and now catching a whiff of her perfume, Cassie was gripped by a conviction: her mum supported what she was doing.

After putting on the rose-sprigged blouse she threw a scarf and a leather jacket on top and set off for a walk along the canal. The sky bore down, a low grey ceiling, and the bitter cold made her regret not wearing a proper coat. She decided to take the stairs up to the high street, to go buy some gloves. Seeing a sign in the window of the Sports Direct that screamed EXTRA 50%

OFF SALE! she remembered they sold ones with touchscreen fingertips.

The next thing Cassie knew she found herself somewhere random on the right-hand side of the store, looking at a display of men's trainers. She stood there frowning for a moment. It wasn't like her to be scatty.

Whoosh. The carpet tiles of the floor loomed closer and she had to fling out a hand to grab hold of the display unit. A jolt of static and the row of trainers dissolved from the centre of her visual field, to be replaced by a jumble of bright colours.

Sweets. Red liquorice shoelaces, acid-yellow lemon sherbets, pink foam false teeth, the violent pastels of sherbet flying saucers. A pick 'n' mix display counter.

Of course. The Sports Direct had previously been a Woolies, and the spot where she was standing had been her childhood Mecca.

Cassie was back in her four-year-old skin – experiencing again the sensory overload of vivid colours, the warm-sticky smell of chocolate, horrid aniseed, sneeze-inducing sherbet. The impossibility of choice – torn between fizzy cola bottles, or the strawberry skulls, or the love hearts to share with Daddy when he came home—

Where's Mummy?! A flurry of panic. Scanning the shop.

There's a man dancing with her. The bag of sweeties she's collected falls to the floor.

Mummy! Adult Cassie hears herself say the word in a half-croak, half-whisper. Feels the hot wet astringency of tears on her cheeks.

Coming to, Cassie found herself still gripping the display unit, a row of Nike Air Max where the sweet-filled hoppers had stood.

A young black guy nearby sent her a look signalling concern. 'You OK?'

She nodded, before making her escape.

Once she'd parked herself in a coffee shop with a large espresso to calm herself down, she went over what had just happened. Was it real, the memory? Had her four-year-old self *really* seen a man 'dancing' with her mother? In Woolies?

Then it struck her: through the eyes of a four-year-old, a man holding a woman by the arms, or in his arms, might look like a couple dancing.

Cassie was familiar with the psychological theory that an adult could recover long-forgotten childhood memories – and was well aware that 'recovered memories' of childhood trauma could be highly unreliable. The brain craved order and pattern, and where it encountered gaps in the record, it sometimes made stuff up just to fill them in.

But. The visceral memory of something being badly wrong was still with her. *OK*, she thought, *let's apply some logic here*. Her mum wouldn't ordinarily have let her loose on the pick 'n' mix alone – four-year-olds having zero concept of restraint. But this time, she had left Cassie to her own devices and gone off some distance – albeit keeping her child within her line of sight. At some point, Cassie had looked for her mum and seen her in the arms of a strange man.

The interpretation of her memory – if that's what it was – was blindingly obvious. Katherine had arranged a rendezvous with a man in a harmless-seeming place. But what had happened between them was hazy. Was he trying to kiss her? Pleading with her to leave Callum? Was she saying no?

187

If the strange man wasn't just a phantom of Cassie's imagination then there was only one interpretation. He had to be Kath's secret lover – the man Callum claimed his wife had been seeing. The man he believed was responsible for her murder.

FLYTE

It was the day after Capaldi had called Flyte and she was briefing one of the female DCs ahead of an interview with an internet fraudster when Josh called out across three desks, 'I've got Cassie Raven for you, Sarge?'

Not allowing a muscle in her face to move, she nodded for him to put it through before dismissing the DC. 'Give me five minutes, would you, Rosie?' Then, turning to face the wall she told Cassie, 'You can't call me here,' in a low voice.

'I'm fine, thanks. How are you?' – her tone sarcastic.

The call from DCI Capaldi in Professional Standards had left Flyte feeling anxious. If he were to find out that she was in contact with Callum Raven's daughter it would be glaringly obvious that her accessing of his police file wasn't a miskey but a piece of personal freelancing.

'I need to talk to you,' said Cassie.

Flyte's lips started to form a no. She'd already stuck her neck out so far for this infuriating girl it could end her career. On the other hand, it made sense to find out what Cassie was up to apropos of her mother's murder: with Capaldi probing another case that Hobbs and Neville had worked on in the 90s there was a real risk of their paths crossing.

'OK,' she snapped. 'But not in public. Come to my place – I'm on earlies so I'll be back by 3 p.m. And be discreet.'

'Thanks. I'll bring cupcakes.'

Snarky little madam.

Flyte hadn't even hung up before another reason for wanting to see Cassie dawned on her. Matt had at last emailed her the medical report on Poppy's stillbirth, but the barbed wire thicket of medical terms – *velamentous cord insertion, vasa praevia, succenturiate lobe* – proved impenetrable. After spending several hours on the phone to the hospital she had tracked down the consultant obstetrician, now in private practice, but hadn't called him yet. If he, or the midwife, had failed to do something that might have saved Poppy, he was hardly likely to admit it. She needed Cassie to translate the report into plain English before deciding on her next step.

When Josh didn't query the call from Cassie, Flyte allowed herself to hope that he'd thought nothing of it, but her optimism proved short-lived.

Joining her in the canteen lunch queue, he craned to see the day's offerings. 'Have they got lasagne on today, Sarge?'

'Doesn't look like it. Some kind of casserole, I think.'

'So, Cassie Raven, eh?' Josh raised an eyebrow. 'What does our very own mortuary Miss Marple want? Has she got another mysterious death she wants us to investigate?'

It was all just harmless banter, but Flyte felt the blood creeping into her cheeks – the curse of the fair-skinned. Of course Josh would wonder what Cassie was calling about: he'd been involved in investigating the death of her former teacher, after all.

The awareness that she was blushing only made it worse. 'Oh . . . it was just about the Appleton case. I'm the FLO on

Bradley Appleton, the suicided boy?' Since she was family liaison officer it was a perfectly plausible excuse but judging by the way Josh was eyeing her face, her discomfiture must be obvious. 'One of his schoolfriends has confirmed he was into self-asphyxiation to get high,' she said. 'So we've requested further tests on the body. Hopefully, it might produce something concrete for the inquest. Which would be great for the parents.' *Shut up now*. Blathering on wasn't her usual style.

Josh diplomatically shifted his gaze from her face to the counter. 'Oh great. Fish and chips! You'll be having the salad as per, will you, Sarge?'

'What the hell do you think you're doing calling me at work?'

She flung the words at her before Cassie was even through the front door.

Cassie glared back at her. 'Keep your hair on. I had no choice – you weren't answering your mobile.'

'I am not some kind of . . . *private detective* at your beck and call! I'm a police officer with a demanding caseload!'

'Well, sorr-y!' she shrugged. Her unrepentant expression, twinned with the facial metalwork and the shaved section of scalp on show, sent Flyte over the edge.

'Do you have any idea of the risk I took, getting that PM report for you? If it should come to light, I'm out. Done. Career over. This is my life! I don't *have* anything else!' The last bit came out as a half-shout.

Cassie blinked – shocked at her loss of control.

Not as shocked as me, thought Flyte.

For a long moment the only sound was the rumble of a passing bus outside the window.

191

'Look, I'm really sorry, Phyllida' – sounding contrite. 'I couldn't be more grateful for what you did for me getting the PM report. It was dumb of me to call you at work.' She twisted one of the bolts in her lip. 'This thing with my mother? To be honest, it's made me go a bit crazy.' A shrug of concession. 'A *lot* crazy.'

Flyte's anger drained away: this ability Cassie had, to turn on a sixpence from bolshy to penitent, always had the power to wrong-foot her.

She made them proper coffee in her Italian machine, which even had a milk-frothing attachment, and served it in her favourite bone china mugs with the pretty wild bird design. In Winchester, she and Matt had a bird feeder in the garden which, if you sat quietly enough, would become thronged with birds. In Camden the only birdlife you saw was the ubiquitous pigeons and the occasional crow pecking at roadkill.

They took their coffees into the living room.

'Nice place.' Cassie nodded, her gaze taking in the ornate cornices and the polished floorboards. 'I'd love to live in a Victorian flat, one day.' She ran a hand along the marble fireplace. 'Do you ever get any sense of the people who've lived here? Like they're around you still?'

'No, thank goodness. I've never done terribly well with house shares.'

They smiled carefully at one another.

'I wanted to ask you about my mother's PM report,' said Cassie after they sat down, her voice businesslike. 'You saw the pictures – the major facial trauma. The pathologist reckoned that happened as she lay on the deck – *after* the back of her skull was caved in by the brick – which was the fatal blow.'

Unable to find an adequate response Flyte made a sympathetic noise.

'So it seems like the murderer chased her, smashed her skull in with the brick, and while she lay there dying, repeatedly bashed in her face. My question is how could anyone do that to someone they loved – not to mention the mother of their child?'

'The brick was tested for DNA, I assume?'

Cassie nodded. 'Plenty of blood from the victim, but not enough genetic material to build a profile of the attacker.'

Flyte nodded: she'd read that in the late 90s a bloodstain the size of a ten-pence piece was required to produce a full DNA profile.

The victim. Flyte understood why Cassie should distance herself that way. Hadn't she spent two years trying to distance herself from the fact of Poppy's death? Only to discover that it simply postponed the reckoning. Studying Cassie's expression, she decided she could speak candidly. 'I'm afraid those kind of facial injuries are not untypical when a man loses control because his wife has been unfaithful – or he *thinks* she has.' She'd seen just such a case while working as a murder detective in Winchester. 'It's an extreme reaction to perceived rejection – I can't have you so no one else will, even to the point of erasing the face I once loved.'

'What if the rejection wasn't perceived, though? What if the murderer was someone who killed her because she really did reject them? A lover, in other words?'

'Listen, Cassie, I can only imagine how tough it must be for you, coming to terms with what your dad did. But the fact remains the police never found any proof of this supposed lover, did they?'

'Maybe they didn't look very hard.' A defiant uptilt of the chin. 'A vaginal swab was taken but there's no mention of the result anywhere in the report.'

Seeing Cassie about to put her mug on the polished wood of her new coffee table she pointedly pushed a coaster over to her. 'Was sexual assault suspected?' she asked.

'I couldn't see anything in the PM report to suggest it. Some pathologists take intimate swabs routinely in a case like this.'

Flyte frowned. 'Look, Cassie, it sounds to me as though the police had good reason to make your father the prime suspect – there was motive, an eyewitness, a dodgy alibi and a history of domestic violence.' But she remembered reading the case file with the growing sense that the case against Callum Raven wasn't a strong one.

'The point is, I don't think they ever even considered any-one else.' Cassie leaned across the coffee table. 'What if the swab came back with a DNA profile that didn't match my father's? Proving that she'd recently had sex with someone else? Could they, I don't know, deliberately lose it somehow?'

'Lose it?'

Cassie lifted her chin again. 'Is that so crazy? From everything I read there was a shedload of corruption going on in the 90s.'

'Well, it's true that testing was done by police labs back then, but the idea that anyone would bribe a technician to destroy evidence . . . well, you're talking serious corruption.'

The sanctity of the chain of custody had been drummed into Flyte during her training. Every piece of evidence, whether from a crime scene, a hard drive, or a body, had to be properly recorded, identified, and stored intact through the system to trial. But she had heard horror stories regarding the often slapdash handling of evidence right up until the 2000s – and now Capaldi's mention of 'irregularities' in another case that Hobbs and Neville had worked on came back to her.

'Have you checked with the pathologist who did the PM?' she asked. 'There might be a perfectly innocent explanation.'

'Apparently, he died in 2005. And Hobbs' boss Neville is dead, too. Which only leaves the sergeant, Gerry Hobbs.'

'What possible motive could anyone have for covering up the result anyway?'

Cassie shrugged. 'Maybe they were protecting somebody? Or maybe Hobbs and Neville had just convinced themselves that my father was the murderer and wanted to bury an inconvenient new lead. The way they promised my grandmother that they'd nail him – it sounds to me like they were personally invested.'

Flyte pulled a sceptical face. 'Look, the likeliest scenario is this: the swab result came up negative for sexual contact and some technician forgot to fill in the box on the form.'

Cassie set her empty mug on the coaster, adjusting it to sit precisely in the centre, before meeting her gaze. 'I went to see Gerry Hobbs.'

'You did what . . . ?'

'I think he has something to hide – when I mentioned the swab he was properly shifty.'

Flaming fishcakes.

So Cassie's freelance sleuthing had already careened into the path of DCI Capaldi's investigation. Like a skateboard cutting up a juggernaut. She was on the point of ordering her to back off, when she caught the mulish look on her face and remembered that issuing orders to Cassie was an approach that could backfire.

'OK . . . so how did this "shiftiness" manifest itself, may I ask?'

'It's hard to explain.' Cassie made a frustrated face. 'I just get a feeling sometimes.'

'Really?' Flyte raised an eyebrow.

'Look, it's my job to notice things, OK?' Cassie shifted in her seat impatiently. 'Like . . . that photo for instance' – she nodded towards the framed photograph in the middle of the mantel-piece – 'obviously it's your dad—'

'Well, who else would it be?'

'I was going to say, you clearly got on much better with him than your mum.'

'What – just because I don't have a picture of her on display?' *The old bat.*

Cassie studied the image, her head on one side. 'No . . . because you cut her out of the picture.'

Flyte blinked. The photo was one of her favourites: she'd been eighteen, in Akrotiri for the Easter holidays and had snapped Pops in his veg patch, one foot up on his spade, holding his army-issue entrenching tool, looking into camera. She'd forgotten that her mother had ever been in shot.

'How . . . ?'

Cassie narrowed her eyes at the image. 'The composition is off-centre, like it was originally framed wider – but it's also the dog.'

Monty the golden retriever stood at the far left-hand-edge of the frame, just in shot.

'It's the angle of his head and jaws . . . like somebody was holding a treat out to him.' Cassie demonstrated.

Hell's bells. Not a treat. A rubber ring that her mother had been offering him. Wanting to get Monty in the picture Flyte had ended up including her mother, too. Nothing a bit of judi-cious trimming hadn't fixed after the print came back.

196

'It's obviously you behind the camera.' Cassie smiled. 'Even though he's trying to look stern, his love for you just shines out of the picture.'

Flyte filed away the feeling this gave her for later.

Even in his gardening clothes – 'in mufti', as he would have said – Pops still radiated the air of an army Major. But his attempts to maintain a parade ground manner at home crumbled when it came to his daughter and only child. *Philly*. His name for her. She could hear her mother complaining still: *I give her a perfectly lovely name and you call her after a brand of processed cheese.* And Pops' fleeting lowered eyelid to his daughter. *On the QT.*

'It's my last photo of him,' said Flyte. 'He died the following year, when I was nineteen.'

'Ahh. You lost him far too young.'

Flyte remembered that Cassie had lost both her parents – and at a far younger age.

'And your mum, is she still alive?' Cassie went on.

Flyte had to stop herself saying, *None of your beeswax.*

'She still lives in Cyprus, remarried yonks ago.' Nowadays their only contact was the regulation Christmas/birthday phone call which invariably ended with Sylvia saying, 'You must come out and stay with us for a few days, darling.'

Always with that killer qualifier. *A few days.*

Any prospect of a change to her mother's lifelong attitude to her only daughter – an awkward but polite froideur – had evaporated after Poppy died. Flyte could never forgive nor forget Sylvia saying: 'You can always have another one, darling, can't you?' Like getting another kitten.

She pictured Poppy's incomprehensible medical report on her laptop. If she wanted Cassie's help deciphering it, she needed somehow to keep her onside while keeping her at a safe distance from Capaldi's investigation.

'Look, Cassie, I can't explain why, but it's really important that you drop all contact with Hobbs – in fact, you need to stay away from anything to do with Camden Police.'

'Why?'

'There's internal stuff going on regarding CID activities in the 90s, unconnected to your mother, which I only heard about after I accessed her case file. Somebody could put two and two together and realise that I did it for you. Searching the database without a legitimate reason is a sackable offence.'

Cassie was eyeing her coolly. 'OK. On one condition.'

'Condition?'

Really, the girl was the living end.

'That you try to find out about that missing swab result.'

'And how am I supposed to find out anything about a result that might or might not have gone missing more than twenty years ago?'

Cassie bit her lip, eyes hooded in thought. 'OK. I'll tell you what I need to know. If the jury at Callum's trial had been told that a key piece of evidence had gone missing, would it have been enough for them to change their verdict, to find him not guilty?'

Chapter Twenty-Nine

Cassie was becoming an old hand at reading Phyllida Flyte, and from her reaction to the mention of Gerry Hobbs – her sudden stillness, the way the muscles around her eyes had tightened – it was crystal clear that he was one of the cops being investigated at Camden nick, presumably for historic dodgy practices. Which would be good news – *if* the investigators were smart enough to pick up on the missing swab result.

But she couldn't just sit around waiting and hoping – the weird episode in what had been the Woolies pick 'n' mix section had only intensified her need to find out the truth about her mum's death.

At the time of her murder, the people Callum spent most time with would have been his bandmates Barney Cotter and Maria Maguire; if he really had been worried that Kath was having an affair – and it wasn't just a clumsy ploy to deflect blame – surely he would have confided in one of them?

Kicking herself for failing to get Maria's number, she googled Barney, figuring that his business would make him easier to find, and followed a trail that took her from Twitter to LinkedIn and finally to Companies House. It had a listing for his music management company Parallel Music, and gave a home address for him and Maria, its only two directors. Cassie knew the road, which she noticed couldn't be more than a ten-minute walk from Prowse Place.

She pitched up at their address mid-morning, finding a tiny little two-up two-down in a backstreet – the kind of Victorian cottage you probably could have picked up for £150k back in the day, but which would set you back over a million now.

As she rang the doorbell, Cassie felt a quiver of anxiety about turning up unannounced, but when the door opened that quickly evaporated.

'Cassie! I'm so glad to see you!' Maria waved her inside. 'Come in! I stupidly didn't take your number so I was hoping you'd track me down.'

In casual gear she looked like the less-glamorous cousin of the singer on stage at The Dublin Castle, although still good-looking, even with barely any makeup and her tall willowy figure swamped by an oversized sweatshirt.

The place was like the Tardis – inside the downstairs had been knocked through and extended out back to create a substantial living and eating space overlooked by a large wall clock – its face the cover of the Clash album *London Calling*, with Joe Strummer smashing his guitar over the spot occupied by the number five.

Glass doors looked out over the garden which had one of those trendy timber-built home offices. Seeing Barney working on his laptop out there, Cassie waved to him. Seeing her, he did a little double-take before waving back.

'He's working on a contract for a local artist. Hip hop.' As Maria put the kettle on she sent Cassie a conspiratorial smile. 'Not my thing, but it pays the bills.' In the stark winter light flooding through the skylights Maria looked older, more ...

ordinary than her blues singer persona – her crow's feet and softening jawline suggesting a hidden vulnerability.

Maria set down the mugs on the dining table before scanning Cassie's face. 'You really are the living image of Kath, you know.'

'Really? I always thought I had my dad's eyes.'

Maria tipped her head assessingly. 'They're the same deep blue, true enough. You know, seeing you the other day, it stirred up a lot of memories for us both. We were wondering if you'd been in touch with Callum – or heard how he's doing these days?'

Cassie shook her head. 'All I know is that since he got out he's been living somewhere in Northern Ireland, near his family.' *Which was true.*

'Of course, it'd be totally understandable if you never wanted anything to do with him again, in the circumstances. But it's only natural you'd be curious.' Maria bit her lip. 'He is still your daddy, after all. And you lost him.'

Cassie was taken aback at the emotion in her voice.

'So, was there something in particular you wanted to ask me?' Maria went on.

'Yes, there is. Do you think there was any truth in what Callum said at the trial?' Cassie hesitated, reluctant to accuse her poor dead mother of infidelity.

'What do you mean?' Maria looked blank.

'His claim that Kath was seeing someone else?'

'Oh, I'd forgotten that,' said Maria, frowning into space. 'It was the first I'd heard of it, at the trial – but then it wasn't the kind of thing Callum would've shared with me anyway.'

'Why not?'

She pulled a wry smile. 'There's no reason you'd know, but your dad and I used to be sweethearts, in the early days of the band – before he met Kath. It was me who broke it off. To tell the truth, Callum was a bit full-on for me' – she pulled a face that combined affection and exasperation.

Cassie was picturing the two of them on stage together; they'd have made a great rock star couple. 'How did he take it?'

'Not that well, to be honest with you.' She grimaced. 'It was lucky really, him meeting Kath so soon after we split. And I got together with Barney, so, it all worked out for the best. But it probably didn't feel right to him to confide in me about their relationship.'

Cassie nodded. If you'd been romantically involved with someone, discussing your current lover with them could feel like a betrayal – both ways.

Maria glanced out of the window towards the studio office. 'It's Barney you should be asking. He and Callum were thick as thieves.'

It struck Cassie as an odd choice of phrase. She wondered again whether Barney had given Callum a false alibi in a bid to get his mate off the hook.

'Does Barney feel . . . guilty at all?' she asked, tentative.

'About what?' From the sudden edge in Maria's voice it was clear to Cassie that she would be fiercely protective of her husband if necessary.

'You know, when he testified in court and the barrister challenged the alibi he gave Callum.'

'That guy was a twenty-four-carat bastard!' Anger brought Maria's Irish accent to the fore. 'The way he deliberately confused him over the timings.' She blew out a breath. 'Sorry.' She glanced out of the window towards the garden office. 'You've got it right, though. Between you and me, Barney went to pieces after the trial – I think he had a bit of a breakdown. He wouldn't talk about it but I could tell that he blamed himself for the guilty verdict.'

Looking out of the window Cassie saw Barney's eyes on them before returning his attention to his laptop.

'The defence didn't call you to back up Barney's account of when Callum was here that night – were you out somewhere?'

Maria shook her head. 'I had a yoga class first thing in the morning so I'd gone to bed early leaving Barney watching the footy. I told the cops I never even heard Callum arrive or leave.' She frowned. 'It's weird but it's all so long ago now that some-times it feels like it all happened to somebody else, as if it's just something I read in the paper.'

'Look, don't take this the wrong way,' said Cassie carefully. 'But when Barney said that Callum was still here watching telly at the time of the murder, do you think he was telling the truth?' Maria's gaze flickered past her towards the garden. 'I mean, it would only be natural for him to want to help his best mate if he was convinced he was innocent.'

Cassie saw different feelings battling it out on Maria's face as she replayed the events of twenty-one years ago. Distress, doubt . . . and loyalty. When she finally spoke, her voice was hoarse with emotion. 'I think Barney *believes* that your dad was still with him. But that might be because he could never accept the idea of Callum being capable of such violence.'

'And you? Do you think he was capable of it?'

Maria met her eyes. 'Truly, Cassie. I've asked myself the same thing a thousand times, and I just don't know.'

Chapter Thirty

Cassie felt her stomach plunge. She'd been hoping that Maria would spring to her father's defence – to say that there was no way Callum could commit murder. And from the sympathetic look in Maria's eyes, she knew what Cassie had wanted to hear.

She touched the back of Cassie's hand. 'Listen. I understand how you feel. I lost my daddy too, you see. When I was seven he left me and my mum to go off with some woman to America.'

So that was why she'd got emotional over Cassie losing touch with Callum. 'Oh, I am sorry,' she told her.

'People had always said I was the apple of his eye.' She smiled at the memory. 'The night he left, he came into my bedroom and said he'd come back for me when I was a bit older. I used to sit at my bedroom window for hours on end waiting to see his car pull up outside. I even had a little suitcase packed, under the bed, ready to go. But I never laid eyes on him again.'

'Did you ever find out what became of him?'

A sad shake of her head. 'I think he must have died soon after he left. You see, I don't think he would have let me down – not willingly.'

Cassie nodded, but she was thinking it was more likely that after remarrying he'd had another child, moved on. Some men did that.

Maria waved a hand. 'That's enough of me and my troubles. What else can I tell you?'

Cassie remembered the article Kieran had shown her, outlining Barney's plans for the band. 'I hear there was a record deal in the offing for *Poitín* just before it happened? Was Kath on board for that?'

Maria nodded. 'After being skint for so long, we all were. We cracked open a bottle of bubbly, the four of us, when Barney told us the news.' She pulled a sad shrug. 'But after Kath died and Callum got arrested, the record deal seemed like a petty thing.'

'Yeah, of course. You must've missed it, though, after Callum went to jail. Being part of the band.'

A nostalgic smile curled one side of Maria's mouth. 'Ah, we had some grand times the three of us. But if the deal had happened we'd have spent our lives on the road. And I get car sick – not a good look on a rock star.' An embarrassed grimace. 'After what happened, then Callum going to jail, I guess it brought me and Barney closer. We tied the knot a few months later. We'll have been married twenty-one years this summer' – a wondering look at where the time had gone crossing her face. 'We're solvent, and I've had a decent enough career. I sang alongside Paul Brady at the *Fleadh* in '98.'

Cassie arranged her face into an impressed expression. *Paul who? And what the fuck was 'the flah'?*

'Ah, listen to me, telling old war stories,' Maria laughed. 'You were probably still in primary school back then.'

Cassie smiled back over the lip of her mug. 'Do you think Barney would mind me asking him a few questions?'

'Speak of the devil,' said Maria.

The door opening behind her made Cassie jump. Barney greeted her with an awkward warmth before heading over to the kettle. His narrow-cut trousers and close-fitting 60s-style roll-neck emphasised his lean frame which together with a wispy mod haircut made him look a bit like Paul Weller.

'You girls ready for a top-up?' His Londonese flat as a pancake after Maria's soothing lilt.

'Cassie wanted to ask you about Callum, sweetheart' – her tone careful but encouraging.

Barney turned to Cassie. 'Sure, go ahead. But I can tell you off the bat, he didn't do it.'

Cassie felt a little surge of hope at his matter-of-fact tone. 'Because you're one hundred per cent sure he was with you at the time of the murder?'

Turning away to spoon coffee into a mug he sighed. 'I've gone over and over that night so many times now, I can't swear anymore as to the timing. But I just know he didn't have it in him to hurt Kath. Like I told the cops, it must have been some random psycho.'

From the look that passed between him and Maria, Cassie guessed that the question of Callum's guilt or innocence had long been a fraught issue between them. Did Barney really believe his best mate was innocent? Or was he trying to convince himself?

'You and Callum were obviously pretty close,' Cassie said. 'Did he ever mention his suspicion that Kath was seeing someone else? Before the trial, I mean.'

His eyes became hooded. 'Callum would never have said anything bad about Kath, even if he thought it. He worshipped her.' He looked at Cassie. 'She was beautiful, your mother, inside and out. And devoted to Callum – and to you.' The last bit sounded to her like an afterthought.

Cassie had the sudden urge to ask, *Was it you she met in Woolies?*

Into the silence Maria asked, 'Are you sure you can't manage another coffee?'

She said no thanks, and asked to use the loo. Upstairs was tiny compared to the ground floor – the original cottage layout, with just two doors and an airing cupboard. Why had she felt the sudden urge to ask Barney if he'd been the man with her mum in Woolies? She had zero memory of what the guy looked like – she'd only been four after all. As she washed her hands, she heard the radio go on downstairs. Hearing Amy Winehouse singing 'Back to Black' she lip-synced along to the lyrics in the bathroom mirror.

Walking back into the kitchen to say her goodbyes it felt as though Maria and Barney had just fallen silent, leaving an atmosphere hanging between them. Had she walked in on something? A disagreement, perhaps?

She was surprised when it was Barney who stood to walk her to the door.

'I hope you get some closure,' he said – the new age phrase sounding awkward in his gritty accent. 'Y'know, for a helluva long time after the trial I really felt like I'd let your dad down.'

'I'm sure you did your best for him.'

A spasm of what could be regret crossed his face. 'Anyway . . . he's done his time now and it's too late to undo any of it.'

She thought how sad it was that three people who'd shared so much should have become so estranged. 'If I should ever hear from him, shall I say he can get in touch?'

'No, no. Better not dig over old ground.'

As she walked away, she tried to decipher Barney's response to the idea of hearing from the man who'd been his best buddy. And concluded that the sudden widening of his eyes could only signify one thing. Alarm.

FLYTE

Flyte had no intention of digging around in the Katherine Raven murder file – not with Professional Standards crawling all over Hobbs' and Neville's history. But she had to admit that the case intrigued her, and despite her protestations to Cassie of a heavy workload, things were actually pretty quiet right now – when the mercury dropped in January, even villains opted for Netflix and chill. Right now the most thrilling case in her inbox was an internet fraud involving fake Airbnb bookings.

Since her last conversation with Cassie she'd been mulling over that missing swab result and the question she'd raised: whether knowing that it had gone missing would have been enough for the jury to bring in a not guilty verdict.

'Geoff Gough, please.'

She'd decided the safest course of action was to call a contact in the CPS, and as a former defence lawyer who'd worked for the Crown Prosecution Service the last twenty-odd years, Geoff Gough was the obvious choice.

'Hello there!' Geoff's golden-brown tones, rich as an oloroso sherry, boomed down the line. 'How is my favourite lady detective?' His hail-fellow-well-met chivalry might rub some people up the wrong way, but she found it oddly comforting. Geoff had recently helped her to get her ducks in a row for a fiendishly complex drug-dealing case which rested on a string of opaque text messages; his advice helping her to charge the main guy with intent to supply Class As.

'This query is purely for my own interest, OK, Geoff? Nothing to do with any particular case.' She had taken the precaution of stepping into the corridor to make the call from her mobile.

'A thought experiment? Splendid.' The sardonic edge to his voice signalled that he was aware she was fibbing but happy to play along.

She laid out the theoretical case of an accused who denies the brutal murder of his wife and claims at his trial that she was having sex with another man – someone whom, if he did exist, police should have traced and questioned. 'So let's say a swab was taken from the body to test for semen – which had the potential to confirm the husband's claim that she had a lover – but it somehow went AWOL. If the missing swab had been brought up at trial, do you think it would have been enough to change the verdict?'

'When did this conviction occur? Sorry, this *theoretical* conviction.'

'Nineteen ninety-seven.'

'When such samples were still analysed at a police lab. Are you suggesting – heaven forfend! – that one of our boys in blue interfered with the post-mortem evidence?'

In for a penny . . . 'Let's say yes, just for the sake of argument.'

'Well, it was by no means unheard of back then. You know, a detective sergeant once told me, after a few drinks, the crucial distinction they made when it came to those kind of antics.' Geoff chuckled, clearly enjoying this nostalgic diversion from the day job. 'A copper who mislaid evidence in return for a backhander was described as "bent for himself", whilst one who planted evidence to get a conviction against someone of whose guilt he was convinced was "bent for the job". The inference being that the latter was on the side of the angels. What other evidence was brought against your fictional accused?'

She ran through it. 'He had motive and opportunity, there was a suggestion of domestic violence, and an eyewitness who put him at the scene, but no concrete forensics. There wasn't enough of the attacker's DNA on the murder weapon to build a profile.'

'It sounds like pretty thin gruel,' said Geoff, 'but then, as we used to say when I was on the other side of the fence, the worse the crime, the weaker the evidence required to convict. Still, I'm not convinced that a judge would have been prepared to allow the defence to make hay regarding your missing swab. It was most likely a simple administrative error – and absence of evidence is not evidence, after all.'

'Shouldn't the defence at least have picked up on the missing result in the PM report?'

'If they were on the ball. But if it wasn't flagged by the pathologist, they might have assumed a missing result equated to a negative result. You say your accused only brought up his wife's alleged infidelity in the witness box?'

'That's right.'

A sigh came down the line. 'Too late for his brief to follow up his allegation and try to make something of it as a line of defence. I presume your accused is out now on licence?'

'Yes, but obviously he'd like to clear his name. Theoretically.' Flyte found herself imagining the daily torture of having a child who believed that you'd murdered her mother – if you were innocent. 'If it were to come to light that the swab result had gone missing, you don't think it would be enough for him to apply for leave to appeal?'

'No. Not without something new and substantive to show that his conviction was unsafe.' Another chuckle. 'I must say, Phyllida, I'm finding this a somewhat novel experience.'

'Really? Would you care to elucidate?'

'It's the first time I've had a police detective consult me regarding how a convicted murderer might be exonerated.'

She didn't say anything.

'My advice is this. The best way to prove a miscarriage of justice would be to trace whoever did murder this unfortunate lady and find some incontrovertible evidence to allow you to charge them with the crime.'

Chapter Thirty-One

There were a ton of reasons why Cassie shouldn't contact her father. Above all, it still stirred up a queasy feeling of disloyalty to her mum and grandmother. And her need to believe him was so strong that she feared his protestations of innocence might weave themselves around her like silken threads until she was completely cocooned.

But she was still confused by Barney's alarmed look at the prospect of being reunited with his former best mate and meeting him and Maria had thrown up more questions she needed to have answered.

That evening – guilt tussling with excitement in her gut – she called the mobile number Callum had given her.

'Cassie?'

She kept her voice cool. 'I just wanted to ask you some stuff about Mum. I don't want to get into . . . the case, the trial, any of that, all right?'

'Sure, darling, whatever you say. I understand.'

She tried to ignore the note of pathetic eagerness in his voice. 'So, could you tell me more about her, what she was like as a person, starting with how you met?'

Callum replayed the stuff she already knew: that *Poitín* had gone down to High Wycombe to play the Oakwood Common benefit gig that Kath had helped organise. 'I remember that night, the moment I saw her dancing in front of the stage. I couldn't take my eyes off her. After the gig I went looking for her and asked her back to the pub where we were staying. We sat up late drinking with Barney and Maria and a pal who worked as our roadie. People peeled off to bed until there was just us two.' A smile in his voice at the memory. 'She didn't go back to the camp that night. And the next day, when they all went back to Camden, I stayed on.'

'But what about the band? Did the others mind?'

A hoot of laughter. 'Yeah, Barney kept leaving messages at the pub telling me to get my arse back to Camden so we could start gigging again. But I ignored him. Me and your mum lived under a bivouac made of bin bags, can you believe that?' A pause. 'But I'd have slept in the road in a thunderstorm for her.'

The love in his voice was unforced and clearly unfaked, but Cassie was aware that all-consuming romantic love was precisely the kind that could curdle into the possessive, controlling – and potentially violent – variety.

Time to rattle his cage.

'I hear she had a boyfriend at Oakwood before you.'

'Oh, you know about him?' His tone soured. 'He was a class-A twat. Kath was totally out of his league. They'd split up a few weeks before I turned up. Kath suspected he'd been shagging a girl who she *thought* was a friend, one of the other organisers. When she called him out on it, he told her that what he felt for this other girl was *the real deal*.' He said the words in a pompous high-pitched voice. 'The bastard.'

The anger in his voice still sounded fresh more than two decades on.

'It made for a bad atmosphere – but Kath was already pissed off with the whole scene: she'd stepped down from the organising committee by the time I got there.'

'Did she say why?'

He paused. 'Your mum was a funny mixture – sweet and determined and a bit off-the-wall all at the same time. She wasn't really cut out for the politics – all the internal bickering over protest tactics, as well as whose turn it was to cook, wash up, empty the chemical toilet . . . After a few weeks we packed up and came back to Camden.'

Political bickering and chemical toilets? Cassie revised her rose-tinted image of the 90s eco-protest scene.

She braced herself to ask the big question. 'What do you think made Mum start drinking? Was it . . . after I was born?'

'Ah no, God love you, it wasn't that!' His accent suddenly stronger. 'Sure, the birth was traumatic, especially since you came a bit early, but once she was over that she adored you.'

'Hmm. What about later, when I was three or four? It sounds like I was a handful.'

'Cassie, listen to me. Your mum had always been on a bit of a rollercoaster with her nerves, y'know? She'd even been on antidepressants in her teens but didn't like how they made her feel. It was like living underwater, she said.'

Cassie was reeling – in a handful of conversations with her dad, Barney and Maria she'd glimpsed a more authentic version of her mum than she'd got from her grandmother in twenty-odd years.

'She must have been . . . challenging to live with. But you claim that you never hit her—'

'—never' – his voice hardening.

She visualised the finger-shaped bruises on her mum's upper arms from the post-mortem photos. 'OK . . . but in those last few days before she died, did you ever grab hold of her by the upper arms?'

'We were having massive rows by then,' he conceded, 'but I never touched her. I remember the prosecution fella saying she had bruises, but I can tell you she didn't get them from me.' A pause. 'She wouldn't even let me see her naked by that time. I thought it was because she was seeing some other fella. Later on I told the cops, maybe it was him who gave her those bruises.'

Woolies. A strange man dancing with Mummy.
Gripping her by the arms, trying to stop her breaking away.

A moment of crystal clarity. Cassie realised that the clandestine meeting in Woolies had taken place just days before the murder. The bruises on her dead mother's arms hadn't been inflicted by her father but by the strange man – a man she'd been seeing in secret.

A wave of happiness broke over her. Callum was telling the truth about the affair. But she wasn't ready to share her insight – not until she had more to go on than the recovered memory of a four-year-old.

'When you were inside, did you ever send Gran money for me?' – picturing the stack of notes that had arrived on her birthday every year after her mum died.

A silence. When he spoke there was shame in his voice. 'I wish I could have, sweetheart, but I was skint. The most I ever earned was a fiver a week in the prison laundry – and it was always getting docked for "misdemeanours".'

'Is that why you didn't get paroled earlier?'

'That was because I would never confess to killing Kath. Apparently, denying the murder "prevented me from exploring the causes and triggers of my offending".' He snorted derisively. 'The parole board is a bit like the Catholic confessional: the length of your penance depends on a full and meaningful confession of your sins.'

'Were there no royalties from the *Poitín* album?'

'Ah no, bless you,' he chuckled. 'In any case, Barney had first dibs on any profits.'

'Really?'

'It was only fair.' Callum sounded touchy – defensive of his former best mate. 'He funded the album out of his own pocket and spent a load more on marketing. I hate to think of the debts I left him with, going into jail when I did.'

Interesting. So Barney had the biggest investment in making the record deal happen.

'To think your nana had me dead and buried all these years!' A dry laugh came down the line. 'How did she account for me having no grave?'

'You were buried in Ireland, she said, near your family. You went back there to be close to them, right?'

When he spoke he sounded hoarse. 'Yeah. My da died while I was away but when I got out in prison Ma looked after me, God love her. I fell into the bottle for a couple of years. Then, when she passed last year, the drinking got worse until I hit bottom.'

Cassie fell silent, experiencing a wave of sadness that she would never know her grandparents on her father's side.

Perhaps guessing what she was thinking Callum said, 'You've two aunties, you know – Ciara and Siobhan – and five cousins, two girls and three boys. You'll meet them one day, once I've proved I didn't kill Kath.'

Cassie pictured herself amid a noisy family gathering, kids running around – the type of scene she'd never experienced as a child.

'How are you doing with the drinking now?' she asked, wondering whether her taste for booze was hereditary.

'I've been dry nearly five months. I'm a fully paid-up member of the Automobile Association.'

'The what . . . ? Oh, you mean Alcoholics Anonymous.'

'I knew that if I didn't get sober, I would never have the guts to come find you and tell you the truth. I just reached step four of the twelve-step programme,' he said, with an edge of self-mocking pride. 'But it's step five I can't quite get my foot up on.'

'What's step five?'

'To admit my wrongs to another person and to a higher power.'

'What, like, God?'

'They don't like using the "G" word, but yeah, whoever or whatever's up there running this shitshow. You see, obviously I can't admit to killing your mum. But the fact that everyone *thinks* that I did it, it's like a mental roadblock that gets in the way of all my real wrongs? I can't even face visiting her grave, not till I've cleared my name.'

Cassie's gaze fell on one of the birthday notes lying beside her on the sofa, with its single line *For Cassandra* – a little looped flourish at the top of the 'C'. If her father hadn't sent them, then who had? She decided to tell him about them.

He fell silent for so long that she thought they'd been cut off. 'Are you still there?'

'I'm still here, sweetheart.'

'So do you have any idea? Who could have been sending me money all these years?'

'Someone with a guilty conscience' – his voice roughened by anger.

'A guilty conscience . . . ?'

'Ah, Cassie darlin'. Isn't it obvious? It has to be the man your mum was seeing. The bastard who took her away from us.'

Chapter Thirty-Two

After her few days of enforced leave Cassie hadn't been looking forward to going back to work – and having to face Dr Curzon – but when she got in, she discovered there was no PM list scheduled. Even Jason had the day off, which meant she had the rare gift of a quiet day with only her deceased guests for company. *Perfect.*

She'd been going batshit crazy sitting at home alone with her questions – the latest being who could have been sending her money all those years. If it really had come from her mother's killer then that surely ruled out the 'random psycho' who Barney blamed for the crime. But was her father right to assume that the cash was blood money from her mother's secret lover – the man who he believed had killed her? Might it have come from the investigating officer Gerry Hobbs? Not out of sympathy, but because he felt guilty that they'd put the wrong man away for the crime?

At least Cassie's dream of her mum weeping had been replaced by ones in which she was vividly alive again. Last night she had dreamed of drowning in a giant pick 'n' mix hopper of strawberry skulls when her mother's face appeared above her, smiling, and lifted her out effortlessly. When she woke in the afterglow of the dream, a new memory arrived: she was wrapped in a giant fluffy towel after a bath, being cuddled by her mum, who was singing her a song she couldn't place.

In the body store, she started the guest inventory, pulling open the drawers of the giant fridge to check each occupant off against her list. The only sound was the burble of the fridge and the gentle hum of the extraction system. But to Cassie it wasn't the hush of an empty room; it was a companionable silence, shared with fifteen others who lay behind the wall of polished steel.

It was a relief being alone for once and not having to lower her voice as she talked to her charges. 'Morning, Mr Iqbal. The undertakers are coming to pick you up today for your funeral. Soon you will be in Jannah with your parents.' She always found the Muslim picture of heaven as a garden of bliss appealing. 'The doctors had to do an examination to see how you died but we managed to fast-track the process for Saira and the family.' Muslims were supposed to be buried within twenty-four hours of death. That wasn't possible if a post-mortem was required but she usually managed to get Muslim guests prioritised and released to the family within two or three days.

Taking the inventory was a routine task which allowed her the headspace to revisit what she'd found out over the last few days. Of course she still had no hard evidence that her father was innocent, but she was convinced that a crucial part of his story was true: Kath really had been having secret assignations with another man. Had that man also been her killer?

The sound of knocking broke her train of thought. Through the glass of the windowed door that gave onto the clean side she saw Doug and, looming over his shoulder, a tall, athletic-looking man in his early fifties, already wearing scrubs over his suit.

A visitor. *Bollocks.* Bang went her quiet morning.

She thought she heard Doug introduce him as 'DCI Baldy', which couldn't be right. And he actually had a fine head of hair, near black and swept back off a high forehead, with an olive skin that suggested a parent with Southern European heritage. Apparently, Baldy had 'dropped by on the off-chance' of getting a tour of the mortuary which made her clench her jaw but the look on Doug's face told her that there was no putting off a Detective Chief Inspector.

After Doug left them, she said, 'Sorry, I didn't catch your name?'

'Just call me Tony.' He smiled at her, his gaze lingering a little longer than it needed to, but then she was used to people gawping at her look. It was always older people; the idea that young people had a monopoly on rudeness made her laugh.

'So, Tony,' she said. 'You must surely have seen inside a few mortuaries in your time?' – adding a smile to conceal her irritation at having to waste time babysitting a cop.

'I certainly have. But these days, police officers spend too much time driving a desk. So, as I was telling your boss – I'm on a mission to change how we train our graduate intake of newbie detectives.' As he rested his intent gaze on her again she noticed his eyes were a deep blue, a striking combination with his Mediterranean complexion and dark hair. 'I want to get our trainees into a mortuary straight away, to familiarise themselves with the coronial system and to observe a post-mortem. I want them to be comfortable with dead bodies, and to have some idea of how to read them, like you do.' He sounded passionate, like it was a pet project he'd been nurturing for a while.

'Amen to that,' she said, warming to the guy. 'We hardly ever see an investigating officer these days. Even at a forensic PM it's sometimes only the CSM and CSIs.' Crimes Scene Managers and Investigators might be trained forensic specialists, but she could never understand why any detective worth their salt would opt not to attend a forensic PM – to see the body, quiz the pathologist, get an understanding of the injuries? Flyte turning up to see Bradley Appleton had been an exception to the norm – and Bradley's was only a category two, aka an unexpected death, not even a suspicious one.

'Exactly.' Tony was nodding. 'When I was a probie fresh out of Hendon it was one of the first things we had to do. The sarge would send you down to watch a PM' – he grinned at her – '*before* lunch, if you were lucky. These days some of the younger detectives never even set foot in a mortuary.'

Having established that he wasn't just some rubbernecking suit who fancied a day out of the office, she gave him the tour with more enthusiasm.

When they reached the autopsy suite he whistled. 'Well, this has had a bit of an upgrade since I was last here.'

'When was that?'

'Oh, long before your time. I worked in Camden nick for a brief spell in the early 2000s. I used to come here to watch forensic PMs, even if it wasn't my case.' He sent her an embarrassed look. 'I know it sounds a bit . . . creepy but I learned so much from the pathologists, the clues that a killer would leave on a body. "Every contact leaves a trace", right?'

'Yep. Locard's exchange principle.' Edmund Locard had been the father of modern forensics.

It was on the tip of her tongue to ask if he'd known Gerry Hobbs or Spud Neville back then. But where would that get her? She could hardly ask if they were the kind of cops who'd take a backhander to cover up a critical swab result.

223

DCI Baldy, aka Tony, cast his searching gaze over the gleaming steel of the nearest dissecting table before indicating the grid of vent-holes around the table's perimeter. 'What are these for?'

'That's the downdraft ventilation system. It sucks any nasties in the air away when we're doing the eviscerations.'

He trained his gaze on her again. 'I suppose you must just get used to it after a while, cutting up the bodies?'

Having long ago tired of this kind of enquiry she just shrugged, non-committal.

'Forgive me, stupid question.' He sent her an admiring look. 'You know, I've always thought of you technicians as the unsung heroes of sudden death.'

Was he hitting on her? He wasn't unattractive, but seriously? He had to be fifty years old.

'Listen, Cassie, I'm planning on setting up a programme of mortuary induction sessions for young detectives. I wondered if you would consider overseeing it. They would pay you more attention than an old geezer like me. And, of course, you would receive a fee for your time.'

Although not exactly posh, he had a nice speaking voice – but now and again he used a London word like 'geezer'. Voice coaching was probably part of the media training senior officers had to go through these days.

'I'd be happy to,' she told him. 'But I wouldn't want paying.'

He beamed, once again letting his eyes linger on her face just a bit too long.

After he'd gone to change out of his scrubs, she tried to decipher the weird way he looked at her. The vibe she got off him didn't feel sexual. The best description she could come up with was *speculative* – like she was a puzzle he was trying to work out. Maybe he was just a bit eccentric and enjoyed meeting a fellow mortuary geek.

Ten minutes later she heard a knock on the glass from the clean side.

'Have a think about my mortuary induction plan.' He handed her a card though the open door. 'I'm set to retire in a few months so I'd like to get it all sorted before I go. If you're interested, let me know and I'll make an official application through Doug. I've written my mobile number on the back.'

As his broad back disappeared down the corridor she examined the card and smiled. Funnily enough, his name wasn't Baldy.

It was Capaldi. DCI Antony Capaldi.

Chapter Thirty-Three

Kieran agreed to meet up for a chinwag after work, and when he suggested the Costa on the canal towpath, east of the market, Cassie readily agreed. Three days into sobriety – a single daily joint aside – she didn't need the temptations of a pub any more than he did and although she usually boycotted chain coffee shops, the Costa did boast a cracking view over the canal.

It was 4 p.m., and the sun was already skulking behind Camden's rooflines of Victorian terraces, but the sky was that clear shade of blue you only got in winter, turning the canal into a rippled ribbon of silver and aquamarine.

'You're looking a lot better than you were the last time I saw you, Cassie Raven. You on the wagon?'

Kieran's sunny expression made it impossible to take offence.

She decided to share her recent encounters with her dad – and her growing doubts about his guilt.

Kieran nodded excitedly. 'Didn't I said it sounded like a flaky case?'

She filled him in on the rest, too: the birthday postal orders, and her father's theory that they'd been sent by her mother's killer, and the childhood memory that had come surging back to her in Sports Direct.

'There's only one possible interpretation,' she said. 'Mum arranged to meet a strange man in Woolies and parked me at the pick 'n' mix so she could talk to him.'

'Fuck!' Kieran shifted about in his seat. 'So, what did this guy look like?'

'That's the thing, Kieran. I have no clue. All I've got is an impression really, of a man holding her by the arms. I'm only guessing, but maybe the reason I got scared was because she looked like she was resisting him?' She screwed up her eyes, trying to picture it again. 'Looking at it through an adult lens I would say that he was trying to persuade or pressurise her.'

Kieran frowned out over the canal. 'What makes you say she "met" him? What if he'd been stalking her and followed her into Woolies?'

'But then why didn't she tell anyone? And Dad says he caught her getting unexplained phone calls at home.' Cassie realised with a jolt that she'd just called him 'Dad', rather than 'Callum' or 'my father'. 'My guess is the boyfriend was upping the pressure and she had no choice but to go out to meet him.'

'So what do you think was going down?'

'I think she'd been having an affair – I remember she used to leave me at my gran's now and again in the daytime, so she'd have had the opportunity. Then when my dad gets suspicious and the rows start, maybe she decides to dump the lover. She meets him in Woolies but he doesn't take it well, tries to talk her into leaving Callum.'

Kieran took a drink of his hot chocolate, nodding slowly. 'Maybe she deliberately met him in a public place because she thought he would kick off. Which could suggest she was scared of him.'

227

'Well, she had grip marks on her arms that would put this meeting just a few days before the murder.'

'So what happened on the night itself, do you think?' Kieran couldn't quite suppress a look of intrigue.

'I'm guessing that the rejected lover was stalking Kath, unable to let it go. He follows her and Callum to the pub. Maybe he hangs around outside? It's only early October so not too cold. Or maybe he's inside, tucked away in a corner? He might even have witnessed their massive bust-up and thinks he's back in with a chance.'

'So then Callum gets thrown out, Kath leaves later on – and he follows her.'

'They end up in Prowse Place, where it all gets nasty.' Cassie closed her eyes, trying to imagine how it went. 'She tells him she won't ever leave Callum; he loses control and reaches for the nearest weapon.'

'OK, I buy that. But I don't get why this bastard would send cash to the daughter of his victim?'

'Maybe when he comes to, he's horrified by what he's done? And then he sees the deceived husband – an innocent man – sent to jail for the crime. Tortured by guilt, he sends cash to the child who's lost both parents.'

Kieran sat back, stroking his upper lip. 'If his conscience bothers him so much, why stand by and see this "innocent man" go to jail rather than confess?'

Cassie lifted one shoulder. 'Sending blood money to atone for something you did is one thing, opting to take on someone else's life sentence is in another league altogether.'

Kieran tipped his head, taking that on board, but still not completely convinced. 'You say the cash is still coming in – and the amounts have got bigger? Would the killer *still* feel guilty, more than twenty years on?'

The objection had occurred to Cassie, too; over time, people had a tendency to construct narratives to excuse their past actions, or even to absolve themselves entirely.

'I don't know,' she said. 'Maybe he found God?' Stung by Kieran's sceptical expression, she said, 'OK, Sherlock, so what have you come up with? Found a murder confession lurking in one of those old fanzines you were talking about?'

'Pete, the guy who collects them, messaged me yesterday, actually. He's left a bunch of 'zines at Bob's vinyl shop for me.' Grinning he added, 'I'd have gone already but I've been a bit busy setting up my little rubber ducky business.'

'Ah sorry, Kieran, I should have asked. How that's all going?'

He pulled out his mobile to show her something. 'I've put up a crowdfunding page to get seed capital so I can order stock from China.'

She sent him a smile. 'Not a phrase I ever thought I'd hear you'd use, back in the day.'

'And I've got some share-space on a stall at the Stables Market, to do some test marketing.' He made a self-mocking face.

'Do I need to speak to your PA to get a meeting in future?'

'She'll always find a space in my diary for old friends.'

He played her the short video on the crowdfunding site, self-shot on his phone. The intro showed him walking through a busy Camden Market before arriving at the canal, where he launched two of his ducks from the towpath – one designed to look like Dr Spock, the other with the cloak and helmet of Darth Vader. It ended with a pitch to camera that poked gentle fun at the typical crowdfunding call-for-investment.

She beamed at him. 'That's fantastic, Kieran. I'll be investing a few quid, obvs.'

He shrugged modestly. 'Well, it isn't going to make me a millionaire, but if it gets me out of the hostel I'll be happy. I miss the laughs we used to have in the squat, you know?'

'So do I, Kieran.' It was true: having always thought of herself as a loner, lately she'd started to find living alone more difficult. 'Look, you know I'm getting chucked out of my flat soon? The council have to offer me something but it could be somewhere out in the sticks, like Enfield.' She bugged her eyes.

'Jesus.'

'I was thinking, what would you think about us getting a place together? I'd pick up more of the rent obvs, and we could only afford a rabbit hutch above a shop or something, but it could be fun . . . ?'

When Kieran didn't respond except to drop his gaze to the tabletop she felt awkward for having brought it up, adding swiftly, 'But if you've got other plans, it's no biggie—'

He looked up, his mouth twisted with emotion. 'No, it's not that. I suppose I just never thought that anyone would ever want to do a proper flatshare with someone like me.'

It was dark by the time Cassie got home. Opening her front door onto the darkened tunnel of the hallway, she imagined what it would be like coming home to light – and Kieran's cheery presence. After convincing him that he was top of her list as a flatmate, they'd agreed to start putting feelers out for a cheap place.

'Macavity?' For the last few days the cat had got back into his old habit of meeting her at the front door, but this evening there was no sign of him.

He wasn't in the kitchen either and she was starting to get anxious when she finally found him squeezed under the sofa. The space wasn't really big enough for him so he'd had to hunker right down on his paws.

'What are you doing there, silly boy?'

He just glared at her – reminding her of his previous distrust after her stay at her gran's. In spite of her cajoling – and a plate of Sheba she wafted under his nose – he wouldn't budge, and in the end she gave up and knocked next door for Desmond.

'Maybe he's had some kind of relapse,' she said as they walked back to her place, 'and thinks you're the only one he can trust?'

But when Desmond got down on one knee on the carpet, with some difficulty given his gammy leg, Macavity viewed him with the same hostile stare.

'Did you hear anything odd today?' Cassie asked. 'Like a thunderstorm? Or another sonic boom?' A few weeks earlier everyone thought a bomb had gone off after a military jet which had been scrambled from an airfield east of London broke the sound barrier.

Desmond shook his head. 'Not a thing.' He got to his feet carefully. 'All you can do is leave him be, darlin'. He'll come out when he's good and ready.'

Desmond stayed for a cuppa and a Bourbon biscuit. But when Cassie went to the draining board to retrieve her favourite mug, it wasn't there. She scanned the worktop and even inside the cupboards – but no joy. It was weird: after drinking her morning coffee she always left the dirty mug by the sink, only washing it up when she needed it again. It would probably turn up somewhere wacky like the recycling bin, put there in a moment of madness.

By the time she went to bed Macavity still hadn't emerged, although he had at least eaten a little of the Sheba she'd left under the sofa. She lay awake for hours, her brain chuntering away – not, for a change, going over father's guilt or innocence – but trying to quiet her jangling nerves which were screaming that something wasn't right. Just after 2 a.m. she got up and went into the kitchen to hunt for the missing mug. It was plain blue china, nothing special to look at, but she liked the way it fitted her hand, and the rim was just right, not too thick or too thin.

'All right, Goldilocks,' she told herself. 'It's got to be here somewhere.' Half an hour later she'd scoured every surface, bin, and cupboard in the place and checked under the sofa and the bed. *Nada.*

She remembered Desmond telling her about a break-in at a flat on the floor below a couple of months back. If someone had got inside her place earlier that day it could explain Macavity's freak-out.

But what kind of burglars stole only a mug?

Chapter Thirty-Four

The next day Cassie came awake with a jolt – and a crushing sensation on her chest. Panicking, she struggled to raise herself on her elbows, before the buzzsaw sound of purring brought her back to reality.

'Hello, you,' she said into Macavity's olive-green eyes. 'Was there somebody in the flat yesterday? Is that why you went loco-cat?'

Stroking the silky head she mulled it over. Burglars wouldn't have much trouble slipping the front door's ancient Yale lock, but why hadn't they taken anything else?

After feeding Macavity she did another tour of the flat. The only item of any interest would have been her laptop, which was sitting on the kitchen table where she'd left it. Now she looked again, she felt a buzz, the kind she got when she looked at a body and spotted something not quite right. The mouse was standing to the left-hand side of the laptop, when – being right-handed – she always placed it on the other side.

Had the intruders accidentally knocked the mug off the draining board, and then taken the bits with them in order to cover up their break-in? Did they plan on coming back, in the hope of richer pickings next time? 'You'll be lucky,' she muttered.

For the first time in her five years living here Cassie felt unsafe: now that the council were no longer filling empty properties, she and Desmond were the last two occupants of her landing. She decided to go into the lettings agency tomorrow, see whether there was anything she and Kieran could afford.

After booking a locksmith to fit a new lock that evening, she called Flyte – on her mobile number this time – remembering the ear-bashing she'd got for phoning her at work.

'Someone broke into my flat yesterday while I was at work. But they didn't take anything,' she told her.

'Are you calling to report a break-in?' Flyte sounded drily amused.

'No. But seriously, Phyllida, I've been thinking about it. Whoever it was went to a lot of trouble to cover their tracks – and I think they might have accessed my laptop.'

'Hold on' – impatience in her voice. The sound of a door opening followed by an alteration in the background noise suggested she'd moved into the corridor. 'Surely it's password-protected?'

'Yeah. Literally.'

'*Meaning?*'

'The password is password.'

Cassie could practically hear her rolling her eyes.

'Listen, it's got to be something to do with me looking into my mum's murder.'

'Really? And how do you reach that conclusion?'

Cassie could picture those perfect eyebrows forming twin arches. 'Trust me, the people who do break-ins round here, they're either kids or junkies. They turn a place upside down and they don't give a toss about you knowing they were there.'

'So, do you want to give me a name?'

'A name?'

'Yes, for the arrest warrant.'

The cynical cop schtick was getting Cassie riled.

'You could start by questioning Gerry Hobbs about that missing swab result.'

'Well, I did ask a legal expert about that. According to him even if the missing result had come out at trial it would have made no difference to the outcome.'

Cassie took this in. 'OK, but what if Hobbs covered up the result because he was protecting somebody? He'd have motive to break in, wouldn't he? Maybe me going to see him made him nervous and he wanted to find out whether I had any evidence?'

'"If" you'd had any evidence.'

'What?'

'You only use "whether" when you are stating two options.'

Christ on a bike! The woman was such a tightass.

'Anyway,' Flyte went on. 'Do you seriously think a retired detective goes around breaking and entering, outside TV crime dramas that is?'

The derision in her voice was the final straw. 'Fine, just ignore me,' Cassie snapped. 'You're not the only contact I have in the cops, you know. I'm on first-name terms with a DCI who turned up for a tour of the mortuary yesterday.'

That shut her up. After a pause she asked, 'Anyone I know?', sounding a lot less hostile.

'DCI Antony Capaldi?' Cassie picked up the card he'd given her. 'Apparently he works at the Directorate of Professional Standards. They investigate bent coppers, don't they?' – grinning to herself.

'What was his interest in the mortuary?' Flyte tried – and failed – to sound casual.

'He wants to set up inductions for newly qualified detectives.'

A long silence, and then Flyte said, 'Look, leave this missing swab business with me. I'll try to find a way to look into it – *informally*.'

'Great.'

'On one condition.'

'Condition?' said Cassie, cheekily mimicking Flyte's response when the boot had been on the other foot.

'That you promise you won't talk to DCI Capaldi about the swab – or mention Gerry Hobbs.'

Cassie left it a full ten minutes after hanging up before dialing a new number.

A deep voice answered, 'DCI Capaldi.'

FLYTE

Flyte pulled up her mother's name in the contacts book of her phone half a dozen times before finally hitting the call button.

'Hi there, how are you?' she said brightly on hearing Sylvia's voice. There was a moment of humiliating silence. 'It's Phyllida, Mother.'

'Ah, Phyllida. What a pleasant surprise . . . You do know my birthday is *next* month?'

Flyte clenched her jaw, determined to make an effort. 'Is it an inconvenient time?' She found herself adopting her mother's clipped and polished diction. Sylvia was 'of good lineage', as she would have put it, and over the years had made it clear in countless subtle ways that in accepting Pops as her husband she had 'married down'.

'No, no, I have ten minutes or so before the gardener is due.' An awkward silence. 'So . . . is there any news on the divorce?' Her attempt at empathy was almost humorous.

'Oh, you know, it's winding its way through the system.'

'Such a shame. Matt was a very . . . agreeable young man, although I could have told you from the start that he was the type who would run to fat.'

'Mmm.'

'Anyway, at least you two are still on speaking terms. That's good, isn't it?'

'Yes, I suppose so.'

'And I must say, it's a blessing really, that there are no children to argue over.'

'A *blessing* . . . ?' It was like a physical blow. Holding the phone away from her, Flyte closed her eyes so she could better picture Poppy's face. When she brought it back to her ear her mother was saying:

'I simply mean that children can cause trouble in a divorce, can't they? All those sad men you hear about, having to take their children to McDonald's.' She said McDonald's the way others might have said Auschwitz.

'I consider myself *blessed* that I had a child, Mother. Even if she didn't survive. And I've been wondering lately – why didn't you support me when I wanted a ceremony for her? Instead of siding with Matt?'

'I just thought that it could only make things worse for you, darling.'

'Worse? How the fuck could it make things worse? My baby daughter *died*!'

The echoes of the F-bomb reverberated in the silence.

'Now, Phyllida—'

'You know what I hope, Mother? That I take after Pops and not you in the human-fucking-being department.'

After hitting 'end call' Flyte stood staring at the screen in amazement. She had never sworn at her mother before, nor hung up on her – had always ducked any confrontation, in fact, just as Pops had.

It felt rather good.

She celebrated with a cup of Earl Grey and a chocolate Hobnob from the treats tin. What had made her call her mother in the first place?

It was tied up with feeling sorry for Cassie, she decided. Having been robbed of both her parents at such a young age, it was only natural that the girl was desperate to save her father from the lifelong parental purdah imposed by his crime. Witnessing her need had made Flyte guiltily aware that she had a mother living with whom she barely spoke.

Well, she had done her best, and it had ended predictably.

As she washed up her cup, she went over Cassie Raven's encounter with DCI Capaldi again. On paper, it was feasible that an under-employed senior-ranking officer in Professional Standards might have a bee in his bonnet about a new generation of detectives who never set foot in a mortuary; on the other hand, she couldn't believe that his encounter with Cassie was pure coincidence.

It was more likely that Capaldi had learned of Cassie's freelance research activities during his investigation of Gerry Hobbs and Spud Neville and decided to look into their handling of the Kath Raven case. But if so, why fabricate an excuse to attend the mortuary rather than approaching Cassie through official channels? She couldn't quite dismiss the feeling that his behaviour was a bit weird.

Whatever his motives, Flyte could only hope and pray that Capaldi wouldn't uncover her connection with Cassie and realise that she'd been lying about her 'accidental' accessing of Callum Raven's record.

Anyway, as Pops would have said, it put the tin hat on any idea of her quizzing Gerry Hobbs about the missing swab.

Chapter Thirty-Five

If his spacious office in King's Cross and the glam PA parked outside was any guide then Capaldi must be a pretty big cheese in the Directorate of Professional Standards.

Seeing Cassie, he broke into a wide smile, prompting a twinge of her previous discomfort. Should she be more cautious? Was this whole mortuary induction plan of his actually just a ruse – an opportunity to hit on her?

After she'd turned down his offer of coffee, he waved her towards a seating area which had an enviable view south-east towards the distant cluster of ultra-high-rise office blocks in the financial district. He followed her gaze out of the window.

'Every year or so they build another one even taller than the last. *Ad astra.*'

'To the stars.' Seeing his surprised smile she said, 'I've learned a bit of Latin – it's a big help with anatomical terms.'

He picked a satsuma out of the wire fruit bowl on the coffee table. 'So have you decided whether you'd like to be involved in my project?' he asked.

'Oh. Sure, I'd be more than happy to help with that.'

'But there's something else on your mind?'

She'd practised what she would say on the Tube journey here: how to get him interested in her mother's murder but without dropping Phyllida Flyte in it. She told her whingeing conscience that she'd never actually promised not to contact Capaldi – only not to make any mention of Hobbs and the missing swab.

Semantics, her conscience replied.

'My father was jailed for murdering my mother back in the late 90s and I think it was a miscarriage of justice.' It felt good to say it out loud for the first time.

'Go on.' He frowned down at the satsuma, concentrating on getting the peel off in one unbroken strip.

'I was wondering if you'd come across the case when you worked in Camden CID? My mother's name was Katherine Raven.' Smelling the sharp-sweet citrus she pictured the molecules travelling over her olfactory epithelium, the back door into the brain.

'The name rings a bell,' he mused, reaching the fruit's equator. He had elegant fingers for a man, except for the reddened skin around the nails, where he'd picked or bitten at them.

She told him the basics of the case and explained that she'd only recently discovered what had really happened to her parents.

'So, you grew up fatherless' – he rested his curiously intent deep-blue gaze on her – 'only to learn that you did have a father after all, but one who murdered your mother – a parent nobody could want. What a terrible thing to discover.'

'Yes, but now I'm not convinced. My father claimed at his trial that my mother had a lover, and the other day I remembered something that happened just before my mother died. A strange man manhandling my mother in Woolies, of all places.'

Capaldi's eyes flickered up to meet hers before returning to his task. 'Even if she did have a lover, it doesn't follow that he was the one who killed her.'

'No, but I've read up a lot on the case,' said Cassie, 'and it's obvious that the police decided it was my dad from the start and didn't even consider any other leads.'

Having stripped the satsuma, Capaldi set the intact curl of peel on the coffee table, where it lay like an orange question mark, before popping a segment in his mouth.

'What did he look like? This man in Woolies.'

The question took her aback. 'Umm . . .'

'I'm wondering whether you could positively identify a new suspect after so many years.'

She shook her head. 'No. All I can remember is that he was a lot taller than my mum.'

He sat back on the sofa. 'So who do you think murdered her?'

'I honestly have no idea. But I do wonder . . . whether the police were covering up for someone? You do read about these things.'

'These "things" are my bread and butter,' he said with a rueful grin. 'But thankfully, the cases of really serious corruption aren't nearly as common these days. Back in the 90s, though . . . policing was a different world.'

Capaldi scanned her face again, as if committing it to memory, but by now she had decided it was just his way. 'Have you had any contact with your father?'

Something, perhaps some instinct to protect Callum, in case the terms of his licence forbade contact, made her shake her head.

'Look, Cassie.' Having dispatched the last of the satsuma, he wiped his hands on a tissue. 'You wouldn't expect me to discuss an ongoing investigation, but I will tell you, in confidence, that I am currently focusing on certain . . . practices at Camden CID in the Nineties. The name Kath Raven does ring a bell, but I've not heard of anything questionable about the case. But you're clearly a very smart young woman so I take what you say seriously. Will you leave it with me?'

'Of course. Thank you.' She became aware of her muscles, ligaments and tendons relaxing – a tension she hadn't even noticed building up over the last few weeks. Capaldi not only had the clout to investigate the case, he was surely intelligent enough to pick up on the missing swab result and to question Gerry Hobbs. It struck her as odd that he'd called her mother 'Kath' rather than the official 'Katherine' – but maybe that was how the cops had referred to the case at the time.

'Have you ever been to Italy?' he asked out of the blue.

'Er . . . no. But I'd like to go to Rome one day. I've always wanted to see the Pantheon.'

'It was your knowledge of Latin that made me ask.' He unleashed a stream of perfectly accented Italian before translating: '*A fool is one who admires other cities without visiting Rome*. Petrarca.' Then, catching her bemused look, he added, 'Apologies. I'm half-Italian, on my father's side. You remind me of my little sister.'

As Cassie plunged earthwards in the lift she decided that Capaldi was certainly a bit off-the-wall, but then as someone who'd been described as eccentric more times than she could count, she could hardly talk.

Chapter Thirty-Six

Cassie was rostered off for the weekend and found herself able to relax – even without the vodka – for the first time since her grandmother had revealed the truth about her mum's death. It was all down to her now-settled conviction that her father really had been falsely accused – underpinned by a feeling of confidence that with Capaldi on the case, finding the evidence to clear his name could be within reach.

Since leaving home at seventeen, Sunday lunch at her gran's had become a comforting routine that Cassie had only missed two or three times in eight years, even when she'd been living in a squat.

For sure, the age gap – make that age *chasm* – between them when she was growing up, chafing to be free of the constraints of school, to start living, had caused some major bust-ups during her teen years, but even her squatting phase had stretched but never threatened to break their bond. It was only really in the last couple of years that Cassie had properly grasped what her grandmother had done for her, taking on a newly bereaved, hyperactive four-year-old in her mid-fifties.

When Cassie had brought home her first dead animal – a magpie she'd found on the walkway outside the flat – Weronika had been sensible enough not to throw a wobbly and bundle her off to a child psychiatrist. Instead of expressing horror, she had admired the bird's beauty and suggested they hold a funeral so that its soul would be freed to fly again. Cassie could still picture the bird's iridescent blue-black plumage on its bed of potpourri inside the shoebox sarcophagus, which they had launched Viking-style onto the canal at dusk.

She knew now that her need to collect dead animals had been tied up with the loss of her mum and dad – a childlike attempt to deny death, perhaps? It probably hadn't helped that her grandmother didn't take her to the funeral: and only now did she understand why – because even a four-year-old would have asked why there was only one coffin.

Weronika had taken the time and trouble to cook a *bigos* – a sauerkraut-based hunters' stew in which the traditional meat and sausage had been replaced by cep mushrooms and smoked tofu marinated in paprika for her vegetarian granddaughter. For Cassie, the biggest legacy of the stroke was the newly sharpened awareness that her grandmother wasn't immortal; and the knowledge that if she didn't raise certain questions now, she might never get the chance.

'Could we look at your pictures of Mama again?' she asked as they sat on the sofa after lunch. Since viewing her mother's PM photographs at the mortuary she'd found herself able to talk about her without getting all churned up. It was like the experience had shifted a gear in her head, enabling her to view her mum as one of the bodies she dealt with at work – no longer her mother, but Katherine Raven, murder victim. She was aware that it was a defence mechanism and a temporary one at that: the grieving process couldn't be postponed indefinitely.

She leafed through the album under her gran's smiling eye, past the early pictures of Kath as a tiny perfect child wearing smart little dresses and coloured tights and into the teenage years when she started to express her personality, wearing her floaty hippy-ish outfits, necklaces made of shells or beads, her wavy auburn hair tumbling over her shoulders.

'Babcia, that police detective who came to visit after she . . . died, Gerry Hobbs, was that his name? Did you ever wonder if it was him who sent money on my birthday?'

That brought a searching look. 'Why would he do a thing like that?'

'Oh, I don't know, it's just he bought me that doll. Wasn't that a bit of an unusual thing for a policeman to do?'

A shrug. 'I think your mama's death upset him.'

Or he was nursing a guilty conscience about something?

'Did the police ever consider any other suspect?'

Another sharp look. 'No. Why would they?'

Cassie's turn to shrug – she wasn't about to ask her gran if Kath might have had a clandestine affair. 'I don't know, I guess when a woman is murdered walking home at night, isn't it usually a random attacker?'

Her grandmother looked at her, head on one side like a bird, a sadness in her eyes. 'Finding out what your father did, it must be a terrible thing, *tygrysek*. It will take a lot of getting used to.'

Her eye fell on one of the photos of her mum in the album in her lap. She wore a long summer dress with a pink-and-red rose design, ruched across the breasts, and one of her signature necklaces around her neck – tiny pink shells strung on a fine silver chain.

For some reason Cassie couldn't work out, her eye kept going back to that dainty necklace. It had set up a questing niggle in her brain, like a mental itch she couldn't quite reach to scratch.

246

Chapter Thirty-Seven

On the way into work on Monday, Cassie dropped into the area's grimiest lettings agency where they gave her details of the one property she and Kieran could afford: a flat above a Chinese takeaway at the wrong end of the borough. It was still an acceptable fifteen-minute walk from the Tube, though, and the fact that the second bed was a box room made it doable if she took on two-thirds of the rent – Kieran's housing benefit should easily cover the rest till his business was up and running.

On arriving at the mortuary Jason told her that Archie Cuff would be doing the five bodies on the PM list today. After feeling a little buzz at the news, she swiftly went hot and cold with embarrassment as she remembered her impersonation of a drunken sex fiend the last time they'd met.

In the autopsy suite, Jason wheeled the first customer over to his table for evisceration, whistling 'Always Look on the Bright Side of Life' while she checked the PM list.

It held nothing too taxing. Three sudden deaths at home, an elderly lady who'd died on the operating table, and an unidentified male fished out of the canal. No decomps, thank Christ – the smell of a decomposed body clung to your nostrils for days – and no high-speed rail suicides. She'd had one of those a few weeks back, from the line into King's Cross, and trying to reassemble the body from a bagful of bits collected by the poor old Transport Police had required 3D jigsaw skills.

'I've got the floater,' said Jason from the other end of the autopsy suite. He waggled his eyebrows invitingly. 'I'm offering two to one on death by urination.'

Cassie disliked the phrase – mortuary shorthand for a drunk who'd decided to have a piss in the canal on the way home, lost his balance and fallen in. Most years they got two or three guys – it was always guys – who'd drowned that way.

As she retrieved her first guest from the body store – an elderly Turkish gentleman called Yusuf Pamuk found dead on the floor of his bathroom – her brain was still chewing over that shell necklace her mother had been wearing in the old photograph, yet still no closer to answering why it was bugging her. After transferring him onto the evisceration table she unzipped his body bag, leaning close to murmur, 'Let's get you out of this ready for the doctor, Mr Pamuk.'

Over at Jason's table she saw him pull the body bag free from the head of the floater, and glimpsed a flash of short-cut hair, darkened by canal water. Sandy-coloured hair.

She went on pulling the bag out from underneath Mr P, but now there was an insistent pinging like an oven timer in her head and it wasn't about the necklace anymore. Suddenly she stopped and headed towards Jason's table. The air seemed to have turned to treacle, making her progress achingly slow, and her legs felt like they had turned to marble, a feeling she sometimes got in dreams.

Finally coming alongside Jason she looked down at the body lying on the table. Her last memory was Jason's moon-like face turning towards her, his mouth opening. She felt herself falling into that great red cavern.

The next thing she saw was a snowy landscape crisscrossed with wavy lines. *Sleigh tracks*?

No. Just the ceiling of the autopsy suite, crazed with cracks. Then the face of Deborah, the admin assistant, looming into her field of vision. The tiles of the floor pressed hard against her back and she sensed that her feet were raised up on something.

'You fainted,' said Deborah, who had an annoying tendency to state the obvious.

Then she remembered. Scrabbled to her feet, knocking Deborah's restraining hand away.

Ignoring the hubbub of protesting voices, she made it to Jason's table, where the drowned man who he'd been about to eviscerate lay – now zipped back inside the white shroud of the body bag.

'Fuck *off*!' Shaking off the hand that had landed on her shoulder, she pulled the zip down.

A joyous leap of hope. She'd got it wrong; it wasn't him after all.

But then it dawned on her. The absence of his perennially cheery expression had made him look like a stranger – for a moment. She smoothed his forehead, damp and chilly to the touch.

'There, there, Kieran. I've got you now.'

'Cassie . . .'

Turning to the voice she realised that the hand she'd shrugged off belonged to Archie, who was still wearing a tweedy outdoor coat. Doug stood alongside Jason and Deborah in the background. They looked like actors in a daytime soap who'd been told to 'look shocked'.

'It's OK,' she told them. 'This is Kieran Byrne.' She set her hand on his shoulder, as if introducing him at a party, his T-shirt damp under her palm. 'He's a good friend of mine.' She felt completely calm. 'I'll call the nick and get someone down here so I can officially ID him.'

Doug nodded uncertainly. 'Are you sure you're OK, Cassie? Why don't you come to the clean side and have a cup of tea and a sit-down while you wait?'

'No.' She transferred her gaze from Doug to Archie, aware that she was turning her head when she didn't need to, like a robot. It felt as if her body needed training in how to be human again. 'Dr Cuff, would you mind examining Kieran?'

'Of course. Give me two minutes to change and I'll be with you.' His eyes sought hers, but sympathy was the last thing she needed.

'You should sit down, at least,' said Deborah. 'You're very pale.'

'I'm quite well, really, thank you.' Cassie was dimly aware that she had started to talk like Phyllida Flyte. 'Jason, would you take over Mr Pamuk for me?' Dismissing the crowd with a nod she returned to Kieran's body.

After extracting Kieran from the body bag, she got him out of his clothes – a black Def Leppard T-shirt, jeans and a puffa jacket, still sodden at the back from his immersion. The canal water smell that rose from his wet clothes wasn't unpleasant. In his jeans pocket there was a wallet with a single twenty-pound note; if he'd had a bank card or any other ID on him it must be lying at the bottom of the canal along with his phone.

Through it all she felt hollow, yet totally calm.

'I didn't expect to see you again so soon, buddy,' she told him, not caring for once whether anyone could overhear her. 'What the hell were you doing in the canal?'

Breaststroke.

'Haha. The old ones are the best. But seriously, Kieran? I just found us a flat, for fuck's sake.'

His face remained stony, lips still set in that unnaturally stern line. Foam was bubbling up from his airways and out of the corners of his mouth – a classic sign of death by drowning. Ignoring the blue roll they would usually use she pulled out a new pack of tissues and used one to gently wipe his lips. 'There.'

She turned to see Archie approaching in his scrubs.

'Right then, let's have a look at this young man,' he said, pulling on nitrile gloves. 'Hello there, Kieran.'

For a moment the kindness in his voice threatened to crack Cassie's composure.

'His name is Kieran Patrick Byrne. He's twenty-nine.'

'Next of kin?'

She shook her head. 'Nobody he's in touch with.'

'Any indication that he might he have been . . . caught short?'

She shook her head. 'His flies were done up.'

Archie ran an appraising eye over the prostrate body. Kieran's arms were tanned – closely freckled might be more accurate – to just above the elbows, where they turned as paper-white as the rest of him. Turning one arm upwards he leaned in to view the inside of his elbow. 'Intravenous drug use?'

Cassie looked down at the purplish scarring along the vein line. 'He had historical substance abuse issues. But he's been off the drink and drugs a couple of months now. He was starting a new business.'

Archie nodded. 'We'll get tox to run all the usual tests, of course.'

But inside she was wondering: had Kieran had a relapse? Falling into the canal ought to be a survivable accident – so long as you weren't too pissed, or off your head on ketamine, to swim to the side and haul yourself out.

Archie was gently probing Kieran's prominent ribs with his fingertips. 'Quite a few fractures here. They're old, though.'

Cassie remembered Kieran hinting in the greasy spoon that his dad used to beat him as a child.

Moving around to the top of the table Archie took Kieran's head in his hands. He palpated his scalp, looking like a new-age cranial masseur, starting at the rear hairline and working from side to side, moving gradually up the skull. Reaching a spot on the right-hand side, just above the ears, she saw his eyes narrowing, the fingers of his right hand going back and forth over one area. 'There's a sizeable haematoma here.'

Cassie felt the swish and yammer of her pulse in her throat.

'Come and see for yourself,' he told her.

The lump – a classic 'goose egg' haematoma – was large and pulpy to the touch, filled with blood.

'Let's get him prone so we can have a proper look,' said Archie, taking the head and shoulders while Cassie took the hips to turn him onto his front. It was easy enough – Kieran couldn't have weighed more than ten stone – but Cassie was grateful to see how Archie used one of his hands to cradle Kieran's head – as if he was still alive.

Leaning in together, Cassie parted the sandy hair at the back of his head while Archie trained a tiny high-powered torch onto the injury.

'A haematoma measuring around four by three centimetres, a few hours old by the look of it,' he said. 'The skin is grazed but not broken.' He straightened 'Impossible to tell from the externals if it caused a TBI.'

Traumatic brain injury.

'Could it have been inflicted by some kind of weapon?'

Like a half-brick.

'I can't rule that out,' he said carefully. 'But it's also possible that he sustained the injury when he fell in. Either way it could have knocked him unconscious for long enough to drown.'

Stripping off his gloves Archie met her eyes. 'Kieran here is going to need a full forensic post-mortem. When the police arrive, would you let them know that I'll be contacting the coroner to inform him?'

A forensic PM was the most thorough investigation a body could undergo. Taking the best part of a day it would be carried out by a Home Office approved pathologist. Its purpose: to establish whether foul play was involved.

Cassie's immediate sensation was one of relief that Kieran's death would be properly investigated, but that soon gave way to a surge of guilt. If this was no accident then there was only one other reasonable conclusion.

Somebody had killed Kieran. Somebody who'd wanted to stop him investigating her mother's murder.

FLYTE

One thing was clear to Flyte from the moment she set eyes on Cassie. Her unnatural calm was like a sheet of glass – and about as robust.

They were in the forensic body store at the rear of the mortuary where the deceased, Cassie's friend Kieran Byrne, was now stored in a separate fridge awaiting the coroner's approval for a forensic PM. On a table between them lay Kieran's clothes and wallet – which Cassie had carefully bagged up in case they held any evidence.

Once they'd completed the official ID procedure, Cassie told her what the pathologist had said about the injury to Kieran's head.

'OK. Well, obviously, we'll be checking out CCTV around the canal,' said Flyte. 'And working out what Kieran was doing in the hours and minutes leading up to his death. That should help us establish whether or not foul play was involved.'

Cassie's face was the colour of skimmed milk. She smiled an inward-looking smile. 'Oh, foul play was involved all right.' Sounding matter-of-fact.

'Do you have any evidence for that? Anything that might help to prove that this wasn't just another case of someone falling in the canal after a few too many pints?'

'He's been sober for weeks.' Cassie tilted her chin upwards. 'The tox report will confirm it. He was starting a business.'

Flyte refrained from pointing out that recovering drunks and druggies sometimes fell off the wagon. 'All right . . . so what do you think happened?'

Cassie touched the evidence bag containing his clothes. Through the clear plastic Flyte could make out a screaming face and spiky letters spelling out 'Def Leppard' on the front of his T-shirt: presumably some sort of rock band.

'I killed him' – she sounded flat-calm.

'Why do you say that?'

'He was helping me investigate my mother's death. I think he got close to finding something out.' A humourless grin. 'Like that was worth him dying for.'

'OK . . . Who would have had an interest in silencing him?'

'You know who.' Cassie's look was defiant. 'The cops. Gerry Hobbs, specifically. The missing swab. It's got to be tied up with that.'

Flaming fishcakes, not this again.

'So you think that DS Hobbs knocked Kieran over the head and shoved him in the canal?' Flyte kept her voice level.

'Maybe not Hobbs. But what if he was on the take and got the lab to lose the swab result in order to cover up for some-body? Look, I don't have anything *you* would call evidence but I'm ninety-nine per cent sure that my dad didn't murder my mother – I think she was probably killed by her lover. Maybe the guy she was having an affair with was someone powerful, some big-time villain? When Kieran started asking around about the murder he might have got to hear about it. Kieran could have stumbled into his path, without even knowing who he was.'

Flyte felt her patience start to fray. 'OK. If you could just give me the details of this mystery lover, I'll get them in for an interview.'

Cassie sent her a look of cold hostility that was worse than any angry outburst.

'Look, Cassie, you have to let me investigate this my way. Give me the names and numbers of anyone whom you know Kieran was in touch with. And details of the hostel where he was staying. OK?' She tried to meet Cassie's gaze but her mind was clearly off elsewhere. 'You've had a serious shock. Let me arrange a lift home for you.'

The girl levelled her gaze on Flyte – the winter sun sidling through the mortuary windows turning her eyes an even deeper shade of blue.

'There's only one thing you can do for me. Find out who killed Kieran.'

Chapter Thirty-Eight

Despite Doug's best efforts to persuade her to go home, Cassie held out at work, even performing two of the eviscerations before making a decent dent in her admin inbox.

Archie came by in his tweed coat before leaving.

'You've had an awful day, Cassie. Do you want to go for a drink? I could buy you a Ruby later.'

This was an old joke, dating from one of their fraught early encounters, when she'd used Cockney rhyming slang to wind him up. Managing a weak smile, she shook her head, remembering with disbelief how that morning she'd been embarrassed at the prospect of seeing him. It seemed so trivial now.

'Thanks, though, for being so great with Kieran,' she told him. 'I was so glad you were the one to examine him.'

'You're welcome.' He scanned her face, his eyes anxious. 'Call me anytime, okay?'

An hour later, at 3 p.m., Doug knocked on the glass and told her kindly but firmly that he'd be coming back every ten minutes until she left the building.

There was something nobody seemed to understand: the only thing holding her together was being in the mortuary surrounded by all her guests – a community which now included her only real friend.

Closing the front door felt like cutting her lifeline to a space-ship to drift into the void. Next thing, she found herself in an offy looking at the bottles of spirits. Discovering they didn't have any Polish brands of vodka, she stood staring at the labels for a long while before picking one at random and taking it to the till.

A movement at the window caught her eye. It was Kieran, clear as day, shading his eyes to see through the glass. He was wearing his perma-grin and his hair was still slicked down, dark with canal water. The sight of him – simultaneously impossible and precious – brought a surge of love and loss. As she raised her hand to wave, he gave a little regretful headshake. She real-ised he was looking at the bottle in her hand. When she looked back up, he was gone.

Had Kieran really returned from the dead, just to stop her buying vodka?

'Who knew you'd be such a buzzkill in the afterlife,' she grumbled, swapping the bottle for a miniature. 'You could give me a clue as to who the fuck killed you instead.'

She met the worried gaze of the off-licence owner. Flinging a fiver at him she left. Outside she checked up and down the street, half-expecting to see Kieran bowling off down the street with his jaunty pirate's limp.

Reaching the canal towpath, she found the spot where Flyte said Kieran had been pulled out of the water. The whole thing still felt almost like a dream, until she saw a fragment of blue-and-white police tape fluttering through the failing light. That hit her like a gut punch, threatening to crack the aura that had enveloped her all day.

Kieran was dead – and she was as guilty of his murder as whoever had knocked him senseless and pushed him in the canal to drown.

She sat on a low wall beside the canal and unscrewed the miniature of vodka. Her gran had told her once that at Polish funerals, it was traditional for mourners to pour vodka onto the grave of a recently buried loved one.

The practice probably had its origins in an Ancient Roman ritual. She knew that they too offered a libation to a departed spirit. Libation from *libare* – to pour as an offering.

Holding the bottle out over the dark green water, she racked her brain for some appropriate Latin saying but in the end she just said, 'Kieran – you were the very best of buddies. I will avenge you.'

For half an hour or so, Cassie sat watching the water and waiting for tears, but none came. After a while she pulled out her phone and opened her contacts. Kieran didn't need her tears, he needed her to make trouble.

FLYTE

After leaving the mortuary that morning, Flyte had joined Josh down at the busy end of the canal, by the pedestrian exit to the market. He had managed to rustle up a couple of uniforms to tape off the seventy-metre section of towpath where she'd calculated Kieran had probably gone in.

The pair of them – an older guy and a younger female – had looked less than delighted at the prospect of a couple of hours scouring the canal-side, especially since an early hint of spring had given way to a fine but freezing drizzle.

'He could have gone in anywhere, couldn't he?' grumbled the older one with a wave of his arm. 'Sarge' – only adding the title after she sent him a meaningful look.

'I talked to the lock keeper, who said that there's barely any current here. The body was fished out just beyond the bridge, but to be on the safe side we need to search all the way down to the stairs there, which he would have taken to get to his hostel.'

The female cop, Kelly, turned to remonstrate with a young guy in a hoodie who was ducking under the tape to get onto the towpath. Flyte approved of the way she dealt with the guy – polite but implacable, straightening to her full five foot seven to boost her authority. After he gave up, muttering abuse, Flyte sent her a smile of approval before saying, 'I'd like you to stay here where it's busy to repel boarders.'

'Sarge?' Kelly blinked in confusion. She had pretty eyes: a golden green.

'To stop people crossing the line,' Flyte clarified. She turned to the male cop. 'Mark, could you take the other end? It's quieter up there but I need you to stop anyone trying to cross the tape.'

She and Josh watched him amble off up the towpath, uniform stretched tight across his over-muscled back and shoulders. He must save all his energy for the gym.

'What are we looking for, Sarge?' asked Josh.

'Anything that might have been used to hit him over the head. And any belongings that he might have dropped during a struggle – his phone and cards are missing.'

'Attempted robbery?' he asked.

'Leaving his wallet still in his pocket?' She shook her head. 'No, my money's on something personal.'

'You think he was bopped over the head and pushed in?'

Flyte hesitated, aware that she might be influenced by Cassie's suspicions. 'We'll have to await the result of the PM for any evidence of that, but from the site of his injury I'd say it's a strong possibility.' She touched the side of her head just behind her right ear. 'I think it would be difficult to hit your head here on your way in.' She twisted her top half to mimic a fall to demonstrate her point.

They started the search, Flyte taking the canal-side half of the towpath, Josh scouring the strip where the path met the grey brick siding, its edge overgrown with weeds and littered with broken glass, beer cans, and fast-food containers.

They worked in silence, using their feet to move something for a better view, occasionally bending to check something out.

A few metres beyond the spot where the fire service had recovered Kieran's body, Flyte saw Josh drop to his haunches.

'Sarge?'

Picking something up in a tissue he popped it into an evidence bag before handing it to her. It was a plain black plastic card, the size of a regular credit card. 'You said he was staying at the Zed?' asked Josh.

Kieran's hostel, Zephyr House: known to everyone as the Zed.

'I nicked one of their customers for pickpocketing a month or so back,' Josh went on. 'I'd swear this is one of their entry cards.'

'Great work. I'll check whether it's Kieran's when I go there.'

'Not sure it tells us anything, though, Sarge?'

She looked up the towpath to the staircase up to the street on which the Zed was located. 'It tells me he was probably on his own. When you're walking along chatting with someone you don't tend to get your door key out of your wallet this early.'

'Makes sense.'

'So maybe someone came up on him from behind. Which would fit with the site of the injury. Turn around a sec.'

She swung an imaginary baseball bat over her right shoulder and towards Josh at head height, following its imaginary arc another few feet out over the canal.

Milo, the young black guy on reception at the Zed didn't seem surprised at the sight of Flyte's warrant card, suggesting that police visits weren't an unusual occurrence. He identified the plastic entry card as one of theirs and showed her upstairs to the room Kieran had shared with three others. Sure enough, when she touched the still-bagged card to the reader above the handle there was a buzz and a click as the lock opened.

'Has something happened to Kieran?' he asked, looking suddenly alarmed.

'Why do you ask?'

Milo nodded towards the card. 'Hey, I watch TV, I know what an evidence bag looks like. It's never good news.'

When she told him, he was visibly shocked. 'I mean, I didn't know him that well, just to say "hi" to on his way in and out. But he was one of those people who always had a smile or a joke for you, you know?'

Kieran's mini-dorm contained four bunk beds, each with its own locked cabinet bolted to the wall. After Milo punched in a code to open the one assigned to Kieran, Flyte fished out the contents. There was nothing of any note – no phone, no drugs, not even a pack of Rizlas – just a modest pile of clothes, a rubber duck wearing pearls and a crown, presumably meant to be the Queen, and a few other personal bits and bobs.

At the bottom of the cabinet she found a pile of photocopies of some crudely produced newsletters on the Camden music scene dated from the 90s and underneath, an old-style vinyl album with two men and a woman on the cover, photographed on the same stretch of towpath where Kieran must have gone in. The better-looking of the two men caught her eye and she recognised Callum Raven from his arrest mugshot.

She bagged it all up to take with her. None of it came under the heading of useful evidence but she guessed that Cassie would value these mementoes of her father's short-lived musical career.

Chapter Thirty-Nine

Cassie still felt out of it, insulated within her bubble when she opened her front door around an hour later.

'I came as soon as I could,' said DCI Capaldi, looking genuinely worried.

'I really appreciate you coming over,' she said, ushering him into the kitchen-diner to put the kettle on. 'Given what I need to tell you, I just didn't feel comfortable coming to your office.' On the phone, Cassie had mentioned only that she had some information about police corruption at Camden nick. She'd been surprised but grateful when he hadn't even asked for further details, agreeing without hesitation to drop in on his way home from work.

Macavity was lapping milk from his bowl but on seeing they had a visitor, he shot out of the kitchen like a firework. 'Don't mind him,' she told Capaldi as she made coffee. 'I had a break-in last week and he's still spooked by strangers.'

'Oh, I'm sorry to hear that. Did you lose anything valuable?'

'Only my favourite mug.'

He didn't comment on that, saying only, 'A young woman living alone, maybe you should think about moving somewhere . . . more secure' – his raised eyebrows making it clear what he thought of her block.

'Oh, I'm already on borrowed time here – there's only me and the guy next door on the whole floor. The council are redeveloping the place.'

Sitting at the kitchen table she told him the whole story – this time including the missing swab result and her conviction that Gerry Hobbs had something to hide. Luckily, he didn't ask how she'd managed to view her mother's PM report – no doubt assuming that her job had allowed her some kind of back-door access to records.

'I can certainly take a look at Hobbs' and Neville's handling of the case, and this swab you think went missing.' His indigo-blue eyes met hers for a moment before looking away. 'But as I said before, even if your mother was seeing somebody it wouldn't automatically make them a suspect.'

There was something different about the way Capaldi was acting but her brain was too fogged for her to put her finger on it.

'As for your friend Kieran's death, it's possible that his interest in your mother's murder is relevant,' he went on. 'But I can't interfere in a current investigation without a very clear connection to one of my cases – that would be way beyond my remit.'

He fell silent, the fingers of his right hand playing a silent sonata on the tabletop. 'So are the police looking into this theory of yours about your mother having a lover?'

He seemed preoccupied. No, more than that. She sensed an undercurrent of something else in his body language – something out of place.

Excitement.

Feeling suddenly cold, she pictured the blood leaving her extremities like a fast-retreating tide. The body's reaction to perceived danger.

Capaldi got up and went to put his mug in the sink. He stood there for a moment before turning to look at her. Behind him in the window the winter sun had sunk behind the roofline but there was still enough light in the sky to throw his face into shadow.

'You're the image of her at the same age, you know.'

She didn't need to ask who he was talking about.

'I've had an alert set up for anyone checking into Kath's case for ever, well, ever since the system allowed it, anyway,' he went on. 'So you can imagine how it felt when I saw the notification ping into my inbox after more than twenty years. After that it was easy enough to establish that this DS Flyte had a previous connection to the Raven family – through you. You and she must have spent a lot of time together on the case of your murdered teacher?'

Had Capaldi been involved in the investigation of her mother's murder back in '97? Was that it? Then she remembered the last time they'd met, the familiar way he'd called her 'Kath'.

'You were the boyfriend.' It was out before she could consider the wisdom of putting him on the spot. Her brain conducted an instant sweep of the surrounding geography: on Mondays Desmond went to his mum's in Haringey, which meant the entire floor was empty apart from her and her visitor.

'Yes and no.'

A curious sensation engulfed Cassie. It was like her whole self had swung up and out of her body on a hinge and hung overhead, seeing the scene as if from above. She wondered dispassionately if this was what people called an out-of-body experience. The dislocation numbed any fear she might have felt, alone with the man who'd probably killed her mother.

'It was you I saw arguing with her in Woolies, wasn't it?'

'I was surprised when you said you remembered that. Kath and I weren't an item by then, hadn't been for years, although I confess I was trying to change her mind. Not that I got anywhere.'

Cassie's brain whirred. 'I don't understand. You dated her *before* she met Callum? How on earth did a girl like her meet a cop?'

'I wasn't born a cop, you know.' This with a return of his old grin.

He came over and sat down opposite her again. 'I met Kath five years before I joined the Met, when I was twenty-seven. After doing psychology at uni I'd spent the next few years . . . drifting. My dad was a builder and I worked for him off and on, but I wasn't exactly a reliable employee and we fell out' – his expression rueful. 'I moved into a squat off Camden Road and scraped a living busking on a guitar outside the Tube. That was when I got involved in the anti-roads campaign.'

'You were at Oakwood Common?' *Click.* It was like a photo she'd once seen shot on a vintage Polaroid, the outline of an image starting to emerge dimly out of grey.

He chuckled at the look on her face. 'It's probably hard now, to imagine me with long hair and a Kurt Cobain fixation. Right after I arrived at Oakwood Kath got me to help her organise a benefit gig, and we fell for each other hard. And in case you're wondering, I make no apology for what we did down there – the politicians were destroying the countryside to build roads. Still are.'

So Capaldi had been Kath's previous boyfriend at Oakwood, the one Callum had mentioned. The one he'd called a bastard.

267

'Anyway, I'm ashamed to say I blew it with Kath.' He stared gloomily at the tabletop. 'I stupidly got involved with one of the other girls. Biggest mistake of my life. It didn't last long because I never really got over Kath.'

'So how did you meet up with her all those years later?'

'After Oakwood I spent a few years working on farms in the West Country – fruit picking, that kind of thing – but finally drifted back to Camden. Still carrying a torch for Kath. One day, I was busking by the Stables Market when I saw her.' He stared over Cassie's shoulder as if replaying the moment. 'She was more beautiful, if anything, and she had you in tow – a mini-Kath but with dark hair and a button nose. I was smitten all over again. Started trying to rekindle things. I found out where she lived and I'd follow her when she went out.'

'You stalked her, in other words.'

His face hardened for a split second. 'You call it stalking, I call it romantic. I was crazy about her. She agreed to have coffee with me once or twice, and it was obvious she was miserable, stuck at home with Callum out gigging all the time.'

Cassie felt so angry she wanted to punch him. 'She was married with a kid! My dad should have knocked your block off. They were happy together and then you ... you turn up and fuck with her head and send her into a depressive spiral.'

He shook his head dismissively. 'Kath was always up and down like that.' Frowning, he put both hands on the table. Shapely but big. Hands she could imagine wrapped round a half-brick.

Her protective glaze had melted away. Now she was just a woman alone in a flat as night fell outside, not a soul within earshot, with a six-foot-something guy who had stalked and, in all likelihood, murdered her mother.

'It's getting dark,' she said, getting up. 'I'll just put the light on.' But on reaching the doorway she made a break for the front door. Turned the latch. The door wouldn't open. *What the fuck?* Rattled it stupidly. Nothing.

She turned to find the figure of Capaldi behind her, blocking the light. 'I double locked it.' He nodded down to the new lock she'd had fitted after the break-in. 'I was glad to see you've improved your security.'

Oh, sweet Jesus. It was Capaldi who'd broken into the flat. That was why Macavity had bolted on seeing him.

She lashed out at him with fists and feet, trying to hit any part of him, to hurt him enough to get time to unlock the door and escape. But he captured both her wrists easily and used his upper body to pin her against the door. He was just too strong.

'It was you,' she hissed. 'You killed her!'

'Shhh. Cassie, Cassie.' His lips were so close to her ear she could feel the moisture in his breath. 'I didn't kill her. I could never have killed the mother of my child.'

Chapter Forty

The fight went out of Cassie and she went back to the kitchen voluntarily – snared by the hooks of his claim, yet desperate for it not to be true.

'You're lying.' She lifted her chin, refusing to sit down.

He shook his head. 'It's true, Cassie. I'm your dad.'

'Prove it.'

She would keep him talking while keeping an ear out for Desmond coming home which should be soon. When she heard his key in the lock next door she would shout her head off – sound travelled easily through the thin walls.

'The moment I saw you with Kath – that very first time – I just knew. You were so like my sister when she was little – that dark hair straight from our Italian dad.' He sought her gaze. 'And my blue eyes.'

'That's it? My father has dark hair and blue eyes.'

'The dates fitted as well. After seeing you with Kath, the first thing I did was to race off to Camden register office to check your birth. Nine months before you were born, Kath and I were still together.'

Every scrap of her being fought the idea. 'So what? I was a few weeks early, I remember my dad telling me.' Her brain was scrolling through her encounters with Capaldi. That intense vibe she got off him which she'd interpreted as him fancying her? Now she realised it was the look of a man who thought he was being reunited with his long-lost child.

Capaldi certainly believed it: his complacent half-smile seemed to suggest his paternity was an incontrovertible fact. Was he just batshit crazy?

Then it clicked.

'You stole my mug.'

'I said you were smart.' He locked eyes with her and she had to admit that his irises were uncannily like the ones that looked back at her from the mirror every day.

He tapped at his phone before pushing it across the table to her, something open on the screen. A lab results document. In the left-hand column, a string of numbers and letters which she recognised as representing each of the regions of chromosomes tested. Three columns: *Allele Sizes; DNA of Child; DNA of Father*. She scrolled reluctantly to the foot of the document.

Probability of paternity: 99.999998%

A dead cert.

Cassie's shoulders went down. As tempted as she was to dismiss it, she knew that even a small amount of saliva from a used mug would yield enough DNA for a reliable match.

Capaldi took the phone from her gently. 'Look, I'm really sorry that I had to go to such lengths to get the sample, but I just couldn't see any other way. It's eaten me up all these years, the not-knowing.'

You could have come and talked to me.

'Are you OK? I appreciate what a shock it must be.' He was trying to look suitably sombre but he couldn't hide his excitement.

271

She just nodded, her brain abuzz. It all made sense. When her mum had hooked up with Callum she was already pregnant by her former boyfriend, and had simply explained away the few weeks' discrepancy in Cassie's birth date as an early arrival.

Capaldi's revelation didn't make her feel any safer. The guy had not only stalked and bullied her vulnerable mother, leaving bruises on her arms, he had thought nothing of breaking into Cassie's flat. And the fact he was her biological father only gave him a stronger motive for murdering her mum after she'd rejected him.

Stay cool and play along.

'Why leave it so long to follow it up, then? I mean, once Mum was dead and Callum was in prison, why didn't you go ahead and claim paternity?'

'After Kath died I was in shock for a long time. My image of the future had always featured the three of us together. I decided I couldn't put you through a custody battle on top of losing both parents – that was unthinkable. I had to accept that your grandmother offered you the best hope of a secure upbringing.'

A spurt of rage. 'But it's not unthinkable to drop this shit on me now?'

He tipped his head on one side apologetically. 'I had my divorce finalised recently. We didn't have kids – we went through the whole IVF process years ago but it didn't work. I suppose I started thinking about the fact I already had a daughter in the world. Then, when I found out that you were digging into your mother's case, it felt like a call to action.'

'So, do you think that my . . . that Callum killed my mother?'

272

He squinted into space. 'I certainly thought so at the time. I went to the police, you know, after it happened, given that I'd seen her just a few days earlier. But several people could vouch for me being out of London at the time, so they eliminated me.' He pulled a sad smile. 'You know something? I owe my whole career to Kath.'

'How come?'

'It was her murder that inspired me to join the police, to become a detective. Looking at her murder again now, I can see that the case against Callum wasn't exactly a slam dunk. Look, if the wrong guy went down for killing Kath then that's terrible, obviously.' He shrugged. 'But nobody can give him back the years he did inside.'

'You're not investigating Camden police corruption, Hobbs' and Neville's handling of cases at all, are you?'

'I'm afraid not.' He pulled a smile of apology.

So the Camden CID 'investigation' had been no more than a cover story, dreamed up so that Capaldi could ask Phyllida Flyte why she had accessed the Kath Raven case. But why had he set up the alert on the computer in the first place? Was it because he had something to fear, if the case was reopened?

'Anyway,' he said, 'proving Callum's innocence isn't really your problem anymore, is it?'

At that moment she heard a faint noise from the walkway, then the clatter of Desmond's key in his front door.

'That's my neighbour. If you don't want me to shout for him then I suggest you leave. It could take some explaining to your bosses, you being here.'

He blinked, as if surprised that she should be throwing him out. *The fucking nerve of the guy.*

At the door he paused to send her a hopeful look. 'I know it's a shock, all this, but I hope when you've had a chance to process it, we can start over.'

'Listen to me. If you contact me or try to come near me again, I'll tell everyone you broke in here. Is that clear, *Daddy*?'

Chapter Forty-One

Cassie felt like the fall guy in some giant cosmic joke. She'd spent twenty-odd years thinking she was an orphan, before unexpectedly regaining a father – albeit one who had killed her mum. Then, just as she started having serious doubts about his guilt, along came a new claimant in the paternity stakes – and just to put the fucking icing on the cake, he was a cop.

She decided she just couldn't deal with it all right now on top of Kieran's death. *Kieran's murder* – she knew in her gut that's what it was and that it had to be linked to his digging into her mum's death.

Right now, she had to persuade Flyte to nail Hobbs to the wall over that missing swab result. She was no longer worried about Capaldi dropping Flyte in it; the Met would take a seriously dim view of one of their officers stalking a young female, daughter or not. If he grassed up Flyte he'd be committing career suicide.

The next morning Cassie dialled Flyte's number, feeling a rush of security on hearing the clipped poshness of her voice. After she'd heard the cut-down version of what had happened Flyte rapped out, 'Meet me at the cafe in twenty-five minutes,' before hanging up.

Twenty-five minutes.

Cassie had to smile. The specificity was so Flyte: not 'around twenty minutes' or 'half an hour'.

When Flyte arrived at the cafe, she handed over a carrier bag.

'These were in Kieran's locker at the hostel. There's an old vinyl record in there. I recognised your father on the cover. And what looks like some music newsletters on Camden bands. None of it's evidentiary, and since he had no next of kin, I thought you might like to have them.' Her tone was business-like but her eyes on Cassie were soft with concern. 'How are you coping with everything?'

Cassie just shook her head impatiently. 'Look, we've got to crack on. You *have to* go and see Hobbs. Capaldi can't touch you anymore, not after what he's done ... You don't think I'm making it up, do you?'

Flyte took a sip of her tea, her eyes narrowed. 'No, I believe you. On reflection the way he approached me was a bit ... inappropriate – a bit cloak-and-dagger – and DPS types are usually straight as a die. He was obviously just using me to elicit intel about your interest in your mum's case.' She shook her head. 'Him breaking into your place, running a DNA test, it's astonishing behaviour in a serving officer. I could talk to my superior regarding how we should pursue it?'

'No, don't do that. Not yet anyway.' The last thing Cassie wanted was Flyte to get drawn into some time-consuming inter-nal politics clusterfuck; she had other plans for her.

'I'll be guided by you as the complainant,' Flyte said. 'The burglary doesn't prove that he killed your mother, only that he was desperate to establish paternity.'

Cassie made a sceptical noise. 'Well, I still think he's lying about something. I just don't know what, exactly. He claims he

276

came forward and gave the cops an alibi for the time of the murder which checked out. Why don't you ask Hobbs about him?'

'Look, Cassie, I still don't have any grounds on which to question Hobbs – at least no defensible grounds, should my boss get to hear about it.'

'Hobbs is covering up for someone!' Cassie burst out. 'Maybe Capaldi – maybe someone else. And Kieran was killed while investigating my mum's murder. How can you not want to question him?'

'I do want to. I just need something approximating a reason.'

'There's no time for that.' Cassie raised her chin. 'If you don't talk to him, I will.'

Flyte's mouth literally dropped open. 'What, and contaminate a potential line of enquiry?'

'Better to risk that than sit on our backsides while Hobbs covers his tracks!'

Their voices had got more and more heated during the exchange. Now they sat in silence, staring each other out.

'It would be nothing more than a fishing expedition,' Flyte huffed. But Cassie could tell she had folded. She was going to do it.

Reaching into her bag Flyte pulled out a sheaf of paperwork and handed it to Cassie, seeming unusually hesitant. Clearly some kind of medical report, it had the name HAMPSHIRE NHS TRUST at the top.

'There is something I'd appreciate your help with, as it happens.'

Meeting her eyes Cassie was thrown by the look she saw there. Phyllida Flyte didn't do vulnerability.

FLYTE

It wasn't the first time that Flyte had put her neck on the line for Cassie Raven and she had a strong premonition that it wouldn't be the last.

Nonetheless, the Kath Raven case had got under her skin, and it was undeniable that some of Cassie's 'intuitions' had been proved right in the past. The girl was a bit spooky – the way she could pick up the tiniest detail that others overlooked. And she was dead right about one thing: DCI Antony Capaldi's behaviour meant that he no longer posed any threat to Flyte's career.

After Capaldi's PA put her through, Flyte wasted no time on niceties.

'I hear you've been paying unofficial home visits to a young female, unconnected with any police matter.' This was a better line of attack than the break-in, which would be harder to prove.

Capaldi dredged up an unconvincing chuckle. 'Watch your step, Sergeant. Remember who is the senior officer here.'

'Oh, I will do. *Sir*. Although I'm told that the higher the rank the greater the punishment for infractions of the police code.'

'Has a complaint been made?' he asked.

'I'm hoping we can avoid that,' she said, all sweet reason.

'What is it I can do for you, Sergeant Flyte?' – his voice as cold and hard as frozen iron.

'I'm planning to interview Gerry Hobbs in relation to the Katherine Raven case, which I have grounds to believe might be connected to a current investigation.' She crossed her fingers for the last bit, like she used to at school: in truth she had sweet Fanny Adams to connect the deaths of Kieran Byrne and Kath Raven. 'And I also plan to tell him that I'm working on behalf of the DPS.' If Hobbs suspected she was freelancing he might cut up rough with her boss, but if he thought the Directorate of Professional Standards was investigating his past conduct, the only person he would dare to consult would be his solicitor. Especially if he had something to hide.

Capaldi's laugh had a trace of admiration this time: almost like he was enjoying the subterfuge. She felt like saying, *You're not out of the woods yet, buddy.*

'All right, Sergeant Flyte. You can say that you are working under my aegis. I'll field any calls I get from Hobbs or his representative. Just don't rattle his cage too hard, OK?'

Now she was sitting in her car in visitor parking at the charity where Hobbs worked; a grainy old photo of him from the *Camden Gazette* up on her phone, and one eye trained on the entrance. She had decided the best approach was a surprise attack at going-home time. After just under an hour at 5.05 p.m., her patience was rewarded. No late finish for Gerry Hobbs.

She followed him to his car, a shiny BMW with the latest reg plate. He was already in the driver's seat by the time she reached him, but at her gesture he opened the window.

'Gerald Hobbs?'

'Who wants to know?'

When she mentioned the magic letters DPS his eyes widened in a gratifying fashion but he recovered quickly.

'If I'm to be interviewed I want a Police Federation rep with me.'

'Look, Gerry. We could do this with wall-to-wall lawyers, a full hearing, the whole shebang . . .' she said. 'But all I'm after is an informal chat, off the record.'

Once she was in the passenger seat her appreciative gaze roamed the squishy leather upholstery and the dashboard which would have looked at home on the flight deck of a passenger jet. 'Nice motor car, Gerry. It's one good thing about the job, isn't it? A handsome pension?'

'What's all this about?' This close to him she could see his naturally ruddy face had grown pale and sheened with sweat.

'It's just a discrepancy I need to clear up. We've received a complaint from a member of the public about the conduct of an old murder case.' Technically true. Pulling out a copy of the pathologist's PM report she handed him the two relevant pages, with a line highlighted. 'Here's my problem, Gerry. As you can see, here . . . the pathologist records taking an intimate swab from the victim, Katherine Raven, but if you look . . . here, at the list of results back from the lab, the swab result is missing. You see the problem?'

'I don't know anything about that,' he said. 'It's a long time ago.' But as he spoke, a bead of sweat broke free and rolled down his forehead – a sight that made Flyte's cold heart sing.

'Look, Gerry, you were the investigating officer and responsible for the exhibits. You carry the can. And I don't need to tell you it's a very serious matter.' A pause to let him consider. 'But I'm throwing you a line here. Tell me the truth before things get really ugly. What happened to that swab?'

Chapter Forty-Two

After Flyte left it was a long time before Cassie could bring herself to open the carrier bag of bits and bobs from Kieran's locker. Finally, she made herself empty everything out onto the kitchen table. Seeing the fanzines and being reminded of everything Kieran had done for her, she felt as if a hand had reached up inside her ribcage and given her heart a tug.

She picked up the album, *Poitín* spelled out in Celtic script on the cover, above the photo of the three band members, down at the canal. It gave her the chills to realise that the spot where Kieran had been found was just a few metres behind them. Barney gazed off-camera, smoking a cigarette, too cool for school; Maria looked willowy and enigmatic in her low-cut long black dress and spiky black choker that showed off her long white neck. Callum was the only one who wore anything like a smile.

She leafed through the half-dozen copies of the fanzine *Camden Sounds* half-heartedly; Kieran would surely have told her if he had unearthed anything of interest. The front page of the September issue was dedicated to news of *Poitín*'s record deal, although it took a far snarkier tone than the *NME* article, reporting that Poitín's *barmy army of fans are up in arms about the cult band selling out. What next?* Top of the Pops?

She could easily have overlooked the band's next mention. It had come in the October edition, in a two-para piece tucked away on the last page under the heading STOP PRESS, clearly hastily added just before the fanzine's release.

Headlined FENDER TO FARMER? it read, *We hear a whisper that* Poitin's *guitar man Callum Raven could be trading his Fender Jazzmaster for a hoe, taking his family to Ireland to try the farming life.* The piece went on: *If true, the departure would scupper the band's move to the mainstream – the brainchild of* Poitin's *manager Barney Cotter.*

Callum and Kath becoming farmers? Had the record deal been going off the rails just before she died? Did Callum get cold feet or had Kath put her foot down at the last minute, freaked out by the idea of him disappearing on tour? Cassie recalled Kieran, over breakfast in the greasy spoon, suggesting that very scenario as a motive for her murder.

She dialled Callum's number. Hearing his happiness at the sound of her voice prompted a jab of pity – and guilt. It felt wrong that she alone should know what Capaldi had revealed. But she couldn't tell him – couldn't even think about the paternity issue right now.

'Just a quick query. Was Mum opposed to the record deal Barney had set up?'

A bout of coughing came down the line, and then he said, 'Well, darlin', she wasn't exactly keen. It would have meant a lot of touring, and she hated the idea of being left at home.'

Cassie racked her brains. What was it Maria had said? That all four of them had drunk champagne to celebrate the news? 'But I got the impression that she'd come round to the idea? That she might go along on tour and bring me too?'

282

'You'd only just started Reception so we decided that taking you away for weeks at a time wasn't really an option.'

'So . . . did you discuss it that night at the pub?'

'Not exactly. But after we had the row, I realised something. I could hardly blame Kath if she *was* seeing another guy, what with me out gigging most evenings. Everything fell into place. The solution for us – the way to make her happy again – was simple. The three of us should move away.'

She could hear the echo of his two-decades-old excitement as he relived the idea.

'My uncle had an unused scrap of farmland in Ireland with an old barn on it. Kath had always had this dream of us all living on a little farm – you know, keeping a few chickens, growing fruit and veg, herbs for the market. We could start over.'

'Why didn't you mention this before?'

'After your mum died, the band, the record deal – it was all just a stupid sideshow. I never even got the chance to tell her about it.'

Cassie's head spun. How had Callum's lightbulb moment found its way into a fanzine? 'Did you tell anyone else about this plan?'

'Umm. Yeah, I went to another pub for a pint on the way to Barney's and Pete was there. I told him about it.' *Fanzine Pete* – who'd clearly wasted no time squeezing this mini-scoop into his next issue.

'That would have meant no record deal – and the end of the band?'

'Yeah.' Callum sighed. 'Look, of course I felt bad letting Barney down, after all the work he'd put in getting us to the next level. Never mind all the cash he'd laid out.'

'So that was why you went round to Barney's – to break it to him.' It was all Cassie could do to keep her voice steady. 'How did he take it?'

He gave a dry chuckle. 'There was a bit of a shouting match, we even squared up to each other at one point. But when he'd calmed down, he was pretty good about it. He asked me to take a day to think it over but he swore he'd accept my final decision either way.'

'And then you headed home intending to share the plan with Mum.'

'Yeah, I knew she'd be thrilled about it. But when I got home, she wasn't there.' He left a pause. 'I assumed she still had the hump with me and had gone to your nana's. I fell asleep on the sofa and woke up to an empty flat.' He fell silent.

'Weren't you gutted to give up on the band – money, fame, all that stuff?'

A bitter laugh. 'There's only one thing I regret, Catkin. That Kath never knew I was ready to give it all up to make things right again between us. And I'd give anything now, just to have her back.' He paused. 'Anything except my daughter.'

Cassie had to bite down on her lip to suppress the turmoil inside her. How would he react to be being told that his father-hood had been cancelled? After promising to be in touch again soon she hung up.

Had Callum's plan to leave the band, scuppering the record deal, been the catalyst for Kath's murder? If so, who would have the strongest motive for wanting her out of the picture?

A phrase from her Latin primer came back to her.

Cui bono?

Who benefits?

There was one obvious answer.

FLYTE

Flyte felt almost sorry for Hobbs. Once he started talking she had to ask him to slow down so that she could understand what he was saying.

'I've been over it a thousand times. I remember Dick Westmacott the pathologist taking the swabs, the bloods and so on, and I can still see the pots right there, lined up on the bench ready for me to label.' He sketched a line along the dashboard. 'I can even remember writing her name and date of birth on the labels, making sure I spelled Katherine with a "K".'

'And the intimate swabs?'

'I just can't remember' – his face contorting with anguish.

'But it was you who labelled the swabs, not the technician?'

'That was how it was done: the labelling and paperwork, even delivering the samples to the police lab, back then it was all down to us.' He opened his hands.

'So you're suggesting that you might have forgotten to label those particular pots? And if they went into the fridge at the lab unidentified alongside dozens of others they simply wouldn't have got tested along with the rest?'

He nodded, looking utterly miserable. Flyte could detect no hint of duplicity in his expression. She couldn't imagine committing such an egregious error herself, but then, she had come to realise that many officers lacked her attention to detail. Or as her boss had once been rude enough to call it, her 'OCD' tendency.

'The thing is, I was under a lot of pressure at the time.' His voice sounded plaintive. 'I remember one of the other sergeants had called in sick so I had to race back to the nick to do a witness statement.' He clasped and unclasped his hands. 'I know it's no excuse. When I got the lab results, with no mention of the intimate swabs, I called them up and they said they didn't have any record of receiving them.'

Flyte left a pause. 'So assuming that what you've told me is true, by this stage you were guilty of a serious oversight, no question, but no actual misdemeanour. You could have taken the consequences, but instead you decided to cover your tracks.'

'I tried to!' he burst out, craning towards her. 'I went straight to Spud Neville, my DCI. I was ready to fall on my sword, take whatever punishment I might get for screwing up the chain of custody, expecting to get thrown off the case.'

'He didn't want to lose you.'

A nod. 'He said that wanting to take the rap was a "noble impulse". Poor Kath had been buried by then, so it was too late to retake swabs and ending what he called "a promising career" would achieve nothing. He said he'd deal with it.'

'How?'

'He just said, "Leave it with me."' Half closing one eye, he lay a finger along the side of his nose, clearly imitating Neville. He pulled an awkward shrug. 'Spud was pals with Dick Westmacott – they used to play golf together. Sure enough when the PM report came back he hadn't flagged the missing result.'

Flyte tried not to show her disapproval. Every time she heard a fellow officer moaning about the ever-mounting burden of rules and regs they had to follow she remembered people like Neville, those relics of the 'good old days' of policing, who had done so much damage to the public's trust in the force.

'I was only thirty and I'd just made sergeant,' said Hobbs. 'In any case, the swab was an irrelevance – Westmacott took them as a matter of course, even when there was no suggestion of sexual assault, like in Kath's case. And corruption in the Met was all over the papers at the time. If it had come out at trial the jury might have thought they smelled a cover-up.'

'Especially as the case was flaky to start with,' said Flyte.

He bridled. 'What do you mean, flaky? Callum Raven was a wrong'un, I tell you. He'd been mixed up with the IRA a few years earlier. He was a wife beater, and he admitted in the witness box that he thought she was having an affair. And we had a solid eyewitness who saw him running away from the tunnel at the right time.'

'By his own admission it was a fleeting glimpse though, wasn't it? And the Turnbull guidelines warn against putting too much trust in the reliability of eyewitnesses' recollections.'

He gave a mulish shrug.

Flyte looked at him squarely. 'What was it that convinced you, personally, that Raven was guilty?'

'I'll tell you,' he said eagerly. 'It was Barney Cotter, Callum's best mate. The one who gave Callum his so-called alibi. Spud and I interviewed him and after we walked out of there we both said the same thing. He was hiding something. It was stark staring obvious he was covering up for his mate.'

Chapter Forty-Three

By the time Cassie reached Maria and Barney's place it was getting dark. She was there on a fact-finding mission, not to accuse Barney directly – that would be stupid, if not suicidal, given what had happened to Kieran just two nights earlier.

Still, it came as a relief when it was Maria and not Barney who answered the door – all dressed up this time, in the outfit she'd worn on the stage at The Dublin Castle: floaty dress, boots, and black choker, this one decorated with rhinestones. 'Come in, come in!' she said. 'Excuse the glad rags – we're going to a party later.'

The kitchen table was covered in flyers for gigs and old newspaper cuttings – Cassie glimpsed Barney's face and the Celtic typeface for *Poitín* among them. Hearing a message ping on her phone she saw the name DS Phyllida Flyte come up on the screen, and shoved it into her jacket pocket.

'Sorry about the mess,' said Maria, clearing the stuff into a pile. 'It's Barney's fiftieth this weekend and I had the idea making up a scrapbook of old gigs, all his press interviews and so on. It's a ton of work, though.'

'He's not here?' asked Cassie.

'He's out at a recording session, but he'll be back later if you wanted to talk to him?'

'No, that's fine.' Relieved that she could speak freely but also suddenly nervous about what she needed to ask, Cassie paused, her eye drifting to a blackboard hung on the wall. On it someone had chalked a shopping list – *Eggs, dishwasher powder, rocket* – and beneath that, in a different hand the scrawled message, *M – Call your Ma!!* Clearly left by Barney.

She decided to take the plunge. 'There is something you might know. Did Barney ever tell you that Callum talked about pulling out of the record deal the night my mum died? He had a plan to take us to Ireland to start a small farm.'

Maria frowned. 'Ireland? It's the first I've heard of it. Are you sure?'

'Callum told me.'

'You spoke to Callum? How is he doing?' Her face softened.

'He's OK.'

Cassie found her gaze drawn back to Barney's message on the blackboard. Something about it was making her feel uneasy but she didn't know what.

Then it hit her: *the handwriting.* That little looped flourish he'd used on the 'C' of 'Call'. She'd seen it before. On the 'C' of 'Cassandra' in the unsigned notes that had come with cash on her birthday – every year after her mum was murdered.

'After Kath died, the future of the band would have been the last thing on Barney's mind – any of our minds,' Maria was saying. 'And after Callum got charged there was no band.'

Cassie tore her eyes away from Barney's looping handwriting. 'Of course. Barney would have been disappointed, though, right? About the deal going south?'

'He would have been gutted, sure. He was still paying off the loan he took out to cut the album.' A sharp look at Cassie. 'Why do you ask?'

Cassie raised her hands in a *don't shoot me* gesture. 'I'm just filling in the blanks, you know.'

Maria looked out of the window towards Barney's darkened office in the garden for a long moment. When she looked back at Cassie her eyes were clouded – like some long-submerged worry or memory had just floated to the surface of her mind.

Cassie had her own worries clamouring to be heard. So it was Barney who had sent her those birthday postal orders every year. The only possible interpretation – that it had been blood money, paid to atone for the sin of murder.

Maria glanced up at the clock.

'Listen, he'll be back soon and I need to pick up fish and chips for dinner.' She stood to pick up her coat. 'If you don't mind walking with me, we can chat on the way. You can eat with us if you like.'

Once they were out on the street Maria seemed to relax, talking about how the area had changed, rolling her eyes at the rash of plantation shutters at her neighbours' windows. 'The place is full of investment bankers these days.'

Had she been worried that Barney might come back while they were talking? Was there something incriminating she wanted to tell Cassie without the risk of him walking in on them? And what about Kieran? Had Barney killed him too?

'Do you remember the guy who was with me, that time you sang at The Dublin Castle?' Cassie asked lightly. 'Name of Kieran?'

'Yes, vaguely. Nice young fella, very skinny though.'

'Did you or Barney see him again after that?'

'See him? What – at another gig, you mean?'

Thinking on her feet Cassie said, 'Kieran is a bit of a muso and he was planning a podcast on the 90s music scene round here. I think he was hoping to interview Barney.'

'Oh, Barney would've loved that. When it comes to Camden bands, wind him up and watch him go!' Maria chuckled. 'Ask him when we get back home. Shortcut through here.' She stepped over a low brick wall to cut through an industrial estate. Entering a darkened passageway behind one of the units they had to walk single file, making it difficult to talk. Pulling out her phone to light the way Cassie saw five missed calls from Flyte and took the opportunity to read her message.

'Tried to call you. Call me back. It's urgent!!'

But Cassie was trying to piece together the night her mum was murdered. Barney had claimed he was with Callum at the critical time – which had presumably been a lie, not to protect Callum but to protect himself. 'On the night Mum died, when Callum came round to see Barney, you were already in bed, right?'

'Mmm hmm,' said Maria over her shoulder. 'Why do you ask?'

'Did Barney come straight to bed after Callum left? Or did he go out?'

'I have no idea; I was fast asleep. Like I told the cops.' The lamps overhead shone a harsh light on her black curls, which Cassie could now see were dyed.

Cassie was thinking back to her last visit to the Cotters, when she'd used their upstairs bathroom. The cottage was so tiny and the walls so thin that she'd been able to make out every word of 'Back to Black' playing downstairs on the radio. If Barney and Callum were having a shouting match downstairs about Callum leaving the band, how come Maria had managed to sleep through it all?

The end of the passage was partially blocked by a pile of fly-tipped building waste – going by the heavily rusted lengths of steel amid the rubble it wasn't recent. Cassie frowned; this didn't feel like a shortcut anymore.

Maria stopped under the orange glare of a security lamp and turned towards Cassie, her lipstick turned purple by the light, the top half of her face in shadow. 'I think I already told you, I had a yoga class the next day.' Her chest was going up and down, her breathing too fast for such mild exertion and her leather choker stood out, shockingly black against the white of her throat. Cassie couldn't take her eyes off it.

She was remembering the images of her mum in the photo album, the dainty shell and bead necklaces she liked to wear . . . and the photographs from her mum's post-mortem report recording the jewellery she'd been wearing that night. A pair of delicate shell earrings. And a leather choker designed to look like barbed wire, broken in two places, which must've been found near the body.

Not my style.

Her mother's words, imagined or otherwise, that had come to her as she viewed the images.

Fuck. The spiky leather choker was totally at odds with her mother's romantic hippy style.

The muscles in Cassie's thighs suddenly went wobbly and she had to put out a hand onto the wall beside her to stay upright. Registered the gritty surface of the brick violating her palm but felt no pain.

That would be the anaesthetic effect of adrenaline, her brain noted, *priming the body for danger.*

Because it had just dawned on her where she'd seen that distinctive barbed wire choker before.

On the cover of Poitín's *album, around Maria's long white neck.*

The cops had assumed the choker was her mum's, when it was actually her killer's. Kath must have had torn it off her attacker while fighting for her life.

The attacker wasn't Barney.

'I . . .'

'You're a stirrer, aren't you? Just like your mother.' Her usual lilt now edged with steel, Maria moved closer, backing Cassie up against the wall. 'Busting up the band just when we were about to make it. For what? To live in a cowshed in the back of beyond.' Contempt narrowed her eyes.

'It must have been hard, to face losing what you'd all worked for.' Cassie kept her voice low and calm, maintaining eye contact, like she did whenever she had to deal with angry, overwrought relatives at the mortuary. 'But you do know the farm was actually Callum's idea.'

Maria wasn't listening. 'Miss High and fucken Mighty.' She spat the words out. 'Then I had to listen to all that crap in court about the *poor little wifey*. Callum was the victim, not her. He was happy until he got involved with her – her constant moods, the booze-fuelled histrionics. Christ, he had to babysit his wife as well as his child.'

Cassie was taken aback at the vitriol in her tone. *This wasn't about money or fame.* Remembered Maria and Callum had dated before he met Kath. 'It was him who dumped you, wasn't it? not the other way round. You were still in love with him.'

'If we'd signed the record deal, gone touring, we'd have got back together, no doubt about it' – utter certainty in her voice.

'What makes you think he wanted to? He had a wife and a family he would never have left.'

Maria sent her a pitying look. 'You think? Just before the shit hit the fan, he kissed me, after a gig.' Her voice softened. 'I knew then that we were destined to be together. Those few years we spent apart were irrelevant. Wife and kid included.'

'Yeah? A kiss. Is that it?' Cassie felt her temper rising.

Maria's face turned stubborn. 'Your father was a beautiful man. It was only natural he'd be torn up by the guilt. But it was only a matter of time – time we'd have had together when the band went on tour.'

'What a crock of shit!' Cassie could no longer restrain the fury she felt on her mum's behalf. 'You were deluded! Callum would never have left Kath. You know what he told me? That she was the only woman *he ever loved*.'

She was about to turn on her heel, get out of there, when her field of vision burst into shards of orange light. For a moment she thought one of the security lights had exploded but then felt wet on the back of her skull. Maria had shoved her full-force into the brick wall. Before Cassie could recover, she grabbed her by the hair and did it again. The impact was sickening.

It's not fair, she wanted to say, *I wasn't ready!* – like the time at primary school when one of the bigger boys had challenged her to a race but started running without fair warning.

Maria's face went blurry then dark. A series of vivid scenes flickered behind Cassie's eyes. *Maria in bed, hearing every word of Barney and Callum's noisy argument downstairs. Creeping out to the pub to intercept Kath. Offering sisterly sympathy. In the tunnel at Prowse Place, dropping back a couple of steps, snatching her moment.* She'd probably picked up the half-brick on the way. Then *bam*! No fair warning.

Coming to, she twisted to push Maria away but only managed a weak shove. *Probable concussion*, her brain noted coolly. *Unhelpfully*.

'Why dig up the past? Why make it all ugly?' Maria hissed in Cassie's ear, one hand holding her by the hair. 'You're just like her. Always wanting all the attention.'

'You . . .' Cassie couldn't finish the sentence.

'Yes. I'm not ashamed to say I smashed her smug face in.'

The hand that had been pinning Cassie's shoulder to the wall disappeared, Maria's face dipping out of view. Blinking to clear her fogged vision, Cassie saw that she'd picked up a length of rusted steel.

Cassie got a flash-frame of her mother's deconstructed face. Then another face. Her grandmother's this time.

Her little eyes were bright and fierce. '*Walcz!*' she was saying. 'Fight!'

The thought of her Babcia losing a daughter *and* a granddaughter was like a second shot of adrenaline. As Maria raised the rusted steel Cassie took her chance. Reached out to grab Maria's choker. Twisted. The leather was wide and sturdy. This one wouldn't break.

Clang! The steel hit the wall behind her, Maria's aim skewed.

A vivid image came to Cassie. The carotid sinus, the nerve junction box where the carotid artery branched into two. Adjusting her grip on the choker she directed its point of maximum pressure on where it was located, in the side of the neck just under the jawbone. Maria's breath stuttered, and she clawed at Cassie's hands. Cassie smelled the iron filings tang of her own blood. She pictured the signal from the carotid sinus pinging up to the brain, and back down to the vagus nerve, instructing it to depress blood pressure.

Two minutes, she told herself. That's all it would have taken for Bradley Appleton to lose consciousness.

It didn't take that long. One second Maria was thrashing around, trying to stop the unbearable pressure on her neck. The next she was in a heap on the deck, one foot sticking out in its high-heeled boot. Utterly still.

FLYTE

Flyte drove like a teenage joyrider through darkened streets to the hospital. She couldn't stop berating herself about what had happened. At least Cassie was stable, Josh had said over the radio. *Thank God.* If only she'd been more explicit in her message.

Despite his error over the handling of Kath Raven's sample, Gerry Hobbs had struck her as a decent and dedicated cop, and his absolute conviction that Barney Cotter had been hiding something had got her thinking. Cassie was convinced that Callum was telling the truth about being at Barney's house at the critical time. If her instinct was right, then what did Barney have to be shifty about?

It was only vague speculation really, until she got a call from Josh, on her way back to Camden after seeing Hobbs.

He'd just interviewed one of Kieran's roommates, who'd said Kieran had been off to a blues gig the night he died. Josh had checked the venue's website, and the line-up of performers. Third on the bill was Maria Maguire.

Flyte had no proof that Kieran had gone to the gig to talk to her – or Barney – the night he died – that would need witnesses, or CCTV images. But at the very least, it made Callum's fellow band members persons of interest to the investigation.

Why in her text to Cassie had she only said to 'call her back'? Why the fuck hadn't she said, 'Stay away from the Cotters'? Some stupid idea about not defaming them without hard evidence.

Hitting a traffic jam just outside the hospital car park she punched the steering wheel hard, hurting her knuckles.

Deciding to leave the car on a double yellow she sprinted into A&E and flashed her warrant card at the desk. She was shown into a family room where a young male doctor arrived to update her.

'Cassie's awake and lucid,' he told her. 'And the CT scan showed no sign of a traumatic brain injury.'

Thank Christ.

'But as I told your constable, she has a couple of nasty contusions on her head and a suspected concussion so I'm afraid you can't talk to her just yet. I'll be keeping her in overnight for observation.'

'Good luck with that.'

He looked startled.

'I just mean you're going to have your work cut out trying to persuade her not to leave,' she explained. 'What about Maguire?' When Josh had called the hospital all they would tell him was that she was still in resus.

'She's doing well considering her heart stopped for at least seven minutes. She was incredibly lucky that Cassie stayed conscious and was able to perform CPR till the paramedics got there.'

The attack on Cassie put Maria Maguire firmly in the frame for the murder of Katherine Raven, a case supposedly solved back in 1997. Flyte visualised the PM photographs, and the way Kath's face had been ... erased. A level of personal animosity that could have been driven by sexual jealousy. Some kind of love triangle between Callum, Kath, and Maria? And did Barney Cotter know what his wife had done?

'OK. I need you to put Maguire on a side ward. A uniformed officer is on the way to be stationed outside.'

For a moment the doctor looked like he might object, but seeing the look on her face he decided against.

Good decision.

She asked him to call her when both his patients were fit to be interviewed. Right now, her top priority was a fireside chat with Barney Cotter.

Flyte's boss, DI Bellwether, had given approval for her softly-softly strategy – a voluntary 'chat' at Barney Cotter's home the following morning. If she dragged him down to the station he might clam up and demand a brief, but a chat in someone's home environment felt less official, making him more likely to let his guard down. And so long as he was cautioned, the interview would still be admissible in court, wherever it had been conducted.

They sat at the kitchen table, Flyte and Josh on one side, Barney on the other. He was pale and his eyes were red-rimmed from lack of sleep but otherwise he seemed calm.

She read Barney the caution using what Josh liked to call her 'terms and conditions may apply' tone of voice, her apologetic smile suggesting it was no more than a tedious but necessary piece of bureaucracy.

She arranged her face into a sympathetic expression. 'How is Maria?'

'She's out of danger, they said. Thank God.'

'So tell me, when did you first realise that she was involved in the murder of Katherine Raven?'

He regarded her for a long moment – the expression on his face difficult to read. When he spoke, his Cockney accent was magnified by strong emotion. 'Do you know what it's like having to choose between two people you love?' His flat London accent underlined the heartfelt emotion of his words.

'Tell me.'

It was a sorry tale. Barney had been 'crazy in love' with Maria from the band's earliest days, but even after they started living together he remained painfully aware that she'd never got over her relationship with his best mate. Meanwhile it was blindingly obvious that Kath would forever be the only woman for Callum.

'I hung in there, you know, thinking Maria would move on, get over him, start to appreciate what I could offer her.' His face twisted into a look of self-disgust. 'Sometimes, on stage, when he was singing and she was waiting for her cue I'd catch the way she looked at him. It was the kind of look she never gave me.'

'But then Callum was charged with Kath's murder. Convenient.'

He grimaced. 'After he went to jail, I asked her to marry me and she said yes.' He raised an eyebrow. 'Like a twat, I thought that with him out of the way we'd have a chance of making it, just the two of us.'

'And did you?'

'It was a hell of a lot easier without Callum around, sure . . .'

'But . . . ?'

He stared up at the ceiling. 'When I was sixteen, I cheated in my maths O level. I had equations and stuff written up my arm. It worked – I got a C. But you know what?' He pulled a

300

quizzical smile. 'I never once put that maths pass on my CV.'
Flyte experienced a spurt of fellow feeling: she'd have felt exactly
the same about a qualification dishonestly acquired.

'The thing is, Maria would probably never have married me if
Callum hadn't gone to jail, so our marriage always felt a bit like
that maths GCE. Fake.'

Flyte gave Josh a little sideways glance, inviting him to prac-
tise his interviewing skills.

'Could we go back to the night Kath died?' he said. 'Take us
through what happened exactly.'

'Callum came round, just like I said. He said he was leaving
the band, taking Kath and Cassie to Ireland, to make a fresh
start. We argued about it.'

'A noisy argument?' asked Josh.

'Yeah, but we made it up before he left.' He raised a palm.
'And before you ask, I admit I'm still not a hundred per cent
sure what time that was, which is why that bastard of a barrister
was able to trip me up in court.'

'Why say you knew the time when you didn't?' Josh asked.

'Because I didn't believe for one second that Callum could
have harmed Kath.'

Josh looked down at his notebook. 'According to her statement at the time, Maria went to bed early. When you joined her,
did she mention hearing you arguing?'

After a long pause Barney replied, his voice hoarse. 'When I
went up she wasn't there.'

'You must have been worried.'

He tipped his head. 'I assumed she'd popped out for cigs –
she used to smoke back then. I dozed off for a bit but woke up
about 3 a.m. I found her downstairs, asleep on the couch.'

'What did she say, in the morning?'

'That she had struggled to fall sleep and had gone out for a walk and a smoke. I didn't even mention the argument because I was hoping Callum might reconsider. And neither did she.'

Leaning forward Flyte fixed him with a look. 'You didn't buy her story.'

'I had no reason not to.' He grimaced. 'Not then, anyway.'

'But then you learned that Kath had been murdered.'

He dropped his head, nodded. 'Maria was always sweetness and light to Kath's face – but she would sometimes bitch about her to me, which I hated, 'cause it was so obviously tied up with her feelings for Callum. So when he said him and Kath were leaving the band, leaving the country, part of me was relieved. But I knew Maria would be furious.'

There was a long pause which Flyte omitted to fill.

Blowing out a harsh breath, Barney raised his eyes to meet hers. 'Later that day I saw her take the clothes she'd been wearing the previous evening out of the washing machine, washed and tumble-dried. The next day I clocked her coat was missing. She said she left it at a gig.'

Barney fell silent but sensing there was more, Flyte waited.

He gave a despairing little shrug. 'A couple of days later, I saw her coming out of the shower and saw that her shins were black and blue, like someone had kicked her hard – repeatedly. She'd fallen over, she said, while out walking in the dark.'

'You didn't believe her.'

'I had to believe her! I was in love with her!' He raised his voice for the first time. 'I still love her.'

Flyte noted the distinction. 'And when Callum was charged with the murder?'

He looked sick. 'It was a relief. It allowed me to construct a . . . parallel reality in which Maria was innocent. Although I always knew deep down that Callum was incapable of hurting Kath.'

'Did you ever ask her the question?'

'Never. But it's been there hanging between us every day for more than twenty years like . . . like a noose.'

'Why are you telling the truth now?'

He straightened his spine. 'It started when I saw Cassie. It was like seeing a ghost. Almost like Kath had turned up to make me do the right thing. I haven't had a decent night's sleep since then, going over how awful it must be for her – first to lose her mum so young and then to be told that her dad had murdered her. Especially when I knew he didn't.'

'Do you know anything about what happened last night between Cassie and Maria?'

He looked at her. 'It's obvious, isn't it?'

'You tell me.'

His eyes hooded. 'Maria tried to kill Cassie to stop her finding out the truth.'

A little thrill ran up Flyte's spine. Of course, his last comment was speculation, not evidence. But hearing him saying it out loud told her something: Barney Cotter would testify against his wife in court.

'You think *she* was capable of hurting Kath.'

'Maria has a vicious temper. I've only seen her in full flight once or twice, but I'm not ashamed to say it scared me. She's been on medication periodically over the years.'

'What kind of medication?'

He shrugged. 'For her nerves, she said.'

'Have you come across someone called Kieran Byrne? We believe he might have gone to your wife's gig on Sunday?'

'I don't know the name.' He frowned. 'I was out late myself on Sunday.'

Deciding it was enough for now, Flyte met his eyes. 'Thank you for your honesty. You are doing the right thing. Are you aware that omitting to mention such significant information when you were questioned by the police is an offence for which you could be prosecuted?'

A sardonic smile spread across Barney's lean face. 'I've been punishing myself in here' – he tapped the side of his head – 'for more than twenty years. All that matters now is Callum clearing his name and Cassie getting her dad back.'

Chapter Forty-Four

Maria's attack had left Cassie with a headache unlike anything she'd ever experienced. It felt like two sumo wrestlers were standing either side of her, each using a paving slab to crush her skull between them.

Worse, when she asked for meds the nurse handed her two round white pills.

'You're kidding me. The one time I can legally take class As and you're giving me paracetamol?'

The nurse didn't appear to find this funny.

'You have had a cerebral concussion. That's a—'

'I know what it is.' Cassie rolled her eyes. 'A transient neurogenic dysfunction caused by mechanical force to the brain.'

She knew she was acting like a stroppy teenager, and that disinhibition was a side-effect of head injury – but she didn't give a toss. In fact, being freed from adult responsibility felt great. If only it wasn't for the pain in her head.

The nurse was droning on about opiates being bad for concussion, *yada yada*.

Cassie felt unmoored from real life, as she had been ever since seeing Kieran stretched out on the slab, but with an added dose of weird from the concussion. She remembered Maria attacking her, but it felt like a scene from a movie, or something that had happened to someone else.

For the next hour or so she tried to sleep but it was hopeless. At half eleven the ward was still a buzz of constant noise, and when she tried to get comfortable the slightest movement felt like a wrecking ball banging around inside her skull. She made a decision. Choosing a moment when the nurse was in a side room, she quietly retrieved her belongings from the bedside locker, and slid out from between the sheets. While getting changed in the loos, she peered at her pale reflection in the mirror, half-expecting her head to be twice its normal size.

How she got to Camden Town Tube station was a blur. She found herself talking to one of the dealers she knew. He was skinny, with big doe eyes – too young-looking for his gold tooth.

'Haven't seen you for a while, fam' – winking at her. 'We was worried you joined the Hare Krishna.'

Then Kieran's face appeared over the guy's shoulder, his hair still wet with canal water. Sketching a half-wave, she told him, 'It's only a bit of weed for my headache.'

'OK, sis, no problem.' The dealer chuckled, slipping something into her hand.

Then, somebody shouted, 'Feds!'

Pandemonium. The last she saw of Doe Eyes was the red soles of his Louboutin trainers flashing off down Camden Road. The next thing she knew some female cop had her up against the wall by the Tube entrance. 'Show me what's in your hand.'

Once in a blue moon, the cops would suddenly go all zero tolerance on street dealing and do a sweep. Just her luck that they had chosen tonight.

When the cop mentioned a caution she pulled a face. 'Seriously? For a tiny bit of weed?'

'Stay there,' said the cop, before turning away to help her colleague put the cuffs on one of the dealers.

Cassie seized the chance to walk away.

But now the streetlights and shopfronts start to blur and shimmer with her every step.

Trippy!

She heard the cop shout, 'Come back here!'

Then a piercing ringing invaded her skull. *A shop alarm?*

Realising that the pavement has turned into a fragile pane of glass, she made a grab for the nearest lamppost – terrified of cracking it. Of falling through.

Faces flooded into her vision. The faces of the dead she had cared for over the years. The battered face of Mrs Perlman, dead of a brain haemorrhage. . . nine-year-old Oliver who went swimming in the canal, foam streaming from his nostrils . . . boy racer Jordan, his neck snapped . . . Hundreds of faces – some slipping past her before she could name them.

So many dead. An avalanche of death.

Finally, piercingly, the ones who she'd known and loved. Her beloved teacher Mrs E, drowned in the bath . . . Kieran's cheery face petrified into stern marble.

Then they fell away too, and she was four years old again, wrapped in a towel on her mum's knee, being dried after her bath. Kath is singing something. *Da-Da da ta da* . . . A Polish lullaby? No. It's 'The Wheels on the Bus'. Looking into her mum's eyes she sees a promise there. *I will always love you.*

Without warning the lamppost slithered sharply upwards out of her grasp, and she hit the glass pavement with a crack.

Chapter Forty-Five

When Cassie next woke properly, the first thing she saw was her old Nine Inch Nails poster tacked up on the wall. The memory of exactly how she'd ended up in her old bedroom at her gran's was slippery. She could only remember snippets and off-cuts. *A bright light being shone in her eyes – paramedic? Doctor? The squawking radio of the female cop. The taste of Lucozade.*

All she'd done was reach out a hand for the glass on the bedside table but within ten seconds her grandmother's head came around the edge of the door. Cassie had always suspected that with hearing that acute she must have bat DNA.

'*Tygrysek!* How are you?'

'Not much like a tiger. But OK. Headache still. How long . . . ?'

'They brought you in the small hours on Wednesday. It is Thursday today. You've been asleep on and off the whole time.' Babcia topped up her water glass from a jug. 'The doctors say you have post-concussion syndrome. You will need proper rest for at least a week.'

Cassie pulled herself up onto her elbows, ready to scoff at the idea, before seeing the look in her gran's eye. And she couldn't deny that even that modest movement had set up a warning thrum of pain in her skull.

'The doctors wouldn't tell me what happened to you – "confidentiality", they said.' She sniffed. 'Do you want to tell me how you banged your head so badly?'

'Not right now, Babcia. But I will do, I promise.' She couldn't tell her what had been going on – not without finding out whether Maria would be charged with Kath's murder and Callum cleared of the crime.

The old lady gave a nod. '*Dobrze*. Now, I expect you would like some mushroom soup?' It wasn't really a question. 'I made it with the dried ceps you like.'

Realising she was hungry, Cassie nodded.

The doorbell rang and her gran said, 'That must be the police lady. I said she could try today – but only if you feel up to seeing her?'

'DS Flyte?' Cassie's hand flew to her hair. 'How do I look?'

That prompted a drily amused look. 'You'll pass, darling.'

Bollocks.

Flyte's flint-blue eyes were soft today, as she asked how Cassie was doing. She lowered her voice to a confidential murmur, 'Listen, I spoke with the officer who did the stop and search on you. We agreed that given your condition at the time of the stop, confiscate and destroy was the appropriate response in this case.'

'Nothing's gone down on my record, then? Thank Christ.' Cassie paused, looked down at her hands. 'Thank you.'

Flyte took Cassie's statement about the attack, a slow and frustrating process given the way the concussion had scrambled her memory, but she said they could fill in any holes later.

'I don't really care about her getting done for attacking me – it'd only be what, assault? GBH? What I care about is seeing

309

that . . . *bitch* . . . punished for killing my mother.' It was a word Cassie had never used till now, but there was no other insult adequate to describe Maria, given what she had done – the havoc she had wrought on so many people's lives.

To Cassie's surprise, Flyte cracked out one of her rare but dazzling smiles. 'I have some good news on that front. Barney Cotter has made a damning statement against Maria and her movements that night.'

'Really?' But her relief instantly gave way to fury. 'So he let his supposed best mate rot in jail for seventeen years knowing all the while his wife did it?'

'I think it took you turning up, asking questions, to force him to face the truth. To have a long overdue reckoning with his conscience.'

Cassie remembered the moment she'd seen Barney's handwriting on the kitchen blackboard and realised it was him who'd sent money on her birthday every year. She'd assumed that it had been blood money to atone for the murder of her mother, when it was actually to atone for the sin of silence.

Between them Flyte and Cassie put it all together – how Maria had nursed a romantic fixation on her old flame Callum for years, an obsession that had tipped into murderous rage when she overheard him arguing with Barney about his plan to leave the band and take Kath and Cassie to Ireland to start a new life.

'What do you think happened?' Cassie asked, still trying to absorb it all.

'Maria must have known which pub Callum and Kath had been drinking in. After creeping out of the house, I imagine she hung around outside in order to "bump into" Kath when she left. Walked along with her. Maybe she wanted to see whether she would go along with Callum's plan.'

'Dad never got the chance to tell her,' said Cassie. 'But if Maria sounded Mum out about it she'd have been dead keen – it was a dream of hers to live on a farm.'

They both fell silent, aware of the alternative reality that might have seen the little family regain happiness in another country.

'In Maria's twisted outlook, your mum was the only thing standing in the way of her romantic reunion with Callum,' Flyte went on. 'If she would just disappear, then the deal, the tour, the grand love affair, would all be back on.'

Cassie remembered that Maria's dad had left his family for another woman, promising to come back for his daughter – and her deluded notion that only death could have prevented him from returning to her. The fear of being abandoned again had tipped an already unstable personality over the edge.

'You do know it was a total fiction, this idea that Callum was in love with her?' Cassie asked. 'He kissed her *once*, when things were going badly at home, and obviously regretted it.' She realised something: if Capaldi hadn't turned up to start hassling Kath, Callum would've had no reason to be suspicious of her secretive behaviour – might never have even kissed Maria. And Cassie's mum might still be alive.

Flyte nodded. 'Female-on-female murder is rare – but when it happens the most common motive is sexual jealousy, often delusional in nature.'

'She didn't love him enough to get him off a murder charge, did she? She was happy to let him go to jail for something she did.'

An ostentatious knock at the bedroom door. Weronika came in, bearing a vase holding an enormous bunch of flowers.

Weronika handed her the card that had come with the latest bouquet.

What have you been up to now?! it said. Signed *Love from Archie.*

Meeting Flyte's eye she felt herself reddening – she'd never suffered from blushing before. Hopefully it was just a side-effect of the concussion and would disappear soon, along with the bursts of disinhibition and the grinding headache.

'He delivered them in person.' Weronika's gaze slid to Flyte and back to Cassie, her expression seeming to say *it's nice to have options* . . . Cassie had always fondly imagined her gran having no clue about her sex life – until recently. It turned out that not only had she known all along that Rachel, Cassie's most serious relationship to date, had been more than just a flatmate – but that she appeared to be unfazed by her granddaughter's sexuality.

'Does she know . . . ?' asked Flyte, *sotto voce,* once she'd gone.

'Know what?' Cassie's eyes widened. 'Oh sorry, you mean about the case?' She shook her head. 'I don't want to tell her anything yet – not until you charge Maria.'

'Sensible. Well, I don't want to raise your hopes, but I spoke to a DNA analyst at the lab and he was confident they'd be able to recover skin cells and even traces of blood left on the murder weapon by the killer.'

Cassie nodded. The rough surface of the brick would have been a great collector of DNA, and modern-day techniques could amplify results from just a handful of cells.

'I've been looking through the PM report again,' said Flyte. 'Your mum had quite a lot of alcohol in her blood.'

'She was a pisshead,' said Cassie, feeling a sudden hot wetness on her cheeks.

'Oh Cassie, I'm sorry.' Flyte looked shocked.

'Ignore me,' said Cassie, taking a breath and waving away the tears. 'It's just the concussion.'

'Of course. I only mentioned it because it helps to explain why she was unable to fight back or escape.'

Cassie nodded again, eyes fixed on the old-school paisley coverlet. Imagining Maria dropping back in order to hit Kath from behind. The defensive kicks her mum had managed to land on her attacker's shins suggesting that she'd turned to fight, had stayed on her feet – at least to start with.

'What about Kieran? You know, if it hadn't been for him, I would never have seen the fanzine, never discovered that it was Callum's threat to leave the band which led to Mum's murder.' Cassie paused to swallow the lump in her throat. 'Maria must have panicked when Kieran questioned her about it and . . . killed him.'

Flyte sent her a sympathetic look. 'It's still early days on Kieran's case. The forensic PM was inconclusive. The pathologist couldn't rule out the head injury being sustained during an accidental fall into the canal. But we're still gathering CCTV footage to put Kieran at Maria's gig and to trace their movements afterwards. If we can establish that she followed him to the canal we can start putting the screws on her.'

'So, what happens to my dad now?'

Flyte eyed her carefully. 'Callum, you mean?'

Cassie felt a twisting in her gut. She'd almost forgotten the unwanted biological father she'd acquired in the shape of Tony Capaldi.

'If we secure a guilty verdict against Maria for your mum's murder, Callum can apply for leave to appeal and the court will overturn his conviction.'

They shared a smile.

'If it hadn't been for your ... ridiculous obstinacy,' Flyte went on, 'he would almost certainly have gone to his grave with the murder on his record.'

Cassie's thoughts turned to Tony Capaldi – her 'real' father. He might have been cleared of suspicion for killing her mum, but there was still something about him and his story that didn't quite add up.

'Did you ask Hobbs if he remembered Capaldi coming forward to rule himself out just after the murder? He claimed he had a solid alibi but he didn't say what it was.'

Flyte frowned. 'Yes, apparently he was up in Coventry for a training weekend.'

'What kind of training?'

'Police training.'

Chapter Forty-Six

Flyte hadn't picked up anything odd about the young Tony Capaldi attending a police event in 1997 on the weekend of the murder. But Cassie had.

Her memory of her last encounter with Capaldi was pin-sharp. He had claimed that Kath's murder had motivated him to join the police – that he 'owed his career' to her. Now it seemed that by the time of her mum's death, he was already in the police force.

Why had he told her such a barefaced lie about when he'd become a cop? Lying there in her old bedroom the question pre-occupied her every waking thought.

It was another twenty-four hours before Cassie could stand without feeling dizzy and exhausted. Friday at noon she finally felt well enough to get up and open her laptop, which Desmond had kindly delivered first thing that morning. After a couple of hours of googling she texted Callum with a simple question.

She had just read his reply when Babcia bustled in with a tray bearing a bowl of veggie stew and some freshly baked bread.

'That's enough of that! You'll wear yourself out. Back to bed with you.'

Cassie complied, for the time being, but not because she was worn-out. In fact, Callum's message had energised her with a cold white fury.

'I heard you on the phone,' she said, taking the tray from her gran. 'Are you off to see Barbara?'

'Yes.' The old lady scanned her face. 'Why do you ask?'

'No reason.' She smiled as she settled the tray onto her lap. 'Have a good time.'

The receptionist called up to DCI Capaldi's office to tell him that Cassie was in reception, and she got the nod to go up.

His PA met her at the lift. 'He's in a meeting but he should be out in ten or fifteen minutes,' she said. At that moment they were passing a long meeting room with floor-to-ceiling glass and Cassie spotted Capaldi, up at the front, running a PowerPoint presentation for a dozen youngish people.

On impulse, she spun round and took two strides back towards the door. Threw it open and marched in. A dozen bored faces swivelled towards her, their expressions turning to curiosity as they checked out the punky-looking girl with the facial piercings.

Capaldi managed a smile. 'Oh, hi, Cassie. I'll be right out if you want to wait in my—'

'No need,' said Cassie, fixing him with a look. 'I'm happy to discuss your fascinating career right here . . . *Dominic*.'

The faces swung back to Capaldi as one, like spectators at a game of tennis, eyes wide, their expressions saying *this is more like it*.

That did the trick.

He led the way down the corridor, shushing the apologies of his poor assistant.

Once in his office he waved a hand towards the sofa. 'Let's sit down and talk about it.' When she ignored him, he perched himself on the edge of his desk instead.

'When you started sleeping with my mother at Oakwood Common, you weren't one of the anti-road campaigners. You were an impostor, on assignment there as an undercover cop.'

A moment of silence as he stared down at his hands. 'Look, Cassie. I'm sorry, truly I am. I was always going to tell you the truth when the time was right. But it's not what you think. I really did love Kath and I bitterly regretted splitting up with her.'

'Bullshit. You didn't fall in love with her. You *targeted* her because she was one of the organisers. So it must have been an irritating setback when she got fed up with the internal politics and stepped back, but you simply moved on to one of the other female organisers. A more promising victim.' It was clear from his expression that her reconstruction of the events of twenty-six years ago was accurate.

Capaldi's lie about when he'd joined the cops had bugged Cassie. Until she'd remembered the covert policing scandal which had emerged in the press a few years earlier. Searching online she discovered that during the 80s and 90s around 140 undercover cops had been sent to infiltrate direct action groups, including anti-roads campaigns like Oakwood Common, in a bid to discover and disrupt their protest plans. The primary tactic used by the mostly male police spies had been to pursue sexual relationships, sometimes lasting years, with female activists.

When their mission ended these cops would disappear with barely any explanation – back to their 'real' lives, wives, partners and children – leaving their 'targets' abandoned and distraught. Some had even been left pregnant or with babies fathered by their bogus boyfriends.

Cassie had read their stories with a mounting sense of fury – and a dawning realisation.

Her text to Callum earlier that day had simply asked if he recalled the name of her mum's ex-boyfriend at Oakwood.

The name Callum had texted back wasn't Tony Capaldi, but 'Dominic Drake'.

'Your "relationship" with my mother was a disgusting lie from the start.' Cassie's voice trembled with fury. 'And I bet if I look up Dominic Drake's birth certificate, I'll find that he was a real person who died in childhood, right?' Horrifyingly, it had been standard practice for cops going undercover to steal the identities of dead children.

'Look, Cassie, I hated that part of it, but I was only twenty-seven.' There was a pleading note in his voice. 'It was what they told us to do.'

'What, so you were "just obeying orders"?'

'Oh, come on, Cassie, there were well-meaning people in those groups but there were also dangerous people trying to stir up real trouble.'

'Can you seriously defend grooming someone and having sex with someone who *doesn't know who you are* – *and* getting them pregnant?'

'Look, I'm not proud of that side of it. But things were different back then. It's hard to explain.' He opened his hands, appealing to her.

Different back then. She'd heard the phrase before, of course – used to excuse the casual sexism, the hand up the skirt, the 'no can mean yes' attitudes of the past ... She had never dreamed that they would be baked into her own history – her very *existence*.

They stared at each other: Capaldi leaning forward from the waist, the supplicant; Cassie upright, arms folded.

318

She pictured the man who'd held her mother in his grip in Woolies that time, a man who now had the face of Capaldi. 'When you came looking for my mum five years later, it wasn't because you'd suddenly realised you were still in love with her.' She saw now that the body language of the man in Woolies wasn't that of a desperate ex-lover pleading for another chance, but of someone trying to intimidate and coerce. 'You turned up because she was threatening to out you to the papers, wasn't she?'

He didn't try to deny it.

By 1997, protest groups were wising up to the police infiltration of their ranks and Kath had no doubt heard whispers on the activist grapevine that Dominic Drake – the biological father of her four-year-old daughter – was a suspected police spy. Cassie tried to imagine how it would be feel to find out that the father of your child was a fraud; that your relationship had been a fiction from beginning to end.

And when Capaldi started to pressure her, Kath couldn't even confide in Callum because she'd never confessed that their little girl wasn't his. So he'd interpreted the mysterious phone calls as evidence of a secret affair. It would have been enough to pitch more robust people than her mother into crisis: no wonder she had turned to her old friend drink.

Capaldi was staring out of the rain-streaked window. 'You know, at Oakwood, when I split up with her, she looked me straight in the eye and said, "Dominic, who are you really, behind the mask?" She was spooky like that, Kath – she had a sixth sense about things.'

A sixth sense . . . An image came to Cassie then – a silvery thread spooling out from her mother to her, across the echoing void. A shared bond.

'What was it like? Living a lie for so long?' – suddenly curious.

'I loved it.' One corner of his mouth curled up in a smile. 'The art of deception, constantly living on the edge of being found out, it's a thrill.' Catching the look on her face he went on, 'Of course I realise now that what went on back then was one hundred per cent wrong. But you have to believe me, when I came to find you, I just wanted to put things right – between us.'

She made a scornful noise. 'I'll bet you've been holding your breath ever since the public inquiry was launched. That's why you put an alert on the computer to see who accessed my mum's file, in case your bogus relationship with her was exposed.' By 2014, the government had no longer been able to ignore the scale of the scandal and had announced a public inquiry which had barely begun and was predicted to run for a decade or more. But if nobody came forward to accuse him of wrongdoing, Capaldi might still escape being named and shamed, or ever having to give evidence.

'When you heard I was asking about my mum's death it must have sent you into a flat panic.' Something dawned on her. 'You didn't come looking for me because you were desperate to get in touch with your long-lost daughter. It was to find out if I'd stumbled on your dirty little secret.'

'If that's all it was then why would I take the insane risk of getting a DNA sample from your flat?' He opened his palms to her. 'How would that help me exactly, if I did end up getting called before the inquiry?'

She hesitated. It was true that the break-in, and Capaldi's declaration of fatherhood, didn't quite fit the rest of the picture. Having managed to avoid investigation so far, why set out to prove he had fathered a child with a target?

'When I first laid eyes on you at the mortuary, everything changed.' He met her gaze, the Aegean blue of his eyes unsettling her anew. 'It was like looking at my little sister. From that moment on, I couldn't think of anything else. When I got the confirmation that you were my daughter' – he paused, his gaze locked on hers – 'I swear, it was the happiest moment of my life.'

Cassie's mind was a-whirl. This part of Capaldi's story rang true. When he'd revealed he was her father, he'd taken a big gamble that she would work out the rest. And she had to admit that, even now, the way he looked at her – like she was the most important person in the world – stirred her emotions. Once again she remembered the first time they'd met, and her misreading his intensity as attraction.

What did it truly mean, she wondered – this man being her father? What was this special thrill that came from learning you shared a genetic bond with another human? The deep blue eyes she'd inherited from him, the discovery that her grandparents had been Italian, the existence of a previously unknown family tree . . . It was a powerful feeling, no question.

But at the same time, completely meaningless.

'Fatherhood is about more than bunch of shared alleles,' she told him. 'You're not even a sperm donor – sperm donors are honest. You lied and lied to my mother before dumping her, and then tried to bully her into silence when she found out you were a cop. You have no clue what it means to be a father. Whatever the lab report says, Callum is my dad, not you.'

She turned to go.

'Cassie!' The raw note of desperation in his voice left her unmoved.

'I never want to see you again. If you approach me – or Callum – I'll make absolutely sure you do get called before the inquiry. Do you want your friends and family to find out the kind of man you really are? Someone who had sex with multiple young women under false pretences?'

Opening the door, she turned to him one last time. 'It's not such a good look these days, is it?'

Chapter Forty-Seven

It was three days later and Cassie had managed to persuade her grandmother that she was well enough to attend Bradley Appleton's funeral. It helped that she was able to say she'd have a chaperone in the form of DS Flyte.

Cassie couldn't attend the farewell ceremony of every guest who she'd looked after at the mortuary – it just wasn't practical. But she always attended the funerals of children and teens like Bradley Appleton, if she was asked, and if she felt that her presence would mean something to their mum and dad.

To many newly bereaved parents, the person who had dealt with their beloved child, who had opened their body, then made it whole again, who had cleaned away the blood and brushed their hair – these actions were akin to a sacrament, and the presence at the final farewell of the person who had performed them seemed fitting. So when Kim Appleton had called to invite Cassie to attend Bradley's funeral, she hadn't hesitated.

As she and Flyte took their places in the last pew at the back of the crematorium chapel, Cassie scanned the crowd for Bradley's goth friends, expecting to see bird's-nest hair and flamboyant outfits. In fact, when she spotted Naenia and the others, she found they'd toned down their look, backcombed hair slicked down in the case of the boys or tidied away in a chignon on the girls.

Good for them. It wouldn't kill them to suspend their right to self-expression for a day.

The ceremony, conducted by a humanist, was as distressing as the funeral of any young person, and yet – like all funerals – strangely uplifting at the same time. Cassie tried not to think about Kieran and her mother, focusing instead on Flyte, who must be reliving her own grievous loss. She sat upright and utterly still, encased in what Cassie recognised as a self-protecting bubble.

After the ceremony, as the mourners filed out of the chapel, the opening bars of Leonard Cohen singing 'Hallelujah' came over the sound system. *Naenia's choice*? If so, it was a good one: its poignant lyricism saluted Bradley's goth-ness without risking offending the older folks.

They were directed into a large, light room where a long table had been heaped high with wreaths and flowers, filling the air with the life-affirming smell of pollen. Cassie was pleased to see Kim and Steve Appleton, who were greeting mourners, holding hands; she had seen too many grief-numbed parents drift irretrievably apart after losing a child.

Seeing her, Kim came over, tugging Steve along behind her.

'I can't tell you how grateful we are, for everything you've done for Bradley, and for us,' she told Cassie. 'And you too, Phyllida. It's made it more . . . bearable, somehow, knowing it was just a stupid accident.'

Since Naenia had given her statement confirming that Bradley had been playing Flatliner – the choking 'game' – it was a foregone conclusion that the coroner's verdict would be accidental death rather than suicide.

'Isn't that right, Steve?' Kim said.

Steve gave an embarrassed but sincere nod. *A man of few words.* His eyes were shadowed with sadness but the anger Cassie had seen in him – against Bradley, the world, against himself – appeared to have subsided.

Kim, by contrast, was talking up a storm about the ceremony, the flowers, the letters of condolence . . . her eyes bright points. Funerals could be weirdly exhilarating for the bereaved – today was Bradley's day, after all, an excuse to talk of nothing and nobody else. And this was the very last time Bradley's mum and dad would be under the same roof as their son.

'I'm guessing it was Naenia who chose the Leonard Cohen?' said Cassie.

Kim nodded. 'She came round the house for coffee last week. She's a lovely girl.'

'I expect that's her wreath?' Cassie nodded towards an elaborate crucifix of black-dyed roses, dotted with a few deep red lilies.

Kim smiled up at her husband. 'Actually, that one's from Steve.'

After the funeral, Flyte drove the two of them back from Golders Green to Camden. She was uncommunicative, clearly submerged in her own grief.

Cassie decided it was better to talk about her loss than to ignore it. 'I ran the medical report on Poppy past Professor Arculus. He's a Home Office pathologist, as you know, but he was an obstetrician earlier in his career.'

'Mmm-hm?' Flyte had become very still – or as still as you could be while navigating the Swiss Cottage gyratory system during rush hour.

'So, as you know, the issue with the pregnancy was an undiagnosed velamentous cord insertion. Which basically means that the umbilical cord didn't attach itself to the placenta correctly as it grew.'

She explained how this anomaly had left Poppy's critical blood vessels exposed and highly vulnerable to rupture during the rough business of birth.

'It's a very rare complication, and in cases like yours, where the problem isn't identified until labour is underway, it's almost always too late to do anything.'

Cassie didn't add that Poppy would have lost her meagre supply of lifeblood – less than 90ml – within ten minutes.

'What about all the scans I had? Shouldn't somebody have picked it up earlier?'

'Not necessarily, according to the Prof. The location of the cord insertion would apparently have made it difficult to spot on a scan. Obviously, you are totally within your rights to get hold of the scan imagery, and take it to a private obstetrician for their opinion.'

'But . . . ?'

'Even if you did find any evidence of negligence it would be a long process and an upsetting one . . .' Cassie hesitated; it wasn't for her to push Flyte one way or the other.

'And none of it would bring Poppy back,' said Flyte.

They drove in silence for a few minutes, before Cassie said, 'Listen, Phyllida – what happened to you is terrible, but you need to know that there was absolutely nothing you could have done to avert it.'

Cassie hoped that her words might do something to help dispel the inevitable *what ifs* that she could almost see crowding around Flyte like a flock of mobbing seagulls.

Another silence, then Flyte cleared her throat. 'If I were to arrange a ceremony of remembrance for Poppy, would you come?'

They didn't have a ceremony? Cassie was careful not to show her surprise.

'Of course I would. Thank you for asking me.'

Chapter Forty-Eight

Cassie had spent a restless night working out how much to tell her grandmother.

Four weeks had passed since the night Maria had attacked her and the previous evening Flyte had called to say that the CPS had given the go-ahead to charge Maria Maguire with murder. Barney's statement now had the backing of forensic evidence: the latest DNA testing technology had allowed the lab to retrieve a second profile from minuscule traces of blood on the half-brick murder weapon. A profile that had matched the mouth swab taken from Maria on her arrest.

Obviously Weronika needed to know that Callum had been wrongly convicted of her daughter's murder and who the real culprit was, but Cassie saw no reason to reveal that he wasn't her biological father. The true story would only upset her grandmother unnecessarily, and anyway, Cassie felt her mum had the right for her secret to be kept.

Now, sitting in the front room with the gas fire popping, Weronika's hand in hers, Cassie watched anxiously as her face paled and seemed to collapse in on itself. After Cassie's words had sunk in, she had a string of anguished questions about why this Maria would want to harm her beloved daughter, but after a few moments she suddenly stopped and stared at Cassie, gripping her hand tight.

'Mother of God, what have I done?'

Cassie patted the hand, scanning her face anxiously. She understood exactly what her grandmother's plaintive question meant. Cassie's father had spent more than half his adult life behind bars for a crime he didn't commit – and she had helped to put him there.

'Look, Babcia, you weren't to know. The police were convinced of his guilt, too.'

'So you say that my Katerina was the drinker, not him?' Weronika shook her head slowly. 'How could I not have seen what was in front of my eyes?'

'Because you loved her and believed what she let you believe.'

'I was wilfully blind! I took against your father from the start, for no good reason. I see that now. He was Irish, he had no proper job, and his manners were . . .' She waved a hand at the triviality of her past objections. 'It's just . . . I wanted so much more for Katerina. I had lost out on studying at university and now she was doing the same – just for a man. You say he was a good husband to her? And that he looked after you.'

Cassie nodded.

'All these years I robbed you of a father.'

There was no point contradicting her grandmother; it would take time for her to come to terms with the mistakes of the past.

'Babcia, darling. The important thing is that Callum is going to be cleared, and I have a father again.' She hesitated. 'In fact, I'm going to see him now, up at the cemetery. He's never felt able to visit Mum's grave before.'

'I'm glad, *tygrysek*.' She pressed Cassie's hand. 'The two of you have so much catching up to do.'

Cassie was relieved to see her colour returning to normal.

'Will you tell him that I am sorry from the bottom of my heart?' Weronika said hesitantly. 'And ask him . . .'

'Ask him . . . ?' Cassie prompted.

'If he felt able to, perhaps he would agree to meet me, so that I can apologise in person?'

'Of course I will. Whatever happened in the past, we're a family now.'

Family. She was part of a family. Cassie couldn't stop herself smiling.

An answering smile lit up her grandmother's face. 'I have always been so fearful of leaving you alone in the world, especially since my stroke,' said Weronika, squeezing her hand tight. 'But now I know that you will have someone to look out for you after I'm gone.'

'She loved geraniums, your mum. Do you remember the tins of them, painted bright blue, like in Greece, lined up along the balcony of our flat?'

Cassie shook her head, watching Callum settle a pot of geraniums on her mum's grave. Despite only being the first week of March, it was one of those freakishly warm early spring days. She was almost too hot in her smart winter coat, but they had both independently decided to dress up for the occasion, Callum in a proper jacket at least a size too big for him.

They stood in silence for a while, looking at the gravestone. It was decorated with a carved relief – the simple bowed head of an angel – the engraved words KATERINA LILIANA RAVEN, and her dates, followed by the words BELOVED DAUGHTER and the Polish translation *Ukochana córka*.

Callum already knew about the murder charge against Maria – Cassie had called him the previous evening – but he

330

didn't look like a man about to have his wrongful conviction for murder overturned.

'It's all my fault.' He turned a haunted look on her. 'You see, I . . . I kissed her, Maria, one night after a gig. I don't even know why I did it. It was just before Kath died, when we were going through a rough patch.' His mouth worked. 'To think that Kath died because I had a moment of weakness.'

Cassie put a hand on his forearm. 'Dad, don't go beating yourself up over one kiss. Maria had already built you and her up into some big fantasy, she probably would've done what she did anyway.'

He still looked stricken. 'I told her afterwards that it had been a big mistake, that I loved Kath. She just smiled and said that we were meant to be together. I mean, I didn't really take it seriously. I never thought for one second . . .'

'Why would you?' Cassie shook her head. 'Look, whatever you'd said she wouldn't have heard you. Psychiatrists call it a delusional disorder – in her head the two of you had a shared destiny, and you were the one who was in denial.'

She'd read a couple of psychiatric papers on the subject and one quote had stuck in her mind. It said that someone suffering from delusional obsession could turn dangerous *if rejection by their love object became impossible to ignore.* The final straw in Maria's case being Callum's plan to leave the band – to leave *her* – for her hated rival.

'She wrote to me in prison, you know,' said Callum. 'I'd forgotten all about it. It went on for years, dozens of letters. After seeing her name at the bottom of the first one, I never read it, nor opened the rest – 'cause I wanted nothing to do with anyone from my old life. I just thought she was writing to me out of pity.' His anxious eyes sought Cassie's. 'You don't think she was writing to . . . confess?'

331

Cassie made a scornful noise. 'If she was going to come clean she'd already had plenty of opportunity. No, she was probably just banging on about how you two belonged together.'

Callum dropped onto his haunches to brush a cobweb and some dead leaves off Kath's headstone; as he got back to his feet it was with the effortful movements of an old man.

The sight stabbed at Cassie. 'We need to come up with an exercise regime for you, get you back in shape,' she said, only half-joking.

He pulled his crooked smile, becoming again the handsome dad of her memory. Funny to think that their shared hair and eye colouring was no more than a happy accident. 'You were always a bossy wee thing, even as a toddler . . .' Then his smile faded as he stared down at the grave. 'So, what happens now?'

'We clear your name.'

Flyte reckoned that Maria's defence would advise her to plead guilty when the case came to court, citing diminished responsibility due to her being in 'an abnormal state of mind' at the time of the murder – which might get her a lesser conviction of manslaughter. Whether she would ever face justice for killing Kieran was up in the air – apparently, the cops were still looking for eyewitnesses having found no CCTV footage to place her with him at the canal. Picturing his cheery grin, Cassie allowed herself to imagine for a moment what it would have been like if they'd got a flat together, the laughs they'd have had, before pushing the thought away. There would be time enough to grieve for him – and for her mum. Right now she had more pressing matters to deal with.

'I've already got a brief lined up for you to meet,' she went on, 'so the minute Maria is found guilty, we can start the ball rolling to get your conviction set aside.'

'And there's nothing that could stop it?'

It pained her to see how difficult he found it to hope.

'No. Even if by some miracle she gets off, the solicitor thinks the judge misdirected the jury by not advising sufficient caution about the reliability of eyewitness evidence. He called the trial "a circus".' Cassie lowered her voice. 'Dad, there's something else you need to know. Kath wasn't unfaithful to you.'

She told him Dominic Drake's real identity and how he'd been trying to hush Kath up before she died. 'That's why she was getting suspicious telephone calls, and why she was so depressed.'

'That bastard!' His eyes wide and angry. 'Why did she not tell me? I'd have . . .'

Because it risked the truth coming out. That Dominic and not Callum was Cassie's biological father.

She felt herself blushing.

He eyed her for a moment before saying, 'Ah, Cassie darling. You know, don't you?'

WTF? He knew already?

'Your mum never said anything but once you were born I did the maths. You weighed seven pound eight ounces! Too big to be an early baby.'

'Did you not ask her?'

'It was for her to tell me if she wanted to.' He smiled. 'Anyway, when I held you in my arms that first time, I knew who your real dad was.'

'Oh, Dad.' Going to him, she let herself be folded into his arms and breathed the remembered scent of him from her childhood – woodiness and male sweat, apples, and cheap aftershave.

Fatherhood wasn't about shared DNA. A dad was someone who made you feel that everything would be all right. Someone who could tell you off when you screwed up without making you feel like a bad person. Who checked under the bed for monsters. Who put your happiness before his own. Always.

Breaking the embrace she took his hand.

'I told Babcia this morning,' she said. 'Of course she's mortified that she helped to put you away.'

He just shrugged. 'What's done is done.'

'She wants to meet you, to apologise. We could go there one evening, have a family dinner together?'

He looked aghast for a moment, before saying, 'You'll have to help me choose a new jacket.' He grimaced down at the one he was wearing. 'She always had me down as a bit of a *gbur*.'

'Not anymore. I think the prodigal son-in-law will be getting the full homecoming feast.' She grinned at him. 'And I expect there will be some humble pie for afters.'

There came a sound she hadn't heard properly since she was four years old. The sound of her lovely, handsome dad cracking up. She noticed he was standing a little more upright too.

'Ah, Kath,' he said to his wife's grave, the laughter still in his voice. 'If only you could see the young woman our little Catkin grew up into.'

Catching a waft of watermelon scent, Cassie thought: *She can*.

The sun setting behind them threw their shadows across Katherine Raven's grave – casting the outlines not of two but three linked figures, as if her mother was standing right behind them, a soft hand resting on each of their shoulders.

Acknowledgements

First of all, a sincere and massive thank you to the many readers who have responded with such warmth and enthusiasm to Cassie Raven. After spending long months tapping away with no real idea how it's going, to discover that a character has hit the spot with readers is an unbeatable thrill.

Recreating the world of the mortuary and getting the science right took a ton of research, and the input of specialists who generously lent me their brains and endured my dumb questions. Any factual errors in the text are entirely down to me.

I'm forever grateful to award-winning Anatomical Pathology Technician, Barbara Peters, who continues to steer me through mortuary matters, the detail of eviscerating human bodies – and the emotional cost of dealing with the bereaved. I quite simply couldn't have created Cassie without her.

Huge thanks too, to pathologist Nic Chaston, who has been so patient and helpful answering a slew of questions on anatomy and determining cause of death. I am especially grateful for her imaginative solutions to those sticky moments when story and science collide . . .

DI Paula James is still an invaluable source of intel on police matters, steering me through the ins and outs of the PNC and document store labelling and much more. (Thank you, Ballgown!)

Thanks too, to pathologist Mike Heath, and to my dear friend and clinical psychologist Kate Gauci. Former coroner Alison Thompson continues to advise on coronial procedure while wrangling her flock of sheep in Wales.

I am grateful to the enormously supportive crime writing fraternity and especially the brilliant Isabelle Grey, aka V. B. Grey, and her incisive feedback on my earliest draft.

And I owe a lifetime of gratitude to my mum, who continues to be an unwavering source of love, wisdom and support.

For helping me to bring Cassie to the bookshelves not just here, but in six other countries, my heartfelt thanks go to the literary legend that is Jane Gregory and the team at David Higham – above all to the talented Stephanie Glencross. I am also grateful to Kath Armstrong who spotted the potential of *Body Language* in the first place.

Finally, a massive thank-you to my publishers Zaffre, and especially to my new editor Kelly Smith whose enthusiasm for the series has been a joy to see. As well as taking Cassie to her heart, her sure-footed input has made *Life Sentence* a far better book.

Now discover forensic sleuth Cassie Raven's first investigation

BODY LANGUAGE

Mortuary technician Cassie Raven believes the dead can talk.
We just need to listen . . .

Cassie Raven is used to people thinking her job is strange –
why would anyone want to cut up dead bodies for a living?
But they don't know what she knows: that the dead want
to tell us what happened to them.

She's eviscerated thousands of bodies, but never someone she
knew, someone who meant a lot to her – until now.

The pathologist says her death was an accident.
Her body is telling Cassie differently.

Chapter One

The zip of the body bag parted to reveal Cassie's first customer of the day. The woman's half-open eyes, a surprisingly vivid blue, gazed up at her, unseeing.

'Hello there, Mrs Connery.' Her voice became gentler than the one she used with the living. 'My name's Cassie Raven and I'll be looking after you while you're with us.' She had no doubt that the dead woman could hear her and hoped she took some comfort from the words.

The previous evening Kate Connery had collapsed while getting ready for bed and died, there on her bathroom floor one week short of her fiftieth birthday. Laughter lines latticed her open, no-nonsense face beneath hair too uniformly brunette to be natural.

Cassie glanced up at the clock and swore. There was a new pathologist coming in to do the day's post-mortem list and with Carl, the junior technician, off sick and three bodies to prep, it was shaping up to be the Monday from hell.

Still, she took her time working Mrs C's nightdress up over her head, registering the faint ammoniac smell of sweat or urine, before carefully folding it away in a plastic bag. The things somebody had been wearing when they died meant a lot to their loved ones, sometimes more than the body itself, which grieving relatives could struggle to relate to. A dead body could feel like an empty suitcase.

'We need to find out what happened to you, Mrs C,' Cassie told her. 'So that we can get Declan and your boys some answers.'

From her first day in the mortuary five years ago it had felt totally natural to talk to the bodies in her care, to treat them as if they were still alive – still people. Occasionally they would even answer.

It wasn't like a live person talking – for a start, their lips didn't move – and the experience was always so fleeting that she might almost have imagined it. *Almost.* Usually they said something like '*Where am I?*' or '*What happened?*' – simple bewilderment at finding themselves in this strange place – but now and again she was convinced that their words contained a clue to how they'd died.

Cassie had never told a living soul about these 'conversations'; people thought she was weird enough already. But they didn't know what she knew deep in her gut: the dead could talk – if only you knew how to listen.

The only outward sign of anything wrong with Mrs Connery was a few red blotches on her cheeks and forehead and a fist-sized bruise on her sternum where either her husband or the paramedics had administered desperate CPR. Cassie looked through the notes. After a night out at the pub watching football, Declan Connery had come home to find his wife unconscious. An ambulance rushed her to the hospital, but she was declared dead on arrival.

Since Kate Connery had died unexpectedly – she'd apparently been in good health and hadn't seen her GP for months – a basic or 'routine' post-mortem to establish the cause of death was an automatic requirement.

Cassie put her hand on Mrs C's fridge-cold forearm and waited for her own warmth to expel the chill. 'Can you tell me what happened?' she murmured.

For a few seconds, nothing. Then she felt the familiar slip-sliding sensation, followed by a distracted dreaminess. At the same time, her senses became hyper-alert – the hum of the body-store fridge growing to a jet-engine roar, the overhead light suddenly achingly bright.

The air above Mrs Connery's body seemed to fizz with the last spark of the electricity that had animated her for five decades. And out of the static Cassie heard a low, hoarse whisper.

'I can't breathe!'

Chapter Two

As always, it was all over in an instant. It reminded Cassie of waking from an intense dream, your mind scrabbling to hold onto the details – only to feel them slipping away, like water through open fingers.

In any case, Mrs Connery's words weren't much help. Cassie could find no history of asthma or emphysema in the notes, and there was a whole bunch of other disorders that could affect breathing. She was still wondering what, if anything, to make of it when she heard the door from the clean area open. It was Doug, the mortuary manager, followed by a younger guy – tall, with a floppy fringe – who he introduced as Dr Archie Cuff, the new pathologist.

Stripping off a nitrile glove, she offered Cuff her hand.

'Cassie Raven is our senior mortuary technician,' beamed Doug. 'She's the one who makes everything run like clockwork round here.'

Although he wore cufflinks (*cufflinks*?!) and a tie, Cuff couldn't be much more than thirty, barely five years older than Cassie. A single glance told her that his navy waxed jacket was a genuine Barbour, not a knock-off – its metal zipper fob embossed with the brand name – and going by his tie, a dark blue silk with a slanting fat white stripe, he'd been schooled at Harrow. Cassie noticed things like that, had done ever since she could remember.

'Looking forward to working with you, Cathy.' He spoke in the fake, demi-street accent favoured by the younger royals, his smile as glib as a cabinet minister's, but it was clear from the way his glance slid over her that she'd already been filed in a box labelled 'minion'.

Cassie didn't often take an instant dislike to someone, but in the case of Archie Cuff she decided to make an exception.

'Me too,' she said, 'especially if you get my name right.'

A flush rose from Cuff's striped shirt collar all the way to his gingery sideburns, but at least he looked at her properly this time. And from the flicker of distaste that crossed his face, he didn't much like what he saw – although it was hard to tell whether it was her dyed black hair with the shaved undercut, her facial piercings, or simply the way she held his gaze. She had to fight a juvenile impulse to lift the top half of her scrubs and flash her tattoos at him.

Doug's eyes flitted between the two of them like a rookie referee at a cage fight, his smile starting to sag. 'Right then, I'll leave you folks to it.' Cassie knew he would probably remind her later of his golden rule: *Never forget, the pathologist can make your job a dream – or a nightmare.*

After Cuff's brief external examination of Mrs Connery, during which they barely spoke beyond the essentials, he left Cassie to do the evisceration.

She placed her blade at the base of Mrs C's throat. This was the moment when she had to stop thinking of Kate Connery as a person and start viewing her as a puzzle to be unlocked, unmapped territory to explore. Without that shift of perspective, what normal person could slice open a fellow human being?

After the initial incision, a decisive sweep down the sternum laid open the tissue as easily as an old silk curtain. Reaching the soft gut area, she didn't pause but let up the pressure to avoid damage to the organs beneath, ending the cut just above the pubic bone.

Within five minutes, the bone shears had cracked open Mrs C's ribcage, exposing her heart and lungs, and Cassie was deftly detaching the organs from their moorings. Once that was done, she used both hands to lift out the entire viscera, from tongue down to urethra, before delivering them gently into the waiting plastic pail. This was a sombre moment, which always made her feel like a midwife of death.

Now for the brain. Going behind Mrs C's head, Cassie repositioned the block beneath her neck. The scalp incision would go from from ear to ear over the top of the head, so that once it was stitched up again the wound would be covered by her hair – especially important since the Connerys were having an open coffin funeral. Combing the front half of Mrs C's thick dark hair forward over her face, Cassie noticed a shiny red patch on the scalp. Eczema? It hadn't been mentioned in the medical notes, but in any case, eczema didn't kill people.

After peeling the bisected scalp forward and back to expose the skull, Cassie reached for the oscillating saw. Moments later she had eased off the skullcap and was coaxing the brain free. Cradling it in both hands for a moment, she imagined Kate Connery as she would have been in life – a down-to-earth matriarch with a ready laugh, surrounded by family and friends in a Camden Town boozer.

When Archie Cuff returned in his scrubs, the atmosphere between them stayed chilly: in the forty minutes it took him to dissect Mrs C's organs, he only spoke to Cassie once, to complain that the blade of his PM40 was blunt. That only confirmed her initial impression of him as the latest in a long line of arrogant posh boys who viewed mortuary technicians as one step up from abattoir workers. A more experienced pathologist would have asked her opinion on the cause of death, and not just to be polite: technicians spent far longer with the bodies and sometimes spotted clues that might otherwise be missed.

As Cuff moved along the dissection bench to rinse his bloodied gloved hands in the sink, Cassie started to collect Mrs C's organs into a plastic bag, ready to be reunited with her body.

'So, what's the verdict?' she asked him.

'There's nothing conclusive to account for her death.' He shrugged. 'We'll have to wait and see whether the lab finds anything useful.' Toxicology would test Mrs C's bodily fluids for drugs, while samples of her organs would undergo histo-pathology to look for any microscopic signs of disease.

'Did you find any petechiae in her lungs?' asked Cassie, keeping her voice casual.

Cuff turned to look at her. 'Why do you ask?'

So he had.

She lifted one shoulder 'I just thought her face looked quite congested.'

I can't breathe.

Petechiae – tiny burst blood vessels – could signal a lack of oxygen.

Cuff looked flustered. 'She was found face down. It's clear from the latest literature that a prone position post-mortem can cause petechial haemorrhage.' He managed a condescending smile. 'If you were hoping for a juicy murder, I'm afraid you're out of luck: there's absolutely no evidence of strangulation or suffocation.'

Cassie knew as well as Cuff did that asphyxia could just as easily have a medical cause, but she stifled a comeback. Dropping a nugget of kidney into a pot of preservative for the lab, she caught sight of Mrs C's body on the autopsy table – her ribcage butterflied like an open book, a dark void where her organs used to be. Above the ruined body, her shiny brunette hair looked out of place.

The light from the fluorescent tubes overhead flared, forcing Cassie to close her eyes, the ever-present reek of formalin suddenly harsh enough to claw at her throat. Behind her eyelids, images flickered: Mrs C's blotched face, the scaly patch on her scalp. She felt her throat start to close and in an instant, everything clicked into place.

'Just popping to the loo,' she told Cuff, before slipping into the corridor, where she pulled out her phone.

'Mr Connery? It's Cassie Raven from the mortuary.'

Ten minutes later she was back. 'Sorry I took so long,' she told Cuff. 'But I just had an interesting conversation with Mrs Connery's husband.'

'Husband . . . ?' He sounded confused at the idea of a body having a spouse.

'Yes. Before he went out last night, she told him she was going to colour her hair.'

'I don't see what . . .'

'He says that she had suffered allergic reactions to her hair dye twice before. Nothing too serious. But this time, it looks like it triggered a fatal anaphylactic shock.'

Don't miss the next case for Cassie Raven

CASE
SENSITIVE

Coming soon

Can't wait till then? Sign up here to discover more about the
world of Cassie Raven: anyalipska.com/meet-cassie-raven